THE FINAL HOUR HAD COME . . .

Death and hatred had shown their faces first in Germany. Soon every man would be familiar with them, everywhere.

In the gathering darkness, one strong light burned clear—the love of Therese for her husband Karl.

Yet how could she fight the evil in men's souls—when she'd never searched her own . . . ?

TIME NO LONGER

"Forceful and moving . . . graphic horror and lyric beauty."—LOUISVILLE TIMES

Also by Taylor Caldwell from Jove

TAYLOR CALDWELL

TIME NO LONGER

A JOVE BOOK

Ten previous printings
First Jove edition published October 1977
New Jove edition published February 1980

10 9 8 7 6 5 4 3 2 1

Printed in the United States of America

Jove books are published by Jove Publications, Inc.,
200 Madison Avenue, New York, NY 10016

THE CITY was getting ready for Easter. Karl Erlich saw rows of white candles tipped with yellow flames in many windows. The snow was falling like flocks of great silent white moths, and the red roofs of the houses were packed with cotton. The winter had been long and hard, and still lingered, in this last snow, through which the scents and humid breath of spring could not yet come. Karl liked walking; he had left his car at home. He liked the feel of the snow against his face, the cold bright wind of night filled with glittering and minute stars. He heard children's voices from somewhere, clear and thrilling. His feet left imprints in the snow; it seemed wrong to break that gentle whiteness. Windows, filled with amber light, shone out at him; he saw the white curtains, stiff with starch in preparation for the holidays. He could see people moving about inside the houses, children with yellow plaited hair, jumping up into their parents' arms for a good-night kiss. People laughed in doorways, lamplight behind them, for it was not so very cold. German laughter, he thought, in spite of old agony and new fear. Bells tinkled down quiet dimly lighted streets. An old man trundled a two-wheeled cart ahead of him; his shoulders and cap were white. He kept shaking the snow from his face, and grinning. His cheeks were red as small wrinkled apples. He wheeled carefully, for the cart was full of dead feathered poultry. Above, the sky was dark and starless, and the snow kept falling and filling the air with its pure breath. A young girl hurried past, glancing at Karl with shy smiling eyes. She had a vivid scarlet shawl over her head and shoulders, spangled with snow-dust. When she ran, her skirts fluttered, showing sturdy legs in white cotton stockings. A servant girl, running blithely in the last snow.

He passed the tall young policeman at the corner, and acknowledged the latter's salute with a kind smile and inclination of his head. The young policeman looked clean and scrubbed and sharp-angled; his uniform was old and patched at the elbows, decently and without shame. Karl sighed, jingled the money in his pockets. Money was scarce these days; he felt guilty because he and his family still had money. So few honest people had money in Germany now. And yet, there were no beggars. Germans did not beg.

The thought made him think of his twin brother, Kurt, to whose home he was going tonight. He frowned uneasily. Kurt had said that only yesterday: "Germans do not beg." But he had added with stiff grimness: "They take!" Karl shook his head, pursing his lips. He even smiled a little ruefully. Kurt was remembering the schloss, which they had had to give up. He never forgot the schloss. If they had lost all their fortune, instead of over half, and had been able to retain that mouldering old schloss, Kurt would have been satisfied. To him, it represented something that was himself yet greater than himself. Without it, he was only a man, only Kurt Erlich, a man like other men. To Kurt Erlich, with his innate hatred of other men, that was intolerable. He could no longer look at his acquaintances arrogantly, and speak of "the schloss." He was not the kind to remind others of his own past illustriousness, or rather, his family's illustriousness. He had to keep silent, or merely boast of things he had which he shared with others. Boasting, too, was no part of him. He never envied other men their money, for money was nothing to him, only pride. He had always despised and pitied men who had nothing but money; they were poor indeed, he often said. So, without the schloss, he was a man without a country, a man without a soul. He never spoke of it, though it was always in his mind, and a gloomy shadow of it was always in his deep-set small blue eyes.

"Damn the schloss!" thought Karl. He had never liked the schloss. He loved the Rhine valley below it, so golden, so green, so vast and broad and silent. When he stood far below in the valley, he had been able to look up at the schloss, a black chaotic shadow against the pale sky. He had been able to smell the warm grass with the sun on it, the exquisite hot perfume of grapes. To him the schloss, glowering and melancholy on its rocks, was an insult to this golden life and golden river and beautiful valley. It was dead, and all that it represented, thank God! was dead. There were some that yearned for the Germany that had produced things like this schloss, but they were sentimentalists who must have hated life. Karl, who loved life and his country, thought the sentimentalists dangerous when they were not funny. He was inclined to believe they were more funny than dangerous.

And that again brought him back to Kurt, and he pursed his lips ruefully again. Kurt lived in a sort of fierce pent joy and excitement these days; he was a somber man, not much given to conversation nor articulateness. But this joy and this excitement flashed out of his eyes constantly, and were the more noticeable because of his taciturnity. Karl had seen his big ruddy hands trembling yesterday when he had spoken of Adolf Hitler, the Austrian sign-painter who had seduced and hypnotized Germans into putting him in command of their country. There had been a fanaticism about Kurt. He belonged to the Party; was one of its first members. He had tried to persuade Karl to join, and had struck his brother across the mouth savagely when he had laughed. But Karl had forgotten. He forgot all of Kurt's monstrous acts through a lifetime, because of his great pity for him. Karl could not remember a time when he had not pitied his twin brother, though sometimes he had laughed gently at him. He sometimes laughed still, but in secret, and ruefully, and even with boredom.

Germany had suffered much, and would probably suffer even more. But she did not need fanatics and madmen and frenzied orators to save her. She did not need hatred nor "vengeance." She needed only a long quiet peace in which to adjust herself and understand herself, and rescue herself from hopelessness and fear.

Karl had now arrived in the broad street on which his brother lived. A fine sturdy middle-class street. The snow here was traced by the wheels of fine sturdy middle-class cars. It was a street of huge solid houses, old-fashioned and ugly, but strangely comforting in this present world of fear and insecurity and change. Kurt's home, which had been his father's and grandfather's birthplaces, and his own, was a ponderous residence whose general hideousness and strength made it one with its neighbors. It was three times the size of Karl's home, which had only to shelter Karl, his wife Therese and his young sister Gerda. But Kurt, who had been born two hours before his twin brother Karl, and who had inherited the greater share of his father's fortune, had to shelter himself, his wife Maria, his two half-grown sons, his wife's mother Frau Matilda Reiner, four servants, and, on the third floor, his adopted brother Doctor Eric Reinhardt. Incidentally, Doctor Eric Reinhardt was the betrothed of Gerda Erlich, Karl's and Kurt's younger and only sister, and the third floor was already under preparation to receive the couple upon their marriage, which was to take place in July.

As Karl lifted the knocker, he thought suddenly, and unwillingly of what his wife, Therese, had said last night. He had remarked uneasily upon Kurt's growing rudeness and almost savage attitude toward Eric Reinhardt, who was a Jew, and expressed himself of some surprise that Kurt was still insisting that the third floor be the home of the betrothed couple. He remembered that Therese had looked at him with her clear gray eyes, so grave yet so smiling, and had answered quietly that the reason for this was not fraternal love for Gerda, though the love was there, but that should the two find a home elsewhere, Karl's visits to his brother's home would be considerably fewer. "Kurt knows quite well," she had said, "that you go to his house as much to see Eric as to see him." That had been her first and only indication that Kurt's passionate love for his twin brother was not a secret from her. Karl remembered that he had flushed with pain, and had changed the subject.

The housemaid opened the door and admitted him into the warm dimly lit hall. She believed that both the Herr Professor and Doctor Reinhardt were in. Karl went into the great old-fashioned living room, with its black-walnut and pale-ash furniture, and found his sister-in-law, Maria, sitting before the fire, sewing. She was always sewing, and never read anything; only her sharp malice and shrewdness kept her from being an ignorant fool. She gave her borther-in-law her knowing and malicious smile, and offered him a chair. "Kurt is with the boys," she said. "He is in a bad temper with them, because of their lack of interest in the gymnasium. Listen, and you can hear him shout! He becomes more choleric every day, because he has so much on his mind. The Party, you know. Really, he is too harsh with the children. He struck Wilhelm last night, very brutally, telling the child he was no true German when he whimpered. That is probably true."

She smiled again, more maliciously than ever, and her small blue eyes became even more knowing in their sidelong glance at Karl. She was a stout large woman with a mass of untidy light hair, coarse ruddy complexion, big pillowlike busts, execrable taste, and enormous hands and feet. There was a heavy necklace of yellow gold and diamonds about the crease which was her neck; the black silk dress was expensive, but dowdy. Karl detested her, and knew that she disliked him intensely in return. He was never comfortable in her presence. It was not that he was constantly thinking of her vulgar origin (her father had been a wealthy hop-merchant). It was because she seemed unclean to him, that he detested her. He always had the sensation that her mind was unwholesome, even obscene, and that she was constantly reading indecent meanings behind the most innocent remarks. She was not too bad-looking, and had been quite pretty in her youth, for her features were small and pudgy and her teeth were excellent. But it was her sly sidelong smiles that most revolted him.

"How is Therese?" she asked amiably, and both her smile and glance were those used when one archly asks about a visitor's mistress.

Karl hated himself for it, but he could feel his ready color rising. "Very well, thank you," he replied shortly, and looked fumingly at the doorway for his brother.

"And Gerda? When I spoke the last time about her wedding linens she said carelessly that she had not yet thought about them. What my mother would have said if I had told her that! The young girls, these days!"

"Gerda is well," answered Karl, holding his temper and looking directly at his sister-in-law. "But she has more important things to think of than linens. She can buy them, but the school cannot buy her influence over her pupils so easily." He bit his lip and determinedly studied the rich hideous old furniture of the room, every piece of which he knew by heart from his childhood.

Maria sighed hypocritically and examined her sewing with minute care while she said: "I have no doubt that poor little Gerda is thinking of other things besides linens these days. It will not be all sunshine for her when she marries a Jew, even if it is our own dear Eric Reinhardt."

Karl regarded her with a fierce frown, though his heart began to beat. "What do you mean by that, Maria?" he demanded. His voice shook a little. "Eric is our adopted brother, as well as a Jew. Besides, he may be a Jew by religion, or parentage, but is a German, too. His father was one of our President Hindenburg's aides, before he was killed at Verdun. Professor Reinhardt was one of the truest Germans who ever lived, and our father's most devoted friend. He left, as you know, his little son Eric, in our father's care, and all his fortune. But you know all this! How can you say, then, that Eric's parentage might cause suffering for him and for Gerda?"

She looked at him pityingly, and with affected wonder. "Do you never read or understand anything, Karl? I know you are interested only in your writing, but you might sometimes lift your nose from your manuscripts and look about you, and read. This is a new Germany, now, under our heroic Chancellor Hitler. He will remake our distressed country; his life and heart are dedicated to her. In this new Germany, he says, there is no place for Jews."

Karl laughed angrily and bitterly. "So that is what is behind all this! You are a foolish woman, Maria, and I offer you no apology for saying it. The Chancellor, in spite of much that is disgusting about him, is a clever man. His Jew-baiting is only incidental scenery on the stage of his real and ambitious plans. It was a morsel he threw the stupid mob, so that it would elect him and bring his National Socialists into power. But now that he is elected, and there is no more opposition, he will forget his Jew-baiting in the press of greater things. Why, German Jews have been in Germany as long, and even longer, than most Germans! They built up Germany; they gave her the illustrious light of scientific genius and some of our most brilliant artists! To eliminate the German Jews from the life of Germany would be to eliminate the glory of the German soul, and reduce us all to savagery."

His voice shook more and more as he added: "But it is ridiculous to discuss this at all. Nothing so monstrous will ever happen in this day."

She smiled evilly. "I still recommend a little attention to what is happening in the world, Karl. I particularly recommend attention to Germany. Few of us like the Jews as you do. Most of us believe them to be enemies of the German people. So, I believe most sincerely that the coming of Chancellor Hitler is the day of death for this alien race in our country."

Karl wet his lips. "Surely," he cried, "you do not hear this terrible imbecility from Kurt?" He no sooner asked the question than he felt suddenly sick and filled with incredulous horror.

Maria gazed at him enigmatically, but did not answer. Her eyes bored into him without expression, as though he were a stranger and she were seeing him for the first time. To her, indeed, he was a ridiculous and disliked stranger, a thinner image of tall and stalwart Kurt, a paler and gentler and more futile image, with his large and luminous blue eyes, long lean face, cropped upstanding light hair and thin broad shoulders. He had a frank and candid expression, yet for all this he seemed older than his forty years, much older than somber and gloomy and angry-voiced Kurt, whose eyes were smaller and narrower and closer, and full of suspicion and coldness.

He was about to repeat his question to Maria, more frantically this time, when he heard his brother's heavy rapid step on the stairway curving from the second floor. He turned to the doorway, and stood up, still pale and enormously shaken.

Kurt never entered a room; he projected himself into it, as though impelled by an explosive force. Yet his projecting had nothing of vivacity and eagerness; there was an iron and ruthless quality in it. Even when entering the old familiar rooms of his childhood, he entered as a soldier enters into alien territory, prepared for anything. He held his big hard body as a soldier holds it, erect and square. His glance was always hostile and challenging.

But this glance, when it encountered his beloved brother, suddenly lightened almost passionately. "Karl!" he exclaimed. "And you were here only Monday!" He flung his arm awkwardly about his brother, squeezed him, looked into his face with smiling and almost breathless affection.

Karl smiled also, feeling the old embarrassed and compassionate discomfort he had experienced from his earliest childhood.

"I'll go away, if I come too often," he said, laughing.

Kurt laughed at this absurd remark, squeezed his twin again.

"If you came every day, it would not be enough," he answered.

"But you rarely come to my home," said Karl, more to make conversation than anything else, for he was still sick inside, and dreadfully shaken.

At his remark, Kurt's beaming expression darkened. He dropped his arm. "How can I come, when Therese dislikes me so visibly? Even Gerda, my own sister, finds me oppressive." His voice was gloomy, almost accusing. "Therese, only the last time, told me insultingly that I was a savage father."

"Therese speaks ignorantly," said Maria. "But that is because, perhaps, her husband is not a father, himself."

Karl flushed. Kurt turned to his wife angrily. "That is none of your affair, Maria. Karl gives Germany poetry and beautiful prose. That is nobility, too. Perhaps as important as giving the Fatherland strong soldiers." But his own voice did not sound convinced, but only loyally hypocritical.

Karl could not help smiling, for all his distress. On another night, he might even have laughed with pure amusement. "It is always the old question: is brain more valuable than brawn? In each nation's answer to that question is the measure of her soul and the shadow of her destiny." He hesitated. He had come tonight only to see his adopted brother, Eric, who had telephoned him that morning that his box from Africa had just arrived. But for some reason, he could not speak frankly about his coming to see Eric to his brother tonight. He waited for the subject to occur by itself, or for Eric to present himself voluntarily.

Kurt laughed indulgently at his brother's last remark, and urged him into a chair. He began to speak of his secondary passion: biology. He was Professor of Biology at the University, where his adopted brother, Eric, was an instructor in psychology. Only with Karl was his voice so boyishly eager, as though he were a child anxiously trying to impress and cajole the only one who understood him, and the only one whom he loved.

"In biology," he said, "we find the true road to the advancement of man. How can we have been so blind, all these years! But now we know that we can breed supermen, bold, heroic, devoted, patriotic, fearless and healthy. True Germans. The superman of Nietzsche is in the loins of the Fatherland; we have only to evoke him." His face glowed.

Karl gazed at him with pity. Kurt was a scientist, perhaps one of the most eminent scientists of this day. His textbooks on biology had been translated into almost all the modern languages. He had made his university famous. But that had been before he had become a fanatic. In his new fanaticism the light of his genius was drowning, like a torch flung into a swamp. Now Karl's pity spread from his brother to all Germany, to all the world, who had been robbed of this lighted torch. It was an awful thing to contemplate, the saddest of all things. It was so deep that he could not reply to Kurt, not even to ridicule his idea.

"Through the mathematical magic of biology we shall get rid of the rabble-curse which produces Communism," continued Kurt with ferocity. Karl still gazed at his brother sadly. In Kurt's eyes he saw again the somber shadow of the schloss, and he hated, with sudden passion, the thing that caused the shadow. It was this schloss that stood in the swamp that was quenching Kurt's genius.

"It should have been destroyed, centuries ago," he thought, and was startled to discover that he had spoken aloud. Kurt regarded him with pleased surprise, and struck him on the arm.

"Well!" he beamed. "I am delighted to hear you say this, for you have always been so gentle about the mobs. We'll make a good National Socialist out of you in time!" But Maria glanced at Karl slyly, and smiled.

Karl was silent. He began to wonder desperately if he was to go away without seeing Eric, and without inspecting the wondrous box from Africa which his adopted brother had brought back during his explorations on his last holiday. But just when his despair was becoming unbearable, and Kurt's voice was a drone in his ears, he heard a whistle, a snatch of lieder, and rapid almost running footsteps on the stairway. A moment later a young man in his early thirties literally burst into the room. He was tall and lithe and dark, with brilliant white teeth and hazel eyes glittering with laughter and vivacity. He seemed much younger than he was, for everything crackled and sparkled about him; his energy was visible in his quick expressions, his rapid words, his vehement gestures. He was apt to fatigue much slower natures; but his friends loved him, felt stimulated by his constantly changing face and moving hands and vivid laughter. But only those who truly loved him, as Karl and Gerda did, ever saw him under the blaze and rush of his vitality. They were quite familiar with his melancholy and his dark depressions; when all the light had gone from him, he wore the face of his people, grave and brooding and sorrowful. Strangers found this handsome young man with the crisp black curling hair rather unnerving and somewhat frivolous, for there were so few for whom he cared sufficiently to let them see him as he truly was.

He had seen Karl only a day or two ago, and had talked to him only that morning on the telephone, but his cry of pleasure and enthusiasm, his quick hug, his delighted eyes, were those of a man seeing a beloved friend for the first time in many years. The air sparkled and fumed about him as he shouted: "Karl! My God, it's good to see you again!"

Karl smiled at him fondly. His slower, gentler nature felt

as though confronted with a warm and delicious fire. He was different from Eric as though from a different world; yet, curiously, the two men understood each other more deeply, more truly, than they had ever understood any one else.

"I'm flattered," he answered. "But how you have changed in these long years since we last saw each other!"

Eric laughed loudly, glancing at Kurt and Maria for mutual enjoyment of this gentle pleasantry. But Maria was watching her husband maliciously. Kurt's face had darkened and hardened, and his eyes gleamed like polished stone.

"Well," said Eric, "it was only this morning that I talked to you and asked you to come tonight. What is the matter?" he asked, diverted, for Karl's cool fair cheeks had flushed suddenly.

"Nothing at all. What should be the matter?" stammered poor Karl. To himself he said: This is ridiculous. I am becoming too sensitive and imagining things that do not exist. I wish Therese had not said what she did last night. But he felt miserable just the same. Everything, these days, was so confused and annoying; events broke in upon a man's quiet and peace like vulgar voices. No wonder a man became supersensitive and saw specters.

But Eric had already forgotten the question. He could think of nothing but his remarkable box which had just arrived. "I haven't opened it yet!" he cried. "I couldn't open it until you came. Kurt has been so inquisitive, haven't you, Kurt?"

But Kurt appeared anything but inquisitive; he was staring at the floor. The hand that held his cigar trembled slightly. What is the matter with him? thought Karl despairingly, and with unusual irritability. However, Eric had also forgotten about Kurt, and seized Karl by the arm. "Come on!" he said impatiently. "It is so late, and I have papers to correct. I can do nothing until you see the box. It is amazing! You will not believe what I shall tell you! You will thank me; there is material here for a thousand novels. I shall say, when your next novel appears: 'I gave him that magnificent idea!'" He tugged at Karl's thin arm again. Karl looked into his eyes; he and Eric often communicated like this, with just a look, just a flicker of an eyelid. Eric understood immediately. He glanced over his shoulder at Kurt. "But Kurt, you are coming, also?"

"I thought you did not care about extending the invitation," said Kurt stiffly. But he came forward, still apparently gloomy and dark, but with a slight softening. He looked at his brother Karl as he answered Eric.

"You are always imagining slights where none exist," said Karl. He was surprised that his voice had an edge on it. I must control myself, he thought. He smiled at his brother, took his arm. "It will not be so enjoyable without you," he added, feeling sheepish. But as usual, the most blatant sentimentality was seized upon eagerly by Kurt. At his brother's words his whole face, his whole stiff body, seemed to melt, to fuse together. He glowed and colored. Karl felt ashamed at these evidences of immeasurable attachment, to which he was accustomed, but which never failed to embarrass and disconcert him. As Kurt took his arm, Karl was filled with mingled annoyance and pity to see how his brother glanced with triumph at Eric, though Eric, had he caught that look, would have been completely bewildered and quite frankly curious.

They went up the stairway. They passed Frau Reiner's room, and Karl had to look in and exchange genial remarks with her. He was the old lady's favorite, and she never failed to express her candid disappointment that he was not her son-in-law instead of Kurt. She was malicious, like her daughter, but she was also intelligent and cunning and very subtle. A terrible old woman, with thin chuckling laughter and an eye. Once Maria had called Karl an innocent, and the old woman had chuckled and shook her head, replying: "Ah, but it is innocence like this which makes us cover our nakedness!" She was a Bavarian, very dark and with black eyes, and a Catholic, all of which made her detest Kurt, who was fair and tall and a Prussian and a Protestant. But none of these identical things made her detest Karl. Last Christmas he had given her a beautiful crucifix, though Kurt had frequently declared that no crucifix should ever enter his house. It was pure gold and ivory and exquisite enamel. Maria had affected to believe that malice had prompted Karl's gift, but both Kurt and Frau Reiner knew differently. It was his innocence. The crucifix remained, in full view, and on a sort of altar. Kurt's expression always became gloomy at the sight of it, but still it stayed. He would have died to defend it.

She asked about Gerda, just to keep Karl in her doorway; she liked to look at him, and listen to his quiet and gentle voice. She had had a lover like him, when she had been young. He made her feel sweet and kind again, for all her knowledge and her years frequently fatigued her, and made her feel dusty and webbed and somehow dirty. He refreshed her, made her believe she was virtuous and simple once more, instead of a terrible old woman with many sins. "Come often!" she cried, as he said good night.

Karl had to stop at the rooms of the boys, too, for both of them, even stiff Alfred, so like his father, loved him more than they loved Kurt. They swarmed about him, looking impatiently at each other. It might have been years since they had seen him. He had infinite patience, and his laughter was not assumed. He was genuinely fond of them and interested in them, and he always saw below the surface, with understanding and compassion. Young Wilhelm had a large ugly bruise on his cheek, and seeing that bruise Karl's lips tightened and paled. He put his arm about the lad's shoulder, and spoke to him with especial attention. The boys were fond of Eric, also; they treated him like a youth, and they all chaffed each other unmercifully.

The third floor was already under preparation. Painters' and carpenters' equipment were neatly lined against the walls. Eric had been moved into two rooms, his bedroom and a sitting room. The sitting room was comfortable and untidy and warm, full of books, heaped tables, sturdy cushioned chairs, lamps and fire and piled papers. Gerda had warned him affectionately that when she was his wife she would see that his private sitting room was well-tidied. She had meant this in fun, but he had taken her seriously, with considerable apprehension. He had gone to the length of installing a thick brass lock on the door, with just one key, which he kept in his pocket.

Eric had brushed books and papers and cigarettes off the large center table. On this table stood a huge wooden box with a hammer beside it. Eric seized the hammer and began to pound at the box excitedly, until Kurt took the hammer from him with a grunt of amused disgust and opened the box dexterously with a few neat blows. Then they all peered in. Kurt gave another grunt of disgust, larger this time; he was disappointed. He had expected, perhaps, to see fabulous treasures of carved ivory, several uncut and unpolished diamonds, weird woven stuffs with gold threads, idols of beautiful woods, and beads and bracelets of crudely fashioned gold. The first thing that came rudely to his attention was an exceedingly bad smell. He recoiled and said: "Feh!" He wrinkled his nose.

But Karl and Eric bent over the box with excitement, regardless of the smell.

Eric suddenly thrust in his hand and triumphantly dragged out what appeared to be a tiny human head made of brown and wrinkled wood with staring glass eyes. It was perfectly carved, and astoundingly lifelike, with real African human hair, all black wool and friz. The little face was evil, and it smiled wickedly, as though imagining the wildest and maddest thoughts, full of obscenity. The glass eyes had a strange glaring expression, fixed and terrible, as though they were seeing awful things beyond the narrow borders of a safe reality.

Eric held it up so that his adopted brothers could view it. The lamplight glittered in the glass eyes. For one moment those eyes seemed like Eric's own, when he was off-guard, and confused. He looked at the little head and beamed affectionately. Kurt was more and more revolted. "Feh!" he said again. But Karl studied it intently.

"I see. It is a real head. I thought the headhunters had been driven away from the Coast."

"Yes, they have been driven away. But this was given to me as a great present from the chief of a tribe. His favorite wife was ill, dying of typhoid. I saved her life. So, he gave me his most treasured possession. The head of his grandfather, who was a witch doctor." Eric laughed with enjoyment. "One witch doctor to another!" He regarded the head with pride.

"A real head!" exclaimed Kurt with horror. "Mein Gott, never let Maria know of this! The horrible thing! I must ask you to hide it, preferably in your cabinet at the university."

Eric and Karl looked at him with intense amusement. "The heroic and strong-souled German!" said the young Jew mockingly but with affection. "Ah, Kurt, you are all alike! Sentimentalists. Full of fire and blood-lust, but horrified at a brutal reality." He put the head down very tenderly beside the box. "I imagine you were a better man than I am, Gilu," he addressed the relic. "You probably used the same hocus-pocus, with possibly better effect. Your patients believed in you. Then, too, you knew a great deal more about the mind and the dark human soul than all the Freuds in the world. What a pair you and Adolph Hitler would have made!"

Kurt uttered a strangled and animal-like sound. Eric and Karl gazed at him in astonishment. His face had turned purple; the veins had swollen in his head. His fists were clenched, and his forehead glistened with water. He was regarding Eric with hatred and fury.

"How dare you speak of the German Chancellor like this! How dare you sully the name of Adolph Hitler by speaking his name! It is sacrilege for your mouth to hold his name; it is blasphemy!"

Eric stared; his mouth fell open. He was covered with amazement. There had never been the rapprochement between him and Kurt as with Karl. He had always teased Kurt, amused at his lack of humor and his heaviness and sentimental gloom; he had even condescended, affectionately. But he had never considered Kurt to be especially intelligent, in spite of the laborious and exquisitely exact scientific research. Eric despised the non-subtle, the humorless, and the ultra-somber. They seemed faintly ridiculous to him, big bears lumbering about with tiny choleric eyes, never seeing the forest nor the flowers nor the clouds. He had also pitied Kurt, and had argued with him endlessly and with patronizing impatience. He had always criticised Kurt, and had made open and good-humored fun of him at times. But he had never dreamed that he had really hurt his adopted brother, for whom he had a mild fondness.

But as he looked at Kurt now, he was thunderstruck. He realized for the first time that his adopted brother hated him, and that the hatred was not new, but a festering thing of many years, only breaking through the surface now, like an abscess. This is what astounded and made him turn as cold as ice with distress and fear. For the first time in his life he was speechless.

"Kurt!" gasped Karl, paling. "This is Eric you are speaking to!" He was leaning on the table with the palms of his hands. Now his arms shook so that they could barely support him. He, too, had seen the hatred.

Kurt swung on him. His face was distorted with grief and bitterness as he looked at his beloved brother. There was a wild and accusing reproach in his eye, which blazed.

"I am well aware that I am speaking to Eric, Karl! And I am even more well aware of what Eric is! That is why I will not have him mention that Name in my house!" He panted; he seemed to struggle for breath. But his eyes, while still infuriated and full of reproach, seemed to plead with his brother also, with a sort of bitter desperation.

Karl regarded him steadfastly, growing still paler. "What

Name, Kurt?" he asked quietly. "The name of a plebeian sign-painter, an Austrian, who is not even a German? Have you gone entirely mad?"

Kurt's bitter desperation and pathetic rage seemed to mount. His face grew even more dusky. His lips shook. He looked like a man about to have a cerebral hemorrhage. "Take care, Karl!" he exclaimed huskily. "Take care! I am your brother, and a member of the Party, but Germany comes before blood, these days. There is nothing but the soul of Germany! There is nothing but the blood and destiny of Germany! There is nothing but Hitler!" And to Karl's utter stupefaction, he raised his arm in a stiff and wooden gesture and cried: "Heil Hitler!"

At this Eric burst out into long and uproarious laughter. He laughed and laughed. Kurt still held up his arm, but all at once he appeared a foolish figure to Karl, who felt his anger evaporating. He was even pathetic, and Karl experienced a quick annoyance at Eric, for his laughter, which made poor Kurt appear so absurd. He was about to reprimand his adopted brother when he caught an undernote in that laughter, and he knew immediately that there was no real mirth in it, but a sort of hysteria and wildness and bitterness.

He knew, too, that something was happening in this room tonight that was momentous and awful, full of prophecy and destiny. Kurt and Eric were symbols of what was happening in Germany, and perhaps in all the world. Karl felt as though he were caught in a dreadful dream, full of monstrous and unbelievable things. He could not speak. He sat down, very slowly and heavily.

Kurt was still beside himself and surging with violence. And then, as he stood there, trying to restrain himself from attacking Eric, he saw his brother's face. Karl had put up his hand as if to shield his eyes from the sight of something unbearable. Kurt could see his pale cheek, his chin, his mouth. He could see his trembling hand, so slender and white.

"Karl," he said impulsively, and there was a cry in his voice.

But Karl did not move. It was as though he were hearing nothing but his own thoughts. Eric had stopped laughing, and was silent. His dark face had a curious pallor on it, and his eyes were fixed on Kurt.

Then Kurt made a gesture that was oddly defenseless and despairing. He turned and went out of the room. He closed the door silently behind him, which was in itself unusual.

There was a long silence after his footsteps had died away. Then Eric began to speak, softly and meditatively, as though to himself.

"I have begun to smell this, this virus, everywhere. I smelt it in my classroom, today, among my pupils. They looked at me so oddly, and once one even laughed, derisively. The others silenced him, but I saw their faces! I smell it in the streets, in the theaters, the rathskellers, the beer-gardens. Strange! I have never thought of myself as a Jew, but only as a German. Other Germans of Jewish blood have felt so, also. And yet, now we smell the virus. There is poison in the air, an effluvia, the breath of pestilence. But where is the serum that can immunize a whole nation? The serum of reason and sanity? It has never been discovered. But until it is discovered, no one in all this world is safe."

Karl dropped his hand. He looked ill and haggard. "Let us not talk of—this, just tonight," he said in a stifled voice. "I'm a fool. I'm just a futile man of letters. I've lived in a cloister. I never knew what was happening. I—I must orient myself. You must forgive me, Eric, but I must have time to think, and understand. You must forgive me for being such an imbecile." He indicated the box. "Please. Eric, let us look at these things."

Eric hesitated, and sighed. Then his irrepressible gaiety came back, partly naturally, partly for regard for Karl. He laughed a little. He picked up the head of the savage witch-doctor and put it on the mantelpiece in a position of honor. Then he raised his arm in Kurt's own stiff salute and cried "Heil Hitler!" Karl watched him. He smiled involuntarily, like a man momentarily diverted from pain. Eric came back to the table and in a changed voice began to talk about the weird things he pulled from the box.

He produced a queer affair which appeared to be two small triangles of black wood joined together at the apex and separated at the other extreme by a peg some two inches high. "This, Karl, is called the 'soul-searcher.' Look, you hold it in your hand and lift the apex to the level of your eyes. But instead of allowing your eye to follow the upward plane of one of the sides, you look through the space enclosed by the sides and then through the aperture. Try it." Karl followed instructions. Eric backed away slowly until his whole face could be seen within the two-inch aperture through which

Karl gazed. The young man smiled and waited, his eyes fixed on Karl.

"Nonsense," said Karl, peering. "I see nothing but your ugly face. Or perhaps you haven't a soul to see?"

"Keep on looking. Besides, there's an incantation which you are supposed to keep on saying to yourself, silently: 'I behold your soul. Nothing can blind my vision to the sight of your soul.' Keep on saying that."

"Nonsense," said Karl again, laughing. Indulgently, however, he repeated the incantation over and over to himself, until he began to feel bored, and Eric's face seemed to grow smaller and clearer and sharper through the aperture, and finally seemed nothing more than a little carved face of ivory brilliantly lighted.

Karl came to himself with a start, as though he had been hypnotized. He ceased the "incantation." Immediately Eric's face again became larger and less clear, the light fading. "What's the matter?" asked Eric.

Karl was silent. He lifted the triangle again with hands not very steady, and gazed through it. He kept repeating the incantation without his previous indulgence and amusement. It affected him like a hypnosis, for no doubt it was just that. The steady concentration of light on Eric's face assisted this hypnotic state, and Karl's own personality seemed to dim even to himself, and he was only vision and murmurous internal words, without thought.

Again Eric's face grew smaller and clearer and sharper and brilliantly lighted, yet, strangely, it seemed to approach closer until it seemed to be at the very opening of the aperture, within touching distance of Karl's hand. The young Jew was still smiling; his expression was gay, his eyes shining with anticipation and boyish enjoyment.

Then all at once Karl felt a cold amazed dread which almost made him drop the triangle. But he controlled himself; now his lips moved feverishly over the words of the incantation, as though he were afraid that he might forget them and break the spell.

He saw Eric's face, tiny, brilliantly lit, carved. But it was a dead face, in light. The eyes were closed, the nostrils distended, the mouth grimacing. Karl looked and looked again; he heard the deep somber beating of a drum, quickening, thundering. He did not realize it was the sound of his own heart. All his attention was concentrated in the vision of that dead face. He had never seen anything else but this, from all eternity, and for eternity he was condemned to look at it.

Then all at once the face blurred, swelled, enlarged. and disappeared, and there was only the aperture with the head of Gilu, on the mantelpiece. grinning and glaring in it. Karl dropped the triangles. His hand was trembling quite violently. He looked up, bemused, and saw Eric standing beside him, grinning.

"Well, what did you see, Karl? Did you see my soul, or my future, or anything? It seems you are supposed to see the future, too; the soul in the future. Very esoteric. What did you see?"

Karl stared at him in silence for a moment or two, then said quietly: "Nothing at all. Except your face—smaller and clearer. That's all."

Eric was childishly disappointed. "No! Is that all? What's the matter with my face? I had half a dozen people, in Africa, look at me through the thing. They all said the same: nothing."

Karl smiled. "Is it possible you are superstitious? You, an authority on the hidden places of the mind? Whatever could be seen through this triangle, for instance, could be, only, the result of the converging rays of light. Such as occurs when one squints, thus making the focussed image clearer. I saw your face, smaller and sharper, but that is all."

Eric laughed. "Let me try." He sat down and focussed the triangle on Karl's face. Karl saw his lips moving silently in the incantation. He smiled again, leaned back and let Eric scrutinize him through the triangle. As he did so, he became aware that he was greatly tired. He refused to remember what had happened in this room between himself and Eric and Kurt; he did not want to remember, yet. He shut his mind, too, against the peculiar thing he had seen through the triangle. Nevertheless, his very grim effort to prevent remembrance and conjecture exhausted him.

He heard an exclamation. muffled and somewhat afraid. Eric had dropped the triangle, and was staring at him blankly, as though seeing him for the first time. "Most extraordinary!" Eric muttered. He had turned quite pale. He stared more than ever. "Most extraordinary." Then he laughed shortly, queerly. "You know, Karl, you have the gentlest and mildest face in the world; a Thomas Mann face. Full of dreamy intellect and noble idealism. Yes, truly; do not smile. And yet, and yet—" He hesitated, resumed, to Karl's amusement, in a bemused voice: "And yet, your face: it was terrible. If this is truly a vision of your face, maybe your future face, you have a terrible soul, a terrible future. I would not like to encounter you, if you wore a face like that directed at me. It was a face that would stop at nothing, when the spirit behind it was aroused. It would not stop at murder, at anything horrible."

Karl laughed with pure enjoyment and a shamed sense of passionate relief. What nonsense! "I tell you, Eric, it is due to the converging of light and lines! I, terrible! Why, I'm even a vegetarian at times!"

But Eric said, without smiling, and in a peculiar voice: "I should like to see Kurt's face through this!" He stood up, and began to rummage in the box again, gravely. "When Socrates said: 'Know thyself,' he must have laughed sardonically."

Karl's amusement increased. "I shall be afraid to look in the mirror tonight. I'll be afraid that Gilu's face will look back at me."

Eric shot a swift glance at the mummified head. Then the glance fixed. After a moment or two, he went back to his rummaging, and said nothing more. But he seemed preoccupied.

"Now, this," he said, bringing out a queer object, "is a phallic talisman." He began to exclaim over the various other talismans and amulets and charms which he took from the box. Karl listened with deep interest. He had always had a sheepish interest in primitive occultism. Eric had an easy and fascinating way of talking, which had made his classes the most popular in the university. Karl was quite enthralled; he leaned his elbows on the table and rested his chin in his hands. His face was mild and sweet and absorbed, the face of a gentle dreamer and student.

"I have always believed, with Shakespeare, that there are more things in heaven and earth than are dreamed of in our philosophy," said Eric. "Now, don't call me superstitious! But my own researches into the dark crevices and pits and caverns of the human psyche have convinced me that here is a submerged continent still undiscovered, and, in a way, frightful. Who knows how deep the crevices are, or what the pits and the labyrinthine caverns contain? A few isolated acts and words, mostly futile or violent, emerge to the surface of the sea, which spreads over this vast and secret world. But that subterranean world is still hidden, full of unsuspected, and perhaps awful things. Sometimes, I feel that psychologists are presumptuous children, who will at any moment dredge horror to the surface, and die of the fright of it, and make all other men die."

Karl laughed gently. "No wonder that Kurt sneers at psychology, and calls it the 'inexact science'! World of dreams. But very interesting."

But Eric said strangely: " 'World of dreams.' But the most potent world of all. Jesus knew this, and could command it. So did all the other messiahs and leaders. And so, perhaps, does Hitler."

Karl looked at him swiftly. He opened his mouth to speak, then closed it firmly.

"It is a world," said Eric, "that is at the command of those who know of it, and have power over it. Confucius, Jesus, Buddha—these had power over it, for profound and beautiful good. And then, there are others, who have the power and use it for evil. I tell you!" he exclaimed, "there are really devils!"

"Devils! Now, Eric, this is really too much!"

Eric shook his head fiercely. "Devils! I've seen them! I tell you, I've seen them! Let me tell you.

"My friend, the chief, took a sort of devotion to me. You see, he was an old man, and all his wives together had given him only a daughter. And then his youngest and favorite wife, taken in last desperation, was pregnant. The witch-doctors had assured him that she would give him a son. She was a pretty thing, with finer features than the other women of the tribe, and had an intelligent look. Then, just before we arrived at this village—it was almost a town, with autocratic rights over three dozen other villages—this wife became extremely ill. When we arrived, we found the witch-doctors leaping about, screaming incantations. A human sacrifice had even been thrown to the crocodiles, and they were preparing the greatest sacrifice—the hurling of the chief's oldest wife into the river.

"I can't tell you how weird it was! The moon was bright yellow above the jungle, and the noises the witch-doctors were making, and the torches, had disturbed all the birds, and they were shrieking and clamoring like lost souls. The village was ringed with fires, and the air vibrated with drums and the wailing of women. How hot it was! and the leaping priests and doctors, painted until they were no longer human and oiled till they shone, made it all seem like an inferno. I heard the distant screaming of monkeys, and the yelping of obscene wild beasts in the depths of the tangled jungles. I could smell the fires and the sweat and the acrid animal odors, and the dried burnished grass. When we came, the dancing and leaping and shrieking stopped, and we saw all their eyes, glistening in the moonlight and the torchlight.

"We had a small amount of typhoid serum left, after we had inoculated the people of another village. We found that this big village had not escaped the plague. But then it had passed. Every one felt safe. Then this young wife had become violently sick, and was dying, big as she was with child. We persuaded the chief to let us look at her. The witch-doctors protested, and threatened us. But the chief had visited the coastal cities, and had a respect for white knowledge. He let us see his wife. There she lay, almost *in extremis*, unconscious. I drove them all out, and shot her full of all the serum we had left, and called the women back to her hut.

"It was exceedingly dangerous, as we soon found out. We were treated hospitably enough, and the chief led us to his hut and ordered food and water for us. But we discovered that we were being furtively guarded. We knew then that we would pay the penalty if the woman died. This so unnerved me that I went back to the girl and nursed her myself all night. My God! I was frightened to death. At one time I thought she was gone. I'll never forget that night!

"Then at dawn she awoke to consciousness and could speak a little. Her fever was down. She was on the way to recovery."

Karl listened, smiling but intent.

"The chief could not do enough for us. I tell you, it was pathetic! He grovelled; he kissed our hands. But the woman's weakness told on her; she gave birth to her child that evening. Again we nursed her through it all, taking turns, driving off the women, though it was a law of the tribe that no man could be present at a birth. Thank God for the chief's brief visits to the coast and civilization! Yes, it was a son. The chief's first son. Small and feeble, but a son. He lived, and so did the woman.

"They would not let us go after that. It was amusing. In some way, the chief seemed to believe that I was directly responsible, not only for the saving of the mother's life, but for the sex of the child! And believe it or not, that child was solemnly given my name! Eric!"

Karl laughed wholeheartedly. Kurt, downstairs, pacing up and down in his library, alone, heard the laughter of Karl and

Eric. He clenched his fists; his sensitive and suspicious German soul was convinced that the laughter was directed at him. He was filled with hatred and rage.

"And so, I have a spiritual son, in Africa!

"The chief wanted the women to strip themselves of all their charms and jewels, for us. We would not allow it, of course. He wanted to give us everything he had. He offered to adopt me as his older son. Naturally, the priests were furious. But I had an idea. I told the chief that I wished to see some magic.

"Now, I had really embarrassed him. The witch-doctors and priests refused with an awful ballyhoo. They prophesied dire things for the tribe if a white man were initiated. I should have been more generous, for I had put the poor old chief in a very bad position. But my curiosity grew stronger as the witch-doctors and the priests grew more hysterical. Finally the chief, in great irritation, told them to shut up and let him think. That again, was the result of his coastal visits. I do not suppose any one had ever dared before to tell them to shut up. After their first stupefaction, they acted like all other witch-doctors and priests do in every other country and nation; they sulked and muttered and threatened, and kept looking at me with fiery and vengeful eyes.

"Then the chief, after a night's thought, decided that I should have what I desired. You should have heard the clamor of the witch-doctors. If they had known what resignation means, they would have resigned."

He paused. Karl, absorbed, leaned forward, smiling but excited. "Go on, Eric, go on!"

"I, only, it was finally decided, should see the magic. My friends raised a fearful clamor. But it was no use. They expressed their opinion of my selfishness very bitterly. But what could I do?

"That night I was awakened by the chief himself, who whispered that the time had come. He was very solemn; he made me promise that I would not hold him accountable for anything that I would see or hear. Then he begged me, for the last time, to reconsider. I told him that I, myself, was a sort of witch-doctor—a very superior witch-doctor! I was in Africa solely, I assured him, to learn of new magic. That seemed to relieve him. My own words made me think: I finally became convinced that I was, in truth, only a witch-doctor, and that Freud was the greatest witch-doctor of us all!

"The chief then went to see the priests, who stood about, muttering and glowering, and he told them what I had told him. They were impressed, though suspicious. One of them asked me what magic I could do. I looked him directly in the eye, and told him truly that my magic power enabled me to change swine into men. Karl, do not laugh! Is it not really true? Does not psychoanalysis free men from obscure and obscene and criminal obsessions? Was not Jesus the greatest psychoanalyst?

"One of the younger priests cynically suggested that I change one of the tribe's swine into a man. I assured him that when the moon was at its full, as it was this night, my magic was reversed, and I could only change men into swine. I offered to demonstrate my power right then, if the young priest would himself volunteer for the experiment, but for some reason he declined. They believed me now.

"We had no torchlight now. We wound about in almost total darkness through the fetid and steaming jungle; the matted vines and vegetation overhead shut out the moon until only splinters and slivers of it shone with a yellow light in the darkness. Never have I smelt such smells, such corruption. All about me I could hear crashes and whines and the breath of beasts. Scores of eyes gleamed here and there and disappeared. And the heat! It was a Turkish bath, sweltering and fuming. I was stung by insects; I stepped on small crawling things. I stumbled, felt thorns and vines tear me. Sweat ran down my whole body. I became sure, at last, that they had taken me into this boiling hell of vegetation and blackness and smells to murder me quietly.

"Karl, if you have ever believed, as all others believe, that vegetation is insensate and has no consciousness, I wish to tell you now that this is not true. This particular vegetation through which I struggled had a foul and malignant life; it demonstrated a gleeful delight in clutching me and tripping me, and revealed a personal hatred. It stank, too, as if my presence evoked an evil soul from it. I was a mass of cuts and punctures when we finally emerged onto the banks of a broad glitter of gold under an open black sky. It was the river. We got into flat boats, all in utter silence, and rowed out towards a small tufted island in the middle of the stream. Now I detected a gloating and anticipatory grin on the savage faces of the priests. I saw the glare of their rolling eyes, saw the glisten of the moonlight on their naked bodies. They were no more human than the drifting log-like crocodiles that infested the water.

"We reached the island, still in silence. The island was very small, and was forbidden to all but the priests and the chief. In the center, in a clearing, was a ring of fire-blackened stones. The priests squatted about this ring, and I squatted too. The center of the ring remained empty, like a small circular stage.

"I expected drums, incantations, hysteria, leaping and screaming. But there was none of this. The priests just squatted like statues of black gleaming marble and did not move a muscle. Even their eyes did not move; I saw the fixed white glaze of them. They looked only at the circle. I was disappointed. I scratched my insect bites, and my haunches ached. But I was the only thing that moved. In that golden moonlight there was the most profound silence. The heat seemed to grow more intense.

"Then I, too, fixed my eyes on the empty moonlit space and waited.

"My mind wandered; I became less aware of where I was. So it was that the first thing I saw in that space did not momentarily alarm or interest me.

"I saw leaping red stars, small and glittering, hurtling about like huge fireflies. I thought at first that they were a sort of tropical firefly, until I saw their number rapidly increase. There was a fixity about their light which showed they were not any sort of insect. They were like a cloud of fiery snowflakes, whirling about, drifting, rushing together, exploding apart.

"I was vaguely startled, and watched with rising alarm as the storm of scarlet particles became thicker. I could hear the muffled breathing of the priests very clearly; their breath was stronger, almost panting, and they sweated. I could hear them shifting on their haunches, as though tormented. I was dazzled, and began to feel a curious cold thrill running along my nerves.

"Then, in the very center of the whirlpool of sparks I saw three enormous human figures, naked and motionless. I could not remember the exact moment I became aware of them, for when I actually did become aware of them I felt a shock of horror. I could not see them very clearly, for through their bodies I could see the opposite terrain dimly, as though they were made of glass. I cannot even tell you if they were white or black. I can only say that they were enormous and human, and had the most dreadful expressions that can be imagined.

"They were smiling. And yet, as I think of it, I cannot say in what particular their expressions were so dreadful. They were bending their heads towards us, as though to see us more easily through the shifting whirlpools of red sparks. Perhaps it was their immobility that was so horrible. I do not know. But I know what it means when it is said that a man's soul swoons with dread, and with a fear greater than the fear of physical death. I felt that in these phantoms was an unnamable loathsomeness and evil and danger; they were the visible signs of those unnamed ferocities and horrors which are fixed eternally beyond the borders of our 'reality.'

"My sensations were indescribable. I was petrified in a sort of hypnosis; I lost consciousness of the other human beings beside me. Only I, and these awful phantoms, existed in a vacuum of hell. I became aware of eternity and wildness and despair and complete terror. I became aware of unreality, and knew it was the only reality.

"Some one shouted, or rather yelled. I did not know that it was myself, until I heard an angry confusion about me, and saw all the priests glaring at me. But I was too frightened to care. The phantoms and the sparks had disappeared, and there was only the empty ring of stones. I examined them. They were smoke-blackened, but cold. There was no sign of any fire at all."

Karl said thoughtfully: "Mass-hypnosis, of course."

"Mass-hypnosis!" cried Eric with impatience. "What do you mean by mass-hypnosis? It is a strange, and even terrible thing, that men dispose of mysteries with a word, pin a phrase upon the inexplicable, and go away, smugly, feeling that meaningless words have solved eternal puzzles. But under the little pink ribbons of words the mysteries still go veiled. Mass-hypnosis! What *is* mass-hypnosis? I know! I've spoken about it often in my stupid complacence in my own classrooms. 'Influence of one powerful mind on a mass of weaker ones.' But what *is* that influence, how does it operate, how can it work without visible sign?

"I grant you that it was 'mass-hypnosis.' But I am also sure that the hypnosis was produced by the phantoms I saw. Evil is always stronger than good; I have yet to see any sort of hypnotism except in medicine, used for a good purpose. Hypnotism works best when the hypnotizer is evil, and the subject disposed to evil more than to good." He paused, then continued in a changed voice: "The influence of the prophets and the saints and the saviors has been very long in the world. Yet one man, like Hitler, like Mussolini, can, with his 'mass-hypnotism,' undo in one hour what these prophets and the saints and the saviors have labored to do for centuries. This proves, without a doubt, that men are disposed to evil, and evil leaders can hypnotize them easily. This proves that evil is the most powerful thing in the universe, when that universe becomes conscious. The things I saw in that jungle in Africa were pure evil, and could be made manifest by the slightest invocation."

Karl was silent for some moments, then he said: "If this is true, and it *may* be true, then it is a good thing that men think very little. If they thought much, and realized, they would all go mad."

Eric smiled wryly. "It is paradoxical, but perhaps it is man's inability to think which has made civilization possible!"

Karl said nothing. Eric waited, but his adopted brother did not speak. So after a few minutes the younger man produced other articles from the box and spoke of them, in a somewhat flat voice. Karl listened, but it was evident that his thoughts were not centered on what Eric was saying. He came to with a start. Eric was showing him three little doll-like images of wood, crudely carved, but all alike. Eric was saying smilingly: "You see how it is? You 'baptize' each creature with the name of your detested enemy. You must believe in the baptism, and it must be done most solemnly, with concentration. Then the creature does in fact become your enemy, mysteriously his own image. After this, he is in your power. Then, you do so:" and he picked up a long prong, like a brass nail, and thrust it into the body of the carved image. "At any spot you desire. Slowly. The wood is soft. You drive it in a fraction each day; the natives say it is better so: the enemy suffers."

"Does it work?" asked Karl, teasingly.

"Yes, it does," said Eric, without a smile. "I have seen it done. Many times. It always worked. The subject suffered slowly, agonizingly, until he died. But he could not die until the nail was driven into a spot that was vital. The torturer sometimes delayed, exquisitely, before administering the *coup de grâce*. The savage mind is very imaginative."

"Is it necessary for the unfortunate subject to know that he is being worked upon?"

"No. Though it works quicker and better for him to know. But I have seen men sicken and die without knowing that they were being 'conjured.'" Eric smiled now. "What explanation have you for this, Karl?"

Karl laughed. "None. I do not believe it. When such a thing succeeds, it must be coincidence. When it fails, the operator probably believes that the 'magic' of his enemy is superior to his, or he conveniently forgets."

A maid brought in a tray with coffee and cakes and the message that the Herr Professor wished to see Herr Erlich at his convenience. Karl nodded, without speaking. Eric was unusually silent as they ate and drank. Then he said, after drinking the last cup: "You are skeptical about everything I have told you?"

"My dear Eric! Is it possible you believe any of the nonsense you have told me? My dear Eric!"

"Of course I believe. But never mind. I shall put all this away, and you need think no more of my idiocy."

Karl watched him return all the occult rubbish to the box. He hoped he had not offended the younger man. It was very painful for him to offend any one, and especially to offend Eric. He was suddenly depressed.

Eric began to speak about Gerda. He spoke as though he were concealing something, Karl thought. But what nonsense! It was only his own imagination which made him suspect that there was something strange in Eric's voice. But probably Eric was offended about the magic, still. So, he answered that Gerda was well and sent him her love, and wanted to remind him of the dinner on Saturday. Eric looked, then, at Karl, and seemed about to speak, and then evidently decided not to say anything. Karl had an uneasy feeling that Eric was concealing something about which he had originally wished to speak. I have really offended him, thought Karl remorsefully.

When Karl was about to go, Eric hesitated, then said, not looking at the other: "I have been thinking of going to America, after Gerda and I are married."

Karl was perplexed. "But I thought you were going to Switzerland on your honeymoon? Can they spare you from the University, all that time?"

Eric put the lid on the box and said in a peculiar tone: "I was thinking of going to America—permanently."

"Permanently!" Karl was incredulous. "America—but why?

Why are you so restless? I cannot believe this! Gerda, I am afraid, would not like America." Already he was filled with a sense of unbearable loss.

Eric gave him a long thoughtful look, in which there was a touch of compassion. "It is all so tentative, Karl. Perhaps it will never materialize. Shall we forget it for a while?"

But Karl said restively, and with a slight querulousness: "You ought not to annoy me with such ideas, Eric. You and Gerda—it would be hard to see you leave us."

Eric said nothing. He carried his box to a cabinet and put it away. When he came back he seemed older and quieter, yet more gentle. The energy that always crackled about him was subdued.

Karl went downstairs. He was met at the foot of the stairs by his brother. Kurt's face was ravaged and sunken, as though he had aged five years or more. He regarded Karl with an expression both dogged and pathetic. "Karl, I must talk to you at once. It is extremely important. Will you come into the library for just a few minutes?" His voice was pleading, and he kept opening and shutting his hands as though under a great strain.

Karl, who had greeted Kurt with some diffident coldness, hesitated. He was always pitying his brother, and this pity fatigued him as pity for no one else ever did. He had compassion for all living creatures, for this emotion rose from some tender deep in himself; but for Kurt it was always attended with this tiredness, a reaction which never failed to make him feel ashamed. "Very well," he said quietly, and followed Kurt into the cool dusky room with its tiers of old leathery books. Kurt had had a high fire built here, for he knew his brother's sensitiveness to chill. Karl felt a pang at this devoted thoughtfulness, and this pang also made him more tired. Even while his conscience bothered him at the thought, he wished, with some irritation, that Kurt were not always so considerate of him, as he was never so considerate of his wife and children.

He went to the fire, and refused the chair Kurt had drawn to it for him. He stood there, looking mildly obstinate and vaguely futile. Kurt, of course, could not sit down, himself. He stood beside his brother with that dogged and pathetic expression increasing on his face. Karl saw that his forehead was damp, and this made his pity torment him again. But greater than his pity was his embarrassment. He knew that the embarrassment rose from a sort of delicate cowardice: he hated introduction into any one's business as much as he hated interference in his. And he understood that Kurt was going to talk intimately. Intimacy with Kurt made him uneasy. He tried to overcome all these emotions by a gentle softening towards his brother. "Yes, Kurt?"

Kurt sighed. "Karl, you must not feel so antagonistic to me——"

"I am not antagonistic." Karl paused, stubbornly, refusing to leave an opening.

"But you are!" Kurt spoke eagerly, approaching his brother more closely. "You are condemning me in your mind for what I said to Eric!"

I shall not get home for hours, thought Karl resignedly. He fixed his eyes upon the other man and did not speak.

"Won't you let me explain, Karl? I have got to explain! It is so frightfully important. It cannot wait any longer."

"Are you not being melodramatic? Besides, in all my life I have never yet encountered anything that could not wait until tomorrow."

"You ought to have been an Englishman," said Kurt, with bitterness. "But this cannot wait. Procrastination is not only the thief of time, but of honor."

"What has honor got to do with all this?"

"The honor of our family."

Karl shrugged; he tightened his jawbone to keep from yawning. But quickening uneasiness tugged at his heart, and for a moment he saw Eric's face. What has happened to the world? he thought despairingly. So much emotion! So much tearing about in the mind! So many dramatics! I detest these intense people. He said resignedly: "You are being histrionic. The honor of our family, I believe, is still intact."

"But it will not be if Gerda marries that—that— if Gerda marries Eric Reinhardt."

Karl felt his heart plunge sickeningly, but he kept his expression quiet. "I do not understand you," he said sternly. In spite of his self-control his breath came quickly.

Kurt gave a gesture of despair. "Karl, where have you been sleeping all this time! Is it really possible that you have been so deliberately cloistered? Do you really not know that the day of the Jew is done in the Fatherland, and that he must be exterminated, either by exile or by the sword——?"

"You talk like a fool." Karl could not keep a quiet violence out of his voice. He paled excessively. "May I ask if you teach this 'philosophy' of yours in the laboratory and classroom? If you do, you should be disgraced and dismissed, for the good of your pupils."

"This is not my philosophy! This is the philosophy of the new Germany. Karl, do you know nothing at all about what is happening?"

Karl's voice shook for all his efforts: "I refuse to believe that Germans could be guilty of such folly! I refuse to believe that my country has gone mad." He paused, resumed with effort: "Is this all you have to say to me?" He turned away, as if to leave the room.

Kurt laid his hand on his brother's sleeve with urgency. His features worked; he seemed overcome with misery and helplessness. Never had he looked so pathetic. But Karl, for the first time in his life, felt no compassion for him. His own lips felt cold and dead and something strangely like hatred fixed his heart into a slow dull beating.

"Karl, whether you will believe or not, whether you know or not, I am telling you what is happening all over the Fatherland. This is just the beginning. I am a member of the Party. Gerda cannot marry this Jew. I shall not allow it. If necessary, I shall appeal direct to the Party leaders. If I have to appeal so, it will do Eric Reinhardt no good. It may even cause his death. I am appealing to you not to force me to this. I—I know your attachment to him." And an expression of the utmost misery and anger filled his eyes.

Karl regarded him piercingly. He knew then that he was indeed a "futile man of letters." He had always loathed men who obstinately would not see the truth. He forced himself to see it, and the sight was horrible, devastating to him. A profound shock went all through his body, as though he were dying. His lips turned blue with the excess of his realization, and he wet their dryness.

"What have you done to my country?" he said, almost whisperingly.

Kurt sighed. His face suddenly changed, became fanatical. His eyes glittered, in the leaping firelight. "What have I done? I, and the others, have saved it! What a glorious destiny we shall bring to the Fatherland! What things shall we not do in her name! The world is ours! Crushed, defeated, broken, Germany shall rise and avenge herself! You smile. But you shall change that smile, Karl! You shall see!

"But first of all, we must purify ourselves. We must rid ourselves of the Jew-parasite, who pollutes our blood and enervates us and makes us less than men."

Incredulous, Karl stared at him. His incredulity had little to do with his brother, but at the things which his brother was conjuring up before him. He could not believe in this dreadful fantasy, this utter madness—and yet, he had to believe. What a world to live in! He had the sensation a man suddenly precipitated into a madhouse would experience. He had the same disorientation, the same bewilderment, the same fear. He forced himself to speak with difficulty: "But what has this imbecility got to do with Eric? Eric, our adopted brother?"

Kurt groaned. "Why will you not realize? Eric is a Jew. And a Jew, in the new Germany, cannot marry an Aryan woman."

Then Karl suddenly understood what Eric had been trying to tell him when he had spoken obscurely of going to America. He realized everything completely. Eric was emotional and passionate, yet Karl knew that Eric's acceptance and understanding of this new horror was not hysterical. Eric was never hysterical; his emotion and passion were always merely surface bubbles rising idly from deep unstirred places within him.

Despair overcame him. Eric would go away. He would lose Eric. He would never see Eric again. He was not used to clenching his fists so; the nails entered his thin fine flesh. He could not do without Eric, who was the only one in all the world to whom he could speak and be sure of understanding and sympathy.

Kurt saw his brother's face, working, twitching, white as death. He saw his eyes, full of wild hatred and repudiation. "Karl!" he exclaimed in a low voice, and took his brother's arm again. But Karl shook him off.

"You shall not send Eric away! I shall not let you do such a thing, such a foul crime! But you have always hated Eric. I never knew why. But your hating him shall not do this thing to him!"

Kurt turned aside. He spoke with quiet intensity: "Yes, I have always hated him." He turned back, and his face was contorted. He raised his voice, literally screamed: "I have always hated him! He turned you against me; he stood between us. He destroyed what ought to have been between twin brothers. I could never come near you; he was always there, with his hateful smile, and his derision. He took you away from me. If I spoke to you, he was there, laughing. He made you despise me. And I am your brother!" He literally sobbed, dryly. "He spoiled my life. I never cared for any one but you. Even when we were children, every one disgusted me, but you. I would have given my life, over and over, gladly, for you! But he made you feel that my life was a silly thing, that everything about me was silly, fit only to be laughed at and ridiculed!"

Karl was speechless; he could hear his own shrill breathing. His nostrils dilated with his rapid breath. He could do nothing but look at his brother, and believe him, and hate him. Never had he been so far from compassion. Always his compassion had been impersonal and detached. A disgusting compassion, he realized now, for it had been tinged with superiority, for all its conscious gentleness. The conscious gentleness of a man of letters, removed from reality, feeling himself above it, and superior to it! He felt a loathing for himself even in the midst of his unbearable agitation and shock and grief and hatred, and terror.

When he could speak, he spoke hoarsely, with enormous difficulty: "You are a fool. No one made you appear ridiculous but yourself. You were always glowering, always suspicious. Eric had but to suggest something for you to oppose it, like a jackass. You were always sullen; pleasantness was unknown to you. You were tedious and tiresome; no one could endure your company, with your sulks and your tantrums. Your jealousy was revolting. You tired me out. Eric was always pleading for you——"

Kurt was beside himself with fury. "He—pleaded for me! He, that Jew!" His outrage made him lift his fist as though to strike his brother.

But Karl, too, was beside himself. All his calm, all his judicious self-analysis, his control, his detachment, were gone. But he was beside himself with despair, with fear for Eric, with disordered grief at the thought of never seeing Eric again.

"Yes, he pleaded for you, when he saw how tired you made me. But you did not deserve his pleading. I have been such a hypocrite all my life! I knew what you were, but I ignored it. My God, how I despise myself!" His lips shook; he swallowed with obvious difficulty and pain. "I ought to have had nothing to do with you, all these years. I should have gone away."

He looked at his brother, and a fierce sadistic delight filled him when he saw how his words were making Kurt suffer.

And yet, a sort of amazement came over him that he could experience such obscene delight; his amazement increased, and with it a curious thrill as he said: "What a swine you are!" But Kurt said nothing; his head had dropped on his chest. His attitude was that of a man who had been mortally struck.

Karl went to the door. There he stopped, looked back. "But you shall not hurt Eric! I shall stop you myself."

He encountered Maria, who was about to ascend the stairs to her apartments. She stared at him, then, seeing his face, she smiled with a covert malevolence. "Are you ill, Karl? What has Kurt been saying to you?"

He lifted his head and gazed at her. She recoiled, shrank together. He went out of the house.

On the way home, stumbling through the new wet snow in the glare of lamplight, he said over and over to himself: What has happened to me? I have committed criminal folly. I ought to have restrained myself, for the sake of Eric and Gerda. I ought to have held my tongue, used guile to help them. But I could not restrain myself! Something over long years rushed to my brain and my tongue. He had tired me for so long. Now, I have ruined everything. I have ruined Eric.

He looked about him, dazedly. The city, the world, suddenly appeared to be grotesque one-sided drawings in children's books. Nothing had substance; everything was two-dimensioned, highly colored, leering, leaning, full of thin shrill light. The painting of children, crude and fantastic, brutally drawn, filled with fantastic creatures without souls or being. Paintings, with Mother Goose rhymes printed beneath them. Or the dreadful drawings of madmen, full of frenzy. The sounds of such a city, such a world, were the close unbearable sounds of nightmare. He thought: I am sick. I shall vomit.

When he arrived home his wife, Therese, was waiting for him. She gazed at him with her clear gray eyes, and knew that he had realized everything in the hours he had been gone from her. She did not kiss him as usual, seeing his face and eyes. She merely said very quietly: "Gerda wishes to speak to you before you go to bed, Karl."

He said suddenly, violently, putting his hands to his head: "Not tonight! I have had enough tonight! Let me alone, tonight!"

Even her lips turned white, but before she could speak again, he had left her and was running rapidly up the stairs to his room. There he found little Gerda waiting for him, sitting before the fire.

"No, Gerda!" he exclaimed, in the husky voice of agony. "Go away, child. I cannot talk to you, tonight. Leave me alone." His voice broke.

She had never seen her gentle detached brother like this, so overwrought, so strange. She stood up. She was very small and delicate, with pale flaxen hair and great blue eyes and pretty pink lips. She appeared much younger than she really was, almost a child. Her expression, her whole appearance, was strikingly like Karl's. She put out her hands to him, pathetically; they were trembling.

"Karl, you know then? Eric has told you?"

He was silent. He regarded her with a distraught manner.

"You know that we must go away from here, perhaps to America?"

He still did not speak. She began to cry, whimpering a little, like a very young child. The tears ran down her cheeks, gathered about her mouth in minute pools.

"But Karl, I need you. We need you, Eric and I. We must go away. Today—today, I had to leave the gymnasium. They said horrible things to me. Because of my Eric, my darling Eric! Karl, you must help us—" She whimpered again. Then, as he did not move, she crept up to him, and laid her head on his breast. She kept shuddering, as though she were very cold.

For a long moment they stood like this. Karl looked down at her little shining head; he felt her clutch him. Something seemed to open in him, like an awful dividing pain. He put his arms about her gently, then with sudden fierceness, like a father protecting his child.

"Yes, yes, dear. Do be quiet, dear. Do not cry like this. I shall help you. Nothing shall hurt you. You shall go away, with Eric. Quiet, my darling. Eric sends you his love."

THERE WAS a feverish gaiety about every one, in the
frenzied last hours before departure. Every one
laughed excessively, rushed about the house, little
cries fluttering after; this was forgotten, then that,
and must be thrust into a box or a bag. A place must be
found for the warm afghan which Therese had knitted for
her little sister-in-law; it was very cold in America, she had
heard, especially in Boston, near the sea. Then, Gerda would
need it on the ship, over her knees, watching the dark polished
waves hurl her into a new world. Then there were the exquisitely bound private editions of Karl's three last novels, all
deep-blue morocco and gold, and all autographed with his
affection. Eric must put these into his most convenient bag,
for use on the ship. Gerda's wedding silver was in its mahogany case, and new silken linens, the gifts of her brother Karl
and his wife, Therese. It was still permitted to take jewelry,
and Gerda's own small fortune had been converted into
diamonds and other precious gems. Then Therese's uncle
had brought Gerda a magnificent krimmer coat and muff; her
trunks were full of valuable gifts from the few of her friends
who had remained faithful to her. What small amount of his
own fortune Eric was allowed to take with him was in the
form of letters of credit and cheques. Roped and garnished
with labels, his African box waited on a chair.

A month ago Eric Reinhardt had been dismissed from the
University. He had expected it; it was not a great shock to
him. Karl had always thought of him fondly as being "emotional." He saw, with humility, that he had been mistaken.
Eric was not emotional. He could become impatient and
agitated over trifles; but over calamities he preserved a bitter
calm, a philosophical humor. He visibly aged, but he indulged
in no passionate recriminations, no outward griefs. He went
about the business of emigration with cold precision and
efficiency. Now he was joining the new University of Exile in
America. His race was inured to misery and uprooting and
hatred, to exile and exploitation and cruelty. After his
initial incredulity and revolt, he accepted the ancient lot and

wasted no time in idle wailing or despair. He never spoke of what had happened to him. It was not new.

His ancestors had dwelt in this part of Germany for seven hundred years, had literally helped to create its prosperity and culture and integrity. They had dwelt here many generations before those aliens who now called themselves "Germans" infiltrated into this region. But to Eric Reinhardt, Germany was already receding from his mind; even now, it had a strange and foreign look to him. The familiar faces on the streets had become alien; the very familiar spots in the city seemed stripped of all the trappings of his memory, like a foreign city which had briefly decked itself in the beloved flags of a visiting stranger, and had now removed those flags, revealing hostile walls behind them.

He had said good-bye to those infuriated friends who had stood with him. German friends. But the words they had said to him, of anger and affection and condemnation for the new madness, were words spoken in a tongue strange to his ears, and only lately learned. For everything that had meant Germany to him was dead. What remained was a convulsed land, where every landmark had been distorted or swallowed up in an earthquake.

Under Karl's solicitous and anxious demands for reassurance, he had said that leaving Germany was nothing now; all his thoughts were turned to America. But when he was alone, he would not let himself think.

He had planned to leave Germany alone, and establish himself in America. Then, he would send for Gerda. But the little frail thing, so fairylike and soft, had refused to be left behind. She had amused and astonished him with her stubbornness, with her mulish refusal to listen to reasonable argument. He was not to go without her; that, she would not allow. Then Karl had interceded in her behalf: Eric must take the girl with him. They could not be married in Germany, but once in Holland, before sailing for America, they could be married. Karl and Therese would go to Holland with the bridal couple, attend the wedding, and accompany them to the ship. And so, after endless argument, it was arranged.

Now that the thing was inevitable, and Eric must go, Karl was consumed with a fever over the delays. He had the obscure but active fear that each day's coming was a new threat to Eric. He could not get him away fast enough. He counted hours, days, weeks. When each passed safely, he was exhaustedly relieved. Eric and he had come closer together in these last weeks than they had ever come before. Yet the very depths of their intimacy and love for each other made them inarticulate, silent. It was impossible for them to speak of their ultimate parting, which must be forever. Once Eric had said: "Next year, you must come to visit us in America," and Karl had turned away, cloven with his pain, and had said hurriedly: "Yes, yes."

For never had he loved Germany so passionately as he loved her in the days of her delirium, and never had she needed all the help of her sons as she needed it now. Eric had been disarmed; he had been robbed of arms to fight. But Karl was still armed; he still had his armor and his sword. He would remain, to fight; he would remain, until he and his kind had conquered, or were destroyed. A sort of exaltation filled him; in the last days, he waited almost impatiently for the departure of Eric and his sister, in order that he might be free to begin the struggle.

During the last weeks Karl had sent numerous letters to friends in Holland and France and England. In each of those letters he enclosed a large banknote. Censorship had not yet been fully established; forty-nine out of fifty were received. These notes were from Eric's fortune, before it had been confiscated. Upon receipt, the friends forwarded the money to a New York bank. So Eric and his wife would not be penniless upon arrival.

After the first convulsion of their lives, Eric and Gerda were jubilant and excited, and more in love than ever. Eric, of course, had left Kurt's house, to spend the time before departure in Karl's home. This period was idyllic for the young people. They stayed closely at home, and thought only of each other. A clear white light came to stay on Gerda's small face; her every look was for Eric. In the presence of this love Karl felt renewed and tender and full of faith. With such as these in the world, surely evil was not the natural state of men, as seemed so evident in these times. He knew what was happening in Germany.

They never spoke of Kurt. It was only on the last night that Eric spoke of him, and then only to Karl. He said straightly and simply: "When we have gone, you must be reconciled to Kurt. Would you condemn a man completely because he had been infected with a virus that was floating about in the air? If you do, Karl, you are no better than those who used to beat the insane, or abandoned the plague-stricken. The fact that he has been poisoned spiritually, and that he is in the midst of a delirium, ought to inspire your pity, instead of your anger." And then he had regarded Karl with the curious expression of the time when he had looked at him through the magic triangle.

Karl answered lightly, and evasively: "You have enough to worry about, Eric. Kurt, at this moment, is unimportant." But he was amazed that when he tried to approach the thought of Kurt in his mind, it was as if he had touched an area of necrosis. There was no sensation there either of hatred or relenting, but only an area blackened, festering and sloughing.

None of them slept that night. And so it was, towards dawn, that every one of them heard the hard ringing footsteps approaching the street-door, and heard the crashing knocks.

Lights flew on in the house, as each member turned on his bedside lamp. They sat up in their beds, their hearts beating with a mysterious dread and terror. Night-calls of ominous import were still quite new in Germany, yet each in his bed knew that something horrible was about to happen to them all.

They heard the sleepy scolding of the servant, as she flopped to the door in her dressing-gown and slippers. They heard her draw the bolts and turn the keys. They heard her shrill voice suddenly stop, as though some one had clutched her throat. And then they heard a man's brutal voice demanding that "the Jew, Reinhardt, appear immediately."

Gerda and Eric met in the hall outside the door of their rooms. They looked at each other with death on their faces. Then Eric took Gerda in his arms, and kissed her, and left her. "I am here," he called. He had pulled his scarlet-velvet dressing-gown over his pajamas. His hair stood on end, like the hair of a boy.

Karl was already in the cold and drafty hall, wrapped in his dressing-robe of dull blue flannel. He looked startlingly old and wizened, shivering there. But his manner and voice were calm. Therese stood beside him, pale and shaken, her plaited hair on the shoulders of her wrapper.

Karl was speaking to an officer in a brown uniform, who was accompanied by two men of obviously lesser rank, also in brown uniforms.

"But Hans, this is preposterous! You were our gardener for many years, and your father served my father. You know us all. When we were children we played together. You carried Eric on your shoulders, for you were a big lad. You know what we have all been: devoted to our beloved Fatherland. And yet, you can come to this house, where you are known and regarded highly, and denounce a member of it as a traitor!"

The officer, a burly, sulky-faced man, shifted his feet and set his shoulders at an angle both obstinate and apologetic.

"Herr Erlich, I know all this. But I have my orders. What am I to do? I know Herr Doktor Reinhardt well." He paused, after saying the last words slowly, almost unbelievingly. "But I have my orders. It is all a mistake, as you have said. There is so much these days— Every one is being questioned." He tried a surly but placating smile. "Probably you, too, tomorrow will be questioned, Herr Erlich. Today, it is Herr Doktor Reinhardt."

Eric came up. Like a wisp of a shadow, Gerda came after him, her clasped hands clenched to her breast, pressing in, as though to subdue a mortal pain. "Hans!" he exclaimed. "What is this, at this hour?"

The officer cast down his eyes; he momentarily sucked in his under lip. He appeared more obstinate than ever, but now obscurely angered also, as though in some way this was all Eric's fault—putting him into this obnoxious position. He said, not looking at Eric, waiting:

"It is not my fault, Herr Doktor! I have told Herr Erlich it is not my fault. What am I to do? I have my orders, to take you into custody, protective custody, for questioning about subversive activities." He ended in a rush, defiantly but desperately.

Eric said nothing. His hands tightened at his sides; blue lines appeared at the corners of his mouth. But he said nothing.

Karl laid his hand on his adopted brother's motionless arm, and said to the officer: "But this is impossible? Eric and my sister leave in less than five hours for Holland. I will tell you! Tomorrow morning I will go myself to your superior officer and explain that Eric and Gerda have gone away, but that I am willing to answer any questions——"

But Eric looked only at the officer and at the lowering vicious faces of his subordinates. Gerda stood beside him now; she had taken his other arm; she had pressed her cheek against it and was staring blankly before her.

The officer was querulously impatient; they saw his facial

muscles quivering. "You make it hard for me, Herr Erlich! What am I to do? The Herr Doktor must come with me; I have an order for his arrest. But your brother, the Herr Professor, is a Party member. This is all a mistake, no doubt. They do not know the Herr Doktor is a member of his family, perhaps. You must go to your brother. He will go to my officer immediately, and the Herr Doktor can be home in time to leave for Holland."

Therese uttered a faint sound in her throat; she put her arm about Gerda, who seemed blind to everything but her agony and Eric. But Karl said with animation: "Of course! But cannot you wait here, Hans? I shall go to Kurt immediately. He will call your officer——"

The officer sighed, flushed with resentment at both his role and Karl's inability to understand. "I am sorry, Herr Erlich. The Herr Doktor must go with me immediately. Those are my orders. No one shall harm him. It will be something to laugh at, before morning. But come with me now he must."

There was a sudden silence. No one moved. But Karl's lips parted as though his heart had been squeezed. After a few moments he said quietly: "Yes, you are right. He must go with you. In the meantime, I shall see my brother." He turned to Eric, who still had said nothing, and had not moved. "Eric, you see how it is. It is a miserable annoyance. But you will be home in less than two hours. Please get dressed."

"Why do you not call him on the telephone, Karl?" asked Therese.

Karl smiled strangely. "No. I prefer to knock on the door. Knock hard, several times. It is something that has not happened at his house as yet."

Then Eric moved for the first time. He turned to Karl, who felt a sudden cold thrill run along his nerves. For Eric's face was the face he had seen through the triangle.

"You are quite right, Karl. I will go and dress." He put his arm about Gerda, and kissed the top of her head. "Go back to your bed, my love. And then, when it is time for you to get up and dress for our journey, I will be back with you."

But she pressed her head deeper into his arm. They heard her exhale a breath like a dying moan. Therese, frightened, tried to disengage the girl. "Gerda dear, do let Eric go. The longer he delays, the less time he will have when he comes back in the morning. Come, do not be foolish. Karl is going to Kurt, and you are making it difficult for us."

But it was Eric himself who had to release himself from her frenzied hold. Finger by finger, he lifted the ice-cold hands from his arm. They were like dead fingers. When he had removed the last one she relaxed all over. Her head fell on her breast and her face was concealed by her flaxen hair. Eric put her in Therese's arms, where she seemed to collapse. He stood looking at her for a moment, then turned away and left her. She did not appear to hear his going, though when Karl anxiously lifted her head he found that she had not fainted. Her blind blue eyes were wide open and fixed; her mouth had fallen open slightly, and her lips were white and cold as stone.

Therese led her into the library off the hall. The servant, whimpering, followed, and turned on lights. "Coffee, quickly," said Therese, putting the girl on a couch and sitting beside her, holding the small fragile body close to her warm and steadfast one. She began to rock gently, murmuring consoling sounds. She kept up that murmuring, hoping to drown out the sound of Eric's going. When the coffee came, she tried to force some into Gerda's mouth. The girl swallowed obediently, like a child. They heard nothing in the hall beyond, not even the closing of the door.

Karl had always gently ridiculed the knocker on Kurt's door. It was a wolf's head, in heavy brass. Romanticism in a gay and ribald man was acceptable; but for such as Kurt to be romantic always seemed overpoweringly absurd. Such as he were usually sentimental; the harder and more obdurate and less subtle a man, the more sentimental he was, thus making sentimentality a shameful as well as a pathetic thing.

But as he looked at that wolf's head, shining dimly in the waning light of the street lamps, Karl did not smile. He remembered nothing of his long walk through the empty dark streets walled with empty dark houses. When he looked at the knocker he had a sickening sensation of shock, like a sleep-walker who had abruptly come awake to discover that his awful nightmare was a reality. He lifted the knocker in a hand that felt numb; he brought it down heavily upon the door several times, slowly and ponderously. It filled all the sleeping dark street with echoes. He could not stop; he kept knocking until lights flew on above and voices, sharp with alarm, were heard, and until the door was flung open revealing the shawled figure of the sleepy servant. In the meantime, the knocking had aroused other sleepers, and heads appeared cautiously in the windows of neighboring houses.

He was admitted to the house. The servant held a lighted candle in her hand, for she had come from her own quarters, where there were no electric lights. He asked for his brother, in the dim remote voice of one who is imperfectly awake. But Kurt was already coming down the stairs, hastily tying his robe about him, and angrily demanding to know who had been making that ungodly noise. When he saw Karl he stopped as though hit by a bullet, and fell back a step, clutching the newel post at the foot of the stairway. His face was a gray blotch in the wavering yellow light cast by the candle.

Karl came towards him and stopped less than two feet from him. He said, very quietly: "They have taken Eric. You must call them at once to let him go." And then he said, without raising his voice: "But you knew, did you not?"

They looked into each other's eyes for a long and terrible moment. The servant saw their two heads so close together, and seeing their expressions she felt a sharp and nameless terror. She backed away, extinguished her candle, and crept up the stairway in a rabbitlike flight. In the darkness below there was no sound, not even that of breathing.

Kurt, with an ice-cold and sweating hand, fumbled for the hall light. It exploded into a fierce white glare. Karl had not moved; his head was thrust forward a little. The flesh seemed to have shrunk upon his face, revealing all the bones like a death's-head.

"Karl," said Kurt in a muffled voice, "let us go into the library. I must talk to you."

He turned away; he could hardly walk. The air in the library was cold and lifeless as that of a vault. He switched on a lamp, and stood there in the bitter white circle of it. Karl had followed him in silence.

"Karl, will you sit down?" asked Kurt. "Do not look at me like that! I swear, nothing shall happen to him. But he cannot marry my sister. I cannot allow that. Why will you not understand?" His voice became thin and strained, and then broke, as though he were about to weep. "Why will you not understand? My sister cannot marry a Jew. Do you know what that means? Do you not know what shame and ruin will be ours?

"I know everything. I know that today she intends leaving with him for Holland, and then marrying him. That cannot be. The Fatherland needs women like Gerda, of pure heroic German blood, to bring children like herself, like us, into the world." He stopped; he seemed to be choking. He flung out his arms imploringly, desperately. "Karl, do not look at me like that! Please, can you not——"

"Then," said Karl softly, meditatively, "you did this thing to Eric? to Gerda?"

"O God!" groaned Kurt. He fell into a chair. He covered his face with his hands, and began to rock to and fro as though in unbearable anguish. "You will not understand. Do you think it was easy for me? Do you think anything but duty would have made me do it? But you have always been cruel and unfeeling to me. You have always hated me. There was nothing that I ever did that was not either ridiculous or contemptible to you. You have never tried to understand the slightest thing about me. If you had made only the smallest effort at any time you would now understand what has made me do this.

"You would understand that I could do nothing else. I went to the local captain of the Storm Troopers, and I said: 'My sister, who is a foolish and misguided girl, intends to leave her Fatherland and flee to America with a Jew. She must be prevented. She is my sister. Issue a warrant for his arrest, on the charge of subversive utterances. At one time he made derisive remarks about the Fuehrer— That will frighten him, that warrant. And then, she must be made to promise to let him go. He will go away, alone.' "

He lifted his head from his hands and looked at his brother. Karl had not moved. He seemed to have dwindled; his clothing appeared too large for him, and hung on his body.

Kurt started to his feet, and again he flung out his arms desperately. "Why do you look at me like that! I cannot bear it. Is there no mercy in you? Is there no remembrance that you are my brother? Is this Jew more to you than I? What have I done that you should look at me that way?"

Only the lower half of Karl's body was in the blazing arc of the light. The upper half was in shadow. His features were almost tenuous. But his eyes seemed to glow and burn with a fire of their own creating.

"Listen to me," he said, very softly, "Gerda shall not marry Eric. She shall remain with me, and Therese. If it must happen this way, it must. But Eric will be released immediately?"

His voice was so soft that Kurt took sudden hope; he, himself, understood nothing but violence. Perspiration of relief appeared on his upper lip and forehead. "Yes, yes!" he exclaimed eagerly. "It was only to prevent her marrying him. He will be escorted in the morning to the border. His possessions are packed? They will be called for, and delivered to him at the border——"

"He will not be allowed to say good-bye to us, to Gerda?"

"No, that is impossible," said Kurt imploringly.

"Where is he now?"

"They will have taken him to the police station. Not to the concentration camp! There he will be held until morning——"

"Then we must go to him, to say good-bye."

Kurt took a step towards him, half held out his hands. "No, Karl, that too is forbidden. I-I tried to arrange that. You must not think so badly of me! But they would not promise. It is better so. Do you not see? It is better so."

Karl's nostrils dilated, and he drew in a thin wavering breath.

"I have your word? Eric will be unhurt? I have heard such—things. He will be delivered to the border today?"

"Yes, yes! You have my word. Have I ever lied to you? Had I lied, how much better you would have thought of me, all my life! But I have never lied. You have my word. This was all arranged. The captain is a personal friend— He knows that Eric—he—is my adopted brother."

Karl thought: I must control myself. I have hurt Eric enough. I must control myself, and not seize him by the throat and strangle him. I must control myself, until Eric is safe. He said aloud expressionlessly: "Then, it is done. I have your word."

He turned and went out of the room. He found himself in the dark hall. He went to the street door. Then he heard Kurt call his name as though from the very bottom of hell:

"Karl! Karl! Is that all you have to say to me? Will you not tell me that you understand?"

Karl took the cold smooth doorknob in his hand. He shook violently from head to foot. A horrible sickness struck him at the pit of his stomach. He thought: I shall be sick, right here. But I must control myself. I must go out. If I so much as turn, I shall take him by the throat——

He went out. His legs bent like rubber as he went down the street. A pale cold green glimmered in the eastern sky.

KARL ERLICH had always believed that truth, like all powerful and awful forces, should be approached with care, and regarded with respect. Like radium, a little of it went a very long way. Only fools tampered with it injudiciously. He, himself, touched it delicately, with gloves.

So he mixed truth and half-truth and falsehood together in his explanations to Therese and Gerda. He told them that Kurt had immediately, in outrage, called up the local headquarters of the Storm Troopers, and had berated the officer in charge. He had inspired them with the fear of God. He had then been informed that the treatment accorded Eric Reinhardt was customary, that all would-be exiles were carefully examined before leaving, to prevent smuggling of currency, and then were immediately escorted to the port of exit. Once admitted over the border, they were, of course, immediately free, and could then communicate with their relatives. This was what was happening to Eric. Within a few hours he would be across the Dutch border. He would then communicate with Gerda— Here Karl paused, and pressed his lips together.

Gerda's stone-white face flushed with the color of life. Light came back into her blind eyes. She would go immediately to the office of the Storm Troopers and join Eric there! They would go to the border together. She must prepare immediately! She laughed a little, then cried.

Karl glanced at his wife. By her pallor, by the steadfast gravity of her look, he knew that she knew he was lying. He took his sister's hand gently, and held it in his warm palms. Then, as he spoke, he felt that little hand grow colder and colder, and saw the white rigidity come back into her face.

"Dear little Gerda, it is not so simple as that. You must have courage, and patience, for a few days. You see, these Nazi imbeciles do not believe in intermarriage between what they call 'Aryans' and 'non-Aryans.' Should you go to Eric now, you may cause him embarrassment, and delay. It is best

49

for him to go alone. Then, in a week, or less, we'll find some way to smuggle you out of Germany——"

Gerda fixed her eyes, full of anguish and terrible questioning, upon him. She did not speak. She seemed to be probing into the very depths of his mind. She remembered Karl's diplomacy and tact on other occasions; she remembered his soothing half-truths, which she recalled resulted from both his natural kindness and his aversion to disturbances and pain. Being of a simpler and therefore more ruthless nature, herself, she had often laughed with mingled annoyance and amusement at him. Now, as she stood there, with her eyes fixed with that anguish and terrible questioning upon his face, she seemed to be imploring: Do not lie to me! I cannot bear it, if you lie to me! Tell me the truth even if it kills me.

But Karl knew that the truth would indeed kill her, and he did not tell it. Instead, he smiled at her indulgently and fondly, holding her hand tighter as if to warm it. "So, you see, my love, you must just be patient a few days longer. In these evil times, one learns patience."

Her lips trembled and parted. She said, with simplicity: "For my own sake, Karl, I must believe you. I do not dare not to believe you. If I did, I should die."

"What a romanticism! Girls do not die because they are not married on the hour previously decided. In the meantime, you must rest and relax. Go to Therese, love, and have your hot coffee, and then lie down for an hour or two. This has been an exciting night, but only the first of such nights for all of Germany."

Therese led the girl away. At the door the older woman paused and glanced back at her husband with an expression of sorrowful understanding.

It was broad daylight now. Karl, pleading weariness, locked himself in the library. Then too, he said, he had a chapter to complete. But in the library he walked to and fro, very softly, almost tiptoeing. Gerda must not know of this constant walking back and forth. She must not know of the almost unendurable anxiety of her brother. A servant brought his luncheon to the library as usual. He could not eat it. He kept staring at the boxes tied and waiting, which had been piled in the library. He kept looking vacantly at the African box. Then he would resume his endless walking.

He glanced at his watch. It was almost four. Eric would be at the border, or practically near it. In an hour, he would be across and free. By twilight, there ought to be a telegram from him, telling of his safe arrival.

At five o'clock Therese tapped softly at the door. He called to her to come in. He tried to smile at her as she entered. She was a tall and slender woman, with light hair and gray eyes and a lovely figure. There was a serenity and dignity about her which awakened respect and admiration in every one. Karl had never lied to her. He never found it necessary. Therese was a brave woman, and to lie to her would be to insult both her and one's self.

She came up to him without hurry and kissed his cold and twitching cheek. "Gerda is almost asleep," she said. "I gave her a sedative. And now, I can stay with you." She added, looking gently into his eyes, "I will stay with you, waiting for that telegram you expect, and which I pray to the Almighty God will arrive."

He knew then what a fool he had been to have denied himself the comfort and courage of her presence all that day. He could not speak. He just put her into a chair and thought: I am always insulting her. He sat beside her and they clasped hands in silence.

She must have made some arrangement with her maid, for the latter came in, just as the twilight was deepening, with a tray of coffee and a light supper. She informed her mistress that Fräulein Erlich was still sleeping, and that when she awakened Frau Erlich would be called immediately. Therese made Karl eat a little, and to set him a good example, she ate also, sitting serene and smiling and steadfast in her chair.

It grew chill and dark in the library. The walls of books receded, leaving nothing but the shadows of nothingness beyond the oasis of husband and wife, who were completely silent now, their cold hands clenched together. No one drew the curtains. The street-lamps, bleakly glaring, sent shafts of empty light into the great room. Rectangles of warm bright gold appeared in the dim nebulous walls of the houses across the street. A wind rose, and began to fumble at the high windows. Karl thought he could hear the beating of his own and his wife's heart in the silence that seemed to transfix his house. All sorts of fantastic ideas moved palely through his mind. He could easily imagine that only those two hearts were alive in all the world, beating slowly yet with gathering terror and doom, knowing that they, too, must be stopped very soon. He could no longer see the African box, but he knew in what corner it lay. All at once he had the idea that the head of Gilu, grimacing madly in that box, could actually see this man and woman sitting in the darkness, waiting, always waiting, and that it was experiencing a sort of obscene and gleeful delight in their suffering. Through his miasma of exhaustion and rapidly-growing fear and dread, Karl's mind could not tear itself away from the thought of that head. He began to think that until that head was destroyed, or buried, no one in this house was safe; danger and frightful death were part of it, emanating from it. Danger and death and evil, all the evil guessed at, and shuddered at, and resolutely disbelieved, but which waited like a dreadful presence outside the brilliantly-lighted rooms of the world.

He felt the warm pressure of Therese's hand. There was something warning as well as heartening in that hand. She had felt his vagueness, his tortured mental wanderings. The street-lights had glinted on his eyeballs, and she had seen such an expression in them. The clock in the hall intoned nine.

"The telegram will not come," said Karl. His voice was hoarse and without emotion.

"My dear," said Therese pitifully, "you must not give up hope. Many things might have caused the delay. After all, it could not have come sooner than seven o'clock. And it is only nine. Think what could have caused the delay! A later train, confusion at the border, the searching for a telegraph office, a delayed train—so many things. Even if the telegram comes at midnight it will not be abnormal."

"Yes, yes," said Karl mechanically. But he listened only for a sound at the door, a ring. Therese sighed; some prescience warned her that the telegram would never come. She began to concoct ways of protecting Karl. For some reason, she felt a passionate urgency to protect him. She felt that it was even more necessary to protect him than to protect Gerda. For all his logic and reason, kindness and patience, wisdom and comprehension, she knew suddenly, with a painful plunge of her heart, that he was more innocent than Gerda, and that this innocence, torn and wounded, might become a formidable poison, which might, at the end, destroy him and others within his orbit. The disingenuous man may be wounded and assaulted many times, growing more cynical and callous with each blow, and reacting to each successive injury with less and less violence. But innocence assaulted became ferocity, became, only too often, madness.

Perhaps, she thought wearily, this was what was the matter with the German people. Innocent, ingenuous, they had been self-insulted against reality. Attacked and wounded at last by reality, their lacerated and outraged innocence had made desperate madmen of them. Karl had always laughed at Kurt, but Therese penetratingly, and for the first time, saw how similar they were. It was this sudden insight which made her understand how frightfully necessary it had become to reconcile the brothers, for the sake of their intimates. She understood, too, that the world would never be safe from Germany's frenzied recoil from reality until its innocent unreality had been restored. The French, who were not innocent, could look on reality and endure it with a shrug, and therefore they were not a threat to peace and all humanity.

In the darkness, holding Karl's hand, she let her tired thoughts wind in and out. Karl was a great artist; he would remain a great artist only if his innocence were kept intact. Disingenuousness never produced heroic music nor magnificent literature, nor painted a divine picture, nor carved a noble statue. Disingenuousness, having become acquainted with reality, could produce, smilingly, only things that were the stature of men. The stature of the gods was beyond its power or desire. A man must believe in the gods to make them manifest in creative art. Disingenuousness, not believing in them, produced mortality, monotony and littleness, and finally expired out of sheer ennui. In innocence, only, was there immortality and beauty.

This year, there was more than a possibility that Karl would receive the Nobel Prize for literature. If he lost his innocence, that prize would be a dying wreath on his grave. Therese said aloud, quickly, from the moving clouds of her musings: "Karl, my dear, no matter what happens, you must not let it hurt you! You are too precious for anything to be allowed to hurt you."

Even she was amazed at his subtlety when he said sadly: "Do you think, Therese, that spiritual integrity, anything, means much if—that telegram does not come?"

Before she could speak in answer, there came the quick sharp ringing of the bell. Therese sprang to her feet, her heart pounding in her throat. Karl stood up, also. They reached the door simultaneously. "Oh, I hope this has not disturbed Gerda!" cried Therese. "Even good news must not break her rest!"

Karl put her aside quickly and gently, and was out in the reception hall before her. Neither saw Gerda, in her night-dress at the head of the stairs, unable to descend, but listening, her flaxen braids over her shoulders and childish breasts, her face white and staring.

The servant was already at the door. She had turned on the lights. But when the door was open it was not a messenger who stood there, but Kurt Erlich.

"You!" cried Karl, out of his hatred and sick disappoint-ment.

Kurt did not speak. He came into the hall, and let the serv-ant shut the door after him. He was as gray and lined as a stricken old man. His dry lips twitched and jerked. His eyes were bright and sunken. He appeared to have suffered some recent and disintegrating shock. He removed his hat, and then held it in his hands, futilely. He seemed to see only his brother.

They regarded each other in an appalling silence. No one moved, except that Therese put her hand to her lips and stared at Kurt, and then at Karl.

After a prolonged moment or two, Karl took a step towards the other man. He had turned as gray as his brother. Two identical faces confronted each other.

"What have you to tell me?" asked Karl in so quiet and steady a voice that Therese shuddered. She caught at his arm; he wrenched it from her.

Kurt made an effort to speak; his whole body was rigidly convulsed in that effort. Finally, he flung out his arms like a despairing man offering himself to the plunge of a sword.

The gesture seemed to release his frozen tongue. "I tell you, Karl!" he cried. "I would give my life to bring him back. He was shot, this morning, when he attempted to escape!"

Karl's nostrils fluttered, distended. Now, he did not feel Therese's hands on his arms. He did not hear her shrill faint cry. Kurt did not hear it either. The two men saw only each other. And no one saw Gerda.

"You mean," said Karl softly, almost consideringly, "that he was deliberately murdered?"

"No. No! You must not even think such things, Karl! My God, Karl, do not look like that! Therese, you must not let him look like that!" Kurt flashed his sister-in-law a frantic and brokenhearted glance, imploringly. "You see, he ran out

of the police station, even before they could question
him——"

Karl shook his head gently. "No, that cannot be. Eric was
not a man like that. He did nothing hastily, though he appeared impatient to the superficial. He did not run away.
They—you—murdered him in cold blood."

Kurt, who was not subtle in the least, cried out in a loud
voice: "Karl, how can you say that of me? That I—I murdered Eric!" But Karl's apparent composure deceived him, as
it had always deceived his uncomplex nature. "Karl, my
brother, you cannot wrong me like that. Perhaps I have been
hasty. But what else could I do? You left me no alternative.
But I had nothing to do with Eric's—. Karl! You must believe that! He ran away——"

Karl's head dropped a little. He began to shake it slowly
from side to side, dumbly, blindly, as if in denial of something too unendurable, too monstrous. Kurt looked at him.
All at once, as he looked at Karl, tears spurted from his eyes.
Therese, stricken as she was, weeping, herself, as she was,
felt a pang at the sight of Kurt's tears. But none of them had
seen Gerda, and now none of them saw her steal away, disappear into the well of darkness beyond the lighted stairs.
The servant had already crept away.

And again, there was silence. The tears still ran down Karl's
face, and Karl still kept up that dreadful dumb shaking of his
head. Therese could not bear the sight of these two men. In
spite of everything, it was for Kurt that she felt the greatest
pity. For Karl, she felt the greatest fear.

Kurt, with heart-breaking simplicity, pulled his handkerchief from his pocket and wiped his face and eyes. The signet
ring on his trembling hand caught the light and shattered it
momentarily. Then he took a step towards his brother. "Karl,"
he said brokenly, "I tell you, I would give my own life——"

Karl stopped shaking his bent head. He lifted his eyes to his
brother's face, and appeared to see him for the first time. "Go
away," he said.

Kurt regarded him with grief and despair, but did not move.

"Go away," said Karl again, louder this time, and in a
strange voice. Under his broad smooth brows his eyes were
like glittering points. He began to tremble violently, though
his expression was still composed.

Kurt, with sudden terror, backed away from him, and took
the handle of the door in his hand. Then, as if his own an-

guish were too overpowering to be controlled any longer, he uttered a deep groan.

But Therese did not hear that groan. She had lifted her head with a jerk. She appeared to be waiting for something frightful. When she heard a dull crash on the street outside, near the door, she knew instantly what it was. Even before the catastrophic short silence was shattered by the terror-stricken cries and shouts of passers-by, and the scream of car-brakes, she knew what they would find, broken and motionless, when they opened the door.

THERESE STOPPED, as usual, to listen anxiously to the steady and yet somehow frenzied walking of her husband, who was locked in his study. She no longer knocked; she knew she would not be answered. And so, she went away, to do her daily duties in the barren silence of the small house. There was no gay sprightly little Gerda to expect in the late afternoons, no animated visitors or telephone calls, no small parties festive and full of song and laughter. A horror lay over this house, and it knew it. The very furniture seemed brooding in a private dark horror of its own. The rooms echoed; the muffled floors murmured and sighed under tread. The light that came in the windows lost its golden vivacity, and became bleak and hard. Therese mournfully decided that she and Karl must leave this house, which was repudiating them, and presenting to them only flat black surfaces, and filling their nostrils with a smell of dust, like the odor of dissolution.

The servant, an old woman, obstinately went about her work, assisted by her daughter. Her manner expressed her low opinion of a house which could manifest such ingratitude to those who had once filled it with brightness. She muttered about leaving, also, but this was only because of her distress.

But Therese knew that it was not the house which was at fault. It merely reflected the emanations of its occupants; it revealed their grief and despair and abandonment, and their pale transfixed inertia.

There was no doing anything with Karl. He kept a white and stony silence, even with his wife. He scarcely ate. Therese believed he never slept. He seemed absorbed in some dreadful dream of his own; there was an air of concentration about him, as if he were being confronted with a problem greater than life or death. Therese knew that this problem was hatred and the weapon of hatred, vengeance. He was plotting against his brother.

Therese felt no fear for Kurt. All her fear was for Karl, and what Karl was doing to himself. Yet, when she tried to speak to him, she found only aphorisms on her tongue, and she knew how he detested aphorisms, even though they were true. All his work was distinguished by an originality and clarity of phrase which had nothing to do with smart sophistication, and the new hard manner of American writers. His originality had a rich patina and majestic outlines, and thus was immortal. It was at once subtle and heroic, like the best of Wagner's music. Even his delicacy was strong and ageless, like an arch of fine steel. The work of Thomas Mann, he once said, had a slow, almost imperceptible unfolding; one rose steadily up a wide and tranquil staircase of marble, and saw the vista at the top becoming clearer and broader with each step. At the final step it was revealed in its entirety. There was no surprise, except the exhilaration at the vastness of utter perfection. But his own work had the simplicity and completeness of a Grecian temple, from the very beginning. The reader always experienced intense amazement and joy.

But Karl worked no more, now, and no one came. Some of the closer friends would have come, in their sympathy and profound shock, but Therese would not let them come. She had only one thought, one preoccupation now: her husband. She was like one who waited at the door of a prison, whose key the prisoner himself held. She heard the prisoner's moving-about; she heard his slow frenzied footsteps. She heard his halts, his faint hoarse cries. She felt his distraction and despair and hatred and rage. But until he opened his door, she could do nothing for him.

His last novel was over half completed. She knew it lay in his desk like a partially-carved ivory statuette. But there it lay, forgotten, for its carver had forgotten it in his most terrible preoccupation with more real, and yet, less valuable things.

Therese was a serene woman, not given to much idle speech. She hated talk for talk's sake. In many ways, she was much wiser and more mature than Karl, for reality, though it frequently revolted her and stunned her, had long ago lost its power to injure her permanently. At times, she gave an illusion of innocence, but she was not innocent.

Though Karl had written realistically of violence and passion and reality, he did not comprehend them objectively, nor discern them operating in his own life and the living life about him. They sprang from a deep subconsciousness which was both in him and without him; he was like a sea-shell immersed in an ocean, an intact identity, yet filled with the waters of the ocean. Now, his innocent objectiveness had been violated; the innocent objectiveness of the universe had been rent open, and, through the rent, violence and passion and reality had burst on his realization for the first time. And so, he was frenzied, despairing, incredulous, frantic, and made to suffer. This was the real cause of his suffering and his hatred. He had written of the frightfulness of all things, but had not truly believed in this frightfulness. He was a prophet overcome with terror at the coming-about of his own prophecies, and frenzied with his need and desire to disbelieve in their actuality.

Therese, lonely and sad, had nothing to do in these awful days but sew and embroider and read. She read all the newspapers. She listened to the radio. She saw and knew all that was happening in a world that contemptuously repudiated honor and kindness and civilization and intelligence and love, and concentrated only on reality. But I can bear this better than Karl, she would think sadly. I never did believe in humanity.

To her calm and passionless eye Hitler, the monstrous Austrian madman, was an innocent of the same breed as Karl. He, too, believed in heroism and destiny and beauty. She could not find him evil. The evil men were the realists behind him, who used his innocence for incredible ends, and to subjugate and entrance all the other innocents. And yet, perhaps after all these realists were not the truly dangerous men. Perhaps the ominous men were the innocents, like Karl, whose self-enchantment made them unable to recognize the enemies when they appeared and made them therefore, impotent to defend the world from the enemies.

If the realists are deadly, thought Therese, how much more deadly is innocence, which insists on its fantasy though the universe perish. Innocence creates the gods, but bewilderedly watches their destruction by a force which it still refuses to believe in, and of whose existence it is obstinately unaware.

One day Karl emerged from his isolation long enough to dine with her and to speak to her with haggard kindness. She imprudently believed that his old enchantment was beginning to weave its web about him again. She spoke hesitantly about Gerda and Eric, and he replied quietly. She even mentioned Kurt, who called Therese each day to inquire after his brother. Karl said nothing. He lifted his cup to his lips with a hand that did not tremble even slightly. Over the edge of it, his fixed eyes were a little vague, but otherwise expressionless.

Then she said: "Karl, my darling, Kurt, too, is as much a victim of what has happened, and what is happening, as Gerda and Eric——"

He put down the cup. Without a word, he rose and left the room. He locked himself in his study. She stood at the door and pleaded with him, but he did not answer. "You are killing yourself!" she cried. But he did not answer.

"Kurt is not the only one who lives in the shadow of the Schloss!" she cried in a louder voice, hoping piteously to goad him. But still he did not answer. And so, she went away.

One night, exhausted, he slept well into the morning. Therese, passing his study, tried the door. It was unlocked. She went in. The desk was bare, waiting. She drew back the curtains, and let the wan sunlight in. Then on a table near the windows she saw Eric's African box.

She had never seen the contents. She went to the table and examined some objects which had been taken from the box and now lay on the polished surface. One was something she thought was a horrid little wooden head with glaring eyes and matted hair. There was something savage and primeval about the face, the grinning stretched lips, the mad fixed eyes. But she was not revolted. In fact, she felt a sympathy for it. It was a face that had looked at reality and had understood it. In the innocent, such a face would inspire madness, and flight. In the disingenuous, it inspired wry amusement and comprehension.

The other object was a crudely carved little doll-like figure without any specific individuality. It's wooden limbs were only partly formed. Therese picked it up and examined it with curiosity. The sharp end of a long brass prong or nail had been inserted in the side of its head. It was not very deeply inserted; just the tip.

Baffled, Therese continued to examine it. An ugly little doll, without beauty, as though carved by a stupid child. She wiggled the brass nail; it was firmly imbedded. What on earth was Karl doing with this nonsense? He hated incompleteness and ugliness, yet in some mysterious way Therese knew that all his absorption these days was centered in this figure.

She held it idly in her hand and stared vaguely into space. She frowned. There was a clue faintly floating about in the darkness of her mind. She grasped at it; it eluded her. But there it was, persistently floating, challenging her to identify it and seize it. She grasped at it again and again, only to have it sink below the surface of her mind. Exasperated, she waited, still staring into space. She tried to relax. The clue bobbed up again, elusively. All at once she knew that the most important thing in the world, now, was to seize it and identify it.

She seemed to see herself as a child, reading something that both fascinated and horrified her. She could feel the book in her hands, and the weight of the flaxen braids on her shoulders. She could even see her long legs in white stockings, hanging over the edge of the crimson leather chair in her father's study. What was that she was reading? Something dark and occult, she dimly remembered. Something strange and ferocious about Africa. Africa!

The clue approached her hand, and she looked at it with fierce attention. And then she saw that it was a ridiculous word: Voodoo.

Voodoo! Her lips parted in a gasp; her eyes, in the bleak light of day, seemed to glare. Voodoo. Black magic, the magic of hatred and obscene murder, and devil-worship. The invoking of evil in behalf of vengeance.

At this, she gasped again, loudly, incredulously. She was filled with a fire of terror for her husband. She could hear the leaping of her heart. She was at once outraged, disbelieving and frantic. She had been a fool! While she had waited, stupidly, supinely, for the prisoner to come out of his prison by his own will, that prisoner had been deliberately driving himself into madness.

For a moment she was revolted; she experienced a disgusted turning-away from her husband. Then she was overcome with pity and renewed terror. She forgot the idiot obscenity that had so outraged her adult intelligence. She forgot her shame and anger for Karl. She forgot the dying innocence that could produce, in its pangs of dissolution, nothing more lofty than this imbecility.

She knew only that her husband was a mortally sick man.

With the haste of repugnance she dropped the little figure on the table, where it lay with the prong in the side of its head. Her mouth was acrid with the salt of fear and helplessness and compassion. What could she do to restore him to sanity, to manhood, to reason?

Dazed, she looked inside the box, and in the welter of disgusting and anonymous objects she saw another of the dolls. She picked it up; again she frowned into space. Groping painfully in her mind for forgotten things, she dimly remembered that, to be effective, an image must be baptized with the name of the enemy. This other doll, intact, without the nail in its head, was an unnamed doll.

Operating almost by instinct now, she feverishly pulled the nail from the head of the first doll. She flung the doll in the box and covered it with the other objects. Then, in the head of the second doll she forced the sharp tip of the prong. She did not quite know why she did this, but something impelled her.

She heard a sound at the door. She turned and saw Karl entering. She tried to smile, then stopped with a sickening leap of her heart. He was regarding her with a face she could not recognize. The red light of madness was in his eyes.

"What are you doing here?" he demanded in a loud but curiously muffled voice.

She put the doll down hastily.

"Karl," she said, with an attempt at indignation. "Why do you talk to me like that? Are you insane? I am your wife, or have you forgotten that, in your selfish preoccupation and disregard for me?"

But he picked up the doll and examined it with the intense concentration of the feeble-minded. Then he put it down carefully. A change came over his face. It lost its inhuman look; it softened. He turned to her, and even smiled faintly, like a dying man momentarily gaining consciousness.

"I am sorry, Therese," he said with almost his old gentleness. "But you know I do not like my things disturbed."

She moistened her pale lips. "You never seemed to mind my 'disturbing' your things before this," she replied with dignity. "Besides, what is all this rubbish? Just poor Eric's silly souvenirs of Africa. They smell. Shall I have Amelia come in and cart them out and throw them away?"

Her tone was casual, if dignified, but she watched him with narrow fearfulness.

He did not answer. He looked down at the doll, and the little savage brown head with its matted hair. He stood there, seeming to have sunken into a dark pit of preoccupation, in which she had no part. The hand which rested on the table had an unfamiliar slackness and distortion about it, to her alert eyes. It was the hand of a man who had suffered unbearable pain, and had collapsed under that pain. With alarm, she saw how emaciated Karl had become, and how dishevelled. His expression, as he stood there, was dazed and unaware, like that of one caught in some delirium from which he could not escape. He raised his other hand, passed it over his head. It was trembling, the nails bluish. His slightly parted lips were the color of lead.

"Karl," she said softly, as though fearing to wake a sleepwalker too suddenly, "come into the breakfast room and have some coffee with me." She did not touch him, but waited, her knees shaking.

All at once he sighed brokenly. He lifted his head and seemed to see clearly and sharply. He looked about him, helplessly. His eyes came to focus on his wife's face, and a burning flush ran over his cheeks, as though he were suddenly and hideously ashamed.

"Yes, I'll have some coffee with you, Therese," he said, in a voice like an echo. He went to the breakfast room with her. He drank coffee. He listened, faintly smiling, to her firm and casual remarks about the weather and the poor quality of the breakfast rolls, and the bad butter.

"It is as bad as the wartime," he said. All at once he seemed vaguely concerned. "Therese, you seem tired and pale. Why do you not go out and walk in the fresh air? It seems a nice day." He lifted his head and looked at the sunshine with the incredulity of a man who has slept, unconscious, for days.

Her heart leapt with hope. "Will you come with me, Karl?"

He hesitated, then shook his head. "I am exhausted," he answered simply.

"Then, will you lie down again, and rest?"

To her joy, he said, after another hesitation: "Yes, I will."

She saw him safely to his room. She helped him undress. When she went out, on tiptoe, he was already asleep. Before he slept however, he had touched his cold lips to the back of her ministering hands.

She felt enormously relieved. And now, to get rid of that frightful box! She went to the study. She tried the door. She could not remember Karl's having locked it, but it was locked.

But she would not let herself be frightened again. She went to her own room to get a book. Then she heard the telephone ringing and went to answer it.

It was Maria, Kurt's wife. Her voice sounded impatient but somewhat concerned. "Therese? Kurt asked me to inquire about his brother today. No, he did not go to the University this morning. He is in bed."

In spite of all her efforts, Therese felt faint and giddy. She clutched the telephone with desperate firmness.

"What is the matter with him, Maria? I am so sorry!"

She could almost see her sister-in-law shrug her massive shoulders.

"You know these men! They scream at a pin-prick. I have no doubt there is really nothing much the matter. He has been complaining for a week or two of an intense pain in his head. But things have been so tragic— It is nerves, or eyestrain, but he is too stubborn to admit he needs spectacles. A confession of age! But there it is: this morning, he said the pain was unbearable, and I have sent for the doctor."

Therese replaced the receiver silently, slowly.

She was trembling violently, as she sat in the chair. A curious prickling ran over her head, seemed to raise her hair. Her whole body was covered with a deathly coldness and dampness.

She clenched her hands convulsively together in her lap; nails entered flesh. She said aloud, staring blindly, savagely, before her:

"I must control myself. I must not be a fool. I must remember that such things do not exist. It is only coincidence! To think for a moment that it is anything else is to confess madness, too."

WHEN Therese, in later years, remembered those weeks following her degrading discovery in Karl's study, she knew that life could never be the same for her. Her calm sensation of personality-integrity was forever shattered. She had thought, being disingenuous, that she could endure anything. She came so often, in these weeks, to the thin end of her endurance, that her natural egotism was profoundly shaken. Another step, she thought, and I would go howling over the abyss, too.

5

Ruin, illness, loss of position and money, loss of health, even death, were all terrors that appalled her, but which she instinctively knew she could eventually control, surmount, adjust herself to, or forget. Her personality would remain intact, for it would never have been assaulted.

But it was the obscure, the dark, the secret and the hidden things, the things that were concealed by an invisible ambush, the things that were only shadows, the intangible horrors in which she did not believe but which affrighted her just the same, that so made her reel on the firm pedestal of her calmness and inner strength. She could sit quietly, and reason them away like a strong wind blowing aside the murky fog. She made herself see the brutal and objective universe, with its blazing light and iron mechanics and inexorable and immutable laws of cause and effect. In the roar and rhythm of this universe fogs and ghosts and miasmas and tenuous horrors were ridiculous, and made one laugh deliciously. The occult things lived in men's grotesque and evil and ignorant minds. They lived in darkness, like all obscenities. But never could they penetrate the clashing machine-rhythm of the universe.

So she told herself, firmly. She continued to tell herself this, firmly, and then, finally, with incredulous despair. And yet, it was mercilessly borne in upon her, while she fought against it with anger and ridicule, that behind the mechanics of the universe was something awful and mysterious and evil and silent, but eternally alert and waiting.

She felt this appalling Something in Karl. And, finally, to her stupefaction, she found that not only was Karl wandering in this dark boundless eternity, full of abysses and shadows of frenzy, but the whole of Germany was so wandering. That shook her to the very heart. There was no escape from the frenzy and imbecility of her husband. She went out into the streets, to shop; she even tentatively called on her old friends. She went alone, to the cinema. And everywhere she discerned this evil madness, this distortion, this murderous fantasy, this flight into unreality, this tragic imbecility.

At first she thought it all the projection of her own mind, which was in too close contact with Karl's. But at last she saw it was not her mind that was at fault, but the fault of the soul of Germany.

Like Karl's innocence, the innocence of Germany (and she had always been the most innocent of peoples!) was wounded and infected. Only the disingenuous, and they were few in this nation, could withstand the assault on vital forces. Like the chronically sick and feeble, they had been vulnerable from birth, and had acquired a twisted immunity.

Karl's disintegration was the disintegration of Germany. His reason, like hers, was gone. Now that the angel with the sword, who had been guarding the citadel of the mind, had been thrown out, the citadel was easily invaded by all the monstrous dwarfs and gnomes and specters and deformities who eternally waited for entry. Man had accepted reason reluctantly; it was a teacher that insisted on his standing always on his hind legs. When that reason was attacked, he fought only feebly, and not with desire, to retain it. He dropped back on all fours, and for a time, at least he felt more free, much more comfortable and less exhausted.

No, there was no escape for Therese, who felt herself the only sane person in her home and in her country. She could no longer stand the streets of Berlin, but would order her car to be driven beyond the city, which was full of such faces and such eyes as Karl's. Everywhere she saw the marks of the same pestilence. But in the quiet summer hills and valleys, in the silent motionless forests torn with sunlight, she could feel her sanity and reason returning. She would sit on the grass and look at the sky, and feel the warmth and peace flowing over her spirit as water flowed over one's body. She could feel strong and poised and even serene again. When she returned to the city she had the feeling she was re-entering a pest-house, or a prison for madmen, and that infection hung in the air like a fog.

Berlin, the most orderly of cities, was still orderly. On the surface. But below the surface were corruption and confusion, wild runnings to and fro, meaningless cries, savage yells, the motions and gestures and voices of insanity. At times, she could almost see this ghastly subterranean life. She could actually smell its pollution. She could see the pale red shadows of it flung upward on the faces of the people, as Faust's face had reflected the shadows of hell.

There was no peace in the newspapers, either. Nothing but the gibberings of violent idiots, nothing but shameful cartoons. (How intrinsically vulgar we Germans are! she thought with disgust.) Nothing but news of enormous new taxes, of rearming, of violence and hatred, of fiendish attacks on the helpless Jews, of concentration camps, of revolting deeds and murders, of blood and agony and death and frenzy. She could hardly believe in what her senses revealed to her. What does the world think of us? she would ask herself in consternation. She told herself with hope, that the world would not believe it. Hitler and his cohorts were too fantastic, too grotesque, for a sane world's credulity.

The most appalling thing, of course, was the disintegration and dissolution of Germany's noblest and most innocent minds under the effect of the virus. There were so many heroic and well-loved minds in Germany, famous minds that all men of all nations adored and worshipped. Yet, Therese, appalled, disbelieving, listened to their voices on the radio, their raving voices thin with hysteria and madness and hatred. She listened to their attacks on the Communists, the imputing of all vileness and disease and crimes and treacheries to the helpless and wretched Jews. She listened to their screaming denunciations of all the rest of the world, the foaming threats, the incoherent dithyrambs. "It cannot be!" she exclaimed aloud, dragged to her feet by this tragic horror, these self-induced and erotic hysterics. She felt no anger, only sorrowful amazement. This pestilence was no less dreadful and killing than the bodily pestilences of the Middle Ages. The bubonic plague of the mind, the suppurating abscesses of the soul, which attacked the noblest and the gentlest and the wisest, as well as the fools.

One night it was announced that one of Germany's greatest scientists who had only recently received the Nobel Prize for his brilliant work in biochemistry, would read a paper to a gathering of eminent scientists and to the German public. Ah, thought Therese gratefully, in the world of science there are no phobias. I shall hear reason again.

But when the scientist spoke, he did not speak in his famous and familiar voice. This voice was higher pitched, thrilling with suppressed hysteria, tremulous, throbbing, keening thinly with hatred and fantasy. His researches, he said (while those like Therese listened appalled), had convinced him beyond the slightest possibility of any doubt, that there is an irreconcilable difference in the bodily chemistry of "Aryans" and Jews. He went on to "explain" the difference, using scientific words and phrases which could only be comprehended by the few. But the German people did not need comprehension; it was enough for them that this man had made this statement. One drop of Jewish blood, he declared, violated and radically changed the other blood into its own "alien" and "unhuman" substance. This proved definitely the profound truth of the "Aryan" theory, and the inferiority of the Jews, who could not, therefore, be counted as men at all.

Therese, listening, suddenly gasped, suddenly burst into convulsive laughter. Her laughter, a little wild, mingled with the vehement voice of the great scientist. All at once she stopped abruptly. Karl, who had been locked, as usual, in his study, had suddenly appeared. He had rushed to the radio, and had turned it so fiercely that the voice seemed to choke on a scream.

"The beast!" he cried. He stood there, his chest heaving, his head bent, his hands clenching and unclenching. Therese, watching, said bitterly in her heart: "But you, Karl, are cut from the same loaf."

Nevertheless, she was passionately relieved that he had come out of his hiding for the first time in days. She asked him quietly, as though she had seen him only an hour ago, if he would join her in some hot chocolate and sponge cake. She waited, quietly enough for his answer, showing no sign of her inner fear and anxiety. When he consented, after hesitation, she almost wept in her relief.

She maintained a normal atmosphere when the servant brought in the hot chocolate pot and cups and cake. She talked casually and indifferently, in her serene voice. Karl did not answer. But she saw that her voice and manner soothed him, relieved his torment. He would sit and listen to her, with his reddened and agonized eyes fixed on her face. He even managed a smile now and then. She spoke only of ordinary things.

Then he said abruptly, which proved to her that he had been listening only to her voice and not her words: "That beast who had been speaking once had a Jewish wife. He was a pervert; she divorced him. He must have loved her, for he has hated Jews ever since." He added with somber contempt: "Perhaps if she had been a German woman, she would not have divorced him."

Therese gazed at him with mortal affront, forgetting everything but what he had said. The blood rushed to her cheeks; her eyes flashed at this unbearable insult. Her voice shook as she asked: "What have I done to you, Karl, that you can say these things to me?"

He did not answer for so long that she began to believe he had not heard her. His chin had fallen on his chest. Then he slowly lifted his head and looked at her. Despite his ghastliness and tormented eyes, he seemed to have recovered reason and humanness again.

"I'm sorry, Therese," he said gently. And then, before she could speak again, he had gotten up and gone from the room, walking feebly, like a man just up from a prolonged sick-bed.

She sat for a long time after he had left her, unable to move. Her whole body slowly turned cold. Her heart seemed a lump of ice. She gave herself up to desolation and grief.

6 THERESE had one enormous encouragement and relief: Kurt was reported, by Maria, to have recovered from his severe head pains and to have returned to his university. He had finally been induced to procure spectacles, not without a violent scene, and these had apparently relieved his disorder. Each day, at his bidding, he had his wife call Therese for news of Karl. Therese had given out that Karl was so profoundly shocked at the deaths of Gerda and Eric that he had had a "nervous" breakdown, and his physician had advised quiet and solitude.

Therese did not like Maria, though she did not underestimate her uncanny shrewdness. But she had never considered her a lady, though her own attitude towards Maria had always been studiously serene, kind and thoughtful. There was a deep antagonism between the two women, for all their apparently familiar and family associations and friendliness. In a way, they respected each other. They were both disingenuous. More than once they had exchanged amused and careful glances at the innocence of their husbands. They had often sat, calm and adult women, with folded hands, and had mused slyly at each other, and had experienced the ageless mutual sympathy of realists in the presence of fantastic children, whose raptures they secretly envied.

For some reason the old sympathy between the two women was growing stronger these days. There was something unspoken but understood between them. Therese, who found all hatreds tedious and boring, when they were not annoyingly dangerous, even called upon Maria in the afternoons when there was no chance of Kurt being there. It was not that Therese hated her brother-in-law; it was simply that she was afraid that her compassion would be called upon for new floods if she saw him, and these days she felt that more draining from herself would exhaust her completely.

When Maria had told her that Kurt had apparently recovered from his indisposition, and she had experienced that enormous encouragement and relief, she had been amazed at her reaction. Then she had burst into wild laughter at

70

herself, laughter in which there was a rare hysteria. Was it possible that she had for one moment become infected by this idiocy? If so, then she was no better than the other fools who infested her country. For days a sense of personal degradation hung in her mind, and personal shame, as though she were guilty of something indecent.

Trouble pressed closer and colder to her as the slow days passed. Not only had she the endless misery of Karl's isolation and strangeness, and the disorientation of the whole household in consequence, but each day brought ghastly news. Suicides, exiles, emigrations, disappearances—all the sorrowful and terrible things that happen in a nation that is going mad. She had to forget her own wretchedness and grief. She saw mourning households whose doors were painted with the obscene yellow of the Middle Ages. When she passed a man in uniform on the street she still could feel no hatred. At first she felt disgust and disdain, and then sorrow, and finally horror. For she felt that these uniforms were the livery of pestilence, the dread trappings of the carnal house. She was overcome with shame.

Confusion seemed to be growing in the country. There was a sound in the air like the dull subterranean roaring of an earthquake that was shaking the very walls of the world. There was a sound abroad like the sound of a coming whirlwind. And in the puffs of the coming destruction the souls of men were already beginning to stir and leap and shiver and tremble like dried leaves in a rising gale. Therese was still able to secure foreign newspapers, though they were becoming harder to get each day, and she observed, with growing despair, that the whole of mankind was as much bewildered and aghast as herself at this vision of the "new" Germany. It mattered not who the traitors were who had brought this desolation about; she read accusations in American newspapers that the British "ruling-class" were responsible for the overthrow of the German Republic, and had destroyed it because of some craven fear of the spread of Communism among the British working classes. There were some who declared that the munitions manufacturers were creating a "national soul and spirit" in Germany, and arousing militarism and racial pride, for ends too revolting and outrageous for easy belief. Others accused the perpetrators of the Versailles Treaty, and the greediness and mercilessness of France, and the perfidy and avarice of Britain. It did not matter.

Perhaps they were all responsible. But that did not matter. What mattered was that doomsday was here and gathering more blackly each moment.

Sometimes she thought: Can it be that outside the affairs of men there are dread insensate tides that sweep over these little affairs, with their painted wooden walls and gilt plaster and spangled solemnities and asinine dignities and childish pomposities? Can it be that these immense and meaningless tides from the seas of eternity roll over it all, and then recede in a welter of matchsticks and broken dolls and rusted toy-wheels? If so, none is to blame, not even the evil ones, not even the innocent, or the fools. The hater and the hated are alike victims; the good and the wicked are destroyed impartially together. The walls of the brothel go down with the walls of the cathedral, and in the heaps of destruction there is none to tell one from another. Mount Olivet and Vesuvius are alike inundated and lost.

In the universal death and torment, men, in the flood, reached up dying hands to grasp at the garments of One who, they hoped (not believed), walked on the waters. Did they grasp Him? Did they see Him? And if they did, why did they not speak of it to other men? And if He truly *were*, why had He allowed the tides to make a mockery and a loathsomeness of all good?

Therese's thoughts, these days, were like hot irons in her mind. She looked in her mirror and thought: I have become old. Sometimes when she saw Karl, on the rare occasions when he dimly emerged, she regarded him with the dispassionate numbness and despair of one regarding a universal symbol. He was a sign on her own door, a sign that appeared on the doors of all men.

A lethargy began to paralyze all her mind and spirit. To overcome this, to struggle up above the thick black waves of it, she called old Doctor Traub who had attended her childhood and girlhood. He was almost as dear to her as her father had been. She trusted him; she knew his understanding and penetration, for all he was not a Herr Professor. He had comprehended the darknesses of the human soul and the strangeness of all life long before Jung had exclaimed over them.

She told him everything without reservation. She looked at him with faintly laughing despair at the end, and pushed back her fair hair with both hands, in a gesture he found infinitely pathetic in the usually serene Therese.

"You see, dear old friend, it is as much for my own sake that I have called you as for Karl's. His disorientation—Germany's disorientation—are undermining me——."

He shook his head with old sorrowfulness. He was a tiny fat little man with beautiful, merciful eyes.

"We—the sane—are all being undermined, dear little Therese. But do not think it is Germany alone! It is all the world. Each people has its own approach to madness. Ours, as you have so subtly said, is by way of our innocence. Others approach madness through a wicked 'realism.' Others through belief in a 'mission,' by which they will either 'save' mankind or murder it for its obstinacy. There are so many ways! Was it not Hamlet who said this is a mad world? But he did not believe it! When he finally did, he went mad himself.

"You, little one, have finally come to believe the world is mad, and so are in danger of madness yourself. For the sake of mankind, we must believe in sanity, in spite of all the evidence against it. We must become fantastic innocents, we realists, and believe in the inherent goodness and progress and divinity of man. Did not Jesus say that only by becoming as little children, innocent believing little children, could we inherit the Kingdom of Heaven? Ah, what a Mind was that! A thousand years is not too long to study a single one of His phrases, and discover the richness and the profoundness of it. The Kingdom of Heaven, unreal, beautiful, strange, peaceful—but the only sanity!

"And now I shall go in to Karl. Do not worry. He will admit me."

Therese hardly believed this. But to her surprise Karl did admit Doctor Traub to his study. She was guilty of creeping to the door where she could at least hear the sound of voices. She heard Doctor Traub's gentle genial tones, and then Karl's reply. Her heart leaped with hope. Karl's voice was calm, quite pleasant, though faint and tired. She could tell by the intonation of it that he listened and answered coherently.

And then her heart sank again. It was not Karl's voice she was hearing, but the voice of a stranger speaking carefully from behind a mask made in the image of Karl. It was a cunning impostor, aware that he must be wary for fear of detection. It was like—ah God! it was like hearing the voice of a living body possessed by a disembodied spirit that had taken complete possession, and was grimly afraid of being exorcised.

Therese put her hands to her head again and felt a sick confusion take hold of her mind. She went away, feeling for each step as though her feet were numb. When Doctor Traub rejoined her in the drawing room she was not surprised at the quietness and gravity of his expression. He sat down very slowly, as though he were bidding for time before having to speak to her. When he did finally look at her it was with a sort of helplessness and sorrowful pity.

"Yes, yes!" she said quickly. "I know! You need not tell me!" And burst into tears.

"Therese," he said, trying for a tone of paternal rebuke, and failing. He let her weep, and as her weeping continued he appeared relieved. When she mopped her face, after some moments, he felt he could speak to her reasonably, for much of the confused distress had disappeared from her eyes.

"Karl," he said, "is quite mad. I say this to you openly. You already know it. We are not children, and must be frank, if we are to help him.

"But it is a deliberate madness, deliberately induced. It is an escape-madness, evoked by a determination for revenge. Karl knows quite well that he cannot obtain this revenge in a sane state; he must induce madness to accomplish it. Too, there is confusion in his mind. He believes that only by becoming confused can he invoke the powers of madness and evil, and succeed in revenging himself for the rending assault on his mind, when Eric and Gerda died. His brother is only a symbol to him of all the forces that have assaulted him, and have undermined his innocence. Again, I must compliment you upon your subtlety. So, in deliberately creating a confused and chaotic and terrible and insane world about him, he can move horribly and easily in it, and project it into reality, where he can revenge himself on that reality.

"I have heard great musicians play furiously and gloriously and divinely under the influence of drugs. They were able to do this by projecting the insane and chaotic world of their drugs into the world of reality. Do you see? Without drugs, these great musicians were only technicians. Without his madness, Karl knows that he would be only a grief-stricken, mortally wounded, but impotent man, helpless before those who have destroyed his innocence.

"Only one man can save him: himself. And how can he

be induced to save himself? I do not know. If I knew, I could save Germany.

"But, my love, you were always wise, even as a child. Perhaps, by watching, you can discern the moment when you can help him. I can only leave that to you. Just as we must leave it to a few wise men in our country to discern the exact moment when they can save the Fatherland."

Therese meditated upon all this for some time, and though her face became more tired than ever, it also became more resolute. The doctor, watching her, nodded his head a little in grave satisfaction.

She asked, in a normal voice: "Did you see that miserable little doll of his with the nail in its head?"

"Yes, I did. It was on his desk. How strange to see Karl's desk so shiningly empty of papers! But there the doll lay. The prong was half in."

"Well, at any rate, Kurt is not having headaches any more," said Therese, smiling miserably. Then both she and the doctor laughed a little, without much mirth. After a few moments, Doctor Traub resumed:

"Karl was always a very reasonable man, full of clarity and logic. Have you ever found anything in him previously that would indicate any instability?"

"No, except that he never, even during his most wry and quizzical and philosophic moments, was aware of reality. He would listen to the most outrageous things with disgust, but the disgust never struck in at his heart. He could argue the most logically, gently and reasonably of any man, but his reason could operate only when it was detached." She added, with involuntary bitterness: "Such reason is worthless."

She paused, and went on in a meditative voice that held a note of strange hardness:

"In these weeks I have read and reread his best books. They are so beautiful, so splendid and lofty. They contain everything that is needed to ennoble man; they project him into a world of divinity and glory and sorrow, of philosophy and peace and adoration. There is violence, too, in his books, and passion and death, and hatred and fury. There is cruelty and bestiality, and despair and greed, and all the other things that make men vile.

"But I dicovered the most curious thing. There is a terrible fault in Karl's writing, and it seems most peculiar that no one ever discovered it before. He has been mentioned for the Nobel Prize; he has won countless other prizes. He is acclaimed the equal of Thomas Mann. Yet no one has ever discovered the appalling fault in his writing which I have just discovered, and which I would never have discovered— unless all this had happened.

"And the fault is this: there is a sort of balance and coherence and calm, even in all the passion and death and hatred and fury and violence and vileness which he portrays. There is *reason* in them. There is a sort of juvenile concatenation. There is poise and logic."

The doctor listened, frowning in thoughtful concentration. But he did not speak.

Therese flung out her hands in despair. "You see! His innocence was guilty of this! There was coherence and reason, because he was unaware of reality. Even his passion was the passion of a man who is asleep and dreaming. Then when he was awakened, and he was confronted with all the chaos, and he saw the broken earth, and the dissolving mountains, and heard the whirlwinds— But I have said all this before. There is nothing left to be said except that Karl, in spite of all that has been printed and spoken of him, is not a great writer.

"He is a great stylist. And the most orderly of writers. But style and order have nothing to do with great writing. In fact, I am becoming convinced that when style and order are so exquisite, so complete, as they are in his work, they prohibit, and inhibit, genius. In his beautiful Grecian temples, with the polished floors and nicely lighted altars, and smooth and calm statues, there is no place for the violent and disorderly and belching gods. There is no place for reality."

The doctor stood up and walked about the austere but lovely drawing room. He studied the few pieces of enchanting furniture, the flowers in a Ming bowl on the white mantelpiece.

Then he turned back to Therese, who was patting her hair into place with a calm expression but trembling hands.

"Do you still love your husband, and Germany, little Therese?"

She was surprised, and did not answer.

"Then, my dear, if you still love them, these dearest of all things to you, your task is to save Karl for the Fatherland. We need men like him—awakened men, not pusillanimous weaklings fleeing from awareness."

Therese still did not speak. She waited. The doctor resumed his pacing; now there was an agitated quality in his steps. But he spoke very quietly:

"Hitler has been in power only a short time. But already he has infected the soul of Germany with his monstrous unreality. God knows how long this will go on, and how grave will become the infection. I—I have lost many friends, even in this short while. I have seen the souls of my other friends become glazed and petrified. I have heard them utter violence and obscenity and imbecilities that are unbelievable. The infection, as in the case of all other infections, strikes most murderously at the young.

"We cannot—we dare not—hate what we see and hear. Not only because it is the hater, and not the victim, who is destroyed by hatred, but because, in hating, we become as these others have become. It does not matter the object which is hated; it is sufficient that we hate, for us to be destroyed."

He regarded Therese piercingly.

"I know, I am sure of it, that when Karl—awakens—he will be a great writer. He will help to save Germany. That is your task."

Therese's pale lips parted as though to utter an impulsive and despairing question, then closed again, like the lips of a woman who has become aware, before speaking, of the childishness of her proposed question.

Long after the doctor had left Therese sat and thought, until the room became dark and the street-lamps outside were lighted. Sometimes she moved as if in unbearable agitation and hopelessness; then she would sink back in her chair, immobile, and meditate again. At last she was completely worn out. She had reached no conclusion, no pain. But a mysterious peace and strength had come to her, not unshakable, but fresh.

When she went in to dinner she found Karl already there, silent, waiting. She glanced swiftly at his face and eyes, and felt her new strength waver. But she spoke normally and cheerfully. He replied with quietness and complete orientation. He seemed rational. He even smiled at the sauerbraten and remarked that this was Eric's favorite dish.

After dinner they listened to the radio. A passionate voice poured out of it—Goebbel's voice. Therese leaned over impulsively to turn it off, but Karl said quickly and loudly:

"No. It is very interesting! I enjoy seeing to what depths we have fallen."

He listened to the end, smiling. He kept moistening his bitten lips. At the end he made no comment. He gently kissed Therese's forehead, and left for his own room.

Does he sleep? thought Therese, torn with sorrow.

KARL was not sleeping.

He sat in his study, to which he had come from his room. He had waited until he had heard Therese retiring, and had heard the creak of her bed. He had listened. Once he heard her sigh deeply. At that sound something momentarily relaxed in him, and he felt a thrust of pain, and with that pain, sanity. He suddenly had a vision; he recoiled from it, putting up his hands as though defending himself from agonizing attack. It was not for some minutes that the thick confused fog closed over his mind again, like water which had mercifully closed over a corpse.

The fog lifted, leaving him in a state usual with him these days. Everything had a bright surface clarity about it, a clarity, however, without edges or substance. His head felt light and giddy; his thoughts were like shining bubbles, but when he tried to seize them they broke in his hands. He was grateful for this, for the mere act of reaching for them exhausted him horribly. Yet he could not help reaching. He was reaching more and more as time went on, and his subconscious mind, in defense, made his body more and more exhausted, made his heart tremble more and more violently.

When he walked about it was as though he floated. He was surprised to find himself colliding with objects, with doors and furniture. He felt the pain numbly, as though under the influence of drugs. When he undressed he discovered large black bruises all over his body. Once he thought: I should be surprised at this, but I am not. The mere effort of thinking this threw him into confusion.

Things fell from his hands; he broke a lamp in his room, dropped a little figurine of ivory, which he cherished. For some seconds he felt actual awareness of distress, then walked away, forgetting. Once he looked into his mirror and thought: Who am I? The face that stared back at him was not his own. It tired and nauseated him to have to look at it. When he shaved he cut himself and cursed aloud at his carelessness, but without much interest.

When he would lie down to sleep it was with the feeling

of utter physical prostration. He would drowse away. Then, just on the edge of sleep his heart would awake like a terrified drum, sounding an alarm, and he would be sitting up in his bed, covered with sweat and anguish and absolute terror. He would be horribly awake and alive; it seemed that every pore of his skin had a separate and pulsing life of its own. And yet, with his aliveness, the clarity was without substance. He would get up, light a cigarette, drink a glass of water. He would find himself colliding with a chair, would drop the cigarette or the glass. Yet everything would be dazzlingly clear and throbbing. It hurt his haggard, red-rimmed eyes. He would try to think in this glittering universe, but his mind felt like thick fluffy cotton against which his thoughts smothered and were silenced.

Often the thought occurred to him: I do not exist. Somewhere, he remembered, there had been something very clever written about this. Montaigne? He tried to unravel the philosophy; the tight-packed ball fell through his fingers, and he closed his eyes against the weariness of the sight of it. Once he said to himself: If I do not exist, then I have only to will not to be. But the effort of willing not to be was more arduous than existing.

Food choked him. He ate practically nothing. The sight of Therese was a pain not to be endured often, for when he saw her the clarity became cold and static and real, and his thoughts became hard and sharp. When he heard her voice he heard the voice of his grief and despair; he heard the call to brave realization. He could not endure it. Once he thought: She is looking ill and tired. I am killing her. But the very thought, in its anguish, aroused anger against her, and a sort of desperate revulsion.

The servants whispered of his irritability and fury. Sometimes the sight of them infuriated him. He filled the house with his cries and recriminations and insults and rage. He crashed doors and hurled furniture. Fortunately, for Therese's orderly household, these fits were short.

Sometimes he hated Therese for the suffering he was causing her. Sometimes he tried to approach her on the level of normal actions and words. But his heart trembled, and the nails of his fingers dug into his flesh. He heard his voice, unnaturally loud and deliberate with his efforts to appear natural for her sake. But when he saw that she was not deceived he abandoned his acting, and shut himself away from her with anger and grief, and relief.

It was only in his study that he could subdue the glitter of the world and acquire substance. Only in his madness and illusion could he feel real. Only with the symbol of his hatred in his hand could he feel organized and potent, and with a purpose. Only at these times could he feel sane.

Once, at the very beginning it had seemed fantastic to him. But that was before his deliberate inducing of confusion, before he had pulled confusion over his head like a frightened child pulling the bedclothes over him to shut out the sight of a dark room filled with specters.

When he had first taken out the doll and had looked at it he had laughed crazily. He had, half-mockingly, baptized the doll with the name of his brother. The mere act of naming the doll gave him a sudden and overwhelming sense of relief and surcease. Confusion had then come over him. He had inserted the nail into the head, just a little way. He had started numbly, then all at once with a fury and vindictiveness which had made his heart leap and strain, and had made red spots float before his eyes.

What Therese did not know was that he spied upon her. She never lifted the telephone but what he listened. He was listening for news of his brother. There was an extension in his study, and he had heard the conversation between his wife and Maria. After that, his exultation made his madness complete, and never again did he laugh at himself.

Once or twice he had a cold lucid interval in which he could actually think: I must finish my chapter. He could actually approach his desk. But when he took up his pen and spread his paper before him something strange and terrible would happen to him. He would watch his hand writing words without coherence; he felt disembodied, a ghost motivating a stiff dead hand. His thoughts blew about almost visibly, like pale spectral moths, without pattern or sensation or purpose. When he attempted to read what he had written the words were meaningless. He forgot the one before the one following, and finally everything was a frenzied confusion again. He would feel his throat tightening, his breast tightening, and a feeling of mortal illness and utter terror would seize him like murderous hands. He would spring from his chair, choking, his heart leaping and tearing, his hands trembling and cold and numb. He would glare about him, like a man hunted to his death, and looking madly for escape. At first he could think, even say aloud, with anguish: What is the matter? What is this thing that has me? But at last he could no longer think this, but could only feel.

Time stopped for him. Sometimes he would wonder, very dully, if it were five minutes ago or yesterday that he held the wooden doll in his hand and thrust the nail in deeper. Finally he was no longer conscious of being awake, of eating, or sleeping. He did not know, of course, that Therese furtively dropped a tasteless and colorless liquid in his evening coffee, and that when he was overcome she would enter his room, where he was lying across his bed, and remove his boots and clothing and lift his head to his pillow.

There was a round tower of black stone in his mind, and a blasted region about it, which he never entered. And in that tower lived Gerda and Eric. He ignored it; he stepped about it, his eyes averted. In some way he knew that in that tower awaited his salvation and his release from himself, and also agony. Once he had a dream. He dreamt that he saw the tower and the door stood open, and Eric and Gerda, standing on the threshold, smiled at him and beckoned imploringly. "I am your sister," said Gerda. "I am your brother," said Eric. "Come in!" they cried together. But he stood, aching to approach them, weeping because of his desire to go to them. But he kept shaking his head. "If you touch me I shall wake up, and I cannot endure it," he answered. They looked at him sorrowfully, then closed the door. He could feel them waiting behind the door.

Whenever he thought of them, they were shadowy and unreal in his thoughts, yet potent with suffering. But there was nothing real for him but his brother Kurt, and his hatred.

There came a morning when he automatically lifted the little doll to thrust the nail deeper into its head. He stared at it, holding it in his hand, and a faint wonder came over him, as though he had never seen it before. He examined it with the minute attention of the dazed and mind-sick, trying to fix its features in his thoughts. Suddenly its vague features took on a strange expression. It was Kurt's face in miniature, and he laughed aloud, with thin ferocity. And then, all at once, it was his own, then Kurt's, then his own again. His laughter rose with a mad sound, and Therese heard it, her heart failing.

He thrust the nail in deeper. And as he did so, a mortal

driving pain assailed his own head. "Do you feel it, Kurt?" he asked aloud. Deeper he drove the nail, and deeper was his own pain. A horrible sort of glee seized him, the sadist's and masochist's glee, the joy which is the joy of self-destruction and torment.

And then, strangely, it was not himself or Kurt he was torturing and killing. It was all the world, which had rolled over him, which had destroyed his innocence. He began to sob; tears rolled down his cheek. His hand twisted and thrust at the doll, and his whole being was pervaded with a mortal suffering and intolerable sorrow.

He was all Germany, full of anguish and despair, and enduring no less than what she inflicted upon others.

8 THERESE said to herself: I know what I must do. I must discover what I am fighting, and for what I am fighting. But how can I discover this? I do not know where to start! I do not know for what I must search, though I know it is most terribly pertinent that I search, and find.

She had the orderliness of the German mind, in which all things were precisely fitted, and in which there was a place for everything. One began at such a point, with such a piece, and other pieces automatically fell into place. She had always firmly believed that in an orderly universe men must maintain order in their own lives and affairs; otherwise, everything was disorder and futility. And now she was confronted by disorder and futility, and a most hideous sense of her own impotence invaded her.

All at once, with a sense of profound shock, she realized that she must first start with herself. This was brutal to her native German egotism, so integrated and so managed with precision. With a sense of outrage, yet with humility, she knew that unless she reached awareness of herself she could do nothing for Karl, nothing for Germany. She must understand everything, before she could help Karl understand.

Her personality was compact and self-sufficient. But now it was shaken and dispersed, like imitation snow-particles in a glass paper-weight. Her personality seemed to flow out from her like a broken stream, and she knew, with sickening clarity, that the world was full of realists like herself, whose realism had become uncertainty and bewilderment. We have nowhere to start! she thought. We have no rock on which to stand. We watch the whole world bursting through the dams of reason. We watch men become the frenzied animals in a zoo. We see them whirl like dervishes to an incantation we can barely hear. We know we must do something, say something, but we do not know what. And how many of us, at the end, must subside into exhaustion and begin to whirl also?

The old half-humorous and cynical phrases were useless now. Civilization, in whose name the realist-intelligentsia could always appeal, and be heard, had become as tenuous and brittle as glass. Civilization was no magic word any longer. It was a puerile phase. It was something to make one smile drearily. Man must have a newer and more invincible magic word to still his whirling and shrieking. There must be another incantation. And it must not be based on man's egotism. It must not be anthropomorphic. It was beyond himself.

Could it be religion? Only a few weeks ago, Therese would have smiled at herself at this thought. Her father had been a bishop. He had also been a realist, and it had been his realism which had made her smile automatically when religion was mentioned. Religion, she had learned, was necessary for the masses. It was harness and reins in the hands of the intelligent and those who controlled a nation. It was the whip which kept the animal which was man in the paths in which he must tread, in order that the masters might have security and peace of mind. The masters had created religion, and had appointed the priests. Otherwise there could be no civilization, no arts, no comforts, no banks, no servants, no progress, no trade or commerce, no cities. There could be nothing which made life endurable and safe for the intelligent, for the masters. There would only be a jungle, and life was chaotic in a jungle. It was all very clever.

Therese had a sudden vision of her father's huge church, so orderly and clean, so dim and infused with many painted lights, so sonorous with organ and song. Then all at once she knew that this church was only a prison-house where ghosts walked, and where men could be frightened into behaving themselves, and making life pleasant for those who feared and used them. There was no vitality here, no love or strength, no courage or kindness, no fortitude or faith. The Church had betrayed mankind, had betrayed God. It had given security and wealth to a few; it had given, in return, no faith, no rock, for the many. It had given the many only fear.

And now a time had come when its vague fear was no longer potent. The curtain that concealed the Holy of Holies had been rudely torn apart by a violent haired hand, and the primitive seeker-after-God had found there only polished empty vessels and a great stupid silence. He had seen only printed words, and the words were dead. The living Word he had come to find, in his terror, was only the stilted ink of the pompous and the stupid, the exploiters and the fat.

Yet, somewhere, the Word surely lived. Somewhere it could

be found. And when it was found, it would be discovered
not to be the whip of the greedy and the crafty, not the drug
which kept the beast in subjection. It would be found to be
the only hope of the world.

But where was it? Was its name God or Love? Was it
called Reason? Therese only knew that in the chaotic animal-
house lived the magic word of order and peace, the golden
key, the "Alif" of which Omar Khayyam had spoken.

Who could find it and give it to the world? Or must each
man find it for himself? But was there time for this finding
now? But on its swift finding, its sleepless search, depended
the existence of a world now spinning like a glittering ball
on the finger-tip of a madman.

As she thought these things, Therese lay on her back staring at the ceiling of her bedroom. She heard the clock in the
hall below strike four. The night was deathly still. She might
have been alone in the universe. Her forehead was damp with
anguish and despair. She lifted her head and listened. She
heard again the disordered pacing of her husband in his room.
"O God!" she cried aloud.

She was seized with unutterable terror.

She was back in her father's church. He was standing before her, in his pulpit, huge and fat and pompous. He was
uttering his usual dead words, so bored, so without meaning.
She heard them clearly, and now her heart began to leap and
strain. Each word was like fire:

"For the vision is yet for an appointed time, but at the
end it shall speak and not lie: though it tarry, wait for it;
because it will surely come, it will not tarry."

The organ boomed, and now all the church was filled with
the sound and the light of a multitude of wings:

"And sware by him that liveth for ever and ever, who
created heaven, and the things that therein are, and the
earth, and the things that therein are, and the sea, and the
things which are therein, that there should be time no longer."

OLD DOCTOR FELIX TRAUB and his wife, Helene, were not rich. They were not even well-off. Helene had only one small servant girl who could not cook. Old Helene did the cooking, and it was excellent, even when so many things were so scarce these days. Doctor Traub was not a "specialist," and so was disdained. He was very old-fashioned. He had only common sense, and common sense was no longer valued. His patients came to him because, like him, they were old or faithful, though even these consulted specialists when they were frightened. He had only one degree, and degrees were so comforting, especially to the neurotic or the simply frightened. He talked brutally and roughly to the pretenders, to the runners-away, and so he was not in the least popular.

He lived with his wife in a little old stonehouse set in a garden at the end of a street no longer fashionable, or even respectable. His study was lined with old disintegrating books, whose rotting leather filled the room with a pungent yet nostalgic smell. Three huge small-paned windows looked out on the garden, which was tangled and profuse and full of color. At the end of the garden stood three ancient trees, crowned with misty sunlight. Here there was silence, though beyond the house the street was not silent. Here one could hear birds, and the muted whispering of leaves, and watch squirrels darting through the high grass.

Therese was admitted by the little servant, who peeped at her under white lashes. The Herr Doctor was in his study; no, he was not busy. She would call the frau doctor, who was busy in the kitchen. The little girl smirked, then scurried away. It was evident that she had a low opinion of frau doctors who basted roasts and got flour on their hands.

The quiet of the old small house settled about Therese, and for the first time in weeks she was able to breathe without pain. The ancient tall clock in the hall boomed. A shaft of pale sunlight lay across worn carpets and polished floors. The black-walnut furniture was hideous, and twisted into fantastic shapes. In a wall cabinet, tiny dainty Dresden figures postured, and stars of sunlight twinkled on the corners of the brass fender and on the faded gold of picture rims. The street outside was hot and glaring, but here everything was dim and still, a little musty, but smelling of spiced dried roses and timelessness.

Therese sat quietly. She became conscious that she had been afflicted with a chronic trembling; now her legs and arms relaxed, and an exhausted pain began to pervade them. She laid her head on the back of the old plush chair in which she sat; she felt the scratch of the starched lace against her tired, quivering cheek. She closed her eyes. She had not been here for a long time. She loved old Doctor Traub, but Helene had always bored her. She was not intelligent, Helene, and she read nothing. She was only kind and good. Therese opened her eyes as though she had received a shock. "Only kind and good." But, dear God, what else was there, after all? She was filled with self-reproach and disgust. What a cool, egotistic, superior fool I have been! she thought.

There was a long, gilt-framed old mirror at the end of the room. She saw her gray haggard face in it. Her small hat was tilted helplessly over her forehead. She automatically straightened it. Exhaustion crept over her like heavy water, and again she closed her eyes as if to shut out not only her pain, but her awareness of herself.

Someone entered the room. It was the old doctor. He smiled at her. He was paunchy and short, and had a little gray beard and small twinkling eyes behind his thick lenses. His dress was untidy; he was given to furious smoking of cigarettes, and the shelf of his paunch was always sprinkled with ashes. His trousers bagged; across his middle was strung an old-fashioned gold watch-chain. When Therese saw him and his wise, pursy, fond smile, she tried to speak, then felt tears crowding into her eyes. She gave him her hand, and he kissed it as a father might kiss the hand of his daughter, without gallantry, but only with affection.

"Ah, my dear, it is good to see you," he said. She saw how his clothing had been deftly darned, and also saw the glazed evidence of an iron on his frayed tie. He smelled of tobacco and soap and earth. He had been in the garden; his short square nails were rimmed with soil. He was good; he was kind; he was sane. He was her friend and her comforter. She cried out in a voice of agony:

"I do not know where to start!"

Insane words, not to be comprehended! But he comprehended. His eyes darkened, became grave. He was no longer smiling. Now his face was old and tired, and ineffably sad. He stood, looking down at her, not speaking. His slow heavy breath caused his golden watch-chain to swing a little, so that it caught fugitive gleams of light. He saw Therese's distracted tears, saw how she wrung her hands. Therese, the calm, the coolly smiling, the superior, the realist. "She has her feet on the ground," he had said once to his wife, but not with admiration, and only with a sort of regret.

"First," he said gently, "you must dine with us."

Helene, twittering, wiping her hands furtively with her palms, entered the room. She was short and stout, like her husband, with graying untidy hair, a homely smiling face, and beautiful kind eyes. A hausfrau, big-bosomed and squat-limbed and shapeless of figure. Like her husband's, her eyes twinkled behind glasses.

"Therese!" she exclaimed. She had seen everything, but pretended not to. "It is so good of you to come! You must pardon me; I have been making Felix's favorite cake. The one with raisins and nuts, that you liked so much when you were a little girl." She bent and kissed Therese's cold moist forehead; she pressed her hand. "Now you are here, you must stay with us."

"Yes," said Therese, but her voice was thick. It is not Helene who is stupid, but I, she thought. She clung to the old woman's hand as though she were drowning.

Helene put her worn fingers on Therese's head, with the gentle touch of a mother. She had no children of her own. She said: "But it will be a little while. Go with Felix into the garden. The last roses have come out. Soon there shall be no more."

"No more," echoed Therese dumbly. No more time, no more roses, no more peace. Her vision dimmed. She felt herself walking beside the old doctor through the wide windows that opened on the garden. Her hand lay on his arm; he kept his warm palm over her cold fingers. They stopped before the profuse rosebushes, whose buds were like splashes of blood among the green leaves. A bird flew over their heads with a rush of wings. A squirrel paused in the tall tangled grass and gazed at them with bright and vivid curiosity. The trees bent, their crowns of gold glittering and breaking. The garden was surrounded by an old red-brick wall, warm in the sun, and dreaming. Bees shrilled over clumps of old-fashioned flowers. It was so quiet here. Therese remembered the old Grimm fairy tales of enchanted gardens, lost in time, lost in dreams, lost in space and reality. This was such a garden. The gate had closed behind her; the world had ceased to exist. The ache that suffused her was the ache of old remembered pain, lessening every moment.

Doctor Traub picked a perfect rosebud, and she tucked it in her thin coat. She bent her head and inhaled the perfume. She was like a sufferer eagerly inhaling the fumes of ether, and wishing to escape torment. They sat down under a tree and looked before them, their eyes misty with enchantment and peace. The ancient house stood at a distance, its panes shining in the sun, a plume of smoke curling over its dim gray roof, its walls stained with green lichen.

Therese sighed. Doctor Traub waited. Because of his paunch he had to sit upright, his short square hands planted on his fat knees. The sun lay on his bare large head. Dignity, strength and solidity emanated from him.

"Is it better with Karl?" he asked gently.

"No," she answered in a dull voice. "It is much worse. I have not seen him for four days. I only hear him, pacing back and forth, and sometimes muttering." Suddenly, frenzy was upon her again.

"I must tell you what I have done! I have gone to the American Consul. I have entered our names on the quota. We must leave Germany." She put her hands to her head. "I must get Karl away from here!"

"And you think that will do any good?"

"Why not?" she cried a little wildly. "Surely, in America, or even Paris, or London, or perhaps Vienna, or Switzerland—! Oh, I have thought it over! I cannot endure it any longer. He will die here; he will go completely mad. And I am afraid that I shall go mad, too! There is something in Germany now, like a drug, and it is in my own food. I cannot live here any longer!"

He listened with intense gravity. He watched her very closely. Finally he stood up and walked away slowly. He bent over a rosebush and pinched off a dead leaf. He looked up at the trees and whistled softly to the birds. He put his arms behind his back, and stood so, looking up, the sun on his tired sad old face. Then, after a long time, he came back to Therese. He sat down again. He gazed at her distraught face. He began to speak slowly and quietly:

"There are some who have had to leave Germany, to save their lives. I do not blame them. There are others who have not had to leave Germany; they have deserted her, in the time of her greatest need. I blame them; I condemn them. They are like physicians who leave their patients on their deathbeds. They have claimed that they can no longer breathe the air of Germany, that they can no longer exist within her walls. They have said stupid things about their souls, and their art, and their love of freedom, and their disgust with the sickness of Germany. Despite their souls, they are stupid, and wicked, and fools. They are cowards, and weaklings, and traitors. They have had no love for the Fatherland in their pusillanimous souls. They have taken from Germany all that they could seize; they have robbed her. They have left her in the hands of her enemies. The ship is sinking; the rats are leaving. The captain and his officers have been the first to desert."

Therese uttered a thin and bitter sound. "Should they have stayed, and eventually been tortured and killed?"

He nodded his head with profound gravity. "Yes, even for that. What do individuals matter, if they have done their work? There is a greater thing than man: men. A man must lose his soul if he is to save others. He must forget his own life, his own safety, his own comfort. These who have deserted Germany have not forgotten. They are greedy little people whose skins are more valuable to them than the agonies of those they have left behind in the prison. Once it was beautiful if a man sacrificed all he was and all he had, for an ideal, for his country, for his people. Now it is no longer beautiful; it is silly. It is much better to run away, where one can eat and excrete in safety; it is as though a worm considered himself of much more importance than the earth."

Therese said nothing; she fixed her haggard eyes hopelessly on the ground. But there was about her a weary impatience and pain.

The grave rough voice went on, becoming more melancholy. "That is what is wrong with the world today, and wrong with Germany. 'The narrowing lust' for comfort and safety and security. Heroism causes a burst of castrated laughter. Self-sacrifice is absurd. Love and strength and manhood excite the jeers of the little men. Austerity and discipline, help for a neighbor, common suffering and honor: these are the forgotten verities. If we do not remember them in time we are hopelessly lost, and the world lost with us."

He looked at Therese with sad intensity.

"You say you will run away with Karl. Where will you run? To Paris? To London? To Vienna? To America? You will find a version of the same madness there which is suffocating Germany. The same plague is there, the same pestilence of the mind. You cannot escape it. It is creeping like a tide, or carried on the wind, like bacteria. The world is going mad; it is driving itself mad. Do not think you can escape the pursuit of madness."

He sighed deeply. His head dropped on his chest. He went on mournfully: "There are some who say that men have forgotten God. Perhaps it is true. For God is all sanity and goodness, all faith and courage and hope. Now it is only the individual, with his own bowels and his possessions, who is valuable. Man has become entranced with himself. He is tired; he is exhausted, for there is no sustenance in self, my dear Therese. An immense weariness and heaviness of spirit has the world by the throat, throttling its will, forcing it to turn away its eyes in a slothful will-to-die. The rest of the world, no less than Germany, is sick with weltschmerz."

He flung out his short fat arms with a tragic gesture.

"There are some who know this, realize this. Their duty is before them, even unto the death. What can be said of these, when they run away? What answer can they make to their consciences, to God? 'Am I my brother's keeper?' Ah, yes, a thousand times! a man is his brother's keeper."

Therese listened; her pale face was intent; her lips opened. Grief filled her eyes.

"But what can I do?"

"You can save Karl. Germany needs him. You must save Karl for Germany."

She laughed wretchedly. "But how?"

"I do not know, my child. That you must find out for yourself. I have told you before. You say you do not know where to start. Start with yourself. How can you give hope to others if you have no hope in your own heart? 'Seek and ye shall find' is still true today as it was two thousand years ago."

He stood up. "And now, Helene calls us. We must not keep her waiting."

They walked towards the house together. The garden was no longer enchanted. It, too, was exhausted, and filled with sorrow. The sun darkened behind a cloud. There she said aloud, suddenly: "If there were only a God!" And her voice was the despairing voice of a child.

Doctor Traub smiled faintly. "Perhaps there is! O, perhaps there is! But always we must act as though there were."

He added: "But this I know: that there is time no longer for man for himself, for man for his gains and his own lusts. There is something abroad in the world——"

10 MARIA ERLICH was surprised when her sister-in-law was announced in the afternoon of a gray summer day. The cool and conventional Therese was not given to casual visits, without a previous announcement. Contained, composed and poised, she always made a point of being expected and being received without the fluster an unexpected visitor almost always occasions.

Maria, though she hardly confessed it to herself, stood in some awe of Therese. She felt at a disadvantage with this daughter of good family and position. Having no soldiers, politicians or clergyman in her own family, she professed to despise them, as became the daughter of a solid burgher born to suspicion of those who ruled. Nevertheless, as is the way with all burghers, she secretly reverenced the aristocracy, for all her contemptuous laughter.

Therese never put on graces or airs, but there was something in her manner which implied that she scorned them, these marks of the vulgar and the insecure and the ambitious. Nevertheless, she chronically irritated Maria, who considered that Therese's simple manners and poise were the greatest snobbery. Maria believed that those who were superior were well aware of it, and affected simplicity. This was all hypocrisy, of course, and very annoying.

She usually received Therese with a jocose smile and gestures, and a knowing look, all serving to hide her uneasiness and sense of inferiority. She had a habit of eyeing Therese with sidelong looks and an air of knowing something to Therese's disadvantage. It was these looks and this air which so irritated Karl, but Therese never seemed to notice, which further annoyed her sister-in-law.

Today, however, the jocund smile, the knowing expression, were absent. Maria's pudgy and usually high-colored face was preoccupied and disturbed. Nor did she bluster at the servant when she ordered coffee and small cakes for her guest. Her flabby flesh seemed flabbier than ever; little beads of moisture were collected above her short pouting upper lip, and about her temples.

The dampness had made Therese's fair hair curl and twine

over her forehead and against her cheeks. But her gray eyes
were ringed in violet, and her face was haggard and strained.
Nevertheless, her manner was, as usual, polite and coolly
friendly, and composed. She remarked on the inclement
weather, and glanced at her damp shoes. Maria vigorously
stirred the fire, and the huge ugly room roared with its infuriated sound, and was filled with red glinting shadows.

"The coldness is unusual for this season," said Maria.

Her dislike for Therese, and her uneasiness, increased. She
said: "How is Karl?"

Therese gazed at the fire, and for a moment Maria thought
she had not heard the question. Then she replied quietly: "I
believe he is improving. He is not so excited. He has slept
the last few nights, and he accepted an invitation to dinner
for next Friday at the home of General Siegfried Heyliger.
The Herr General is my second cousin, you know."

Maria fumed with envy. The General and his wife had
been scrupulously cordial when she had met them at Therese's home, but they had not extended any invitations. She
laughed shortly.

"What a bore that old man is! Please forgive me, Therese,
but you do know the dullest people!"

Therese smiled slightly, without offense, and refused to be
annoyed. She did not reply. After a few moments, during
which Maria's face reddened, she asked: "And how are Kurt's
eyes? And his headache?"

She was not interested, and believed that Maria would
merely shrug and answer that all was well with Kurt. She
was surprised to see that Maria's expression changed to one
of great disturbance.

"I do not believe it is his eyes after all. His headaches continue. As for myself, I think he is only neurotic and upset
about Karl. He speaks of him constantly."

Therese, paling a little, leaned forward the better to see
Maria in the dim shifting light. "He is not better? His headaches are worse?"

In a loud angry voice, Maria said: "Much worse. He broods
night and day. When the telephone rings he trembles. It is
really too bad about Karl. He is punishing his brother too
much. After all, Kurt only did his duty."

She stared furiously at Therese's white drawn face with
the curiously brilliant eyes.

"Oh, I know that you condemn Kurt, too, Therese, in

spite of your aristocratic silence! And yet you had no particular love for Eric and Gerda. You see I know you quite
well, in spite of your cool pretty manners. You were jealous
of Karl's affection for his sister, and annoyed because he
spent so much time with that—Eric. I saw it all!"

Therese's pale lips twitched. She gazed at Maria with a
shocked look. Was I, then, so transparent, so small, so mean?
she asked herself. But no, surely, I loved poor little Gerda.
Ah, poor little Gerda! And Eric, whom she had accepted and
whom she had always treated with affection and courtesy.
But had there not been times when she had felt very tolerant
and progressive because of this very affection and courtesy?
Had she not considered herself very amiable, for Karl's sake?

"He is right: I must begin with myself," she said in a trembling voice.

Maria stared. "Who is right?" she demanded.

But Therese did not answer. She was standing again in the
enchanted garden with old Doctor Traub, and her heart was
sick with self-disgust and bitter humiliation. I, no less than
all the others, am guilty of the madness of Germany, she
thought. Of the madness of all the world. She pressed her
hands convulsively together, and was conscious of hideous
coldness running over all her body. Her soul quivered as
though stricken by lightning, and fainted with sorrow.

Maria fumed again, this time with impatience.

"You are always so cryptic, Therese. I suppose that is because you consider yourself an intellectual. But intellectuals
are in bad repute these days in Germany. So futile and pallid,
so impotent and whining."

She expected that at last her insults would arouse Therese
to affront. But Therese looked at her with dazed eyes.

You are quite right, Maria. Only I know how right you are."

Maria's mouth opened with astonishment.

Therese went on in a faint muffled tone: "I do not condemn Kurt too much. You see, Maria, Karl and I are also
guilty. Karl because he refused to see and refused to act. I
because I was so smug and so tolerant."

Maria's astonishment grew. She felt superior to this broken
woman with the tears thick in her gray sunken eyes. And
because of this new and exhilarating superiority her malice
subsided, and she experienced a throb of kindliness.

"I am glad you are so sensible, Therese. Tolerance is a
disease. We Germans have been too tolerant of the Jews, our

enemies. I was always surprised at your magnanimity towards Eric Reinhardt. I never wanted him in our house, but Kurt insisted. I could not understand Kurt, who disliked Eric so much. Now we are all awakened; the Jews must die, or be driven from Germany. I prefer they die. Wherever they are they will always be a source of infection for the world."

Therese said, in a dim, slightly wild voice: "I did not know why I came here today, but now I know!"

Again Maria stared, frowning. "I am glad if I have helped you," she muttered sullenly. "In any event, I am pleased that you do not condemn Kurt. If only Karl were so sensible." She sighed with exasperation. "There is something indecent in Kurt's love for his brother, something obsessed. I always thought so. Karl infuriated him frequently, and they never understood each other. But still there was that obscene affection in Kurt. Such a foolish look would appear on his face when Karl entered a room, and he would listen to everything Karl said with the passionate preoccupation of a lover. I had hoped, this time, that Karl's ridiculous rage against Kurt because of Eric Reinhardt would disillusion him, and make him aware of the degradation of Karl's unspeakable admiration and attachment to that—Jew. But it was too much to hope."

She went on gloomily: "And now, when there is so much change and joy in Germany, and so much pain in Kurt, he speaks of nothing but his brother, and listens for him, and calls a dozen times a day to see if there is any message."

Therese said again in that faint muffled tone: "Ah, my God, poor Kurt! Poor Karl!"

Maria was deeply touched. "It is so kind of you to say that, Therese. If you could only bring them together again."

Her fat peasant face was suddenly twisted and grotesque with suffering and love. And Therese, seeing this, felt her heart open with grief and understanding.

She had seen herself revealed; she had instinctively sought something here, and she had found it. Now she could go. She must be alone with herself, to bind up her wounds and endure her anguish in privacy.

Just then her two nephews entered the room. Vaguely she became aware that they were in uniforms of some kind, and on their sleeves were fastened swastikas. She liked neither of them, though Wilhelm, with his young thin grave face and cropped light hair, resembled Karl, and Alfred, bulky, vigor-

ous and extrovert, like his mother, was always affectionate
with her, and openly admired her.

Wilhelm clicked his heels and bowed stiffly over her hand,
with a murmured word. But Alfred kissed her heartily and
asked after her health. She smiled at him as she had not smiled
at Wilhelm. He was so wholesome, with his round hard red
cheeks, his knowing eyes like his mother's, but merrier and
gallant, his broad young shoulders, and the smell of clean
virile young manhood about him. She never smelt this virility
in Wilhelm, for all his steady intelligent eyes and thin erect
body. Often she had wondered how she had come to admire
and love an intellectual like Karl, for like all her class she
distrusted fine-drawn and too unhuman intellectualism. She
glanced up suddenly to see that Wilhelm was regarding her
fixedly and a little sternly. Then her glance sharpened; there
was something in his aspect which sinkingly reminded her of
Karl's present look and distraction.

She rose hastily. "I must go," she said. "Please have my
car called, Maria."

"But are you not going up to see Mother?" asked Maria.
"She is so fond of you."

"I am afraid that is a slight exaggeration," said Therese
with a faint smile. "However, it would be only courteous."

Alfred conducted her up the stairway. "We see so little of
you and Uncle Karl lately," he said, warming her with his
admiring eyes.

"Your uncle is still ill," answered Therese, with that strange
tightening of her heart which always came upon her when
Karl's name was mentioned. "He misses his sister."

The hand under her elbow stiffened, and when she glanced
at the youth she saw that his eyes had become hard.

"There are things worse than death, and Uncle Karl should
realize that," he said coldly and in an oddly mature voice.

Therese involuntarily paused on the landing. Behind her was
a great tall window through which came the gray and spectral
light of the dark day. It gave her face a leaden pallor.

"Alfred, how can you talk so? You know nothing of honor
or dishonor!" The youth had never heard such a voice from
his aunt, so tremulous and shaken, yet so thrilling with anger.
He could hear her loud uneven breath. He was taken aback.
"How old are you? Eighteen? You are hardly a man, but you
mouth man's words. Go back to school, Alfred!"

He colored with his father's own bullish violence, and dropped her arm. His body seemed to swell and grow taller. He was no longer youth, loving and gay, but frightfulness and ferocity. She could see his face, suffused and savage. And yet, when he spoke, his words were quiet and controlled:

"I no longer go to school, Aunt Therese. Neither does Wilhelm. Haven't you noticed our uniforms? We have men's work to do, for we are men now. We have a new Germany today. We are preparing for anything and everything. For unity and strength, for power and war."

Therese looked at the uniform. She had seen increasing numbers of these uniforms on the streets, but had not noticed them objectively. At her nephew's final word she was filled with horror, and forgot everything else.

"War! Are you mad, Alfred?"

He smiled; his eyes disappeared in cunning and contemptuous wrinkles. He took her arm again with a new masterfulness and an open disdain.

"Grandmother is waiting for you, Aunt Therese."

She was literally propelled up the stairs; she stumbled once or twice. She had the sensation that she had become old and impotent and shameful. The grip on her arm did not relax; her flesh was bruised when he deposited her upstairs. She turned to look at him, speechlessly. He smiled at her with irony and knowingness. He lifted his arm and said: "Heil Hitler!" Then with intensified irony he bowed, clicked his heels, turned and ran lightly down the stairs.

"He thinks himself a hero," she thought. But then, was not all Germany posturing now in the attitudes of Wagnerian opera? Heroic and grandiloquent attitudes, absurd yet frightening. Lohengrins and Tannhäusers and Siegfrieds in a madhouse, wrapping tattered banners majestically about them. They did not know that Germany was old and tired, as was all the world. But Germany had become a Faust, insanely selling her soul for a spurious and dreadful youth which had no verity in it. Under the new litheness and activity, under the shouting and the leaping about, lurked an old dying man, drugged and feverish, revenging himself for his impotence by sadism and wild threatening screams.

She did not know she was laughing convulsively until she heard Frau Reiner's shrill penetrating voice near by. "What is it? Is it you, Therese? Why are you laughing so loudly? Come in, come in!"

11 FRAU REINER, tiny and wicked and incredibly wrinkled, dressed in rich black silk, many chains, a scarlet shawl over her bowed shoulders, her little withered hands glittering with rings, sat near a huge window draped in red velvet. Her diminutive feet, elegantly shod, rested on a round blue footstool. Her dyed black hair was elaborately coifed, and dressed with jewelled combs, in the manner of her youth. Her cheeks were vividly painted, her lips crimson. Thick, almost fetid, perfume flowed from her, impregnated all the vast, high-ceilinged room, with its frescoed cupids, gilded plaster walls, crystal chandelier and heavy Victorian mahogany furniture. In one corner of the great room was, an immense canopied bed, covered with heavy yellow lace and a puff of sky-blue satin. Amber candles burned in the dim grayness of the room before the crucifix which Karl had given the old beldame. A stout maid fidgeted about the dressing-table smoothing piles of lace-trimmed silken underwear such as a harlot might have worn.

As Therese entered, the old woman grinned. Her false white teeth shone in the sacred candlelight. Her little black eyes snapped and sparkled evilly. Vitality crackled about her, an obscene and quenchless vitality which was ageless and full of rascality. The grin became a leer. She leaned forward, the better to see Therese. The old witch of the garden, thought Therese, with an almost hysterical senselessness.

"Come in! Come in! Why do you stand there like a ghost, Therese?" cried Frau Reiner, peremptorily pointing at a chair near her. She turned to the stout maid. "Get out!" she shouted.

The maid started, dropped a gilt mirror, overturned a crystal bottle of perfume. Then, in complete terror, she ran out of the room.

"Clumsy trollop!" screamed the old woman, pursuing her with a voice like a yapping dog. "Ah, for the days when we were permitted to thrash our wenches! The world has gone soft."

The hot stale air of the room was flooded with the renewed

scent, and Therese felt nauseated. If the odor had been floral it would not have been so bad. But it was a thick and viscous odor, sweetish, overpowering and pervaded with corruption. Therese thought of a corpse stickily scented to close out the stench of decay. She put her cobwebby handkerchief to her nose and involuntarily closed her eyes against a sudden retching of her stomach. She had long suspected that under Frau Reiner's silks and embroideries, shawls, rings, bracelets, chains and incenses, was an unwashed body.

She heard the old woman's sharp vitriolic voice: "Well, Therese! You look ill. But tell me: how is my dear Karl?"

Therese forced herself to open her eyes. She was choking, as though from some noxious gas. The room swam before her.

"Karl? I believe he is a little better. He is beginning to show some interest in life."

Frau Reiner grunted, eyed the younger woman. "Do you know what I think? He needs a mistress. When a man shuts himself up and has vapors, and gets a disturbance in his soul, he needs a new body in his bed."

Therese found herself laughing helplessly. "I am sure that if that would help him I should have no objection."

The old woman's eyes narrowed cunningly. "Therese, you were always a cool selfish creature. Did you know that?"

Therese answered quietly, to the great surprise of the beldame: "A week ago I would have denied that with indignation. Now I know it is the truth. I have been too absorbed in Karl and myself, and the picture we presented to the world as a genius and his devoted wife, who lived only for him and cared for nothing else. I have been concerned with niceties. Now I know there are no niceties. I have tried to serve delicately brewed tea in thin cups in the midst of earthquakes and pestilences."

There was a little silence as Frau Reiner's eyes probed her ruthlessly. "Humph," she said at last, surlily. "I used to wonder if you would ever realize anything. At your age the lesson must have come hard."

"I am only thirty-eight!" said Therese quickly, with offense. And then she smiled at herself, drearily.

"But now you have grown much older," remarked Frau Reiner in a grudging voice nevertheless tinged with approbation. "It is always good to grow old. One is allowed to live, at last."

Therese wondered how soon she could escape. She glanced

quickly at her watch. Within an hour Kurt would be home, and above all things she shrank from meeting him. I will give myself a polite five minutes, she thought.

The old woman settled back in her chair to the tune of her jangling bracelets and chains. "Yes, it is true: only when one is old can one be free. If one is healthy, the appetites, in large measure, are still retained, or at least one can laugh at past appetites without regret." She paused, Therese made no comment. Frau Reiner added in a loud tone: "What are you doing to help Karl?"

Even she was taken aback when the usually imperturbable and composed Therese cried out as if from the depths of some personal hell: "I have first to begin with myself! And I do not know what to do!"

Even in her distraction she thought that Frau Reiner would consider her mad or hysterical, and laugh at her contemptuously. She braced herself for this contempt with something like distraught hatred. But the contempt did not come. Instead, Frau Reiner's wrinkled tiny face became shrewd and thoughtful. She played with a chain, and the candlelight flashed in the links. Then she nodded slowly:

"Yes, I can see that you must begin with yourself. I might say, you must begin with Germany. You see, I know Karl as you never knew him, you woman preoccupied with the delicacies! But to begin with Germany would be impossible. You have a hard enough task with yourself. I think, however, that you have gained some understanding."

Therese pressed her lips together to stop their trembling and to quiet her nausea.

The old woman resumed in a hard slow voice: "Has it ever occurred to you that you and your kind, your nice, tolerant, reasonable, superiorly-smiling kind, all realism and selfishness, have done more to bring about the madness in Germany than any ridiculous sign-painter and his criminals, or the wretched people themselves? Just as the selfish, well-bred, cowardly, gentlemanly fools in all other nations will bring about the ruin of their own countries?"

"I am beginning to see," answered Therese, almost inaudibly. She gazed at Frau Reiner with desperate humiliation and deep surprise.

Frau Reiner shrugged: "Your kind has no bowels."

Therese thought to herself hysterically that her bowels just at this moment were only too factual.

"And Germany, just now, has no use for bowelless men. Say what you will about the National Socialists, they have begun to show evidences of intestinal activity. The wrong kind, of course. They have taken castor oil. Instead, your kind should have exercised and promoted natural and healthy activity. But you did not. You let the people take castor oil. And in the end you will take it, too, because you will admire the activity and think it vigorous. You will not see that the purging will destroy Germany. At the last she will expire from exhaustion. But not before she has destroyed other peoples, too. That will be your crime."

Therese did not speak. The old woman continued: "Your kind, so cool and without hysteria, has hated emotion and passion. You have prided yourself on this, as evidence of your 'civilization.' You did not know that you were quiet because you were in a stage of rigor mortis. Pah, you disgust me! I hate corpses. All you have given the world is cynicism, hopelessness and confusion."

And then it seemed to Therese that the smell of decay in the room came not from the old woman and her perfumes and fetidness, but from herself.

"Life," said Frau Reiner, "is not nice and unemotional and tranquil, and full of books and commerce and the status quo. It is violent and terrible, hot and full of smells, and noises, and furious comings and goings. It is really very vulgar. It is not ashamed of its stenches. Why do you not wrinkle your arisocratic nose, Therese? A short time ago you would have done so."

The old woman's face was a grinning mask of contempt and satisfied hatred. "Selfish, correct, conversational idiots! Did you not know that anything the world has gained for itself, everything beautiful and splendid, its justice and its decencies and its tolerances, were not won for it by you realists, you sensible ones, you reasonable gentry. They were won by the heroic, by those passionate souls who regarded martyrdom as an accolade, by the unrealistic who considered sacrifice and death as small things to pay for the liberation of men. Your kind laughed at them in their generation; you have always killed the prophets, you Pharisees!"

She gazed at the crucifix, in its halo of amber flames. She nodded grimly. "*He* knew all about you. He hated you. He knew that your gentlemanly selfishness and smiling derision were of more danger to the world than the Caesars, the

Mussolinis, the Stalins and the Hitlers. Because you betray the people to them."

She burst out into thin cackling laughter, and rocked in her chair. Therese gazed at her with the unwinking eyes of terror and revelation. The witch in the enchanted garden had broken in with storm and fury, and in the lightnings Therese saw herself.

"I am trying to do what I can!" she cried out wildly.

Frau Reiner chuckled with sadistic glee. All the hatred of the bourgeoisie for the aristocrat glittered in her tiny fierce old eyes.

"I am an old wicked woman with many sins. I have lived a long time. I know what life is, and I have loved it. You never knew what it was. Hitler knows what it is, in his distorted madman's mind. He feels the weight of the triviality and exhaustion you attenuated fools have brought upon the world. He smells your decay. He knows what you have done in your selfishness and 'realism.' You have made life too complex; you have put too many chains on it. He will simplify things. But he will simplify them by a greater surge of madness, by cruelty and death, by fire and sword."

She shrugged, shook a withered fist at Therese. "I would not mind if only you died. But others will die with you. My son-in-law, my grandsons, all of Germany. Perhaps all the world. Because you have never thought anything was worth fighting for, or dying for. If Germany is to live, you must learn to fight, to live, to die. However, I am sure you will not. You will prefer to run away to some remote place, where, for a little while at least, you can continue to be reasonable and cool and calm and comfortable."

She paused, snorted. A disordered silence filled the room, as though violent deeds had transpired there, and violent voices sounded.

Complete nausea, of both mind and body, had Therese in its clutch. She lay back in her chair and struggled with it. Time and reality vanished for her; she floated in a gray mist. She was filled with a deadly sense of guilt. I have betrayed Karl, she thought.

Then into the dim and violent room there floated pure and poignant notes of music. Some one was playing the piano downstairs in the music room. One by one the notes mounted the long staircase, entered every room, like a host of majestic archangels with lighted faces. Everywhere was the sound of their voices, grave and mournful and full of sorrow. It was Wilhelm who was playing below, Therese knew, for she had often listened to him with delight. He was playing Beethoven's "Moonlight Sonata," and it was the voice of the angels.

Even old Frau Reiner listened; her head drooped on her sunken breast. The light darkened at the windows. The crucified form seemed to move in the light of the candles, as though aroused to life.

Tears floated into Therese's eyes. She clasped her hands passionately together, and simply. She looked at the crucifix, and it seemed to her that the answer was there for any eye to see. God and strength, passion and goodness, fortitude and self-forgetfulness, struggle and life.

And now the music below suddenly rose triumphantly for all its sorrow. Wings appeared to beat against every wall and every window, to flash against the sky and light the earth. Its tempo quickened; the voices cried out sternly and joyfully. Life had risen from its grave, wounded and stricken and beset, but it had risen and was on the march.

Therese, unable to bear the stress of her emotions, rose from her chair and left the room. She descended the staircase. When she had almost reached the bottom, the big old house was filled with silence, and there was no sound.

And then, so abruptly that she almost screamed out, Wilhelm appeared below her, and gazed at her strangely. "I must talk to you, Aunt Therese, at once," he said.

12 BECAUSE of her own distraught condition, Therese saw distraction in Wilhelm's thin young face and still fixed eyes. But nature, habit and convention were too much for her. She had always shrunk with well-bred fastidiousness from receiving confidences. And, she now admitted to herself, from having the smooth serenity of her thoughts disturbed by the heated emotions and despairs of others. She would always avert her eyes from the indecent spectacle of another human being standing naked before her. But not because of delicacy, and only because of selfishness. The cry for help would make her only faintly indignant, that any one should dare enter the cool and ordered rooms of her spirit where she dwelt in self-pre-occupation, and should dare to demand anything of her which would remove her from her own tranquil affairs. Her lack of curiosity was not admirable; it was only that no one but herself and those she loved were important to her.

This nature, habit and convention now made her cry out to herself: I have too much to harass me to listen to this schoolboy! Her face became cold and distant, and full of polite reserve.

"My dear Wilhelm, I am in such a great hurry. Can you not wait for another time?"

He did not reply. He was barring her way, one hand on the balustrade near her own hand. He was very quiet. He only looked at her. His eyes bothered her, as well as irritated her, and she dropped her own. It was then that she noticed his hand on the balustrade. It was trembling violently. It was this contrast between his self-control and his hand which made her hesitate. Then she sighed.

"It is not far to walk. Suppose you walk with me? I shall dismiss my car. I shall be glad of your company, and I like to walk. I do not think it will rain." She added, forced by her habit: "But will it not wait?"

He stood before her, in his new uniform. He was too thin, and very tall. He was more like Karl than ever. But this did not soften Therese. She had always been annoyed at this

106

resemblance, and had politely disclaimed it when any one pointed it out to her. How dare any one resemble the one whom she loved, and so make him common clay! Her egotism was outraged.

He took her arm, not masterfully, but gently and courteously. "Thank you, Aunt Therese," he said.

Maria suddenly appeared. "What are you doing, Wilhelm?" she asked.

"I am taking Aunt Therese home," he replied, in his polite young voice.

Maria was pleased. Wilhelm was her favorite son. Many had pointed out to her the close resemblance between this son and Karl Erlich, the famous writer who must eventually get the Nobel Prize. She snorted, scoffed, pretended to be contemptuous, but was secretly delighted. Let them laugh at her plebeian background if they wished. Some day her son would be greater than Karl Erlich. She said: "That is quite right." She offered her flabby puffy cheek to Therese. "Dear Therese, come again very soon. And give our love to Karl. We are so worried about him." She added: "But will you not wait for Kurt? He will be so disappointed to have missed you."

Therese, who had been hoping that Wilhelm might be detained by his mother, was quickened to action.

"I am so very sorry. But I must go at once. Give our love to Kurt."

She and Wilhelm went out into the gray twilight. A damp wind had arisen. Therese drew her furs closer over her shoulders. She always dressed simply but with exquisite taste. Maria tried to imitate her, but succeeded only in appearing dowdy. Her black cloth suit, its somberness relieved only by the red of a rose near her left shoulder, was beautifully cut. It set off her slim tall figure and good bosom to elegant advantage. She had bought it in Paris. Her small black hat was Parisian, too, and enhanced the poise of her head, and the glinting waves of her fair hair.

They walked together in silence, past the tall ugly rich houses, so old and so graceless. Here and there an ornate lamp stood lighted in a window behind lace curtains. Brass knockers on the doors gleamed. Limousines were discharging ladies at various points, and recognizing Therese they greeted her cordially and would have detained her for conversation had she not indicated by her formal manner that she did not wish to be detained. The western sky was torn with thin scarlet, through which the dying sun attempted to appear. "It always shines at sunset, no matter what the day," she had heard somewhere. All at once her eyes were filled with tears. She began to hurry a little. She forgot Wilhelm for a moment, then when she became aware of him walking beside her, she felt her old distaste rising.

Wilhelm she liked least of her husband's nephews. She had never known why. He had taste and breeding, and reserve and gravity. He was a gentleman. Perhaps it was because he was so young. Therese had never liked the young, even when she had been young herself. They bored her and irritated her. Vapid, immature, green and inexperienced, they either distressed her with their bombast and noise, or disgusted her with their gravity and knowingness. Mature and experienced herself, she hated immaturity and narrowness of experience. They were so boring, so tedious. She could never be indulgent or maternal with the young. She liked them best when she did not have to see them. And now she was so hampered, when she needed so desperately to be alone and think, by a schoolboy with his silly troubles!

"What did you wish to say to me, Wilhelm?" she asked, with an attempt at affection, yet in a voice that implied that nothing he could have to say would be important. Perhaps he would tell her now, and she could dismiss him, and be alone.

He did not answer for a long moment. Then he said, in an oddly muffled voice: "Really not so much, Aunt Therese. But I must have some one to talk to!" Suddenly his voice was sharp and strained and breathless. "I have no one to talk to!"

She sighed resignedly. "You have your mother, who loves you, and your father, who is a brilliant man. And your brother, and your schoolmates, and your professors!" (Oh, the absurd exigency of mankind, who never have any one to talk to except the whole world! The silly impertinence of it, the ridiculous egotism! And now she must be bored by the vaporings of a schoolboy, who had begun, in his adolescence, to believe that his soul and glandular disturbances were of worldly significance.)

He gave a peculiar slight sound, then said: "My mother only loves me. You cannot talk to one who only loves you, Aunt Therese! That is not a point of contact."

She had hardly listened to his first words, then, when the impact of what he had said finally entered her consciousness she felt a plunge of her heart and an awakening of her senses. She actually stumbled, and stopped for a moment. She gazed at him, like one aroused suddenly from sleep. "Wilhelm! Yes, yes, child, I know what you mean." She stood, looking at him with profound recognition.

They were unconscious of those passing them towards Unter den Linden, and who glanced at them curiously, wondering what intensity had this slim young fellow in uniform and this distinguished older woman.

"And my father," went on Wilhelm, gazing at her with dumb misery. "He loves only Uncle Karl, and thinks only of the Party. Alfred? He is less my brother than the brother of any stranger. My professors!" Now his young face darkened and grew tighter as though with grief. "I have no professors. We have left school. I thought I heard Alfred tell you today."

"I had forgotten," she murmured. She moved on; he stepped to her side and took her arm.

They reached Unter den Linden. Here, Therese became conscious of the renewed activity of which she had been only vaguely aware recently. The shop windows glittered in the faint bright light of the sunset. There were many customers within, buying with a sort of gay fever. Busses and cabs moved with a quickened tempo. The crowds stepped livelier. There were many uniforms and military cars. From every building fluttered the vivid black, red and white of swastikas. Cries and greetings of "Heil Hitler!" resounded behind, before and at each side of Therese. It might have been a holiday. But to Therese it was dread delirium, in which the patient had been electrified to a last mortal motion before dissolution. There was no use trying to talk to Wilhelm in the febrile press. They finally turned down the Wilhelmstrasse, and, as though they had consulted each other, they crossed the broad strip of grass into the park.

It had suddenly become warmer. It was as though the fever and heat of Unter den Linden had pervaded the air, like the emanations of a blast furnace. Therese loosened her furs, and Wilhelm took them on his arm. The park was full of nursemaids and children; the girls were shrilly gathering up their charges and preparing to leave. It was still summer, but yellow faded leaves were drifting down on the grass. Here and there a young fellow in the same uniform as Wilhelm's chattered gayly to a nursemaid, or saluted a passing officer. Now the air and the sky were dimming swiftly. In this duskiness the flower-beds glowed strongly, as though throwing out light of their own. They wandered among the trees and finally found a quiet and isolated spot near a small pond. The water was the dull polished hue of lead, and as still. Trees bent towards it, staring at their dark pale shadows. Lily-pods floated on it, immobile, and the red and white flowers were closing into buds. They sat down on a bench facing the water. The heavens were a gaseous gray, without substance. But in the west the scarlet had brightened to long tongues of fire. It made the trees on the opposite side of the water look as if a conflagration burned behind them. A wall of solitude closed about them. They might have been alone, though behind them was the Wilhelmstrasse and its important office buildings, and to their right, beyond the trees, were the walls of the United States Embassy.

Therese noted that for all the isolation and quiet of the place Wilhelm kept glancing about him uneasily. His eyes searching every tree and every distance. Seeing her watching him, he said, with a sad laugh: "One has to watch for the Gestapo. They are everywhere. I believe they spring up from the ground."

She listened, incredulously. "Oh, Wilhelm, do not look for shadows!"

"Shadows," he repeated. His young face, in that dusky light, became sharp and suddenly clear. "That is what we must look for, always. They are more potent than realities. Germany is full of shadows. Soon the world will be full of them, too. Terrible shadows."

She was startled again. She regarded him closely. Was this really a schoolboy, immature and obsessed with the workings of his adolescent glands? She had never known Wilhelm, she reflected, with a feeling of stupidity. She had graciously watched him grow from childhood into manhood. She had received his awkward kiss for Christmas, Easter and birthday presents. But he had never touched her thoughts or her consciousness. She had never really seen him. She did not answer him. She was too filled with her own dolorous and heavy thoughts.

He began to speak in a rush of words, not as though he were speaking to her, but to the pond and the trees. He must speak, and it did not matter if she listened. The words burst from him; he could not contain them. No matter who else listened, he could not hold them back.

"I wanted to study music, when I had finished with the gymnasium. Paris, Rome. Mother had half-promised. Father never listened to me. It was all my life! It was not just the music. I felt it was only a door that might open the world to me. I wanted to know all the world. I believed that if I did, I would find something in it that was an answer to all the sorrow and pain in it. I—I might even find God there.

"Somewhere, I knew, there was an answer. It seemed terribly important to me to find it. Important for everybody. Every one looks, at some time in his life. Perhaps it might be given to me to find, or to help find. Goethe, Schiller, Lessing—Mozart and Beethoven and Wagner. They had heard the answer, somewhere. They tried to give it to us. But so few of us have ears to hear. Even when we heard, the voices of these men came to us muffled; we heard only a few scattered words. But there would be others who would hear a few more words. Some day the whole sentence would be there! I wanted to find only one word, to add to all the others."

It seemed to Therese that fingers were fumbling at her raw heart. And now her whole conventional training, her whole timorous selfish nature, her old shrinking from the sight of nakedness, struck at her full force. She did not want to see! Even though she, too, looked for the answer, she did not want to see. She thrust away the desperate fingers that fumbled at her wounds. Her face grew cold.

"And then, Wilhelm?" she said, in her usual cool voice.

If she thought to stop him, to stop his fumbling, she was disappointed. He did not hear her. His eyes, bright and fixed, were turned inward on his own despair and agony.

"And then," he continued, his tones feverish and broken, *"This* happened. *This* thing came which shut out even the words we had already learned. *This* shut me, and others like me, in a prison. There is no window in the prison. Tomorrow, we shall not be released. Soon, the whole world will be in the prison. I know it, I feel it! What then, is there to live for?"

She glanced about her, uneasily. What if some passerby heard this raving, which had become loud and incoherent? Perhaps this passerby might think, with amusement, that this schoolboy was making some shameful and passionate declaration to a woman old enough to be his mother.

"Do be more moderate, Wilhelm," she said, almost sharply. She took the furs from him and put them on her shoulders with a gesture that was like a slap in his face.

He seized her arm; he thrust his face close to hers. She could feel his breath. "Aunt Therese, do you not feel it, too? This death? This ruin? This raging destruction under our feet?"

"I think you are very immoderate," she answered, trying to release her arm. He stared at her. The eagerness and fever slowly subsided on his face. He withdrew his hand. Now he was looking at her with dumb anguish and accusation. But he did not answer.

She said, keeping her voice judicious, and even a little severe:

"I think the thing that troubles you, Wilhelm, is that you will now have to dirty your hands. They make you work hard, do they not? It will not hurt you to use your hands at honest labor."

He looked at his hands. Once they had been white and smooth. They were calloused and brown now, and the knuckles pushed through the thin skin.

"You young people have been so irresponsible and soft," said Therese, all her old dislike of the young in her tones. "You have wanted a soft cushion. You have refused to grow up. You have whined and complained, and never worked. It is time for you to be men." She became aware of her malice, and was momentarily ashamed, though she knew she had spoken only the truth. "Believe me, Wilhelm, I am not trying to be unkind. But you must be a little more realistic, and understand that you must work."

She expected him to become immediately boyish and awkwardly confused, as all young people become in the presence of unheated adult ridicule. She expected him to stammer: "Oh yes, I know I must work." Apologetically, and nonplussed. Placating, hoping for her favor, as a child hopes for a pat on the head.

But he said nothing at all. He had turned away from her. She saw his young profile, keen and clear, against the last fading light. That profile, so still, so absorbed, almost marble-like in its resignation and agelessness, frightened her. A swan, its white plumage vivid, gleaming, silently sailed out upon the dark and motionless pond. It stood poised over its own spectral image, bent its long curving neck, and appeared to meditate. Behind it, the trees were massed darkness, without form. The sky floated with vague ghostly violet, and the fire faded from the west. There was no sound, not even the purr of a distant bus, nor the most distant voice. Therese felt unutterably alone. Wilhelm had gone from her.

"I do not mean to be unkind," she murmured, hoping to awaken life again in that desperate marble stillness. (Oh, why had her egotism, which always felt itself unique and superior, and resented a common touch, done this to this suffering boy?)

He said, as if speaking to himself: "Work. Yes, I have always wanted to work. That is why this is so hideous: I cannot work. There is no work for me to do. If it had all waited just a few years more, when I would have known how to work, how to fight it. But I do not know. There is our superior officer: he is strong and terrible. He is old. He knows what to do. But what he does is evil and dreadful."

His voice changed, became a cry: "I do not know where to start, or what it is that I must do!"

Therese felt cold. These were her own words, her own cry. She could not endure it. She stirred abruptly. The swan lifted its long prehensile head and gazed at her steadfastly. It was like some ancient image, without pity but with the most awful understanding.

Therese had only one thought now: to escape this fumbling hand, this nakedness, this cry for help. Her old timorousness and distrust for emotion filled her with heat and anxiety. At all costs, he must be made to dress himself again in decent garments and leave her alone.

"I am sure you are too imaginative, Wilhelm. Things are never so horrible as they appear to the young. This—is all just a phase in history. It will pass tomorrow, or the day after. Germans are so stable, so controlled, you know. Do not take it so much to heart, child."

"And I am sure it is not only Germany, but the whole world," he said, so quietly that she could hardly hear him. He looked at her fixedly. There was no misunderstanding in his eyes. He knew all about her. He knew her timorousness, her coldness, her selfishness, her egotism; he knew that she comprehended, but denied the comprehension. He did not even accuse her, nor show contempt for her. He merely gazed at her as a marble image gazes, without wonder and without hope.

Now it was she who felt stripped naked, and ashamed. Her

pulses throbbed. A pain shot across her eyes. She averted her head, and as she did so, she stood up. He had to rise with her. And then again he stood looking at her, with that unendurable and all-seeing eye.

"Wilhelm," she began, miserably and confusedly searching for the proper words.

He extended his hand to her. Her gloves lay in it.

"Your gloves, Aunt Therese," he said, formally.

She took them.

"Shall I see you home now?" he asked, in the same formal voice.

"No!" she cried out, her sensations compounded of wretchedness and anger and compassion. "Please leave me, Wilhelm. I want to be alone for a few minutes."

He bowed. He did not protest. He turned quickly and walked away. She watched him go. He disappeared among the trees. She turned back to the pool and the swan. All the light had completely gone, but the pool was livid in the darkness. The swan hovered over his image.

Therese shivered. She looked at the sky. The violet gas had drifted away into depthless darkness. The light was leaving the pond, and leaving Berlin. It was leaving Germany. It was leaving the whole world.

"Oh!" she exclaimed, aloud. "Why did that wretched boy have to upset me so!"

And then she knew. He had seen her face in his mother's drawing room. He had recognized his own anguish in her face. He had been drawn to her as one tormented is drawn to another. He had come to her for help, and she had driven him away.

"I should have sent him to Doctor Traub," she thought.

Ah, yes, there was the solution. She ran towards the trees through which Wilhelm had disappeared. She called him. There was no answer. Night insects began to shrill in the grass. A wind, lonely and mournful, filled the trees. A nightmare sensation fell over her. It seemed to her enormously necessary that she find Wilhelm. She ran through the nightmare, through the trees, calling him. She was like one calling for the dead. Her voice took on a note of frenzy.

But when she emerged at the edge of the park, he was nowhere in sight.

KARL CAME down to dinner.

He was like a blind man feeling his way through passages once familiar to his sight. There were the same sightless eyes, the same pathetic feeling, the same slow step and sad confusion. Therese watched him come. The opening, dividing pain so close to her these days began to stir in her heart. Her first impulse was to go to him, as one goes to assist the blind, to lead him to his place. She resisted, however, prudently. Though she was so keenly and sorrowfully aware of his gauntness, his pallor, his bright fixed eyes and drawn lead-colored lips, she put on her best and most engaging smile and assumed a matter-of-fact attitude.

This was the first time he had appeared at dinner for a week. To judge from Therese's attitude, he had never missed a meal with her.

"Good evening, Karl!" she said, in a sprightly voice. "Lotte has made your favorite cheesecake. Is it not a lovely evening? Shall we walk after dinner?"

He stopped abruptly in the doorway, gazing at her, searching for her, as though startled at hearing her in a room he expected to be empty. The sightlessness in his face was almost unbearable to her.

Then he smiled. "Good evening, Therese." She could hardly hear him, so muffled and thick was his voice, so uncertain and exhausted. He sat down. His hands trembled as he unfolded his napkin. He dropped it. He fumbled for it on the floor. She saw that his bent head was graying. These visible threads of anguish made her close her eyes on a spasm of torment and grief. She appeared not to notice, and kept the smile firm on her lips.

"And a really excellent roast! It is remarkable that Lotte was able to get it, in these days. I am afraid it will have to last us the week."

He lifted a glass of water to his lips. The lamplight was shattered into brilliant flashes of light on its crystal. His hand was so thin that the bones appeared to thrust through the fair and delicate skin. She saw that his lips were cracked, as though he had been through a prolonged fever.

He began to look about him, dazed and numb. And then she knew that he had not consciously intended to come into the dining room. But habit had taken him by the hand and had led him down. He was confusedly wondering how he had happened to come here. He was a stranger in the room, a wanderer led in from a wild storm, bewildered, disoriented and afraid.

Automatically he lifted spoon and fork to his mouth. They returned to his plate almost as full as they had left it. He chewed slowly, and sometimes paused, suspended in the very act. He is dying, thought Therese, something squeezing with agony in her breast. He was dying, and Germany was dying. The whole world was dying. She felt that she was in a universal graveyard, where the dead and the expiring convulsively embraced each other. A sense of complete horror overwhelmed her. It seemed to her that she felt the touch and taste of wet clay on her lips. She struggled against the horror. She had experienced this same sensation in nightmares. But now there was no awakening.

Or could there be an awakening? In that universal graveyard, surely there were some whose blood was still warm, whose sinews were still strong! But were they enough?

We must struggle for reality, she thought wildly. We must not be overwhelmed by the hideous dream. We must believe in the sunlight, and in fires, and candlelight, and books, and laughter, and gardens, and health. We must believe in order. Never must we allow ourselves to believe that the graveyard is reality. If we do, we shall end in the grave ourselves.

But the horror held her. She had a dreadful impulse to rise with a scream, and flee. But where could one flee? Into the darkness and the homeless night?

She became conscious that Karl was gazing at her fixedly.

"Are you ill, Therese?" he asked, and his words and manner were gentle, if deadly tired.

Her heart throbbed. She wanted to burst into tears. She tried to restrain herself. Karl had seen her weep only once, when the hopes she had had for a child had been cruelly dissipated. She remembered how distressed and broken he had been at the sight of her weeping. She bit her lips fiercely.

If I cry he will take me down into the graveyard with him,

and I shall never be able to rescue him, she thought. So she made herself smile.

"I have had a little headache," she answered. His thin profile was Wilhelm's. But she had driven Wilhelm away. But she had so much to do! She must save Karl. She dared not diffuse her strength.

Immediately, she saw that her words were the worst she could have uttered. He put his uncertain hand to his head. He smiled, terribly.

"My head aches, also," he said, almost jubilantly. Then he paused. His mouth fell open; his eyes became glazed. "Or is it my own head?" He appeared to meditate. "Or another's? I do not know. Therese, if one's head aches, like this, it means that every one's head aches, too? It is a universal pain?" He leaned towards her, eagerly, across the gleaming damask. Hope and madness made a light on his ghastly face.

Despair seized her. Impotence turned her body to ice. She could not struggle. She thought: I must give in. It is more than I can do.

But the thought awakened her German pride and doggedness.

"I shall give you some aspirin after dinner," she replied, practically. "My headache was quite bad, but it is gone now. You should have told me before."

The madness on his face subsided. The sufferer had opened his door and had glared out for a moment, tortured. Now he shut the door again. But behind the door he lurked still, muttering awful things to himself.

"I think the evening air will be good for both of us," she went on.

He did not reply. Old Lotte crept into the room and stared at him fearfully. Therese refused to let her catch her eye. She made her expression stern and controlled. She watched the old woman remove Karl's almost untouched plate. She smiled, nodded to Lotte, allowed her own plate to be removed. Lotte said, in the voice of a servant allowed many things in a household because of long service: "You did not like the roast?"

She implied that any one who did not like a good red roast in these days was reprehensible and outrageous. All at once the tight horror in Therese relaxed. Lotte's words awoke her from the nightmare. She laughed.

"Lotte, we appreciated it too much! We hardly dared eat it! But look how much is left for tomorrow, and the next day!"

Lotte grunted suspiciously. She eyed the roast with a dolorous expression. "It will not last so long, Frau Doctor. No one brought ice today. Now, if we had an American refrigerator ——"

It was a sore spot between Therese and Lotte, this old quarrel about refrigerators. Therese seized on it with an almost febrile delight. It was the light of sanity in a universe of dark, swirling madness.

"Now, do not argue, Lotte! I shall not have one of those noisy things in the house. The Herr Doctor must not be disturbed when he writes. You know that." Her tones were a little too loud, like one who talks through ether, rejoicing in the sound of life.

Lotte grunted again, ill-naturedly. "I talked to the Muellers' Gretchen this morning. The Herr Professor vowed he would have no refrigerator. But the Frau Professor bought one just the same. He never hears it, in his study."

Therese leaned towards her husband. "Karl, would you mind one of those electric refrigerators? I am quite exhausted by Lotte's stubborn arguments. If you do not mind, I shall get one and that will be one controversy ended."

He stared at her blindly. He wet his lips. He swallowed painfully. Then he looked at Lotte, thereafter returning his eyes to Therese. Lotte waited eagerly, but with a look that implied that she had no real hope.

His voice was rusty when he said: "Get anything you want, Therese."

Lotte exhaled a triumphant breath. She marched out of the dining-room, bearing the plates like triumphal wreaths. Her short broad back expressed her victory over the obstinate Frau Doctor, whom she regarded as her own child.

"Thank you, Karl," said Therese.

But he had already forgotten her. She no longer existed for him. He rose and began to feel his way to the door. She opened her lips to call him, then closed them. Impotence darkened over her again. She heard him walk, stumbling, up the stairs. She heard the door of his study open, then close. She heard the click of the lock.

The window looking out upon the garden was open. It was very dark outside. There was nothing to be seen. But she heard the uneasy threshing of trees, the thrilling of insects. She sat without moving, her hands in her lap. The lamplight flickered on the table, caught gleams on the silver on the huge old mahogany sideboard. Shadows of dim light passed over the walls, with their crimson wallpaper. There was no sound. Therese's mouth opened, and she gasped, like one in a vacuum.

She looked about the empty room. She looked at the empty table. There were only two chairs at its long spotless expanse. The silver on it winked and glittered in the light of the crystal chandelier. Gerda had sat here, at Therese's left hand, and Karl's right. All at once she was there again, young and fragile and smiling, lamplight on her flaxen hair and in her deep blue eyes. So intense was the illusion of her presence that Therese murmured: "Gerda!" And there were tears in her own eyes and an overpowering sensation of bitter grief in her heart.

Gerda continued to gaze at her, smiling and intent. Therese saw her lips moving, but she could hear nothing. But what Gerda said appeared to have entered her consciousness, for the taut breathlessness relaxed, and her limbs released their twisted muscles.

Gerda was gone. Therese looked about her in a daze "She was here," she said aloud. "Gerda was here! I know it! She is not dead at all! It is I who am dead, and Karl. We are all dead."

Lotte entered the room. Seeing Therese alone, she started, squinted her eyes, looked about disbelieving. "The Herr Doctor is gone?" she asked incredulously.

"Yes," replied Therese. Her whole body was trembling. "He could eat no more. He went to his room."

"But I heard you talking to him, just now, Frau Doctor."

"You are mistaken, Lotte."

The two women gazed at each other intently. A look of fear came over old Lotte's face. She thinks I am mad, too, thought Therese. Wildness laid its hands on her. She was not responsible for her words. "Fräulein Gerda was here a moment ago," she said.

Now she will think I am completely insane, thought Therese. But to her stupefaction, Lotte quietly laid the cheesecake in its silver dish on the table. Her old gnarled hands shook a little.

"She is often here," she said, softly. "Sometimes in her room. Sometimes on the stairs. I hear her laugh. Once, she played the piano for me, and then she turned to me and said: 'Lotte, did you like that?' "

The old woman straightened up, drew a long breath. Her

face was pale and moved. "It is not I alone, Frau Doctor. Lottechen has heard the Fräulein, too. We are not afraid. In Herr Professor Mueller's house, Gretchen has seen his father, who died ten years ago. When we have our nights off, we servants talk of how often we have seen the dead, lately. In the streets, in the houses, in the churches. They are everywhere. Just as they were everywhere when Our Lord died. But we are not afraid. They smile at us, and speak to us. Germany is full of ghosts. But it is as though we are dead, and they are alive."

She looked at Therese steadfastly. "Do you know what I think, Frau Doctor? I think the Lord is here again. Walking in the world. I think we are going to have a terrible time. I think it is the end. It is doomsday."

Therese made herself smile indulgently, as a mistress smiles at a garrulous old servant who believes in the occult, and witches. But her curious shaking did not subside.

"What imaginations you have, Lotte! But that is the peasant mind, of course. You are always seeing doomsdays."

Lotte shook her head obstinately. "This is the real doomsday. You do not believe it, Frau Doctor? But you shall see! We are only peasants, but we feel it in our bones. You shall see!"

Doomsday. The garden was still now, like death. Even the insects were still. The light flickered on the walls.

Suddenly, profound coldness encased Therese's body. Reality receded from her. She was in an appalling and unknown universe where anything could happen. A universe full of dark tides and mysterious terrors, conscious and watchful. Within the doors of the little world, there was light and minute activity. Outside the doors, chasms waited, and bottomless pits opened silently.

She said: "You have forgotten my coffee, Lotte." To herself she said: "We know nothing. Nothing at all."

She watched the old woman leave the room. She was all alone. Terror darkened every wall, and the air was full of its odor.

She sat in the drawing-room. Lotte had peevishly protested at building a fire in the shining grate. But this was mere habit. She grumbled at everything. But her old sunken eyes were bright with concern for Therese, so pale and shivering.

Therese looked at the fire. She saw its warmth, but did not

feel it. She could not control herself. At times, she was conscious of disembodied visitors. They were all about her.
Vaguely, she heard a bell ring somewhere. Lotte came into the
room pursing her lips.

"Herr Professor Erlich is here, and wishes to see the Herr
Doctor," she said, disapprovingly.

Kurt! Fright made Therese start to her feet. "Oh, he cannot see him! Tell him to go away, Lotte! Tell him the Herr
Doctor is ill."

"I told him, and he said: 'It is a lie.' "

Therese was panic-stricken. "Under no circumstances must
he see the Herr Doctor!" She paused, moistened her dry lips,
glanced around the drawing-room with haunted eyes. "I will
go into the library. Show the Herr Professor there."

She went into the library and waited, wringing her hands
convulsively. She had some moments to wait. Then Kurt
entered. She gazed at him without speaking, overwhelmed at
the change in him. His large and burly figure had shrunken;
his shoulders were bent. The slight gray at his temples had
widened. But the change was strongest in his face, which
was heavily lined and drawn. His small bellicose eyes were
sunken and bright with suffering, and there was a constant
tremor about his hard wide mouth.

He saw her, but looked beyond and about her. "Good
evening, Therese," he said hoarsely, and in a preoccupied
tone. "Where is Karl? I must see him at once."

"Please sit down, Kurt," she said, trying to keep her manner
natural.

"I must see Karl," he repeated, and now his voice broke.

They stood facing each other. Therese calm, the man looking about him like one completely distraught.

"I am sorry, Kurt, but that's impossible. Please sit down."
She seated herself. He sat down also, automatically, on the
edge of his chair. He kept wetting his lips. His eyes implored
her, like the wounded eyes of a dying animal.

"You see, Kurt, he is still very ill."

The pathetic suffering vanished from his face. "Therese,
that is not true. Maria told me today that he is accepting
dinner invitations. When I heard that, I was happy. I knew
that he must be better." There was a cry in his voice. "I
must see him, Therese!"

She fumbled desperately in her mind for the proper words.
Fright rose in her. How could she control him? If she could

not, he would force his way into Karl's presence. Her imagination fainted with horror at the thought. She said coldly:
"If you insist upon seeing him, everything that I have been
able to do for him will be ruined. Kurt, have you forgotten
that you caused the death of his sister, and his best friend?"

His eyes lighted with rage against her. "Gerda was my sister, also. Perhaps you have forgotten?"

She stared at him. Suddenly she was filled with hatred for
him, and violence. There, like a speared bull he sat, leaning
towards her, panting, the man who had brought this dreadfulness upon Karl, the man who had brought death and agony
to Germany. He personified all the forces and storms that had
battered her with such ferocity; he was the earthquake which
had thrown up the earth on which she stood. She lost her old
compassion for him.

"Kurt," she said, quite quietly, but in a shaking voice which
she could hardly control, "I have forgotten nothing. And I
know that if Karl sees you, he will go entirely insane, or even
attempt to kill you. I—I should not have permitted you to
come into this house!"

Like all Germans, he was taken aback at this counter-as-
sault. He tried to stare her down. When he could not, the
rage receded from his tormented face, his panting became
lower and more controlled. Now he was once more pathetic
and moving. He said at last imploringly: "Therese, cannot you
see that I must talk to my brother?" His large and brutal hands
involuntarily extended themselves to her; he was a victim
begging for his life. "Maria tells me that you spoke to her
very sensibly today. She said that you admitted I could not
have done anything else than what I did. When she told me
that I said to myself: 'Therese was always a practical and
intelligent woman. She will help me.'"

Therese pressed her hand against her breast; her heart was
leaping; the blood was drumming in her ears. She struggled
for calmness. Deceit, she saw, was her only course. She made
herself smile faintly.

"Kurt, I would do anything to help you. But this is impossible. Believe me, I am telling you the truth. The moment
Karl shows signs of real recovery, I will call you. I have no
desire to keep you apart. It is really painful to me to see your
estrangement. But there is nothing else I can do at this time."

Because truth was so mixed with her deception, he believed
her. His hands fell limply to his knees. The mournfulness of a

stricken beast gave a dignity and almost heroic resignation to his face.

"I know, I know!" he murmured, brokenly. "You were always my friend, Therese. You did not like that Jew, either!" A new change came over him. His fists clenched; he beat them wildly on his knees. His face took on a hideous rage and ferocity. "It is all that Jew's fault! God, why did he not die before my father took him into his house! He was always there, laughing at me. He taught Karl to laugh at me. He taught Karl to hate me! And there was never any one but Karl in all the world for me!" He gasped; he drew in a deep breath. There was a heavy wheezing in his throat. Suddenly he put his hands to his temples, and clutched them, his fingers trembling violently. His eyes disappeared in wrinkles of physical anguish. He groaned.

Therese was terrified. She sprang to her feet and rang the bell for Lotte. When the old woman appeared, Therese cried to her: "Wine! Bring wine at once!"

Lotte stared, paralyzed, at the rocking and groaning man. A strange expression of grim exultation sparkled in her ancient eyes. "Lotte!" cried Therese, harshly. Lotte started. She scurried from the room. She came back almost instantly with a tray of wine and glasses. Therese splashed the wine as she poured a glass. Her teeth chattered. She thrust the glass at Kurt and commanded him: "Kurt, you must drink this!" Lotte, from the doorway, watched, her hands folded under her apron, a grin on her lips.

But he did not reach for it. She pressed it against his lips. He swallowed. Beads of sweat ran down from his forehead, which was pulsing with unbearable pain. His temples were knotted with swollen veins. He was a man *in extremis*. Shudders passed over his body. He swallowed again and again, the wheezing like a death rattle in his throat. Finally, he thrust the glass aside. He fumbled for his handkerchief. He wiped his face, which was the color and wetness of clay.

He looked at her with simple and humble apology. Red veins threaded the whites of his suffused eyes. There was moisture in his pinched nostrils; his forehead continued to drip. The water was like tears, bursting from all his pores.

"I am sorry, Therese," he said, not able to raise his voice above a whisper. "But—there is such a pain—here." He touched his temples with fingers still visibly trembling. "As if —if a spike were being driven into my head, into my brain."

Therese exclaimed incoherently: "No, no! It is not possible!" The glass fell from her fingers and was shattered on the floor. She exclaimed again, full of passionate repudiation and horror: "It is not possible!"

Even in his torment, he was startled at her words and manner. He stared at her blindly. "But it is possible, Therese. They say it is—my eyes. There is a strain—" His attempt at reasonable talk collapsed. He whimpered in his throat. He continued to wipe his face. Now he did not look at her. He was filled with shame at his plight and his betrayal of his suffering. He even hated her because she had seen his weakness and pain.

"The fools have wanted to take an X-ray of my skull," he mumbled.

"Then by all means have it taken, Kurt!"

Her vehemence finally penetrated to him. In spite of what he was enduring he regarded her with surprise, quite touched at her solicitude. He saw that she was genuinely overwrought.

"Thank you, Therese," he said, with a gentleness quite alien to him. He was more and more convinced that she was his friend. Her face was so pale, her eyes so distended.

She thought to herself: Karl and Kurt. They are both symptoms of the soul of Germany, both dangerous and equally responsible for her plight. Both madmen. I must hold myself tightly, otherwise, I shall be mad, too. She sat down near him, trying to stop the tremors that thrilled along her nerves.

But in spite of herself she thought: Some way, I must find out if Karl has discovered my changing of the dolls!

He said apologetically: "The pain comes on me at unexpected times. Between the times, there is just a dull aching in my head, like an abscess. And then, without warning, I have a seizure. I—I sometimes collapse. But it is really nothing! he added, hastily. "One must not think of oneself these days. There is so much to be done."

But what he had endured, and the friendship for him which Therese had displayed, had broken down his usual dour reserve and bellicose egotism. He had a desperate need for sympathy and understanding.

"I have only one consolation, my son, Alfred. He is a true son of Germany. You must know Captain Baldur von Keitsch? He is my son's commander. He speaks highly of Alfred. He has recommended him for aviation instruction. Alfred is without fear, and is enthusiastic over the new regime." He paused, and gazed at Therese with a kindling expression pathetic to see on his drawn face. "I have no fear for Alfred. Who knows? If he continues as he is now, he may even be brought to the attention of Herr Hitler, himself! We need such as Alfred in these heroic days. For soon the world shall hear from us, and tremble!"

His eyes darkened. "But my son Wilhelm. I have little hopes for him."

Therese wanted to be silent. She was not interested in Wilhelm. But she said, responding to an unfamiliar impulse towards interfering in others' affairs.

"Wilhelm is a fine boy, Kurt. You must not press him too hard. He is very sensitive." She added, the impulse stronger: "Sometimes I think he is very like Karl."

She had thought to please him, and soften him towards Wilhelm. But to her amazement he was again angered. Moreover, he was outraged.

"Like Karl! There is no one like Karl! It is sacrilege to say so!"

She could not be affronted. She could only marvel at this fresh manifestation of reasonless love, and feel its pathos. All her disgust at Kurt, and her hatred for him, vanished. Her heart melted, and she felt the sad tug of compassion.

Her emotions, and what she had gone through, had exhausted her. She could not control her thoughts. Her head throbbed and beat. She was full of a universal pity. If there were angels, so must they feel for all men, even for such men as Kurt Erlich.

She was aghast at her own words: "Kurt do you believe in doomsday?"

He had been absorbed in his own dreary thoughts. He now stared at her, blinking rapidly.

"Oh never mind, Kurt. I am afraid I am just a little disturbed."

He was never of a complex mind. He rose to his feet. He had to catch at the back of his chair to steady himself.

"Therese," he said humbly. "Please tell Karl I was here. Tell him I ask him for only a moment. Just a moment, Therese!"

"Yes, yes, Kurt. Of course. When he is able to see you. You understand—his feelings, just now?"

But he merely bowed his head, and walked out of the room like an old man.

She sat in a long and shivering silence. The clock tolled out its hour. Everything was very still. The fire died in the grate. The room was suffocatingly hot, but Therese was numb with cold.

After a long while had passed, she tiptoed up the stairs. She was surprised to find that Karl's study door was slightly open. She pressed her hand against it. It opened wider. A lamp burned on his shining desk, empty of everything but the open witch-box which Eric had brought from Africa. But Karl, himself, was not there.

There was a fetid and breathless atmosphere in that room, as though invisible obscenity lurked in it. Therese held her breath. Where was Karl? She crept towards the box, and looked within. The substituted doll lay on top of all the other debris, and the brass nail was sunken deeply in its head. She did not know why she was so intolerably relieved, why her body relaxed. Karl had not discovered the substitution then. She wanted to burst out into hysterical laughter.

She turned. On the mantelpiece stood the head of Gilu, the witch-doctor. The wicked eyes seemed to watch her intently. The lamplight made its grin wider. It was laughing silently. It was sentient and evil. It was alive and full of horribleness and understanding. It was the evil of the hating and gloating forces outside the walls of reality, waiting, sleepless, and forever triumphant.

She stared at it and it stared back at her, exultant, contorted with obscene mirth. She was seized with an impulse to lay her hands upon it, to throw it into the fire. She actually took a step towards it.

She heard a slight sound behind her. She started violently. Karl stood there. She saw his face, sly and gleeful, alight with madness. And then she knew that he had known of Kurt's presence, that he had heard every word.

"Were you looking for me, Therese?" he asked gently.

She put her hands to her face with an appalled gesture. She shrank from him.

"No! No!" she almost screamed. And ran from the room.

To be natural, always to be natural with Karl, no matter what happened: Therese knew that was her only course, until she could actively help him. They were like two people fallen into a pit, full of slime, the walls precipitous and with few footholds. Karl was sinking in the slime. She knew that she had a single foothold, and that with pain and anguish, she could rise to a higher one, and then another, until her footing was firm and she was out of the quicksand. Then and then only could she reach down a hand and pull him to safety. In the meantime, as she struggled from one precarious hold upwards to another, she could only call words of calm encouragement to him. She could only try to make him believe that this was a normal fall, and nothing to despair over. In a moment or two longer, they would both be free, climbing upwards strongly to the light and safety. Never, even for a moment, must she allow him to see her own hopelessness and terror. If she did, she would fall back forever into the slime with him, and they would go down together.

So, when on the morning of Friday she knocked lightly on the door of his study, and his slow dragging step approached the door, and he opened it, she smiled at him with her old sprightliness. He had not had anything to eat, but she ignored this.

"Good morning, Karl! Did you work late, last night? I did not hear you this morning. Karl, you have not forgotten we have dinner with Siegfried tonight?"

He stared at her blindly. His clothing was dishevelled. He had not gone to bed, or rested. But the smile was determined and fixed on her face.

"Siegfried?" he mumbled, passing his hands over his head with a dazed gesture.

She pretended to wifely exasperation. "O Karl, how forgetful you are! But you always affected to forget dinner with Siegfried. I wish you liked the dull old creature more."

Her heart leaped with painful hope when she saw his smile, a little sheepish. For one instant his bloodshot eyes became

127

normal, and there was even a faint twinkle in them. The prisoner had come to the door, and was looking at her shyly. She wanted to put out her hand with a cry to him, but she dared not.

"But he is dull, Therese," he said. His voice was hoarse and weak, but it was more natural than it had been for some time. He shifted uneasily, and regarded her with pale suspicion. The prisoner was closing the door again. "But, my dear, you must excuse me, after all. I am sorry, I had forgotten. I—I do not feel like attending any dinners."

She held back the trembling of her senses, and assumed an air of marital annoyance. "O Karl, I did so want to go! I feel like a party, even if it is a dull one. Why can you not oblige me in this?"

A sudden fever of despairing impatience possessed him. "I cannot go, Therese! Do you not understand? I can talk to no one! But go yourself. He is your father's cousin, and it will not be odd if I do not accompany you."

Her tense fingernails ran into her palms. She struggled for calm.

"Very well, Karl. But I shall not pretend I am not annoyed at you. However, go back to your work. I shall not disturb you." She pretended to be hurt. "I shall send Lotte with your breakfast."

She turned away. She expected that he would shut and lock the door immediately. She walked slowly down the stairs. But he had not yet closed the door. She knew that he was watching her. She did not let herself falter. She even hummed lightly, loud enough for him to hear her. When the door finally closed, just as she reached the bottom of the stairway, and she heard no ominous click of the lock, a light perspiration broke out over her. O, God be thanked! she had gained one small higher foothold.

Her relief was so intense that she felt hysterical. She went into the garden to regain composure. It was not a garden like Doctor Traub's. Her aristocrat's instinct was simple and formal. A line of tapering poplars caught the morning sun on their pointed crowns at the rear of the garden. She had no walls, but the trees were a colder and more forbidding barrier than any sun-warmed bricks or stones. On the other two sides were rows of evergreens, pointed and fronded, giving the garden a chill and rigid air. There were no flower beds, and only a long sweep of green grass, sparkling with dews of the past night. Therese was fond of the cool purple of iris. Though it was late in the season for them, they stood in formal sheltered rows near the poplars, their drooping amethystine petals frosted with moisture. There is no place to hide here, thought Therese. She was startled: Why had she thought such a thing? All at once she hated her cold bare garden, which offered no seat for the tired, no consolation of warm color, no smell of hope. It was like herself, egotistic and selfish. She could not endure it. She returned to the house. Lotte was just descending the stairs with an untouched breakfast tray in her hands.

"The Herr Doctor refused it all, except for a cup of black coffee," she said, her disapproval of such scandalous conduct in these days making her small old eyes sparkle.

"I must have rosebushes, many of them! and phlox, and lilacs, many frowsy bushes of them, and yellow daisies with black hearts," said Therese.

Lotte stared. "Are you well, Frau Doctor?" she exclaimed, full of concern.

Therese laughed drearily. "I have just been in the garden. For the first time, Lotte, I have realized how ugly it is."

Lotte nodded. "I have always thought so, Frau Doctor. It is like a church, without painted windows, without music, without a pulpit and a priest."

"He never said so, Lotte, but how the Herr Doctor must have hated it!"

Lotte eagerly welcomed this admission to confidence. "Yes, yes, Frau Doctor, it is so. He hated it. I knew it. He would go out for air, but he never remained but a moment."

Therese was silent. The old simple peasant had known the places in Karl's soul which she had never known, herself. She had been too self-absorbed.

She had never really known anything, and, at the last, she had not even known her own soul.

She went alone to the house of her father's old cousin, General Siegfried von Heyliger. She had often gone alone, for Karl had always been bored and impatient with the General, who talked of past wars and past glories and found nothing good in the present, and who incessantly complained of the softness of the new youth, and the decadence of the martial spirit in Germany.

The General lived in an enormous old brown house in a

section of Berlin that smelled of musty and dignified age.
Men like the General lived in this section, men who lived in
the past, old soldiers with fierce white mustaches, saber scars,
big bellies, pensions and hideous ancient furniture. They
talked constantly of Heidelberg and duels, wars and beer tav-
erns in ivy-covered little towns. They were meticulous and
gallant with ladies, ceremonious and polite with the brutal
politeness of the Teuton. They despised the French, admired
the British, and never mentioned the rest of the world, which
was obscene, irrelevant and filthy to them, and not to be
spoken of by gentlemen and soldiers. Politics were the amusement of the vulgar and the degraded. In short, they knew
nothing at all. Karl had said they were fat old ghosts in
tombs, chattering about their youth and their campaigns,
unaware that outside the tombs the world rushed by, full of
noise and life.

The smell of the past was thick in the moldy ancient house.
The carpets threw up a filmy cloud of this past. The great
fires burned without present warmth. The portraits were of
old soldiers, and Bismarck, and the Kaiser. A foggy patina of
blue mist covered the immense sofas with their curved bulky
arms, dimmed the long thin mirrors with their marble bases,
shrouded windows already shrouded with yellowed silk. The
ceilings were lost in plastered gloom; the walls, covered with
the deep crimson of Victorian wallpaper, flickered with candlelight. Over black-marble mantelpieces were crossed sa-
bers and likenesses of ancestors, scowling ferociously, and
wearing medals. A marble stairway wound heavily upwards
from the hall, and red velvet curtains swung gloomily at
every doorway. Even the servants were old, and crept about
with frightened and inward expressions. For the General
was famous, or infamous, for a villainous temper, and every
one was awed and overwhelmed by him. Even Therese called
him "General," not presuming upon their relationship. Even
his wife called him respectfully by his title, and not in their
most familiar moments would she have dared address him by
his Christian name.

But he was fond of Therese, whom he had dandled on his
knee when she had been a child. He had allowed her to play
with his medals. He had told her great and heroic tales of
campaigns in which he had figured prominently. "Ah, there
are no days like those in these days," he would sigh. Marshal
Hindenburg had been his closest friend. But he never spoke

of the old Marshal these days. His lips were closed against him. Nor did he ever speak of Adolf Hitler in connection with his friend. It would have been like speaking of a crawling, writhing panderer in connection with an emperor. Such things were so indecent as to approach sacrilege. One ignored them, as one ignored shameful necessities of the body. But one could tell that he was thinking of Hindenburg when his face darkened with grief and bitter sternness.

He was one of Berlin's most famous and best-loved generals. Each year, he had been given a banquet by the younger officers, during which his stories had been listened to with respect, if with boredom. He was a great beer-drinker. He detested the new fashion of drinking harsh spirits. Only beer was served at the banquets. But this year the occasion of the annual banquet had been ignored. He had waited for the announcement. He had had his medals polished, and his uniform prepared. But there was no announcement. However, the next morning the most prominent Nazi newspaper in Berlin had derisively, and with enormous politeness, announced that General Siegfried von Heyliger had had a birthday, and Berlin felicitated him, but was too engaged these days in a new and more vital order to bother about old generals, who, the paper hinted, ought to be dead anyway, as they were a hindrance to the new and more vigorous Germany of today. There were many such old soldiers, the paper hinted, who refused to believe that the Germany they knew had happily gone, who refused to believe in life and modern power, who lived in the past and were only old moldy corpses dragging at the chariot wheels of the new Germany. Germany had an affection for them, certainly, and respected their pasts. But should they dare interfere, as they sometimes did, with the march of the iron feet of German youth, they would be taught a lesson they would never forget. Away with the past! It was dead (and apparently, the generals were dead with it). Heil to the future, to victory, to youth, to war and valor and the new Germany!

Upon reading this, the pathetic old General had momentarily collapsed. His innocence (and how innocent were these grand old warriors!) was torn and bleeding, brutally assaulted and thrown down. His flesh felt wounded; he was mortally stricken. The light of the horror blinded his eyes. He could not look at it. He had raged for hours, stamping and foaming through the house, after his first numbing shock.

He cursed and threatened everything and every one, except that obscenity that had wiggled its snakelike way from Austria into the heart of Germany. Even in his extremity he could not bring himself to speak that loathsome and putrid name. It would be like giving vent to some indecent sound.

Old warrior friends came to sit with him, as mourners come to the coffin of a comrade. They had sat with him, not speaking, mourning for themselves as well as for him. They, too, were innocent. They could not understand. They could only suffer. They sat about him, in silence, and he sat, too, not speaking. Then at last, he tried to speak, but when he did so he gave only a strangled murmur, and then had burst into the terrible, bloodlike tears of the old and the lost.

But he was still too innocent to be broken permanently. At least, Therese, knowing the foul story, hoped this was true. After a few days he said: "I am glad, I am proud, that I have been removed from the lists of the Nazis! I belong to Germany, and Germany belongs to me. We have only to wait!" Soon, his walk was even heavier and more majestic than ever. There was a sparkling of waiting triumph in his eyes, and he developed a knowing, secretly lofty expression, as though privy to important confidence. His dignity was more in evidence than it had been at any time. He became more intolerant, more insistent upon discipline in his household, more exacting, more stern. He was like a man attempting to hold shut the iron door of a citadel with the weight of his body and his bleeding hands. He had given up, for some time, his twice-daily walks, reserving his old strength for a stroll at sunset. Now he walked again at dawn, marching rigidly through the streets, and his neighbors could hear that ponderous pacing through the quiet of the echoing morning. Against his doctor's orders, he exercised, rode, fenced, walked, and resumed in all a vigorous life. He took on new color and vitality and fierceness. He induced his comrades to do likewise. They were less, or more, simple than he, and complained. But he bullied them violently into obedience. Soon, they were doing military exercises in his garden, much to the scandalized amusement and concern of the neighbors, who still had much affection for the old regime.

Therese had often heard her father's cousin laughed at and called "a typical old military idiot of the military school— really very stupid, you know." She had agreed, secretly. But now she was not so sure. As the days passed, and she saw more of the General, she listened more closely to his expressed contempt for "the rabble," his proud repudiation of all that the mob represented, his gentleman's aversion for the mongrel horde, his passionate belief in the eternal durability of the virtues of austerity, courage, discipline, class pride, valor, birth, breeding, and restraint. "The Old Junker," as her daintier friends called him disdainfully, represented something which Germany had lost, but which surely she must regain if she were to survive. He might be overweeningly egotistic and narrow; he might be utterly devoid of the "culture" and sophistication of the twentieth century; he might be an innocent; he even might be stupid. But he was a rock in a weary land, rugged but indomitable, simple and uncompromising. He was the Old Army, in many more ways than one.

She watched him, tonight, as he came towards her, and never had she felt such affection for him. He was nearly six feet six in height, and unbelievably broad in proportion. His feet and hands were enormous. He had a huge broad face, truculent and fierce, the color of ripe tomatoes, and fringed with snow-white silken sideburns. His thick white mustache curled upwards, a fixed replica of the Kaiser's. The ends, waxed and brittle, pointed inexorably to little blazing blue eyes, choleric and bellicose. His prow of a nose jutted arrogantly; his lips were broad, almost spatulate, and wore their usual expression of intolerance and ferocity. He was almost completely bald; his round pink skull, like a dome of rosy granite, shone in the candlelight. He wore his dress uniform, old-fashioned in cut, but impressive, and his many medals and ribbons formed a shield on his massive breasts. He even wore his sword, clanging, at his side. One of his crimson cheeks was wrinkled and drawn by a deep sabre cut received in his gallant and turbulent youth.

"Ah, liebchen!" he exclaimed fondly, in his deep rumbling voice. He took both her hands and kissed them with paternal affection. "You are a rare visitor, but like everything that is rare, you are precious."

She smiled at his old-fashioned gallantry. She was pale and cool in her classic gray gown, shot through with pale threads of silver. Her light smooth hair rose above her serene forehead like a glimmering wave.

"But you are not looking well," he said, squinting at her anxiously. "You are thin. But your color is remarkably high."

Had she put too much rouge on her drained face? She hoped not. But she had had to do something to hide her fatigue and pallor, and her colorless lips.

He now noticed the absence of Karl, and asked after him. His tones were a little reserved, for he was suspicious of Karl, and timorously disliked him as one of those intellectuals who always found him stupid.

Therese explained that Karl was unwell. The old General, in spite of his words of concern, was visibly relieved.

"Ah, that is bad. He works too hard, perhaps? Or, he still grieves over his sister, the little Gerda? That poor child. We have come on bad days," he added, shaking his monumental head, his great face darkening. "I am sorry that Karl is not here. I have invited one of his acquaintances, the writer, Herr Doctor Paul Lesser, who greatly admires him."

Therese knew that Paul Lesser was a very minor if pretentious writer, and Karl detested him and always avoided him. She was glad that her husband had not come tonight, for Karl would have inevitably gotten into one of his irritable, impatient arguments with the affected tyro. It was always as if Karl were outraged that amateurs and would-be artists dared invade the sacred porticoes of literature, and dared lift their donkey-voices among the columns. Their talks about the "meaning of art" infuriated him. "One might as well talk about the 'meaning' of the sky, or the sun, or the earth," he would say. "Only the pseudo-artist is solemn and sententious about his 'art.'" Inevitably, he would become insulting, and only bad feelings followed. Karl, at these times, was impossible.

Visible regret now showed in the General's expression that he had gone to the trouble of inviting Paul Lesser, and having to endure his high-flown conversation. To the General, the pseudo-artist and the real artist were the same thing. They all wrote, did they not? It was sufficient for him, and horrible in any event. Now he was saddled with the pretentious fool. It was really too bad of Karl. Nevertheless, one artist was easier to endure than two, even if those two became engrossed with each other. Too, the women always loved artists. Possibly one of them would be absorbed in him, and take two undesirables off his sweating hands.

The General's wife now came fluttering to greet Therese. She was his second wife, and childless, as had been his first. She was considerably younger than he, a slender, agitated, gasping woman, and a fool. Therese pitied her. It must be a dreadful strain to live with the bellowing General. She had once been pretty; now at forty-five, she still bore fragile if worn traces of former beauty in her bright, strained blue eyes, a little popping, and withered, rose-leaf skin. Her blond hair was elaborately curled and swirled, and she had coquettishly tucked a pink rose in its masses. Her smile was fixed and artificial, showing good if large and prominent teeth in a perpetually anxious grin. Always, before greeting any one else, she would shoot an apprehensive glance at her husband, to see whether he would need placating. Her pale-pink chiffon gown floated about her as though constantly disturbed by unseen winds.

She was delighted to see Therese, for the General could always be counted on to be at least temporarily amicable in her presence. She kissed Therese with thin but genuine enthusiasm, and Therese held her breath to avoid choking on the passionate and overwhelming perfume which flowed from the other woman. Poor Martina had always harbored the coquettish belief that she was a femme fatale, and still harbored it, despite stringy shoulderblades, flat bosom, and puckering skin. She was amiable, vapid, voluble and incoherent. If she had any ill-tempers, vices or conceits, they had probably all been beaten and flayed out of her fleshless body, leaving only anxieties, smiles, apprehensions and alarms behind, with a warm-water flood of sentimentality.

"O my darling Therese, how delightful to see you!" she cried in her shrill but gentlewoman's voice. Therese guessed, from her tone, that she had not had an easy past hour with the General, for her manner was too hysterically gay. Her conjecture was correct, for the General was now glowering behind her back. Therese further guessed that some of the guests were entirely Martina's fault, and Siegfried had been punishing her with his usual lack of tact, his usual fury and abusiveness. No wonder the poor creature was delighted to see some one who could exercise some control over the huge boar, and like Circe, make him a man again.

Therese never knew whether Martina liked or disliked her. Probably the unfortunate soul never liked any one or disliked him. She had no time for likes or dislikes, absorbed as she was in the furious vortex of the General's own daily preferences. Therese had no aversion for Martina, as she usually had aversions for the shallow and the weak and colorless.

Therese explained to Martina that Karl could not come, but had sent his regrets. Martina listened vaguely, her popping, strained blue eyes darting about. She hardly heard. She thought that she had heard some sound from the General, and was anxiously intent on it. But she murmured: "Of course, of course!"

"And now, let us go back to the fools," said the General, in a heavily playful voice, flashing a look of violence at his wife.

"The General is so amusing, is he not?" bubbled Martina, with a desperate little laugh, and a look of complete and embarrassed terror on her face.

"Oh, very, exceedingly," responded Therese, laughing slightly, and giving the General a fondly admonishing smile. At her arch glance, he had to smile himself. He was immediately in a better temper. He ceremoniously offered his arm to Therese, leaving his wife to trail behind. He could always be placated, Therese knew, by references to his enormous wit and humor, neither of which he possessed in the slightest.

Four gentlemen and three ladies were waiting in the drawing-room. The atmosphere had completely subdued them. They sat in the dim gloomy light as close to the fire as they dared, utterly swamped by the tremendous mahogany furniture and cold, prism-hung lamps.

The men rose ceremoniously, but the first thing that Therese noticed was that the huge and scowling portrait of General von Hindenburg was missing from its station over the black-marble mantelpiece. It had hung there for several decades, longer than Therese could remember. It had been taken down; the room it had dominated seemed to have lost its soul and its character. Nothing had replaced it; the space was dark and blank against the rest of the wallpaper, which had faded. Nevertheless, that sharp dark rectangle was more significant than the portrait had been. The eye was drawn to it inevitably, with a feeling of lostness and mournfulness.

Therese was pleased to see that among the guests were Herr Professor Herman Muehler and his English wife. The Herr Professor taught literature and poetry at the University, and was one of Karl's few close friends. Tall, slender, bent, though he was still in his forties, gentle-mannered and sardonic, he inspired instant respect because of the aura of integrity and thoughtfulness which surrounded him. His dark hair was thin, and he was partially bald. He was not handsome; his nose had a Hebraic formation about it, though he was of the purest "Aryan" stock. His features hinted of a Hapsburg strain for he had the jutting underlip, forgotten when he smiled his singularly sweet smile, and eyes set too close together on each side of a high bridge, and too high under thick black brows. One saw instantly that he was the only gentleman present among the other guests.

His wife, Elizabeth, was a comfortable cosy little woman with pink cheeks, dowdy clothes, and a gay smile. She was famous for her good sense and excellent housekeeping and warm hospitality. She was much more German in appearance, conversation and manner than her husband, but Therese rightly suspected that under it all the Briton lurked, watchful, a little amused, more than a little opportunistic, and completely hard-headed. She was no fool.

Of the other three men she knew only one, Herr Doctor Paul Lesser, the intellectual and the pseudo-writer, who was experiencing a fitful popularity in Berlin at the present time, due to his theatrical and somewhat violent last novel, *The Passionate Land*. She knew him only slightly, as he was one of Karl's pet hatreds. A bachelor, and intolerably affected, he wore British clothes and a monocle. The monocle gave him, at first, an illusion of virility, immediately belied by his fat puffy pink face and querulous, pulpy pink lips. His eyes were prominent and full of belligerent conceit and arrogance. But there was about him a certain effeminacy and weakness, which, combined with the arrogance, made one think of a masculine woman. His voice had the hoarseness and insistence of such a woman's, and he had a certain affected way of pronouncing adjectives and phrases as though he valued and enjoyed them as a gourmet enjoys exquisite cooking. "Words," he would often say, "are the colors on a palette. One must choose them as carefully as an artist chooses them." He struck attitudes. This, Therese found the most annoying thing about him. She could not forgive his affectations, of speech and poses, though well understanding that these were the protective dress of the incompetent and the inferior. He was the fool warned of by the Koran—the fool that did not know he was a fool.

She turned away from him with distaste, without allowing him to kiss her hand and rhapsodize about how charmed he was to see her, and how prostrated he was not to be allowed to converse once more with Karl. She looked with relief at the other strangers, waiting for introductions.

Captain Baldur von Keitsch. The son of one of the General's old friends. A huge stout smiling man in his forties, uniformed and medalled and epauletted to the last inch. Once his face had been delicate and handsome, and the ladies of Berlin had been hypnotized by his leanness and his extraordinarily deep gray eyes. His voice was rich and beautiful, and warm as new milk. Now he was enormously stout and bulging, and even his military uniform could not detract from that expanded belly, immense jellylike buttocks and swollen thighs. Nevertheless, he was still handsome, and his full-colored broad face, his jovial smile, his brilliant eyes, and his charming manner, still had power to undo women and make men his indulgent and affectionate friends. He was not a fool. Only a few guessed that he was a dangerous man, completely foul, completely without a single touch of humanity, compassion, honor or integrity.

Therese had never met him before. He beamed down upon her warmly. He kissed her hand lingeringly. His eyes dwelt upon her with amorous boldness, seeing everything, and full of licentious admiration. He was no plebeian; a reptilian mind as sharp as steel, and as supple, meshed behind that open masculine face. Therese, with the new sad prescience which had come to her these dolorous days, knew of this mind immediately. It was a profound shock to her. Never, in her austere and remote experience, had she met such a man before, or, at least, never had she recognized him. Despite the horrors of the present, her calm and judicious mind had repudiated much of what she had heard. She had called it "hysteria" and "melodramatic exaggeration," and even "propaganda." Now she believed everything, and was disgusted at her previous aristocratic incredulity. She had refused to believe that the Germany she knew could be guilty of such men. Objectively, she had known it; subjectively, she had rejected it. The merging of her two awarenesses paralyzed her with horror. The spots of rouge on her cheeks stood out like badly painted patches on her extreme pallor. Nevertheless, she retained her calm dignity and poise over the sickness in her heart when she was introduced to the next gentleman, Herr Heinrich Schmidt.

He was all elegance and polish, dark, slender, tall and handsome, with the most charming and magnetic smile she had ever seen. She had heard of him, from the newspapers, from the whispers. What his position was with the National Socialist Party no one knew exactly, but that he was extremely potent and actively sinister was known to all. His manners were exquisite; he was a man of rare intellect. His father had been a personal friend of the last Kaiser, and his blood was excessively noble, coming as it did from a long line of Junkers, professors, scientists and scholars. His mother had been Baroness Hermine von Markowski, related to both British and German royalty. Immensely rich, mysterious in his activities, a personal friend of Hitler's, fascinating and almost beautiful, he was irresistible to both men and women. The latter incoherently raved of his profile, his waving dark hair, his white smile, his lovely courtesy. He was a bachelor. It was now rumored that he was to be attached to the German Embassy in London, because he was well-favored by the British and had been educated at Oxford, and was alleged to be an Anglophile.

After he had kissed Therese's hand, he gazed at her ardently.

He said: "I know your husband, Frau Doctor. We need men of his accomplishments in the new Germany."

Therese replied: "My husband is ill. Moreover, he is not interested in politics. He is a man of letters, you know."

Herr Schmidt smiled slightly. "Even men of letters must realize that we have a new order, and the Fatherland needs every hand and every brain."

Therese paused. She looked into those actor's eyes, and the familiar painful thrill ran along her nerves. She had known instantly that Captain Baldur von Keitsch was dangerous. Now she knew that this danger was the danger of a wild beast's. But this man was all evil, all deadliness. She had the appalling sensation that she was face to face with a serpent, the embodiment of wickedness. I must keep my balance, my control, she said to herself, trembling. I must not let myself be swamped by my own imagination.—But she knew, in spite of this, that her awakened senses were not lying. The cataracts of habit and convention had been removed from her eyes, and she saw with a clarity and sharp dreadfulness as she had never seen before.

Was it possible that such men had always existed in Germany, discreetly hidden and camouflaged by necessity and conventions? Or had the new Germany suddenly given birth to these monsters, or, by its insidious toxins, had made smiling madmen of gentlefolk? She was inclined to believe the first. Evil always existed; it awaited only the moment of release to rise above civilization and restraint. The sickness quickened in her heart. What hope was there for the world in these days? For she knew it was not only Germany who was so hideously menaced. It was all men. The disease afflicting Germany afflicted the whole world. The epidemic smoldered everywhere, though it had shown its first scarlet signs in her own country. There was no place to flee; there was no refuge anywhere. It was this ghastly realization which turned her face even more pale, and dried her quiet lips.

She turned from Schmidt hastily, with a movement of flight. She seated herself as near as possible to Herr Professor Herman Muehler and his English wife. Frau Muehler regarded her with her friendly but wary smile. She saw that Therese's hand trembled slightly as she sipped her fragile glass of sherry. Her eyebrows rose a little at this evidence of emotion.

"And how is Karl, Frau Doctor? We have been so worried about him. Herman speaks of him constantly, and misses his visits."

Therese reflected for a moment, as she often did, that in spite of Karl's austerity and shy reserve, people soon learned to speak of him by his first name. But few dared to approach her so intimately, though she knew that she had a more approachable personality, and liked her fellows much more than did Karl. It was still a mystery to her. She could not understand the intimacy towards Karl, even in those only slightly acquainted with him.

She answered: "He is still—unnerved, I am sorry to say."

And then she knew the answer. Karl, in spite of his restraint and aloofness, was naive and simple. He did not know nor comprehend others. Objectively, in his social contacts, he had seen only smiles or faces, or heard only what it had been intended for him to hear. His innocence had insulated him. And so, he could respond to others in the way they wished him to respond. He took them at their face value, and believed what they desired him to believe. They had had no need to protect their nakedness from his candid but unseeing eyes. He took their protective costumes to be the costumes of their souls. They meant nothing more or less than what they said. Their conventional deeds, to his simplicity, were the expressions of themselves. Accordingly, they could relax their wariness and suspicion and distrust in his presence. They could deceive him. They saw themselves reflected in his eyes as they wished to be reflected. His conscious mind, Therese realized drearily, had never caught up, until now, with his subconscious mind. It was his subconscious mind, all-seeing, all-understanding, which had made him a writer. But in spite of this, he had not been a great writer, for his conscious mind had been asleep. Now he could be great, if ever he could overcome his cowardice and the dreadful wound to his innocence, caused by the merging of his two minds.

She added, unaware that she was speaking aloud: "He has been asleep. Now he is awake. He cannot bear it, yet."

Frau Muehler raised her brows again, with a faint smile of amusement and condescension. She did not like Therese. Therese always saw the things she was not intended to see. Therefore, it pleased Frau Muehler to watch Therese's sadness, and listen to her make unconventional and naive statements.

But Herr Muehler, who had been listening with unobtrusive intentness, said suddenly and softly: "Yes, yes, he has been asleep. I understand that. It is painful for such a man to wake up."

Therese looked into his gentle brown eyes, so tired and understanding, and something hard and suffering broke in her. Her lips trembled; she felt the sting of tears against her eyelids.

He nodded, and his smile was like the touch of warm comfort. "But he will wake up, and find his way back. Do not be too afraid, Frau Doctor."

Therese had always liked him, with as much liking as her selfishness would permit her to like any one not important to her. Now, realizing what he was, what greatness of soul shone behind those nearsighted and weary brown eyes, she loved him. She did not see Frau Muehler's covert and superior British smile. She did not see her discreet ridicule because Therese had stood nakedly indecent for any one to observe.

The warmth of her love and gratitude pervaded Therese like a heartening fire. She was conscious of a renewal of her waning strength. "I am not so very afraid now," she said, steadily.

"Do I understand that he has had a nervous breakdown?" asked Frau Muehler, with an air of concern.

Her husband replied quickly, but he looked at Therese: "All Germany is suffering from a nervous breakdown. But it is not only Germany; it is all the world. We intellectuals have helped to bring this about by creating psychological confusion, faithless realism, and liberalism without a tangible purpose or goal." He added, as if to himself: "In our stupidity, we have not realized that men must believe in something."

They had not seen the approach of Herr Schmidt, and they started when he spoke, smilingly: "You are quite correct, Herr Professor. Few men of your profession are so discerning and understanding. But now, the National Socialist Party has come to the rescue of Germany, and all other nations. We are giving men something to live for."

A curious hardening and reserve passed subtly over the professor's face. He said quietly, looking at Schmidt with piercing intensity: "I am afraid, Herr Doctor, that we do not speak of the same things, though our words are similar."

Schmidt shrugged slightly. Frau Muehler glowed at him, and smiled with a little disloyal malice. "Do explain what you mean, Herr Doctor," she said.

He pulled a small but heavy chair before them and sat down negligently. "Thank you. It is a matter of great concern to me. You see, it must all be explained, especially to those who should be the natural leaders of our youth. And I happen to know that the Herr Professor is very much loved by his pupils, and has much influence with them. It is so very necessary that he understand."

Doctor Muehler said nothing. But his gaze became more piercing.

All Schmidt's charm radiated itself upon the two women. His handsome face took on itself an expression of passionate earnestness and fascinating naïvete. It was evident that he wished them to believe in his sincerity and enthusiasm.

"Two absorbing faiths have always sustained mankind—God or war. The intellectuals have taken away God from our youth, by their cynical and critical attitude towards all things, and their absurd attachment to what they call 'truth.' "

He paused. He glanced at the professor quickly.

Doctor Muehler nodded his head. "Yes," he said, very quietly, "that is true." But the hardening and reserve on his gentle face became more discernible.

"And so," went on Schmidt, with an almost disarming

earnestness, "National Socialism, with its demand for single-minded self-dedication and sacrifice, with its fanatical religion of the State, has been able to obtain the passionate loyalty and devotion of our youth. It has given it a reason for living, and called out all the noble heroism which makes mankind full of majesty and dignity. It has promised youth greatness, strength and war. War against corruption at home. War abroad, if necessary, against those who would strangle Germany. It has destroyed the complexity of Jewish-Christian civilization, and has given Germany one faith, one leader, one hope, and one goal."

"In other words," interrupted the professor, softly, "it has corrupted the natural urge of mankind to self-sacrifice and devotion, to sinister ends."

Schmidt looked at him with a suddenly evil intensity. He smiled.

"Is it evil to give men a reason for living, Herr Professor?"

"I repeat, we say the same words, but we do not mean the same thing," said the professor, coldly. Now an astonishing thing happened. The professor's eyes became vivid with hatred and understanding. The two men regarded each other with a fixed stare. Therese felt a sudden devastating fear.

"I am afraid," almost whispered Schmidt, with a regretful smile, "that you are too much of a liberal, Herr Professor."

"Why? Because I believe the noble instincts of men can be used for a noble purpose?"

The professor lifted his eyes and fixed them unseeingly on the old General and Captain von Keitsch, who were conversing boisterously near the fire.

"We are guilty," he said, in a low musing voice. "We have delivered our children up to you, without a word and without a warning. Because we have been weak and stupid. We have laughed at duty and piety and order. We have given our children a heaviness and tiredness of spirit, and a feeling of futility and sickness. We educators have emphasized that the individual is all that matters, his own happiness and self-expression. We have said: 'Every man for himself. You are your sole concern.' How wicked and blind we have been! We thought we were very clever! We emasculated thinkers! We thought that men could live by intellect alone. We laughed at 'souls.' We jeered at the ancient idea that the business of men is the welfare of all men. We told them that the burden of living, and duty, courage, abstinence and moderation are the imbecilities of a generation now outmoded and narrow of mind. We smiled indulgently at the name of God. We smiled at duties and obligations and discipline. We said: 'These are the chains which fetter a free spirit.' We did not know that no man can be free if he discards his responsibilities. The unchained and irresponsible man is a prisoner."

Schmidt smiled gaily. "You may deny it, but we do mean the same things, Herr Professor!"

It was then that Frau Muehler spoke, with a smile:

"Of course you mean the same things, Herr Doctor! The professor speaks of it constantly. He knows that the liberals and radicals have brought about the corruption of the youth. He is much upset about it. He said only recently: 'The National Socialists have done what we should have done. They have given our children a religion.'"

She went on, with unusual animation, and with much nodding: "I, myself, tell my relatives that they must not believe the stories of the atrocities and terrorism which Communists and Jews tell of Germany. Some of them are quite concerned. I received a letter from my cousin, Lady Elizabeth Colston-Hepwaithe, just the other day. She is quite a humanitarian, and was silly enough to give refuge to some Jews who were driven out of Germany. She wanted to know what was happening to Germany. I wrote her that she was being misled, like so many of my people, into believing that all manner of horrors were going on here. I told her that no changes are ever accomplished without some suffering, but that in this instance, only traitors and subversive elements were being punished. So different from other revolutions, when the innocent suffered, too! I told her that I had never seen the German people so happy, so alive, so hopeful as they are today."

Therese regarded her in stiff and formal silence, her polite training making her face noncommittal and detached. The little Englishwoman's bright and sensible face was aglow with well-bred fervor. Her commonsense voice, cultured and musical, impelled attention. Herr Doctor Schmidt surveyed her with pleasure and approbation. But her husband looked at her with a strange expression.

"The British," he said, in a curiously tight voice, "have always suffered from brutal indifference, expediency, or innocence." After a slight pause he added: "I prefer to be charitable. I prefer to believe it innocence."

He turned to Schmidt. "Have you heard much of the Gestapo, Herr Doctor?" he asked.

Schmidt's sparkling eyes shifted only a trifle. "I know some of the officials. Clever and competent men, Herr Professor."

The professor continued to regard him steadfastly. "Ah, yes. So I have heard." He paused again. "They might have been interested in this conversation, perhaps?"

But Frau Muehler had become too much animated to hear undercurrents. "So much melodrama!" she exclaimed. "So many dramatic stories! Why cannot Germany be left alone to complete her regeneration?"

Her husband gazed at her for a long and weary moment. At last he said gently: "My dear, it is not regeneration. It is degeneration." He threw a sharp and gleaming glance at the listening Schmidt. "That might interest the Gestapo also?" He resumed, turning to his wife: "Do you know why Germany must now be the concern of all the rest of the world? Because she is suffering from a frightful contagious disease. And what does one do with a diseased and dangerous person? Ignore him? Or quarantine him?"

Without waiting for a reply, he stood up, not apologizing, but walking away with an oddly shaken gait, as though his thoughts were too terrible for control. He left a hole of silence behind. Therese's fear for him soared up into terror. She had heard all the undercurrents. Only a little while ago she would not have done what she did now. But now she rose, too, and followed the professor to where he was standing alone at a distant window. He was gazing fixedly out into the night, the folds of the dusty crimson velvet draperies falling about him. When Therese stood beside him, he did not look at her. It was as if he was expecting her. He said in a low, broken voice: "That man—he is a Gestapo officer. I heard it before. I know it now."

She put her hand on his arm and said pitifully: "You are so agitated. What do creatures like this Schmidt matter? The Gestapo! It is not important! Germany will rid herself of his kind soon. I am sure of it."

He moved his head despairingly. "Therese, I tell you it isn't just Germany! It is all the world. It is every man everywhere. Germany has just been the first to show the infection. That is what makes it so hopeless." He breathed deeply; his thin hands clenched. "You heard my wife, Therese. She speaks for—for the rest of the world. That is why I cannot have the slightest hope."

Therese was silent. She stood beside him, her hand still on his arm. Waves of desolation swept over her. When he spoke again, it seemed that he was only echoing her own thoughts.

"Last night I thought of going away. To England. To America. To France. And then I saw how hopeless it all was. There is no place to go! Therese, we are going down in ruins, all of us. Perhaps it will be five years, or ten years. Then the end will come. It will never be the same for us, in our generation. Peace, security, hope, civilization: these are all doomed. One by one, each nation will go down. Some by treachery, some by greed, some by expediency, some by cowardice, but all with violence and confusion and death. They will say it is Germany's fault. Just as they say a single man with smallpox began an epidemic. But they will not realize it is because they have no immunity of their own!"

He sighed despairingly. "There is just one immunity. A year ago, I would have smiled at it. Just as pseudo-intellectuals smile at it in other countries. Now, I do not smile. They, too, will have to learn their lesson."

Now he turned to her. His ugly, kind, thin face was pale and glistening with grief. "Do you know what that immunity is, Therese? It is God. What does it matter if some say that religion is nonsense? Perhaps it is. I do not think so. A doctrine which insists upon compassion, frugality and strength, courage and faith, justice, sternness and duty and gentleness, is not nonsense. It has its roots in the very earth of being; it draws its saps from the universal verities, the established facts. Why did we not see this before?"

"But what can you do, yourself, alone?" Therese was not conscious that she had cried out.

He was silent a little. Then an exalted gleam flashed into his eyes.

"I did not know, until now, Therese! But now I know!"

Just then dinner was announced.

BECAUSE the father of Captain Baldur von Keitsch **15** had been his particular friend, and because the Captain filled some of the requirements of the old General as to what constituted the good soldier, he was pleased to have him sit on his left, where he could talk to him. Moreover, the Captain paid him that deference so delightful and necessary from a younger officer. So his father had sat, at the left of the General. He was dead now; his son had many of his physical characteristics, and this gave to the General the comforting sensation of continuity and stability in a world which he was uneasily suspecting showed some evidences of irresponsible revolt against all the things he revered and honored. The Captain understood the things that went through the old man's mind, and he artfully catered to them for his own purposes.

He had spent some years in Paris on a mission of apparent friendliness and governmental cooperation. Only he, and his associates, knew what had been the real purpose of those years. He had become accustomed to the civilized and delicate cooking of France, and had come to loathe the hearty, filling meals of Germany. However, he made it a point to compliment Martina on her dinner, saying that he was experiencing again some of the delights of his stay in Paris. The poor woman bridled, confessed that she had a French chef, and cast a blushing simper about the table. She was rather susceptible to the gallant Captain, and his praises filled her simple facile heart with joy. He was so agreeable; he rarely contradicted. His warm and charming smile embraced every one's opinion with sympathy, while his flat reptilian eyes invaded one's inmost secrets.

"It is fortunate for Germany that we have still men like you among us," said the General, beaming upon his friend's son. "I have detected signs of a disorderly turn of mind lately. In the name of discipline, there is such a lack of true discipline and honor. They tell me it is just youthful exuberance and excitement." He shook his head. "I am sure they are wrong. We were exuberant and excited when we were

147

young, too." He smiled coyly, straightened his great flat back
and curled his mustaches. He inferred that he had been quite
a dog in Heidelberg. He glanced at his wife, and showed frank
contempt as he visibly compared her with the lush barmaids
and mädchen of his youth. "But under it all, we realized that
there was a basic necessity for discipline, respect, honor and
the soldier's code. Perhaps it was because we young officers
were gentlemen. From what I hear, the young men in command these days, and even the older ones, are not gentlemen." He frowned forbiddingly. "What is this? Are you
encouraging the mob to rule Germany?"

The Captain smiled amusedly. "I am still a gentleman, I
hope, General."

The General shook his head irritably. "Of course, of course!
There are a few of you left. Otherwise, I should lose hope.
But you still encourage the mob. We young officers had a
proper contempt for the people, who are only cattle. We
were scrupulously polite to them, certainly, but they knew
their places. They never presumed. It was all understood.
There was first the soldier, the gentleman, and then the pro-
fessions, then the bourgeoisie, and then the common people.
Each class realized its responsibilities to itself, and to the
Fatherland, and neither would have wished, or dared, to invade another class. Thus each class had its own pride and
rigid self-respect, its own kind of honor, its own immutable
code. This made for order and tranquillity. Now, if I hear
aright, there is a mongrel mixing of all classes, with the
worst in the ascendant. Is that democracy?"

The Captain's smile broadened. "I would hardly call it
democracy, General. It is National Socialism."

At the word "Socialism," the General exploded with indignation and scorn. "Socialism! Marxism! Nihilism! Atheism!
Anarchism! They are all the same, pestilential!"

The Captain did not reply. His warm and sympathetic smile
became as fixed as a grin. The General leaned towards him,
as though pathetically desirous of being reassured by the
younger man's presence.

"There is no honor among thieves and plebeians," he
urged. "You will not permit this appalling state of affairs
much longer?"

"Of course not," replied the Captain, soothingly. "This is
just a phase of the revolution."

At that ghastly word, the General's flushed face paled.

"Revolution!" he stammered. "Revolution! What revolution?"

The Captain became more and more soothing. He glanced about the listening table; his right eye closed in a wink as he encountered the gaze of Doctor Schmidt. "Every change is a revolution, General," he said reassuringly. "I use the word loosely, for want of a better."

"That is the trouble with the world today!" cried the General. "It uses words loosely, not understanding the impact. Revolution! But you young men are always given to extravagant phrases." He smiled with difficulty. "I hate the word. For me, its connotation means untenable change, a convulsion, a catastrophe. To you, probably, it means a shifting of cabinets! Do be more careful, Captain." He still smiled, but his marble-like blue eyes pleaded pathetically.

Doctor Muehler leaned forward and said gravely and quietly: "General, Captain von Keitsch is not using words loosely. When he says revolution, he means revolution."

There was a sudden silence about the dinner-table. Martina's thin eyelids fluttered distressedly. Her smile was painfully fixed and touching. Was her party to be ruined? How she detested politics these days! People got upset so, and said the most incredible and astounding things, which did not make for harmony. As for herself, she thought, she never understood politics. Why could not people forget them? The roast goose was really delicious, but there it lay on plates, cooling in its sauce, and every one's face was so strange.

In the meantime, the Captain and Doctor Muehler faced each other across the damask and crystal expanse of the table like two deadly duelists. They did not take their eyes from each other, though Doctor Muehler continued to speak to the General:

"I am sorry, General, that you must be disturbed. But truth is always disturbing. The fact remains that Germany is in a mortal convulsion, brought on by such men as our good Captain here, and," he flicked his bitter glance at Schmidt, "and our 'honorable' Doctor Schmidt. They say to you: 'This will pass.' It is the drug they are giving to all of Germany. And so you, soothed and lulled, say to yourselves: 'This will pass. It is only today. We must not alarm ourselves too much, or allow our serene judgment and tranquillity to be disturbed to the dislocation point. One must not become unduly excited, or hysterical; one must remember that events change constantly. It is all a matter of keeping balance, and believing steadfastly in the old sane order.' "

Doctor Lesser, the writer, nodded portentously. "Naturally, that is the only thing to believe, the only sensible thing."

But Doctor Muehler ignored him as too insignificant to be noticed. He still stared fixedly at the Captain, whose smile had taken on a vicious quality. He went on:

"But how terribly wrong such an attitude is! How frightful! How dangerous! For I tell you, General, and all of you, my friends, that this will not pass. It is not today. It is tomorrow, and a thousand, thousand tomorrows, all the generations of our children and the generations of all the world's children, for an era or more to come. It is not the immediate event in Germany alone. It will not matter if Germany is destroyed, or destroys, and the world is dragged down with her. That will change nothing. The end is here. The convulsion of nature is already shaking the foundations of a thousand cities, all over the earth."

Every one stared at him. The General's eyes bulged with gaping incredulity; Frau Muehler had flushed uncomfortably; the writer looked superior and aloof. But the Captain and Schmidt riveted their gaze on Muehler with a cold and curious contemplation and thoughtfulness. As for Therese, an ice-lump of fear settled in her chest, as she saw the look of these two men. She wanted to cry out: "Stop, Herman, these are murderers!" She wanted, at least, to warn him. But he did not look at her. And then she was glad that he did not. She knew that some abscess had broken in him, and that in the breaking he was experiencing an ineffable relief.

"You are talking nonsense," said the General, bluntly, but there was a plea for desperate reassurance in his voice. "Nonsense," he repeated, looking about the table, and the word sounded like a miserable question.

Doctor Muehler went on, quietly, musingly, as though speaking to himself:

"The change will come only when the hearts of men change, and that may not be for half a thousand years. But we must work sleeplessly for that change, even if it does not come in our lifetime; we must urge our children to work for it, and their children, telling them that there is no hope for them until it comes. All this, in Germany, in the world— this pestilence of the mind, this disease of the soul—is the result of wrong thinking. Men thought wrong, until the

Protestant Reformation, which lifted a whole world from a darkness in which there were only the little lights of the priests, which they jealously guarded, and which they refused to give to other men. The Reformation snatched the candles from the priests, lighted a million lamps, drove feudalism from the face of the earth, built universities and schools open to all men, set in motion the machinery of freedom and liberty and enlightenment. For the first time, since the fall of Rome, we were able to see, and see clearly."

He paused, then resumed in a melancholy tone: "And then what happened? The old unscrupulous forces of evil, which are always alive and always waiting, rose up again on their mission of destruction. The heroic Protestant Reformation, which had freed men from slavery, ignorance, blindness and superstition, became the materialist's and the industrialist's Reformation, and men were lost again. Lost in a wilderness of machines and dusty, futile science. Lost in the dry cant of pedagogues and politicians and profit-seekers, the philosophies of exploiters and low fellows. The Protestant philosophy of justice and enlightenment and mental liberty became the philosophy of cynics, weary even of their own words. They said that men can live by bread alone, provided there was sufficient bread." He paused again for a moment, then continued, his voice sad and heavy: "But it is still true that men do not live by bread alone, but by the word of the Living God. Suspicious of theology, which had once enslaved them, the Reformation brought a critical atheism, which was, in its way, as destructive and as enslaving as the old Roman hierarchy."

Schmidt, smiling his fascinating smile, inclined his head. "In many ways I must confess I agree with you, Herr Professor. I still think we mean the same things, though you deny it. I agree that you pedants have helped to bring out the present world-ennui and confusion. You have always resisted change. You refuse to recognize the change. You prefer to operate in a vacuum, a nice fur-lined vacuum, filled with words."

The Captain laughed genially. "Herr Professor, at heart you are really a National Socialist. We believe as you believe. You are still confused, but I am sure we can complete your enlightenment."

"I do not believe in oppression, cruelty, wickedness and violence," said the Professor tiredly.

"But there are elements that must be suppressed, elements which are impeding the new Protestant Reformation in Germany," urged the Captain. "And then, after we have consolidated Germany, our mission will extend to the rest of the world."

Martina smiled happily. What had promised to end in heated quarreling had become merely a pleasant and cosy discussion. She glanced about the table. But she met no smiles, no answering glances. Every one's attention was fixed on Doctor Muehler, the Captain, and Doctor Schmidt with a breathless intensity. Martina was bewildered. How difficult people were these days, spoiling agreeable dinner parties with long faces and sepulchral voices!

Doctor Muehler regarded Schmidt fixedly.

"You mean—war," he said, in a flat and weary tone.

The Captain shrugged. "Why not? War is the vitalistic expression of the people. They must have something to fight for, and sacrifice themselves for."

"War!" cried Therese, repudiatingly.

"War!" exclaimed the General, bewildered. Then he added with an almost childish simplicity: "But with whom?"

Doctor Muehler regarded Therese gently. "Yes, my dear, war. You see, they really mean war, at the end. On all the rest of the world. That is their lunatic's obsession.

"But I mean war, too, but not their kind of war. Tyrants and oppressors and conquerors come like storms, like earthquakes and tidal seas, like winds and fires. Each generation confronts them. Each generation must decide whether there are things worth fighting for, and dying for, or whether personal survival is more valuable than the welfare of its children, or slavery sweeter than liberty and justice. It must decide whether it prefers a sword and a vision, even unto death, or life so impotent and sterile, so shameful and rabbitlike, that it contains no hope and no light. The history of tyrants is always the history of the pusillanimous. Oppressors are only the visible symbols of a people's cowardice, a world's ignominy and littleness of soul. They, like Hitler and Mussolini, like all madmen and tyrants, are not symbols of the vitalism of the world, but the signs of its decadence, its degeneracy, and its corruption of spirit."

The Captain said with ominous quietness: "I do not like your remarks about our Fuehrer, Herr Professor."

But Doctor Muehler continued to speak to Therese, whose face was as white and still as the tablecloth:

"The pattern of war will always recur, in every generation. For in each generation monsters and madmen are born, and will, to the end of time, seek to subjugate, rule and destroy. We must teach our children that such a pattern will inevitably recur in their lifetime and that it is in the nature of things that they will come face to face, sometime in their lives, with these monsters and madmen. It must be their duty to resist and annihilate them, to the very end, even to an end that may be the grave.

"If we do not teach them so, not only we shall die, but they must die, also, shamefully and weakly, without even the consolation of a vision to sustain them in the darkest hour."

There was a sudden sharp silence after he had stopped speaking. Frau Muehler's sensible face was suffused. Her eyes sparkled angrily upon her husband.

"What emotion, Herman! What fantastic extravagance! I have never heard you talk like this before." She was outraged.

He regarded her with gentle sadness. "You are right, Elizabeth. I never talked like this before. But it was not from lack of courage. It was just from stupidity. And blindness. I thought this would pass, too. Now I realize it will not pass."

Doctor Lesser, the writer, gave vent to a superior cackle. "It is not the function of the teacher, and the artist, to give vulgar attention to the passing event," he said. "Really, Doctor Muehler, you are stepping down into the base politician's chair." He glanced around the table with an egotistic humor: "It is the artist's true function to interpret life, not to attempt to guide it."

Doctor Muehler gave him a look of supreme contempt.

"So speaks the intellectual," he said, with bitter insult in his voice. "So speaks the shrilling impotent eunuch. But when I denounce you, I also denounce myself. I know, now, what I must do."

The Captain and Doctor Schmidt laughed outright, as though overcome with an inner amusement which had now burst out. Martina laughed, too, breathing with relief. After all, she thought, it was only an agreeable discussion. The General looked about, uncertainly. He smiled, though with bewildered uneasiness. Elizabeth Muehler, intensely relieved by the laughter, shot one glance of cold reproof at her husband, then smiled sensibly. Really, Herman was impossible. He had insulted almost every one tonight, but not one had taken offense. How truly tolerant and civilized were the Germans!

But Therese neither laughed nor smiled. She was as white as death. She was consumed with an awful fear. She knew that Doctor Muehler was signing his death-warrant, and there must be some way to save him yet.

Yes, there must be some way to save him, she thought desperately. She did not like the sparkling fire in his eyes, the rigidity and exaltation of his face. He must be saved, saved like Karl, for Germany.

SHE HAD HOPED the air would free her from the increasing, ominous dread, the vague fright. But it did not. She could not forget the faces she had seen. It was like looking at the faces of bestial executioners. The executioners of Germany. She drew in a hard breath. I must control myself, she thought. She tried to stop the trembling of her flesh. I shall be ill, down in bed, hopeless, she reprimanded herself severely. Then what could I do? But it was no use. She could hardly walk when she alighted from her car. The cool air struck her like a freezing blast, though it was still summer.

The house was quiet. Only a single yellowish light burned in the entry. Old Lotte would always arise when her mistress returned, but Therese shrank from any contact with any one, even with this simple old creature. She stood in the hall, holding her breath, listening. There was no sound at all. She climbed the stairs as noiselessly as a ghost. She expected to hear Karl's incessant fumbling pacing, hollow in the midnight stillness. But she heard nothing. Now she breathed easier. He must be asleep.

She paused before his study door. She saw a faint gleam of light under it. She pressed her hand against the door, and it swung silently open. A dim lamp burned on his desk. Then she started. There were disordered papers on the desk, covered with handwriting. It was not possible! It could not be that he was writing again! It could not be that while she was sinking he was recovering! She tiptoed to the desk. Sheet upon sheet, covered with disordered, straggling writing. Tears blinded her. She sank into the desk chair, gripped the edge of the desk. He must have been writing for hours. He was not distinguished for rapid writing. Each jewelled phrase and shining word came to him slowly, perfectly, laboriously. Then she was struck with the shambling, leaping, incoherent lines, so different from his usual small, neat, precise writing.

Was that a faint, murmurous sound! Her head jerked up; she listened. She saw that Karl's bedroom door was also open a little. She went to it. The lamplight on the desk fell within

like a pale misty shaft. Karl was in bed, asleep. He must have
stirred and murmured in his restless nightmare, for his head
was hanging over the edge, and one arm was flung down-
ward so that it almost touched the floor. He slept, but his face,
so haggard, so gaunt, was not composed. It was tight with
some sorrowful preoccupation, some despairing resistance.
He looked curiously defensive, lying there, in his attitude of
exhausted abandon. She knelt beside him, not daring to touch
him lest he wake, but it seemed to her that her heart poured
out like a flood towards him, protective, grief-stricken. My
darling, she said silently. My darling, perhaps it would be
better if you died. Died in your sleep, like this. Perhaps it
would be better if all the innocent died in these days. For
when you awaken, how dangerous you are, how appalling!
There is no room in the world for awakened innocence. It is
better for us if you die. We can recover. But you cannot recover. You can only devastate and destroy, in your mad fury
of vengeance. It is not the cold, the balanced, the matter-of-
fact, who raze cities and light them into flames. It is the
innocent who cannot bear their awakening. God protect us
from you!

She rose to her feet, heavily, painfully, as though she had
become old and stiff. She closed the door silently. But not
before she had lightly touched his fallen hand with her trembling lips. She went back to his desk, and stood, looking down
at his writing. She sat down, and began to read. The char-
acters were disordered; some of the words had letters missing.
Others were unintelligible. But she could still read. And then,
as she read, her pulses slowed down to a slow agonized
beating, and it seemed to her that all the world was listening
to the voice of assaulted innocence, which must some day
rise to a crescendo of avenging madness.

It was soon evident to her that this was not tonight's work
alone. The ink was different on some pages; the writing, at
first, was small and precise, only becoming towards the middle, incoherent and scrawling. He had been writing for a
long time. Some of the pages had drifted to the floor. None
were numbered. She was not sure which was the beginning
or the end.

". . . I can feel a deep and expanding smile in myself;
finally, it seems that the whole world is smiling that helpless,
evil smile. A dull ache began to move like an independent
creature behind my forehead. I felt it moving; I listened

to the rustle of its whispering voice. Then the Thing began to caper wildly behind my forehead. I heard a sound as though it had clapped its hands. Everything was listening, the room, my body, the furniture, the lamp with its little bright red licking tongue, the trees, the distant sky. Then the Thing, having aroused all the universe, was satisfied, and listening itself, gloating.

". . . I can feel nothing in myself except implacability, of vengeance to be accomplished, of inexorable purpose. In life there is nothing else. Not even grief. . . . I am writing here by lamplight. I write. The pen scratches loudly. Now a thousand pens are writing, recording terrible things, and they become thunder in the black silence. I cannot endure the sound. I must stop writing tonight. . . . I put down my pen, but still the thousand pens go on writing, and the sound scrapes my mind, my soul, all my consciousness until I must scream aloud. I am being flayed. I can see my own flesh, bleeding from countless small wounds.

". . . Tonight there is a storm. I watch those flames darting from the black heavens, listen to the shudder and crash of that thunder, the roaring of that rain, and the bending and groaning of the great trees. It is a beautiful storm. I shriek and howl with it.

"I am in the storm, part of it, breathing it, thundering in it. Where do I begin, and the storm end? It is very confusing. . . . What is that voice? Is it only the wind? I strain my ears, and I hear Eric's voice in it, calling in anguish. But I shall not listen! I am afraid of what he is calling. . . . I slept deeply for the first time in many months. To awaken was like emerging from the blessed nothingness of death into the torment of life. Then I noticed a curious thing. Every object was suddenly, thickly, outlined with an intense and glowing scarlet, like fire. This scarlet burned every familiar object, the posts of my bed, the window-sills, the curtains, the trees clasped against the sky, my very fingers as I lifted them. My chair by the window was outlined in that red incandescence. . . . The sun brightened rapidly, and I saw that its rays were also outlined in this bloody light. Was this fire? Was the whole world about to go up into flames? How beautiful, how delightful! How my heart sank with exultation. The whole world, and everything in it, the murderers of Eric, the murderers of Gerda, the murderers of Germany and myself!

"I opened my door. I remarked to myself on the absence of heat and smoke in this conflagration. All was dark and silent without. I crept down the stairs, went through the house, opening doors, halting, listening. Not a sound. But every object had its outline of glowing and living light. Then I knew. My sight had become prenaturally sharp. What I saw, I was convinced, was the decay, invisible to others, of all things, the slowly eating and remorseless decay of life, going on hour by hour, day by day, year by year, age by age. I laughed with delight. I could see it, this decay. I could watch death eating, burning, dissolving all things. Nothing could escape. . . . It was soon evident to me that I, myself, could will this decay, or stop it. It was in my hands. But I would not stop it. I would will it to go on, until every last leaf, every last man, every last clod of earth, was dissolved into a river of fire. Then I would be avenged. Eric would be avenged."

Tears were running down Therese's face now. She closed her eyes. She thought she must faint with her horror and grief. She could not bear to read. She stood up, saying to herself: It is all over. There is nothing I can do.

She stood, looking down at the disordered, stained sheets of paper. She held herself rigid against her trembling. She must go on. She must read to the end. She must follow that tortured soul down into the abyss, to give him her hand, and to die with him if she could not save him.

She sat down again, and resumed her reading:

"A strange, pleasing phenomenon has happened, though I hear no comment about it from any one. The sun always shines, now, with a dark bronze light, and the air on the brightest day is spectral. The trees no longer show clear green leaves, but they are brownish and decayed, blasted. The grass is not green, but has the dull copper tinge of autumn fields. At night the moon shines molten. There is a chill over all things, a smell of decay thick in the nostrils. Surely they must have noticed that summer is not here, and that winter has settled eternally over the earth.

". . . Last night I saw Eric. For many days I had been in a sick dark fever, when I never knew whether the horrid images and faces and terrors I saw were real or a dream. And then, last night, the fever left me.

"A low mournful wind suddenly rose; it crept, murmuring, about the eaves, tried the windows with ghostly hands. Thinly howling, it went on its way, setting the leaves on the trees to a shrill hissing, and then fleeing off into the night. My brain was sharp and clear, and my eyes picked out the red outline on all the dim objects in the room.

"Then, I saw Eric. He was standing near the window, and was half turned towards it. He had not changed, though he had lain in the earth. The moon had come out, faint and fugitive, and fell on him. He appeared to be thinking, to be utterly oblivious of me. Long moment after moment passed as he stood there, not moving. The wind returned, howling with renewed strength, and the moon fluttered in it. . . . I noticed a strange thing. The red outline had not touched Eric.

"Then he lifted his head and looked at me. He smiled. His lips opened, but I could hear no sound. I knew he was speaking to me, and that if I wished, I could hear him. But I cried out: 'No, Eric, I shall not listen to you! Go back to your grave, which they dug for you. Some day when I have avenged you, I shall listen.'

"He still spoke, and I refused to hear. I felt a sudden rage. Why had he escaped from the earth into life again? Why had they not sodded him down so that he could not rise into torment and agony once more? Why had they not nailed down his coffin so that he might not have burst the screws, and escaped?

"We looked steadily at each other, moment by moment, and never did his expression change. Yet I felt in him a sad, understanding pity. I heard him sigh. The sigh was taken up in the wind, which echoed it dolefully, carrying it away over the barren earth, up into the lightless skies. Then he was no longer there.

"I know why he has come. But he shall not deflect me from my purpose! He was always the Jew, compassionate, forgiving, understanding. Do they not know that they bring death upon themselves? Do they never long for vengeance? But I know, and I shall do what I wish to do, no matter how often he comes and how often he pleads! Pleads for his murderers. . . . But, perhaps he was pleading for me. . . ."

Therese clasped her hands to her breast. She stared passionately about the room. It seemed to her that there was some invisible presence there, warm, steadfast, gentle and comforting. "Eric!" she whispered, aloud. "Eric, Eric, help me!" She sobbed convulsively.

"The Thing behind my forehead has told me that I must

know all dreadfulness, all horrors, if I must avenge Eric.

"How little men know! They think they are small and impotent and helpless. They do not know that they can will all things. How little they know of my mysterious wisdom, of my new gift to peer behind the thick veil of illusion into the wild and frightful country of reality. Their silly illusions are the illusions of timid childhood. I look beyond. My brain is like a portal through which flow the dread truths of God and creation. I know I can destroy and ruin and bring death and desolation to all the universe. . . ."

Therese cound hear the muffled thudding of her heart. She looked about the quiet, lamplit room, wildly. Was this madness? Perhaps it was not! Perhaps it was truth! One man's insanity, one man's open burning brain, one man's mad effluvia flowing out to cover the earth, to pollute, twist, destroy and inundate it. Surely it was not delusion. One had only to think of Adolf Hitler, with his red and howling dream, to know it was not delusion. Suddenly all the air seemed permeated with her own terror and realization. It was possible to project from one's own brain an engulfing flood of death. Karl was seeing clearly. Before the vision of such appalling horror she felt her heart fainting away. What could any one do against it? Against the knowledge of such as Hitler, and Karl Erlich? Against those who could evoke the spectral and monstrous forces behind the little frail wall of human existence?

She pressed her hands against her temples to stop their agonizing pain. Who knew what was life, and what was death? Man had hung a little curtain at the door of his little house, and shivered behind it. He forgot what went on outside. To reassure his quivering self he laughed childishly at mysteries, scoffed at dread premonitions, denied the shrieking terrors that blew at his curtain and invaded his dreams. He refused to believe that one man, by throwing aside the curtain, by opening his eyes and seeing, could permit entry to every man's house of the unspeakable things that swirled through the corridors of the universe.

She could not control her tired and shuddering thoughts. She looked about the study, with bemused and aching eyes. The head of Gilu was alive in the lamplight. It grinned at her; its eye-sockets gleamed. It was the Spirit of Evil, bursting through the thin curtain of reality. She stared back at it, numb and impotent, feeling her consciousness disintegrating. A dark mist fell over her vision.

She was again in her father's church. She could hear the rolling and surging of the organ, like a great sea. The waves fell over her, lifted her up, tossed her down, filled her heart and her soul. There was only blackness and death in and about her.

Then over the thunder and the waves she heard the singing voice of a man, singing as she had heard him sing a hundred times or more. Then she had listened with indifference, even boredom, with an air of politeness. But as she listened now, the voice was a light over the storm, triumphant, rising, breaking through the darkness: like an eternal light:

> ". . . . But Deliver us from Evil,
> For Thine is the Kingdom, and the power,
> and the glory,
> Forever and ever . . . ."

Dawn had come. The sky was suffused in a pale and milky light. The tops of the great garden trees floated in a clear radiance. The radiance brightened, became enhanced. The trees were like prayers in it.

17 SHE BATHED, DRESSED. Her body was laden with an immense fatigue. It felt that it was not a part of her, but a weary burden which she must drag with her. She passed Karl's door on her way downstairs. She could not control her exhausted thoughts. She had seen doors standing closed all her life. But there was such a finality about this door. It was like a door shut on a corpse.

Lotte was surprised to see her so early, and was about to mention it when she saw her mistress' face. "The Herr Doctor has not stirred yet," she said. "We have heard nothing of him."

She added, in a carefully matter-of-fact voice: "He was so restless last night. He walked about for hours. When I brought him his hot milk I put two tablets in it, instead of one." She went on grimly: "Then he slept."

Therese was too tired to speak. She sat down, drank half a cup of coffee. She said at last: "I want the car, Lotte. No, I do not care for anything to eat. I am going out."

"So early, Frau Doctor?"

"So early."

Lotte hesitated, eyeing Therese with indecision. "Frau Doctor, do you remember how I spoke of ghosts? Or, perhaps you think I am a silly old woman, and you do not believe in ghosts, after all?"

Therese lifted her hollow eyes, and smiled palely. "Did I say that, Lotte? How can one believe, or not believe, in anything?"

Encouraged, though a little puzzled by this ambiguous remark, Lotte went on, a trifle defiantly, with a wary eye out for incipient amusement from Therese: "You remember, Frau Doctor, that I told you about the Muehlers' girl, who had seen the ghost of the Herr Professor's father? She had seen him often. She was not afraid. One is not afraid of a ghost, when one really sees such an apparition. It is the thought of one which is so terrifying. When one comes face to face with a ghost, one can adjust oneself, learn to accept it, even to understand."

She paused, doubtful of the effect of her words on Therese.

To her intense surprise, Therese had begun to regard her with strangely-bright tired eyes.

"Yes, yes, Lotte," she said, in a still, peculiar voice. "I understand, perfectly." She added, as though speaking to herself: "It is the idea which is so terrifying, the unknown in which one does not really believe."

Somewhat disconcerted, but not entirely reassured, Lotte went on:

"Last night the girl saw the old man's ghost again. She met him in the dark hallway. She asked him: 'What are you doing, Herr Muehler?' You see, she knew him well; she had known him before he died. He smiled at her, and said: 'I am listening.' Now, the Herr Professor and the Frau Professor were dining with the General, and there was no one in the house last night but the girl, the cook having left. But the girl was not nervous. It was only in remembering, that she was disturbed. But now she was quite tranquil. She talked to him as though he were alive, and indeed, she told me, he was quite solid, and colored, with his little white beard really distinct. She even wondered, she said, if she ought to invite him into the drawing-room, where they might talk at ease. It was all so very natural!

"She was even curious. She said: 'To what are you listening, Herr Muehler?' And he answered: 'To my son.' Now, that was a little absurd. The Herr Professor was not in the house. She began to think. The more she thought, the more it was absurd. She expected the ghost to disappear, but, as she watched it, it went into the Herr Professor's bedroom and sat down in his chair near the bed. Then she regretted that she had been so impolite, and had not invited him into the drawing-room. But he was always a cosy man, she remembered, and preferred kitchens and bedrooms to drafty drawing-rooms. He looked very satisfied. He picked up a book and began to read. It was very pleasant, seeing him sitting there, under the lamp, reading. She saw how his spectacles shone, and how his beard nodded, as he apparently agreed with the writer. She said, a little nervously: 'You seem so real, Herr Muehler.'

"And then she was startled, for he laughed. It was a real and living sound. He looked at her, and answered: 'But I am real, my girl. I was never so real in my life!'"

Lotte waited. But Therese was listening with hard attention, her cup in her hand. Lotte shifted on her old aching feet. She continued, more and more defiantly:

"The Muehlers' girl, Frau Doctor, is a very sensible creature. She asked herself: 'How can a ghost be real?' So she
said: 'But you are dead. I am alive, and I know you are dead.'
And do you know what the ghost answered? He said: 'No,
my child, I am not dead. It is only that you are sleeping. I
am awake.'

"Now, that was ridiculous. The girl knew she was not
sleeping. She was standing there, still in her apron, and she
had her candle in her hand. She was on the way to her bed,
but she was not sleeping. She pinched herself. She felt the
pinch quite strongly. But one does not argue with a ghost.
There are tales that they can become very unpleasant, when
contradicted. So she merely nodded solemnly, as if in agree-
ment. At this, he was very amused. He laughed, quite loudly,
and his eyes danced behind his spectacles.

"She was very sleepy, however. She wanted to go to bed,
for she rises early. But it did not seem polite to leave the
ghost. So she asked if she could bring him anything. He was
so real that she could understand that he could drink coffee
and even eat. But he shook his head. 'No,' he said, 'I am
waiting for my son. I shall never leave him again. When he
goes, I shall go, too. But not until he goes. He will need a
lot of comfort at the last, and it will comfort him to see me
the first of all. We have such a lot to say to each other.' "

Lotte waited to see the effect of this extraordinary story
on her mistress. But Therese did not laugh. She did not even
smile. She gazed at Lotte fixedly, and her face paled more
than ever. She put down her cup with a clatter, and terror
stood in her eyes. "No! No!" she exclaimed, in a low voice.
She stood up, abruptly. Lotte saw that she was trembling
violently.

The old woman was seized with compunction and self-
reproach. "I have not frightened you, Frau Doctor? If I
have, I am a miserable old wretch! You have so much to
bear!"

Therese put her hands to her head. She closed her eyes. She
had again that ghastly sensation of disembodiment, of being
swirled about in a dark universe where unreality was the only
reality, and there was only horror.

"Oh, Frau Doctor, I have really frightened you!" cried
Lotte. "Do not listen to me. Besides, she is a very silly girl,
and goes about with her mouth open, constantly. And very

stupid, too. She makes up a lot of stories, and most of them are lies."

Therese dropped her hands. She forced herself to smile. "I am not frightened, Lotte. But I am really in a hurry. Will you call the car, please?"

Lotte scurried out, shaking with her passionate self-reproach. While she waited, Therese kept smoothing her hair distractedly with her hands. She put on her hat and coat, which she had brought with her. Her flesh was cold and rigid. "No, no!" she repeated, with a sort of anguish.

When she was in the car, riding steadily through the clean, wide, sun-washed streets, and breathing deeply though spasmodically of the fresh bright air, she was able to orient herself. She thought to herself that her home had become a dark and airless tomb, in which specters walked, and there was only grief. She felt herself a widow. She felt that she was going down into hell, like Orpheus, to rescue one already dead, and bring him back to the living earth. But first, she must traverse the blood-lit caverns herself; she must learn the way in order to guide him. But have I lost the way? she thought, despairingly. I go deeper and deeper into terror, into loneliness and darkness, and perhaps I will not know the way back. Perhaps I will be trapped down here myself, with Karl. There is no end to the dreadfulness.

Her head ached crushingly. Her sleepless body seemed to creak like a rusty door. How long can one endure? According to the whispered tales of the concentration camp, it was astonishing how long one could endure. She wondered if she had the fortitude to endure, and to go on, searching for Karl, going deeper and deeper into hell.

Now, as air and light and sound poured into her car, and sanity returned, she wondered if she were not more than a little absurd in going on this errand. What could she say? What could she do? Perhaps she would appear only ridiculous. She had so far recovered sanity that when the car stopped at the door of the Muehler house, which was not far from her own, she was able to say to the driver: "Just a moment, Frederick. I will wait here a moment."

She sat back on the seat and pondered doubtfully, looking at the quiet house with the lace curtains fresh against the windows, and the flowers growing thickly on the sills. No doom hung there; no shadow of terror. A plume of gray smoke rose idly in the air. The window-panes shone in the early morning light. Behind the house, the trees hung, heavy with warm sun. Here was reality, and health. The dark mists swirled behind her, receding. She was indeed ridiculous! She glanced at her watch. It was just a little after half-past eight. What on earth would they say to her, when she burst, haggard and exhausted, through the door, imploring? But worse, what would she say? Doctor Muehler would be finishing his coffee. Streaks of sun would lie across the golden-yellow liquid. He would look at her with his kind and quizzical eyes, a little wondering, but pleased to see her. But his wife might not be so pleased. She had little imagination, for all her cleverness. She would politely urge a little breakfast on Therese. She would sit at the table with them, smelling the yellow buttered toast. And they would wait. It would not be hard to talk to Doctor Muehler. His sympathy and subtlety would understand even the ravings of a prostrated woman, whose clarity of vision had been clouded by sorrow and the blackness of a nebulous dread. But his wife—it would not be easy to talk in her presence. She would smile, that calm superior British smile, and she would listen. Finally, she would think Therese a fool.

And she would be quite right, thought Therese. Her irresolution grew. Should she wait outside until Doctor Muehler came out, and then drive him to the University in her car? She knew he usually walked. Perhaps that would be best. If she were indeed a fool, it was better that such a kind and gentle man alone see her folly. He would appreciate her coming. He would not think her interfering and hysterical. He would understand.

Her chauffeur, she suddenly observed, was watching her narrowly in his mirror. He was a young man. Suddenly, she remembered that she had never liked him, for all his competence and respectfulness. He had been in her employ a year. What did she know of him? Through half-closed eyes, she watched him watching her. Was it only her imagination that he seemed cynical and brutelike and crafty? Where did he go on his evenings off? She remembered that Lotte had mentioned that she had seen a uniform in his room, with a swastika on his sleeve. Therese had barely listened. All the young men these days loved uniforms. Germans loved uniforms. It had not been significant. Now she wished she had asked Lotte what sort of uniform it was. How little the selfish and the superior know! she thought.

She pulled herself together. There is enough horror without imagining more, she thought. The first thing I will imagine is that he is a spy. This will never do! This is still Germany, still summer, and the sun still shines. Everything is peaceful. Indeed, she was a fool. When she remembered Lotte's story of the ghost, she smiled involuntarily. Frederick was still watching her. He thought she was smiling at him. He returned the smile, touching his cap with a quick military flash of his fingers. His eyes were bold and admiring in the glass.

She was filled with healthy annoyance at his presumption. Instantly, her exhausted disorientation vanished entirely. How silly she was. Because there were some crimes, some darknesses, some horrors, in Germany, because she had come into contact with some of them, she thought the whole world had been spinning into madness! She could readily see what could easily happen to the sane if they allowed themselves to think too much, and imagine too much.

She leaned forward to tell him to drive on. At that instant, the door of the house opened and a servant, with a pail of steaming suds and a broom, appeared. She put down the pail, dipped the broom into it and began to scrub the white steps. Had she not looked up then, and had she not seen the car, Therese would have gone on. But the servant saw her, and recognized her. The situation had become even more absurd. She could not go on now. Frau Doctor Muehler would hear the story, of how Therese had been seen lurking before her house, and she would wonder. Therese could see her raised eyebrows and quizzical look.

She nodded curtly to Frederick, who leapt from his seat and opened the door, saluting. She ignored him. She approached the servant, who stared at her blankly. "Is Frau Doctor Muehler at home?" she asked.

The servant stammered that the Frau Doctor was still at breakfast. Therese was forced to summon as much dignity as she could, and entered the cool hall, where shafts of sunlight lay on bowls of flowers and polished chairs and mirror. The servant followed her, wiping her hands on her apron. Feeling more and more ridiculous, Therese said that she would go at once into the breakfast room. There was no need to announce her.

She liked this house. It was ugly, and the colors fought with each other. But there was a homeliness about it, an English homeliness, warm and confiding, not too formal. The furniture in the drawing-room was covered with gay summer chintz. The English had no taste. But they made up for it in an inviting atmosphere. She walked down a narrow carpeted hall, and entered the breakfast room. She heard no voices. But she found the Frau Doctor sitting alone at the breakfast table, calmly drinking coffee and reading the headlines of the newspaper.

When she saw Therese, she stared as blankly as the servant had stared. But she recovered her poise immediately. She wore a flowered wrapper, and her light brown hair was braided and wrapped about her round sensible head. She looked younger and fresher, and the wrapper concealed her dumpy figure. Her complexion was as dewy and bright as a girl's.

"Frau Doctor Erlich!" she exclaimed. But that was her only expression of surprise. "How very nice! Have you had your breakfast?"

The coffee and fresh kuchen had come to Therese's nostrils in a powerful and inviting wave. Her strong body, having thrown off the paralyzing inertia of terror, responded to the smell of the good food. She smiled, as though with self-deprecation. "Yes, thank you. But, do you know, I believe I could drink another cup of coffee, and eat some of that kuchen!"

The Englishwoman graciously ordered another cup for her guest. If she were extremely surprised at this early morning visit she concealed it. Therese looked about her, glanced through the open window at the riot of grass and flowers in the garden. Birds were filling the glittering air with cheeps and trills. It was very pleasant. The rigidity passed from Therese's limbs. She removed her gloves and laid them aside. The other woman watched her without appearing to do so. How eccentric she thinks me! thought Therese, behind her pleasant smile. It was intolerable, to be thought eccentric. She cast around in her mind for placid and commonplace things to say. Should she tell her hostess that she had come out for an early shopping tour? And that she wished her to join her? But one merely called up on such an occasion. Moreover, she was not on such terms of intimacy with the gracious but reserved Englishwoman as to be able to drop casually into her home at any moment.

The Englishwoman saw her confusion behind the dignity and placidity. She knew very well that this was not a casual visit. But she wished to put Therese at her ease, though she thought everything so peculiar. But one never knew with foreigners, she remarked to herself. They did the most unpredictable things. Even Herman was unpredictable. Look at this morning, for instance.

"Do you know, Frau Doctor," she observed, with some sprightliness, "I have never enjoyed myself so much as I did last night. Such stimulating conversation. I was quite excited at times." Her smile asked indulgence for her excitement. "But then, Germans are always stimulating, and have so much of interest to say. I am afraid that we British are quite dull, and our conversation leaves much to be desired."

She spoke German perfectly, but with an English acent, thus making the gutturals a little softer, the vowels a little more clipped. Her reserve, this morning, was not so evident. She was making a good-natured attempt to put this pale woman at her ease, for all Therese's apparent eccentricity.

Therese laughed lightly. "The General does not always have 'exciting' dinner guests," she said. "They are usually duller than dry bread. But did you not find that Schmidt a trifle detestable?"

The Englishwoman raised her eyebrows at this forthright question, which she thought somewhat in bad taste. "No, I am sorry. I really found him very enjoyable, and extremely intellectual. I quite agree with him."

Therese, to her dismay, heard herself saying, with unusual warmth:

"I think he is detestable. It is such men as this that give Germany a bad name. Do not think we are all like that." She drew a deep breath. Her composure was rapidly disappearing under those amused but politely reticent eyes. "If we do not get rid of them soon, we shall have a bad reputation in the world, I am afraid."

The Englishwoman poured herself another cup of coffee. How peculiar and gauche she must think me! thought Therese, with mortification. She was suddenly quite sick with her passionate desire to be away from her. Why on earth had she come!

Forcing herself into an attitude of tranquil indifference, she asked:

"But where is the Herr Professor?"

Now the Englishwoman was not smiling so maddeningly. "He left very early, much earlier than usual. He said the summer was going so rapidly, and he wished to enjoy the morning sunshine. I have an idea that he did not sleep so well."

Instantly, the flower-filled sunlit world vanished into gray dimness for Therese. Her dread, her fears, her terrors, rushed back into it like clammy mists. Everything took on its old grotesque quality of nightmare. She leaned towards the Englishwoman and asked in a stifled voice:

"He has gone? My God, I should have come earlier!"

Herman's wife put down her cup abruptly, and stared. "I do not understand," she murmured.

Therese stood up. She wrung her hands, and her ring flashed in the sunshine. "He is in terrible danger." she said. She glanced at the door, reached it, closed it, returned to the table. "Do you think he has arrived at the University yet? Do you think we can reach him before he has gone into his classroom?"

The Englishwoman was propelled to her feet. The two women stared at each other across the table. Frau Doctor Muehler's fresh color disappeared.

"What is the matter? What danger? I do not understand you, Therese."

It was the first time she had called Therese by her first name, but her agitation had broken down her reserve. Wrinkles appeared in her smooth skin.

"You do not know Germany, Elizabeth!" cried Therese. "You do not know Germany today! We are all mad, here. But Herman is sane. I knew there was something in his mind. . . ." She flung out her hands impotently. "Please try to understand, Elizabeth. Herman is about to do something which will ruin him. Perhaps kill him. How do I know? I do not know, really. But I feel it. There were frightful men at that dinner last night. You do not know how frightful! A little while ago I would not have known, either. But now I know. I saw Herman watching them. He was resolving something. Something which will ruin him. He could not help it! They were goading him. He was seeing something I have been seeing for a long time. He could not endure it. He talked, and they listened. That is danger enough. But there is worse danger. The thing he has in his mind to do. . . ."

Her voice, dwindled, gasping, incoherent, filled the breakfast room with the hysteria and the disorientation of doom. Elizabeth Muehler listened, paling more and more. She moistened her lips. She stared fixedly at Therese. She fumbled for her chair, fell in it. A thick silence pervaded the atmosphere after Therese had done.

"We must call him at once!" cried Therese, finding her voice again. "We must stop him!"

The Englishwoman was silent. Then her eyes, fixed so piercingly on Therese, narrowed. Her color returned somewhat. Her hand reached for a silver spoon, played absently with it.

She thinks I am mad, thought Therese. But she was not humiliated. She was merely frenzied.

"Call him at once!" she repeated.

The Englishwoman's lips opened. "You are so upset," she murmured. "Please sit down, Therese. Let us talk about this calmly."

Mortification caused Therese to blush, in spite of her distraction. She sat down. She stammered: "You are British. You cannot conceive of the things which happen in Germany now." Even to herself she sounded inept and stupid.

The Englishwoman paused. She struggled to regain her poise and serenity. It was evident that Therese had shaken her. She was visibly but politely annoyed. What emotion! What hysteria! What imagination! Her thoughts flitted across her eyes. Really, this was too much. But these foreigners were always emotional. They did and said such incomprehensible things. It was very irritating, especially at breakfast. She had not thought it of Therese, who, at times, seemed so British in her reserve and manner, and was so well-bred. Her disappointment in her own impeccable judgment increased her annoyance.

"It was very nice of you to come," she said in her low calm voice. "And I appreciate your apprehension for Herman. But he is really very sensible and cautious. He would do nothing that would cause any—any unpleasantness."

"You do not know Herman!" exclaimed Therese, more and more mortified, more and more enraged against this woman who made her feel so silly and badly bred.

This made the Englishwoman smile with complete amusement. Her eyebrows jerked. "I have only been married to him for a long time," she murmured. She went on, hoping that her attitude would convince Therese of her enormous bad taste, and thus calm her: "I am sorry to have to admit that many Germans today seem so—unnerved. But why? Changes of government are quite common in England. No one becomes quite so upset. It is very usual. Of course, there are always a lot of speeches, and the lower classes become agitated, and the newspapers are often more than a little violent. But no one gives it much thought, really. Everything goes on just the same. Everything adjusts itself. One has only to wait. You see," she added, in the voice that an adult uses in speaking to an overwrought adolescent, "we British have been through many changes of government policy. But everything always returns to the comfortable mean. National excitement is just a way of getting rid of excess energy. But mankind, after all, is inherently sensible and healthy. And I know enough of Germany to realize that things will settle down, and adjust themselves. The danger comes in getting—excited, and going to pieces. One must not allow this."

Therese was seized with a horrifying impulse to slap that serene and slightly-smiling face.

"Have you heard of the Gestapo, Frau Doctor?" she exclaimed.

Elizabeth lifted her eyebrows again, and smiled. "Yes, I have But who listens to vulgar tales? There are such liars, you know. And the Jews, who were never really Germans, you know, are an excitable and volatile people, full of lies and imaginations. They have spread these absurd stories. During the war, we had an Intelligence Bureau, too. Every nation has to have one, during a period of national stress. Fortunately, however, the Jews did not begin their usual lies and agitations against the government. What a detestable people they are! Always stirring up trouble and contention. That is because they are all Communists at heart. They love confusion. It is during periods of confusion that they can seize advantage, and money. Therefore, you see, understanding this, I do not give much credence to the disgusting tales of the Gestapo and the concentration camps." She paused. Her face became cold and more than a little vicious, "Sometimes, I almost wish they were true. It would be such a relief to every one of breeding and decency if all Jews were eliminated." She added: "Just because some of them have been detected in their crimes against Germany, and have been properly punished, there is such an outcry. Touch one of their precious skins, and all Israel screams. Really, it is too disgusting!"

Therese listened to the end. Her mortification and agitation disappeared. She felt as cold as death, and as impotent. Her heart was cold, too, and beating with a mortal pain.

"Have you forgotten, Elizabeth, that the Gestapo killed Eric Reinhardt, my husband's adopted brother? He did nothing. He was a good and loyal German. They murdered him. Murdered him in cold blood. You knew him. He only wanted to live in peace. When Germany made that impossible, he wanted to go away. I have never seen any one so wretched. What had he done? Nothing."

The Englishwoman assumed an expression of regret. "Yes, I know. That was rather bad. It was very unfortunate. But sometimes the innocent must suffer with the guilty. I often thought if he had not tried to escape. . . ."

Frenzy seized Therese again. "Will you not listen? Will you never learn? He did not try to escape. We—we saw his body. He was tortured to death!"

Distaste for this excessiveness made a wrinkle appear in the Englishwoman's smooth brow. "Really!" she murmured. "You make it sound as though we were living in the Middle Ages again. . . ."

"We are!" cried Therese. "The most dreadful things happen! Men are not civilized. They never were. The laws of society made them hide their bestiality. But in Germany we have no laws any longer. We are being urged to be bestial. And so, it comes out, like a turgid geyser bursting through the earth. You do not know! You will not see! This is not Britain. This is Germany, without laws. The whole country is full of beasts." She clasped her hands together convulsively. "I saw Eric's body. Kurt Erlich made them send it to us. I cannot describe it! My God! O my God! When I saw the body, I was glad poor little Gerda was dead. I was so very glad!"

She looked at Elizabeth Muehler. "And unless we do something, at once, you will see Herman like that!"

Now, this is really too much! thought the other woman, fully angered and affronted now. She forgot her breeding in her great indignation. "How can you talk like that?" she demanded, her voice no longer quiet, but almost shrill. "How dreadful of you to say such things! You are not only a disloyal German, Frau Doctor Erlich, to imply such things of your own people, but you are positively offensive! You must forgive me, but you are really responsible for my saying such things to a lady in my own house! I never thought it possible that I should be so frank, so—well, insulting. But you force me to talk like this. No one would harm Herman. But truly, this is madness! This is the Twentieth Century. I—I have no time to listen to such nonsense."

There was a sudden silence between the two women. The Englishwoman breathed loudly and jerkily. Her face was flushed scarlet. Her eyes snapped with her anger. She had pushed her chair away from the table.

And then, in the hallway, the clock tolled the hour of ten. Slowly, ominously. The Englishwoman heard it. Therese heard it.

"I have no time," repeated Elizabeth Muehler, with bitter coldness, and deliberate insult.

Time. Time no longer. In her sick and whirling bemusement, in her mortal illness, Therese thought incoherently: There are so many times. So many changes of times. Time no longer for man's little private world. Time no longer for mankind. Time no longer. Time only for death and madness, for fortitude and courage. For the last cry of faith and peace against fury and terror. . . . She put her hands to her head, in her old gesture of despair. Heavy impotence paralyzed her whole body. She thought: If I could only die. If I could only sink into nothingness and darkness. For, at the end, I can really do nothing at all. Nothing at all against blindness and stupidity, nothing against inertia and smiling fools. Nothing, until it is too late.

"Too late," she whispered.

She felt something hard pressing against her lips. She opened her eyes. Elizabeth was standing beside her, with a distressed, changed face. She was pressing a glass of wine urgently to Therese's white mouth. The servant, intensely interested, was standing in the doorway, a decanter in her hand.

"Oh, I am so sorry!" the Englishwoman exclaimed. "Forgive me, for being so rude, Therese. There, my dear, drink. I am afraid you fainted for a moment. You are really so ill! I am a brute. Please forgive me. There, one more swallow. Do you feel better now?"

She wiped Therese's pallid face, on which little beads of moisture stood. She flung wider the already open window. Distressedly, she fanned Therese with her handkerchief, which was impregnated with a delicate odor of lilies. "Please, let me take you to my room. You must lie down. I should have remembered you have so much to bear. But my temper—my deplorable temper. . . . And you were so kind to come . . . about Herman. I should have understood."

I must lie down, thought Therese numbly. If I do not lie down, I shall collapse. A violent craving for rest pervaded her. A passionate desire to relax, to sleep, to forget. She began to push herself to her feet. The servant and the English-woman took her arms. She felt herself being helped up cushioned stairs. She felt herself sink onto a chaise-longue. She heard blinds being lowered, the murmur of voices, a warm shawl being placed over her feet. She felt a cool and solicitous hand on her forehead. But she could not open her eyes. Complete prostration rolled over her like black waves.

She thought to herself, dimly: It is no use. It is too late. There is nothing I can ever do. If I could only die. Nothing matters. I can struggle no longer. I can only give up.

She surrendered to her appalling impotence, to the darkness, to the deathly cravings of her body. She began to feel herself sinking into unconsciousness. Her limbs relaxed as the limbs of the dead relax. She embraced unconsciousness as an addict embraces the sensations of his drug.

She must have slept. But it seemed to her that she was not completely unconscious. She could hear a faint and swirling ringing in her head, extending to all the universe. Her flesh felt like clay. The nausea increased somewhere in her body. Once or twice she tried to move, but iron weighed her down.

The ringing was more insistent. She floated to the surface of unconsciousness. She thought that she must have slept a long time. By sheer force of will she raised her languid arm, and tried to focus her eyes, in the dimness, on her watch. It was almost half-past eleven. Her arm fell to her side. She looked about her. She was in Elizabeth's boudoir, large, ugly, warm and quiet, and full of comfort. She was all alone. The bell which had awakened her had stopped. She could hear the twittering of birds outside, and the stillness of the house. Leaf shadows fluttered against the drawn blinds. I must go, she thought.

And then she heard a cry, Elizabeth's cry, wild and broken. The cry was repeated, not once, but several times. She heard the scurrying of servants, and their own confused faint screams.

The nausea seized her as she tried to rise. She bent double, retching dryly. Sweat burst out over her as she forced herself to her feet. She swayed. She pressed her hands over the spot in her breast, which was being pierced by hot daggers.

"Too late," she said aloud, simply as a child speaks.

18 HE HAD GONE out earlier than usual. He always walked to the University, which took at least forty-five minutes' rapid walking. Now he left the house fully one and a half hours before the time of the convening of his first class. His wife recalled later that he had kissed her with a little more than his usual tender kindliness, and had looked into her eyes with a sort of sad inquiry. He had walked away, with his peculiar, rather shambling gait, his satchel under his arm, his crooked pipe between his teeth. But he had been very calm. No one could have guessed that he knew he was going to condemn himself to imprisonment, torture and death. He had been so quiet, so matter-of-fact, so almost indifferent.

But he did not arrive at his first class before the usual time. He walked very slowly, sometimes stopping to look at the thick green trees, or speak to a child or a dog, or glance into a perambulator. He might have been a petty bourgeoisie strolling to his little shop or office. But with every breath he drew, he drew in the air of the life he loved, the life of Germany, the essence of its soul. He was no longer a shabby, gentle, quiet and kindly man in his middle-age, renowned for his learning, his literary tastes, his intellect and his knowledge, but a young man again, strolling to the university where he would learn, not teach. The world was new for him again, and the tranquillity of his youth was in his eyes, like a serene benediction. In this frightful hour, he could think: How tranquil were the mornings of my youth! The whole world was swelling about me. It was peaceful, but beyond the peace I could hear all the tumult of living, waiting for me beyond the calm threshold of the university and the classroom. I really lived then. There was nothing I could not do. There was nothing heroic for which I would not die. I knew then that the very reason for life was a noble purpose to which I might sacrifice myself.

In the selfless devotion of youth there was a living joy, a beauty and a glory. But somehow, he thought, the crowding years shut out the vision, and at last there were left only narrow walls, dim windows, a waning fire, and a loaf of bread. Years do not bring wisdom; they bring only timorous selfishness, and the little prison of self-protectiveness.

But now he was free! In his body there was the awakening tingle of taut muscles finally released. He was not Herr Professor Herman Muehler. He was young student Herman Muehler, willing, eager, to die for what was good, and longing for the heroic opportunity. His father had been a Swabian, a scholar, a German Republican, though he had also been only a poor second-rate shopkeeper with a vision and a large simplicity of heart and mind. His mother had made a mesalliance in marrying him, for her father had been a Prussian army captain, a Junker. But she, too, had had his qualities of heart and mind, and intense blue eyes that saw straightly and uncompromisingly. Every quality with which they were endowed they had bequeathed to their son. They were satisfied that, though they could leave him no money and no position, they had given him the best of themselves. At one time Heinz Muehler had dreamed of going to America. He had even gone so far as to sell his little shop and buy tickets. But at the last he could not leave Germany. It was as if he had some sad prescience of what Germany was to become. To leave her in her convulsions would have been dastardly. In small places, in the huge darkness, he knew it was his duty to keep his little lantern burning, in order that Germany might find, in the encroaching gloom, some haven, some refuge.

Like all the other Germans of his kind, he had a passionate love of scholastic learning. Herman would not keep a shop. He would be a Herr Professor! Sometime before, he would not have cared. But his wife, the daughter of a Junker, had not quite forgotten her birth. She had not forgotten that both Beethoven and Goethe had been close friends of her grandfather. Herman must be worthy of such an ancient friendship.

They lived to see him appointed instructor in literature at the University. They died shortly before his marriage to the Englishwoman, whose father had been a great liberal and a great gentleman. They were satisfied. Frau Muehler also was secretly delighted that the Englishwoman had a fortune of her own, and seemed a sensible young miss with no nonsense about her. At the last, she must have had some misgivings about a noble life which had no material prospects.

But knowing that there was some treachery in this misgiving, she kept her thoughts to herself.

Herman had been deeply touched at his young wife's passionate attachment to Germany, and her complete entry into its life. And then, finally, he saw that she was not really attached to Germany. She was attached to the artificial form of its rigorous aristocracy. She said, frankly, that she was delighted at the narrow confines of its class distinction. England, she observed, was losing this very necessary distinction. All sorts of inferior people were creeping into the ranks of the titled and the distinguished. One found the daughters of brewers and shopkeepers standing in line at the Court of St. James's. England was losing her flavor and her strength in the brackish water of inferior classes. Germany was still immune, still rigorous. In time, she began to detest her native country, and all her enthusiasm was given to Germany, in which she found nothing wrong.

Herman found that he had married no republican, no Swabian, no liberal. But he was a gentle and tolerant man, not given to arguments or tempers. He adjusted himself to his wife's ambitions, and thenceforth told her nothing. They remained childless throughout their marriage, and though his wife complained, he was secretly glad. He became the spiritual father of those few in his classes who were like him, who could be counted upon to light the little lanterns and keep them burning, even if they died for it. The lanterns might be struck out, but the oil would flow from the broken vessels, ignited, and, perhaps, some day, setting a great fire which would burn away all that was dark and corrupt in Germany.

But I have become tired, after all these years! he thought, as he strolled peacefully towards the University. He had watched the lanterns go out, one by one. It had given him a dreadful grief. But he had kept silent. He knew why he had kept silent, now. It was because he had forgotten the words he had once known. His own lantern had become dry, and he had no oil for the others.

And then, from some mysterious source, he had been given oil again. He had lighted his lamp. He held it in his hands. It would be struck out of his grasp, but the ignited oil would flow, and who knew but what it would find another lantern and light another lamp.

Never had he felt so happy, so peaceful! He forgot everything, his wife, his life, his sadness, his timorousness, his tired and fruitless indifference. He was young again. He could hardly contain the joy that made his heart palpitate. The world of his later years had vanished like a nightmare. The old world he had known, fresh, airy, bright, full of excitement and happiness and hope, was about him again. He had no wife, no home. He had only the University, and the promise of his life. He was no Herr Professor. He was a student, with the lamp in his hand.

He sat down on a bench under a tree, and removed his hat. He refilled his pipe, crossed his long shabby legs. His satchel lay beside him. The sun came softly on his head through the large leaves. He smiled at everything. The tired and disillusioned wrinkles on his worn face relaxed, disappeared. His brown eyes shone with exquisite pleasure and peace, and even some latent excitement. He smiled at everything. All at once he thought of Therese Erlich. I should like her to know, he said to himself. Then, she will not feel so wretched and so despairing, remembering me. I should like to tell her how happy I am, just now. He had a momentary impulse to call her, and tell her. Then he remembered that she lived in the dark and shifting nightmare, still. She must find her way out of it alone, into the daylight. Moreover, she might call to him out of the nightmare, and kill the brightness. I must be selfish for the last time, he remarked to his impulse.

He did not feel like a condemned man. He was free. Out of the tranquil aura of his freedom he could look at all things with a beatific detachment. He had lost his life. He had saved his soul. The simplicity of his thought seemed so beautiful, so satisfying, so lovely, that tears rose to his eyes, and he was compelled to remove his spectacles and wipe the mist away.

He had told his students that the way to living was through the narrow door of knowledge. But he knew that he had cluttered that open door with the rank growths of form and complexity, confusion, theories and futility. Now he understood that the moment knowledge lost its clarity and simplicity it lost its meaning. It became full of words, formless and chaotic. It choked out the light and left only a dimness in which nothing could be seen. It did not say: "This is the way of life." It said: "There is no light."

Knowledge had emphasized man's littleness of soul, and

impotence. It had said to him: "Who, by taking thought, can add one cubit to his stature?" It had not told him that he could increase the stature of his soul, and that the man of learning was the high priest of despairing people.

So deep was he in his musings that he was hardly aware of a young man's voice calling to him with pleased surprise: "Herr Professor! Herr Professor!"

He looked up, to see a young man in the uniform of the Storm Troopers approaching him with outstretched hand, eager gait, and affectionate smile. At first he did not recognize the young man, who was so stalwart, so soldierly, so lean of body and hard of face. He adjusted his spectacles, and peered. Then at last he saw it was Joseph Buerger, one of his most promising students of two years ago, one of those he had thought of as a lamp-bearer in the gathering gloom. The shock of what he saw now, the metamorphosis of a student into a robot, so profoundly shocked him that he turned quite white. But his smile was gentle, his handclasp warm and kind.

"Good morning, Joseph. I did not recognize you at first."

Joseph saluted stiffly, still smiling with affection. Then he sat down beside Herman and beamed upon him.

"How I have wanted to see you! It has been so long. I have been in Munich for the past year. Now I have come home, for I have much work here. I said to myself only yesterday: 'I must see the Herr Professor again, very soon!' How could I ever forget the years in your classroom, and the things you taught me!"

Herman regarded him with piercing sadness. "What did I teach you, Joseph?"

The young man paused; his smile became fixed. He colored. Herman laid his hand on his arm, and shook his head a little.

"Never mind, Joseph. You see, it was not important, after all. Nothing I have said lately has been important." He added, after a moment: "For, I know now, I had nothing to say. I, too, had forgotten."

The young man protested. "You taught us to love Germany, Herr Professor! I remember that."

Herman's eyes slowly travelled over the uniform. His expression became increasingly sad.

"And what I taught you has brought you to this, Joseph?"

"To this? Are you not proud of me, Herr Professor?"

Herman was silent. He clasped his hands together. Age

and mournfulness shrank his face. He seemed to huddle in his shabby clothing.

Joseph's eyes hardened, his lips tightened. "If you are not proud of me, Herr Professor, it is because you do not understand. I have been chosen for important work in Berlin, after my work in Munich. Is that not an honor you can appreciate?"

Herman lifted his eyes and fixed them sorrowfully upon the other's. "What was your work in Munich, Joseph? Beating and murdering the helpless and the innocent? Oppressing the defenseless? Trampling down all that was good and gentle in Germany under your robot's boots? Helping to kill the soul of the Fatherland, and serving mountebanks and monsters who are no more a part of Germany than the decaying fungus on a tree trunk is part of the tree?"

Despair galvanized him. He flung out his hands. He looked at the sweet blue sky, and the pattern of leaves against it.

"If I have brought you to this, Joseph, then it would have been better if I had died first."

A flash of blinding anger and fury made a glare in the youth's eyes. He tried to control his voice; it came, stifled, from his lips. "If you were any one else, Herr Professor, I would take you into custody for this! You are a traitor to the new Germany."

But Herman only smiled slightly and with even more mournfulness.

"Yes, Joseph. I am a traitor to the new Germany."

He sighed. "But more than that, I was a traitor to you. Joseph, you must forgive me. Years from now, you will remember me, when you are in despair, and full of hopelessness. You will say: 'He gave me no staff, no rod to comfort me. He gave me no lantern to guide me. He taught me the dead austerity of literature and pedantry. When the hour of trial came, I had no sustenance, no bread. What I have done, he is guilty of. The grave I must lie in, without hope, he dug for me.' You will hate me then, Joseph."

The young man listened. Slowly, the anger and the fury left his eyes. He paled. The hardness dissolved from his face, and the softness of the student took its place. All at once the uniform was incongruous on him. He looked at it. He looked at the swastika on his arm. He was terribly shaken. His eyes were dark with the horror of memories.

Herman stood up. He picked up his satchel and put it under his arm. He put his hat upon his head. He was an old man.

"Herr Professor," muttered Joseph.

But Herman walked away. His step was slow and feeble. The young man watched him go. A pattern of light and shade lay on his bent shoulders. For a long time afterwards, Joseph sat on the bench, his head bowed, his fingers placed over the swastika on his arm as though to hide it.

He was not too early for his first class, and his largest, after all. They were already assembled, the young men. Some of them were in the new uniform. Because he was so popular, many students had to stand at the rear of the room. They preferred the discomfort to being in the class of another. His classes always ended on a burst of involuntary applause, and utter silence always prevailed when he was speaking. They all loved him. They delighted in his phrases, his gentle ironic humor, his sudden flashes of lyrical prose. They loved his lack of affectation, his warm humanity, his tenderness for them, his friendliness and simplicity. A word of praise from him would send a student off in a rosy daze, which lasted for hours. When he entered his classroom, every eye turned to him in excited anticipation, affection, and respectful pleasure. When they greeted him he would return the greeting with kind delight, as though grateful, and a little confused and surprised.

They greeted him as usual with glances of affection, smiles, anticipation. Many of them stood up, thrusting out stiff arms, and crying: "Heil Hitler!" Their mates watched this demonstration with indifference or amusement or approbration and some with contempt.

But all of them remarked that the Herr Professor seemed preoccupied, even distracted, and that his stooped figure showed marked decrepitude and listlessness. He mounted his platform. He listened to their greetings. He smiled, and it was the smile of a man in deep suffering. Only his eyes were intensely bright and alert, though sunken behind their spectacles.

He lifted his hand. Silence fell immediately, respectful and waiting. Books were open. His satchel lay unopened before him. All at once every student was aware that something momentous was about to take place, something frightfully important. The silence in the great room became thick and breathless. Every head strained forward, and every smile was wiped away. The very sunlight, streaming through the ancient windows, had an ominous glitter in it. Beyond the room, with its closed doors, other classes were convening with joyful noise and bustle. But in this room there was an abrupt and heavy silence.

He looked at them all. His eyes travelled slowly from face to face, as a man looks at a jury, despairing and impotent, but pleading. He spoke, his voice slow, lifeless, almost inaudible at first:

"I stand before you. I am no longer your teacher. You are no longer my students. You are judge and jury. I am the condemned man. I am self-condemned, waiting for punishment. For I have betrayed you. Today I am confessing my betrayal to you, hoping only that you will understand, and hoping that out of your hatred from me you may take hope and strength for the dark and terrible future."

They were amazed. They stared at him, hypnotized, blinking. They glanced at each other, as though seeking enlightenment. He saw their faces before him, a little pale, altogether bewildered. He loved them. He was a father confronted by the eyes of his betrayed, lost children.

He said, speaking as though from the depths of profound exhaustion and pain:

"A year ago, even a month ago, or a week ago, or perhaps a day ago, I might have saved you. I did not. That was because I did not quite know myself. Now I can only show you the way to salvation, to save yourselves. Tomorrow, perhaps I can have the consolation of knowing that I have saved a few, if not all. I must borrow a metaphor from a certain Book which few of you know. I must be like the sower it relates, whose seed fell on stony ground, or perished in the hot byways, or was trampled upon on the highway. But perhaps a few of the seeds will fall in fertile earth, and a new harvest shall grow, to feed the soul of a starving Germany."

He opened his satchel now. He withdrew from it an old book bound in flaking black leather. They stared at it, incredulously, and then at him. He did not open it. He merely pressed his hands on it, and leaned on it, as though it were a rock and he a passer-by, faint with sun and lostness.

Now his face was strained and passionate with pleading and anguish.

"I have taught you that there is no such thing as good or evil. I was an academic fool, dry and ironic, throwing ridicule on the old and 'narrow' concepts of theologians. In the academic and scientific worlds there was no good or evil. Art was beautiful, and beyond good or evil. Science saw nothing but survival and theory. This is what I have taught you.

"And I have taught you to look only for form and line, for phrase and liquid movement. I have taught you sterility and the pedant's castrated laughter. I led you into the temples of Art and showed you beautiful shapes and dead lips. I did not light a fire on the cold altar for you. I said: 'There is no altar.' I asked you to admire the shapes in the empty, dusty light."

He paused. He was breathing with difficulty. "I did not tell you, because I did not know, that anything which is dead, even Art, is without value. I did not know that its function is to live and breathe, to bring a warm beauty and comfort and living hope to men. I said that in a poet's meter, in an artist's prose, there was the delight of perfection. But the message in them I did not know, and so could not tell you. Once I knew. But I had forgotten. My crime is my forgetfulness."

Not a young man moved nor stirred. They might have been statues before him, showing awakened life only in their intent eyes. The grayness of his exhaustion and sorrow deepened on his face. But his voice was still quiet.

"Now I know what I had forgotten: that good and evil exist in the narrowest and most rigid concepts. But we must always try to remember, without sentiment, and without reproach, that men are inherently evil. But what do I mean by 'evil'? I mean those uneliminated instincts of primeval life, such as self-preservation, murder, violence, and the madness which is the consciousness of wild beasts. Civilization has called these instincts evil, because they conflict with an ordered society in which civilization and its beauties and its goodness can survive, and in which it can go about its slow and painful duty of eliminating man's primitive nature.

"There are a few men everywhere who are fully men, having freed themselves of this nature. They realize that all men are slowly crawling up from the primordial ooze, but the majority crawl so slowly that their crawling is almost imperceptible. It is the duty of these few to assist the upward crawl. If they fail in their duty, as I have done, the movement is slowed, will even stop, even though men like me throw pretty flowers upon the ooze and try to call attention to the form

and shape of their petals and their leaves, while men struggle
to their death in the mire beneath."

He lifted his hands with the slowness and heaviness of a
sick man trying to rouse himself. He looked at them with
despair.

"How can men like me satisfy our consciences if we run
away, or keep silent, and let the ooze envelop once more
these poor, half-conscious beasts? We must stand on the
high banks, or even descend into the ooze, to give hope and
strength, to urge and expostulate, to reach the blind deaf
ear, to hearten the inevitable groping towards the light!"

His hands dropped. He leaned again on the book. His head
fell on his breast. Not one young man moved a muscle. Only
lips parted, as though it were an effort to breathe in that
atmosphere of grief.

He lifted his head. They could hardly endure the wild sorrow in his eyes.

"I did not go down into the ooze to you, to help you and
hearten you. I ignored the ooze. I called attention to the
flowers I threw upon it. I gave you no staff and no rod. I
gave you nothing by which you might live. And when the
darkest hour came, I did not give you my hand, nor did I call
to you. You sat at my table, and I did not give you bread.
The table was set with vases and ancient vessels of beauty,
and I called your attention to the shapes and the colors of
them. But there was no water in them to quench your natural thirst, and no wine to inspirit you. I thought you could
live by form alone. And so, you sat there, and one by one
you died. And the light went out, and I was alone in the
darkness."

They listened. Some thought the darkness drifted into the
room like mist, obscuring faces, changing them. Some thought
the room was filled with dying men. They looked at the professor, and it seemed to them that he was all lamentation
and despair, all misery and agony.

"And so," he said, in that strange, but penetrating and
whispering voice, "the darkness spread over Germany. And
now it is spreading over the whole world. Men like me
watched it spread. We saw the lights go out, one by one. We
did nothing. We thought to ourselves: 'It will pass.' But it is
not passing. It is growing thicker and thicker. And those
who should have lighted it had only empty lamps in their
hands. We sent you out with empty lamps! We drove you

into the darkness without a single taper to guide you, without a single call to bring you home!"

His voice had risen. It had become a cry. The students shivered. Some of them uttered faint strangled sounds. But some shot to their feet, crying out savagely: "You are a traitor! You are an enemy of the new Germany! Heil Hitler!"

Instantly confusion prevailed. The turmoil in the hearts of the young men became visible in their contorted, moved, or enraged faces. Many shouted to their fellows in uniform: "Sit down! Take off those swastikas! Be quiet!" Some leaped to their feet and began to strike out with dull blows. Others, terrified or infuriated, struggled to reach the doors, shouting. Cries of "traitor!" "Herr Professor!" "Down, you dogs!" echoed through the great room. Others cried: "He is not finished! Let him speak! Speak, Herr Professor!" And then, fainter and deeper, there were groans of "My God! O my God!"

But Herman watched it all with blind eyes. He swayed a little as he stood on his lonely platform in the midst of that wild and gasping confusion. He had opened the Book. He was looking for a place. It was his awful preoccupation, the tears on his face, his fumbling hands, his bowed head, which brought momentary and suspended order into that room. The young men at the doors, flushed, uniformed and infuriated, paused, and looked back over their shoulders. The young men in their seats leaned forward, the better to listen and see. Dust rose from the floor, choking, turned to gold in the ominous sunlight. And now again there was intense silence.

He looked up. He held out his arms to them. He smiled at them with love and sadness and tenderness.

"I must go away now. I must leave you. I must wait for the death your murderers and your destroyers will prepare for me. But I have this last word for you. Go out, and remember that you can light the empty lamps I have given you. You, by taking thought, by simplicity and fortitude, by hope and faith, by fearlessness and courage, by gentleness and compassion, can save Germany yet, can save the whole world. It is in your hands to do this thing. It is my punishment that I cannot. But I shall leave you with some consolation if I know that you will set your hands against madness and fury, against hatred and oppression, against cruelty and tyranny, against all the spirits of evil which have broken down the gates and have entered the city.

"You must be prepared to fight to the end, and to die. Your work is before you, stern and dreadful. It can end only in agony and death. But you will know that your deaths will be like a fire on a high hill, helping to lead others home, and to peace. That is all I can leave you now: this hope, and all my love, and all my prayers for you."

He lifted the book. He began to read. His voice was like a great strong wind blowing through the echoing halls of the ages from the lips of a man who had never died, and whose spirit wandered forever among the spirits of men:

"Even the youths shall faint and be weary and the young men shall utterly fall, but they that wait upon the Lord shall renew their strength; they shall mount up with wings as eagles; they shall run and not be weary; and they shall walk and not faint."

Every man listened, and to many it seemed that the words sounded like a trumpet, a promise, and a deliverance. All of them, in spite of themselves, were inexpressibly moved. The words were written in fire, invincible and unquenchable, powerful and singing.

He closed the book. He looked at them all, and all his heart and soul was in his eyes, all his pleading. He lifted his hands as though to give them a blessing.

"God be with you, and keep you," he said, and there were tears in his eyes.

They were silent. Some of them wept openly. Some of them extended hands to him. The young men at the doors hung their heads. He stepped down from the platform, and moved towards a door. The uniformed students hesitated.

And then, one by one, as though ashamed, they fell back, and he went out alone.

19 THERESE had not even approached the environs of the University since Eric Reinhardt's death, though before that she had been a frequent visitor. There was so much there of sanctity, age, urbanity, wisdom, peace and promise, so much of hope and tranquillity. She had seen the libraries of New York, Washington, Paris and Vienna, but the library at this University, even allowing for the partisanship of a national, seemed to her to be vastly superior. Everything that was good in Germany, the very soul of Germany, was in those quiet corridors, the lofty still rooms armored with books. No matter what storms raged in the souls of men, here was sanctuary, here was the voice of enduring greatness.

But today, it was like a house of pestilence to her, a mockery of health and life, a graveyard. The voices of the dead stood mute on their shelves, and there were holes in their ranks, burned out by the fire of hatred, ignorance and bestiality. Heine, Wasserman, Mann: they were absent, and so many more! All at once, even in her distraction, there rose the fierce hope in her that some day Karl would be so honored by his absence, and that in the public squares the Germany of today would pay him the supreme honor of burning his books! In that way the very soul of his writings would ascend to heaven, would blow over the world, impregnating the minds of men with immortal ashes of thought and nobility. She thought of the funeral pyres of the past, both of men and books. How their incandescence had lighted the dark places of the world with everlasting flame, showing the pits and caverns, and the bridges of progress winding thinly over the abyss! Only by heroic death, selfless, pure and unafraid, could the masses of confused mankind find their way, safely and strongly, to the fields of peace. "Greater love hath no man . . ." Through her exhausted and incoherent thoughts, it was strange how often these days the quotations of her father (who had been so banal, so gross, so inept and so stupid) would cry out like trumpets. Perhaps it was because not even the tarnish of selfish, narrow and circumscribed minds could forever blacken the shining silver of truth.

She waited in the library, feeling that here was not life, but death. She waited for Kurt Erlich. She remembered, with loathing, that he was a member of the Party. He might be able to help Herman Muehler. She had left Elizabeth Muehler more composed, after that one heart-breaking and agonized cry. Strange, the composure and fortitude of the British! Once, she had believed they came from lack of imagination. Now, she believed they came from some rocky core that could not be shaken.

The library was dim and hushed. She sat in a leather chair, watching the doorway, unconscious of the bent heads of students at distant tables. An old man entered uncertainly, shadowy in the dusk. His steps were faltering; he peered about him, fingering his spectacles. He was bent and tired, and moved as though he could barely see. There was an air about him of distraction and hopelessness, of engrossment with private suffering and despair. Therese watched him with sympathy. Suddenly, a shock forced her upright in her chair, her heart beating with dread and fear. For she saw that the old man was Kurt Erlich.

Incredulous, disbelieving, she stared at him. What a dreadful change had taken place in the burly and vital man! She could hardly recognize him. Even when he saw her, and came towards her, smiling a little, she repudiated his identity. She had not seen him since that night he had visited her home, demanding to see his brother. That had not been so long ago— surely, O God! not more than a week or so ago! But years had passed over him in the interval. His flesh had shrunk, his hair whitened. Furrows were cloven deep in his gray, fallen face. His clothes hung upon him like the clothing of a scarecrow. About his watery and blinking eyes were wrinkles of suffering and sleeplessness. His shaking lips were dry and colorless. He had not shaved recently; she saw the glimmer of silver on his sunken cheeks, his bony chin.

"Kurt!" she gasped, staring at him with distended eyes.

He sat down beside her. The mere effort of walking had made him breathless. In his left temple there was a large bruised spot, purple and suffused. She saw it. The horrible sickness so familiar to her lately struck at her heart. Her legs relaxed suddenly with it, and she could taste salt in her mouth.

"Kurt!" she gasped again, and closed her eyes against the sight of him.

He leaned towards her, and took her hand. "Therese," he said. His voice was hoarse. His breath in her face was fetid, like the breath of the dying. She had a sudden paralyzing fear that she would be sick, right there before him, in the library. She struggled to control herself, to still the tremors of her revolted stomach. She swallowed the flood of salt water in her mouth. Her leaden face was covered with a film of cold sweat.

She forced herself to open her eyes. Everything swam before her. She tried to smile. For a moment she had forgotten, in her extremity of physical illness, why she had come. She forced herself to remember, forced herself to shut out his face, his dying aspect.

"Kurt, something dreadful has happened." Her whispered voice could hardly be heard. "They have arrested Herman Muehler—they said he was a Communist—subversive. I do not know. But you can do something, Kurt?"

He bent his head. She saw his skull through his whitening hair. It gleamed a little through the dusk. She saw that it was bony and narrowed. The veins pulsed in his sunken temples, as though he were enduring physical agony. His jaw had dropped open, like the jaw of the dead. This gave him a preoccupied but somewhat imbecile expression.

"What can I do?" he whispered in return. But he seemed to be speaking to himself, and not to her. She seized his arm. She was horrified, even then, at the thinness of it, through his clothing.

"But you are a member of the Party! You can surely speak. They will listen to you? You know Herman well. You know he is no Communist. He has been often at your home. . . . Kurt, you must do something!"

He looked at her from the caverns of his eyes. "I know nothing," he whispered. "I know nothing at all." All at once a wild thin fierceness animated him. "Nothing at all!" He put his trembling hands to his temples. "I have never known anything! Now, I do not want to know!" He seemed galvanized with terror. "Go away, Therese! Let me alone. I can stand no more."

A moment before she understood she exclaimed: "How can you be so base!"

And then, looking into his nightmare-dull eyes, looking

into his dying-man's face, she understood. The horror had him too. Realization had not brought him clarity. It had brought him frenzied insanity and despair. It was a man *in extremis* who glared back at her blindly. He was not seeing her; he was seeing the Thing she saw in these unspeakable days. He had awakened, like a thousand, thousand others, only to be unable to bear the light of understanding, only to die, not by violence, but only by horror.

She fled from him, as one flees from a corpse. She heard a whimpering sound behind her: "Karl? My brother?" Her feet carried her like wings. She reached the shining afternoon light. She breathed deeply. Her heart was rolling in her chest. She stumbled down the stairs. She was impelled by the wild conviction of pursuit. She reached her car, and literally fell in it. The chauffeur watched her intently as he closed the door.

There was nothing, now, that she could do for Herman Muehler. She was certain of it. But slowly, as her heart and her terror calmed, she began to cast about for help.

There was the General! He was still Germany. He was still potent. She would go to him. She glanced at her watch. It was almost evening. She would go to him tomorrow. In the meantime, she would return to Elizabeth Muehler, and give her what comfort and hope she could.

The car stopped. She was at her tomb of her home. She looked at it in the evening sunlight. All at once, she could not endure it. She tapped on the window. "Frederick, I did not want to come home. Drive me at once to the Muehler house."

20 WHEN THERESE was admitted to the home of the General, with Frau Professor Muehler, she was informed that the Frau General was not at home, but that the General was "at work" in the garden. The two ladies seated themselves, and waited for the old man to enter the gloomy, blue-misted drawing room to receive his guests.

The late summer air was warm and golden outside, and faintly smoky, but here in the drawing-room there was a dank and stifled chill. Therese shivered. The chill entered her tired and aching bones. She glanced at Herman's wife. The Frau Professor sat in silence, in a sort of white, stony calm, her eyes a little glazed and fixed. While Therese watched her, she lifted a white handkerchief to her lips and dabbed them delicately, and then resumed her posture of unhurried waiting. Therese marvelled at such composure. She remarked to herself that the poise of other Europeans was the result of long and painful effort, but the poise of the British was part of their nature, which fire and flood and death and horror could not shake, though they might destroy. At another time, earlier than this, she might have thought such composure a sign of cold heartlessness. So Germans thought, and the French, and others. But Therese, whose prescience was so quickened these days, knew what anguish lay behind that repose, what utter despair stood in speechlessness behind those unhurried eyes.

She wanted to offer consolation, but in the face of that hard and motionless quiet words of sympathy were abashed. However, she knew that there was more than quiet there; there was also the rockbound strength before which more volatile, more vehement, more hysterical peoples were helpless. She did not like the Englishwoman more for her insight into her nature; but she admired her profoundly.

To any other woman at such a time she would not have said what she said now: "My cousin's house is the most dismal place in the world."

The Frau Professor glanced about her quietly. She even smiled a little.

"But I like it. It reminds me of the English houses."

Therese looked about the room. She had always despised it, and had been amused at it. But all at once it seemed inexorable, immovable, a shelf of rock in a tilting world. The heavy walls and massive furniture were a promise of solidity and succor. They repudiated agony, calmed hot despair. So long as houses like this remained in Germany, she could not go entirely mad.

The General came in, charging into the room like a bald mammoth. He looked less formidable today, for he wore a white woollen shirt and a pair of huge old gray trousers. His pink face streamed with sweat, which he kept wiping with a handkerchief like a small tablecloth. It was evident that he had been exercising. The whites of his eyes were suffused, and the motionless air of the drawing room shook about him like heat waves.

"Ah, Therese," he roared, pleased and surprised. Coming from the bright sunshine, he did not at first see the other woman, sitting like a stiff statue in the dimness. He had eyes only for Therese, and he blinked at her. He wiped the pleasure from his face when he saw her own. "My dear, Karl is not worse?"

"No, General, he is not worse," said Therese, giving the old man her hand. He kissed it with an air of relief. He said: "Martina is not home. She is gadding again. Where do you women gad?"

"Oh, everywhere. Anywhere." Therese smiled slightly. "But I did not come to see Martina, General. I came to see you."

"Me?" He was delighted, but somewhat bewildered. "How can a lovely girl like you waste her time on an old man?" But he bridled. It was then that he saw the other woman. "Frau Professor!" he exclaimed. He blinked.

Therese laid her hand urgently on his arm. "General, we have come to you for help. Something terrible has happened. The Gestapo has taken Doctor Muehler into something they call 'protective custody.' We came to you because you are the only one who can help us."

He stared, astounded. His great fleshy underlip pushed in and out. His eyes started. "Muehler? Impossible. What for? Are they mad? What has he done? Herman!"

"We do not know. They would not tell us. They merely

said something about 'subversive activities,' and 'treason against the State.' We do not even know where he is, but they must have taken him into custody either at the University or while he was on the way home. They said, at the University, that he left at 11 o'clock, which is extremely unusual, except when he has been ill."

The General was appalled. He was also infuriated! "The cattle! The swine!" He clenched his fists until they resembled red rocks. "Are they mad?" he repeated, incredulously. He swung about to the Englishwoman. Her calm and quietness reassured him, made him uncertain. A woman in such a situation should have been prostrated, broken. But there the cool fish sat regarding him without emotion. He scratched the back of his thick scarlet neck. "But, is it so bad, Frau Professor? Perhaps our Therese is a little—unnerved?"

The pale fixed lips of the Englishwoman parted. She said: "It is very bad, General." And then he saw her eyes. He had seen eyes like these in the faces of dying men on the battlefield. They affrighted him, filled him with terror and vicarious suffering.

"Oh, we cannot permit this!" he cried involuntarily. He began to tug at his knitted shirt. "We shall go at once! We shall drag him out of their hands! We shall slap their faces, the dogs!"

He panted. His great face turned crimson. His little eyes were blue lightnings. He literally ran out of the room, shaking the floor as he went.

"You see," said Therese to Herman's wife. The Englishwoman's marble face relaxed. A faint color came into it. "Thank you," she said softly. And then, to Therese's grief, she began to cry soundlessly, and proudly. She dabbed at her eyes. But her attitude made it impossible for Therese to go to her and comfort her.

In an amazingly short time the General returned. Therese stared at him blankly. He was in full uniform, medals, sword, helmet and all. He had not worn this particular field uniform for a long time. His girth had increased, and the gilded buttons strained across his middle. But he was formidable again, and as imposing as a heroic statue of stone. The spike glittered on his helmet; the ancient eagles above his thick white brows gleamed with majesty. He was the Emperor-King of Lohengrin. He was a Viking. He was Thor and Odin. He was Germany, repudiating a mongrel horde of yapping jackals. Even

Therese, who was always a little amused by him, was awed. There was a sound about him like invisible trumpets. His military cape hung from his gigantic shoulders, carved and heavy. He was no longer faintly ridiculous.

"Let us go," he said abruptly. His ancient car was waiting, tall, narrow, but polished. The footman and the chauffeur, seeing him in full dress as they had not seen him for many years, sprang out of the car and stood at attention, their old faces pulsing with pride and passionate emotion. He sat between the two women, his hands folded over the top of his great sword with its faded tassels. He stared straight ahead, not boisterous now, but gloomy and more than a little terrible. He did not seem to breathe. Vengeance, outrage and disgust had turned his red face to the color of gray granite. His waxed mustache bristled. But he said nothing.

They arrived at the Gestapo Headquarters. A measly little clerk was telling a group of prisoners' relatives that they could not see the Public Prosecutor, and that they were doing their sons, fathers, and husbands no good by their impudent insistence. The clerk had been a subaltern in the army. He was glorying now in his exalted position of being able to bully his betters. He beamed sadistically at the heartbroken women. He rubbed his feeble hands and almost crowed. At one time he had been drawn to the Communist Party. His hatred for those of distinction and blood was still manifest in his shining rodent's eyes.

The General strode ponderously into the bare office, his feet shaking the dusty boards. The weeping women fell back. The clerk stared, blinked. Then slowly he rose, and slowly, mechanically he saluted. He dropped his eyes. He was terrified. The General stood before him as a man stands before a cur.

"The Public Prosecutor, at once!" he said, in a tone which denied the manhood of the weasel before him. "General Siegfried von Heyliger, His Majesty's Field Marshal."

The clerk trembled. He bent almost double. He saluted again. "Yes, General, yes, yes, General!"

The General stood alone in the center of the room. The sobbing women were silent. Therese dared not approach him. He was looking about him with scorn and detestation. Then he saw the large posturing portrait of Adolf Hitler hanging on the wall, draped in swastikas. He was galvanized. His mighty body shook with rage and contempt. His eyes were outraged. His face swelled, became purple. In two steps he reached the portrait, looked into its eyes. There was something portentous, something frightful in his attitude. Then deliberately he withdrew his sword, cut the cords that held the portrait. It fell to the floor, and the glass shivered. He looked down at it. The mad eyes stared back at him, malevolent. He shuddered. Then he stepped upon the face. His booted heels ground the face to a mass of twisted paper. Then he stepped back, again shuddering as though he had touched something loathsome. His expression had in it horror and repulsion. It was as though he had had a glimpse of an unclean monster, and that even his act of destroying it had polluted his flesh.

The women fell silent. They could not look away. Their pale and tear-stained faces were transfixed. He stood there, not moving, standing on the fallen swastikas. Again he was Odin, in a shuddering triumph.

The clerk scuttled back into the room, panting. "The Public Prosecutor will see you at once, General!" he stammered, saluting and cringing. Then he saw the General, standing on the degraded flags. He saw the smashed portrait. He gasped aloud. But the General turned on him eyes so terrible that he quailed. He shank back, flattening himself against the wall. The General, followed by his two women, passed him without another glance. The other women, affrighted, slunk from the room.

The Public Prosecutor, in the dread uniform of the Gestapo, rose, smiling courteously. He was a quick, lithe, middle-aged man with a fox face. He saluted smartly, came from behind his desk and drew out a chair for the General. He ignored Therese and the Englishwoman. "What an honor, General!" he murmured.

But the General did not sit down. He surveyed the other man with fiery contempt. He held his sword in his hand.

"I demand the immediate release of Herr Professor Herman Muehler," he bellowed.

The Public Prosecutor's smile faded. His pale eyes narrowed. He scrutinized the General intently. Then he glanced at the women.

"Are these ladies interested in this case, General?"

The General fumed like an enraged bull. "I do not introduce ladies to men of your class, Herr Prosecutor!" When he spoke the title it was with an emphasis of cold affront and disdain.

Therese was alarmed. This was the wrong way to approach this man, she thought. Now he would be angered. To her surprise, however, he smiled with amusement. He regarded the General almost with indulgence. Then he bowed ceremoniously.

"General, my father was one of your favorite officers. Major von Stedtreiter. I am Fritz, his second son."

The General's eyes bulged until they resembled protruding blue-veined marbles. Under his huge white mustache his lips parted blankly. "Eric von Stedtreiter! It is impossible! He would have no son who so degraded himself!" But it was evident that he was disturbed. He finally sat down, stiffly, a monument of a man, with his hands on his sword.

The Prosecutor lithely came from behind his desk again, and offered the two ladies chairs. They sat down. Therese had taken great heart. She made herself catch the officer's eye, and smiled at him sweetly. He visibly quickened, and shot a bold look at her. Quite inspired, then, he returned to his desk.

The General, still taken aback, mumbled, with a wave of his hand: "This lady is my cousin, Frau Doctor Erlich. Perhaps you have heard of her husband? The writer, Karl Erlich." It was evident from his surly, preoccupied tone, that some virtue in him was shaken from its base.

"Karl Erlich! Ah, who has not heard of Germany's greatest artist!" The Prosecutor bowed deeply to Therese, who smiled again. A faint dimple appeared at the corner of her mouth. The man must be placated. It must become a cosy affair, this, to assure the safety of Herman Muehler. "And the brother, is he not, of Herr Professor Kurt Erlich? Who does not know such men!"

"And the other lady—this is Frau Professor Muehler, wife of the gentleman you have in your custody," muttered the General. He drew a deep breath. He had paled, and there were beads of sweat beginning to drip from under his helmet. Suddenly, he could control himself no longer. He burst out in a fury: "But what are you doing, you son of Fritz von Stedtreiter, the bearer of his name, in this rathole? What are you doing in this nest of that Austrian gutter mouse?" He shook his head. "I cannot believe it! It is too disgusting to believe."

The Prosecutor was not affronted. His amiable smile grew broader. "General, this is another day. The old regime is dead. Pardon me, allow me to finish. Germany has begun again. She is climbing the stairs to the light. What does it matter what heads she uses as stairs?" He was a volatile man, and his mood changed, became respectful, but somewhat stern. "I must repeat, this is another day, General. But we are not inhuman monsters, in spite of Jewish lies. We seek only justice. And so, I am at your service, and I can assure you that I shall do anything in my power to assist you in this deplorable affair."

"What 'deplorable affair'?" demanded the General, irately. "You talk like a fool." His thought veered. "Were you not in the army, also?"

"Yes. You shook hands with me once, and congratulated me on my regiment." He smiled, as though at some past childishness.

"And you are here, in this place!" muttered the General, helplessly. His flesh was the ghastly color of quicksilver.

"I am at your service, General," repeated the other. He touched a bell. Two young men in the uniform of the Storm Troopers entered the room. "Bring me the dossier of Herman Muehler," he said. While they waited, he looked at the Englishwoman intently. "I believe you can assist us a little in this, Frau Professor. And I can assure you that only by being frank with me can you help your husband. Tell me: did he take an active part in the Communist Party, or was he merely a passive member?"

The General snorted violently, but the Englishwoman, composed though she was, showed every indication of bewilderment and indignation.

"The Communist Party? That is absurd. Herman despised the Communists."

The officer raised his brows. His air implied that he was merely gently amused and impatient at an obvious and very crude lie. "You are mistaken, Frau Professor. We have his dossier. He was one of the first important Berlin members of the Communist Party. He entertained prominent members in his own home. We have it in his dossier."

Now, for the first time, Therese saw the Englishwoman's composure crack. Her pleasant and sensible face turned white, not with fear or confusion, but with honest anger. She became rigid in her chair. Her eyes flashed.

"And I tell you, Herr Prosecutor, that that is a lie! A vicious lie! From the very first my husband expressed his revulsion for the Communists." She had difficulty in getting her breath, so intense was her indignation. "I am British, Herr Prosecutor, of an old family. Herman, even had he wished, which is ridiculous, would not have insulted me by bringing such creatures into my house."

The Prosecutor was silent. He drummed thinly on his desk.

And then Therese knew. It was no use. They were determined to torture and kill Herman Muehler. They would tack all sorts of lies upon him, to justify their monstrous deeds. Denials meant nothing. They were determined to do this thing. An enormous sickness struck at her heart, and she grew faint.

The troopers returned with the dossier, and then, as at a signal, they stood behind the Prosecutor, who delicately began to turn pages. "Ah, here it is. In full. He has been under investigation for a long time. But we hesitated, out of sheer magnanimity, to arrest him, hoping he would finally be convinced of his errors. It is not necessary to tell you the full contents of this report. But it is here. However, we should have done nothing, except perhaps warn him, had it not been for what he did yesterday."

He closed the cover of the dossier with a slapping sound, and looked at them cruelly. He no longer pretended to any sly friendliness. "Frau Professor. If you wish to help your husband, you must tell me the truth. You must tell me the names of some of the Communist leaders who infested your house. We can get nothing from your husband, who continues to lie. But I will tell you what I will do: I will put in a recommendation for leniency for him if you, yourself, will give me the names."

The Englishwoman looked at him with filmed eyes. "I do not know any names," she said. She whispered this. She could not speak aloud, so great was her anguish. Her hands visibly trembled. "He told you the truth. I am telling you the truth now."

He shrugged, as though regretful of such obstinacy.

The General could no longer control himself. He struck his sword upon the desk. "What is this? What are you trying to get this poor woman to say? Do you want her to lie? Do you want her to incriminate innocent people?" His great face swelled, turned purple with apoplectic blood. "Enough of this infernal nonsense! I demand the release of Herman Muehler immediately, and I warn you now, you shall suffer for this outrage!" He inhaled, and his breath came like a dying wheeze. "What has happened to Germany? I cannot understand."

Alarmed, Therese rose and put her hand on his shoulder. He shook it off, violently. "Go away, Therese. Sit down. I cannot believe this! It is beyond my comprehension. It is a nightmare!" He struggled to his feet. "Where is Herman Muehler? Bring him to me at once, and I shall take him home with me. I am General Siegfried von Heyliger, the personal friend of the President. If I am delayed another moment, it will be worse for you, you renegade son of Fritz von Stedtreiter!"

The Prosecutor did not rise. Instead, he lifted his eyes to the General, and they were gleaming with amused malignity. He no longer pretended to friendliness and junior-officer respect. His foxlike face became evil and vicious.

"General," he said coldly, "when will you and your kind learn that your day is done in Germany? When will you learn that you in part are guilty of Germany's condition? You and your rigid 'honor,' your pettifogging, childish inadequacy, your silly 'codes,' your arrogance, domineering insolence! This is a new day, and unless you keep your mouth shut, unless you conform and cooperate, or, at least, keep out of the way, we shall deal with you as though you were no more than a common criminal. The Army! The Junkers!"

His face was full of pale and livid malevolence. And contempt. He spat to the side, resumed his glazed and wicked staring at the old soldier. He could hardly conceal his exultation, his hatred, his ecstasy at the General's dreadful humiliation. Behind him, the troopers grinned impudently.

Therese was prepared for anything. She was prepared to see the General strike the younger man. She was even prepared to see him run through. But she was not prepared for the expression of appalling illness which spread over the old man's shaking flesh. She was not prepared to see him overcome with such dreadful horror. She was not prepared for that look in his eyes. And then she knew that he understood. She knew he saw, not the Prosecutor, but a frightful vision. The old man, stupid, hidebound, fierce, rigid and uncompromising, without imagination, now had a vision. He was paralyzed before it. He was dying before it.

The Prosecutor repeated exultantly: "Your day is done! Sit down, General!" His voice rose to a mad pitch. He made the "General" sound like an obscene epithet, full of jeering and unclean innuendo. And the General stood before him, his uniform seeming all at once to be too large for him, and wrinkled, covered with fungi, its buttons tarnished, its epaulets drooping, its sword rusty, its helmet absurd. His cloak hung about him, and it was the cloak of Don Quixote, mildewed and ragged.

His flesh knew these things; his soul knew them. His majesty was gone. Germany was gone. The whole world was going. It had made majesty and heroism contemptible, fit only for the laughter of rabble. It had exalted brutishness and coward-ice, dishonor and ignominy. It was the canaille on the steps of the Louvre, the Roman rabble at the gates of the Palatine. It was the galloping of asses among marble columns. And before that galloping the marble pavement cracked, and the stench of manure drowned out the odor of incense.

So must the General's soul have known. It was not the Prosecutor's words which were killing him. It was the thing he was seeing.

The General sat down. His eyes were glaucous. A piteous trembling shook his body. The sword lay at his feet, unnoticed, forgotten.

Therese stood beside the old man. He did not feel or see her hand on his shoulder. She was overcome with her sadness and despair. She had forgotten Herman Muehler. Herman's wife was weeping, not loudly, but silently, her tears streaming down her face. And the Public Prosecutor watched them with sadistic glee. There was a mad gleam on his face. Behind him, the troopers waited, like wolves.

The Prosecutor lightly flipped the pages of the dossier, satisfied at last at what he had done. His voice, cold, thin, but harsh, reached the dim ears of the women.

"I will be completely frank with you. There is nothing you can do. Either you, or this—the General. Nothing. You can appeal directly to Papa Hindenburg himself. He can do nothing. You can appeal to all your friends, to von Blomberg, to Goring. They can or will do nothing. You see, I wish to save you time and misery, and false hopes." He grinned. The mad gleam brightened on his face. He clenched his fists and beat them on the dossier. "Because such criminals as this Muehler must be stamped out. Destroyed. They are a danger to Germany, and are her enemies."

He looked at Therese. She gazed back at him, calmly, silently, her gray eyes shining and very still. For a moment he was abashed by her look, by her beauty which had become the beauty of a slender bared sword. No matter what he might do or say, he could not tarnish that shiningness. For some curious reason, he wanted her to believe he had some justice on his side. He frowned.

"I owe you no explanation, Frau Doctor Erlich. But you seem to expect one. I will give it. On Monday, this Communist criminal stood before his class, and incited them to riot, to treason. He urged them to help destroy the new Germany. He was overheard by a loyal teacher, who was standing by the door. The teacher called witnesses. They were horrified by what they heard. They went and called the Gestapo. Before the criminal had been able to run twenty yards from the University, he was taken prisoner. I cannot tell you where he is, now. But I can tell you there is no hope for him, because of the things he caused to happen."

Therese said, coldly and scornfully, her tone denying everything he had told her: "And what did this poor man cause to happen?"

He stared at her with admiring animosity. Then he simulated anger and righteous fury: "That night, over twelve of his students attacked some Storm Troopers who had just arrested a filthy Jew. They were armed. Two of the Troopers were shot. Fortunately, a crowd gathered, and began to beat the students. But they kept up their treasonable shouting. So some of the crowd, poor misguided wretches, attacked the Troopers. Two were shot, and one was beaten to death. Then the police took a hand, and the rioters were arrested. Besides the students, nearly fifty civilians were taken into custody." He paused, and added weightily: "So your Communist professor caused the death of fourteen persons in the streets. More arrests were made that night, of students. Therefore, sixty people are now in custody, and of this number nearly half will be executed. The rest will be shipped to concentration camps." Again he paused, then went on in a sepulchral voice. "You can see, now, that your friend is a murderer, and that whatever he suffers will not cover a fraction of what he did."

Therese listened. Her limbs became stone cold. Her eyes shone like bitter ice. But the Englishwoman had stopped her weeping. She was gazing steadfastly at the officer. She began to speak so quietly, so unemotionally, that Therese started violently as at a strange sound.

"There have been times, since my marriage, when I have thought I had made a mistake, and that I had imagined the promise I saw in my husband at first. But now I know I have not made a mistake."

She stood up. She turned to Therese, with such calm, such pride, such composure, that Therese could only stare at her blindly.

"We are wasting our time, my dear. Let us go."

Before that courage, that steadfastness and strength, Therese's impotent despair slunk away. She hesitated. But the Englishwoman's eyes, so bright, so tranquil, so strong, gave her fortitude. She bent over the General, who had been sitting like granite, unmoving.

"It is all over, General," she said, gently. "Let us go."

He started. He looked at her with his glazed, unseeing eyes. He tried to get up. He was an old, broken man, visibly disintegrating. She had to summon all her strength to help him get to his feet. She could feel the rigid tremors rippling over his great shattered body. But he obeyed her like a numb sick child. The Englishwoman went to his side, and assisted Therese. The old man took a few feeble steps; his monumental head fell on his breast. They left the room, holding him between them. His cloak had slipped from one shoulder, and trailed behind.

The Public Prosecutor watched them go, smiling evilly. He began to laugh, throwing himself back in his chair. He laughed and laughed, striking the desk before him savagely and gleefully. The Troopers snickered.

Then the officer saw the General's sword, lying on the floor by the chair where he had been sitting. His laughter stopped abruptly. He got up, and lifted the sword. It was heavy and ponderous in his hands. The sunlight glittered on its edge. But along its length there were faint rusty spots, like dried blood.

It lay in his two hands, the faded tassels drooping. Its carved hilt glittered. It was ancient. And useless. Its day was done. But there it lay, mighty and potent, and all at once it was no longer useless, but a symbol.

The officer stood so still, like that, with the great long sword in his hands, that the Troopers became uneasy.

That night, as Therese sat alone in her dark unlighted drawing-room, unable to abstract any warmth from her dim red fire, she was called to the telephone. It was Frau Professor Muehler. Her voice, assured, quiet, passionless and tranquil, came to Therese's ear, without faltering, and without grief.

"Therese, my dear. I just wanted to tell you that Herman is quite safe. Quite safe. They have just sent me a box. His ashes. And now I will go back to England. There are so many there that must be told. Told so many things, Therese!"

IT WAS STRANGE, thought Therese wearily, how so many of the Biblical phrases (so trite, so tiresome and so childish she had once thought them), came with ominous pertinence to her mind these days. Now one tolled heavily in her thoughts: "All thy waves and thy billows have rolled over me."

21

I can stand no more, she told herself, but all the time she was girding herself, bracing herself, for the more her prescience told her was to come. There was no end to it. There was no end to the dreadfulness that had gripped her husband. He was the specter that haunted her gloomy house, whose whispering footsteps echoed overhead, who was not there when she sought him out. When she sometimes passed him in the halls he would look at her blindly without seeming to see her, and she had come to the state where she allowed him to pass her, not speaking. Sometimes she said to Doctor Traub: "It is hopeless. He has died." But the doctor would shake his head and say: "Patience. Patience, liebchen. You can only stand, and be ready. For surely he will find his tortuous way back. He must not find you absent when he does."

So, she waited, hopelessly, sorrowfully, her only comfort the warm kind hands of Felix Traub and Helena. She went to them very often, sometimes every day, and they spoke simply and sympathetically, taking her into the garden and walking with her. "Patience," they said, knowing that she was one of them as she had never been before. "Patience," said their staunch old house and the fires that were being lighted in the golden early autumn, with its mists and mellow trees and brightening hills.

One day, as she sat alone at luncheon, old Lotte came in, with a card. Therese took it listlessly. She was not receiving visitors. But she was surprised when she read the name: "Madame Henriette Cot." The smart French proprietress of a chain of Berlin beauty salons, one of which, the smartest, Therese had once patronized. She knew the Frenchwoman

205

only slightly, and did not like her, though she had been condescendingly pleasant to her.

"How strange," she murmured. Was it possible that the woman was calling to see her about her long absence?

She said, "Lotte, please tell Madame Cot I am not receiving any visitors. My husband is ill."

Lotte set her hands on her broad hips. "I told her so, Frau Doctor. But it was no use. She was very urgent. She seemed quite agitated."

Therese frowned. "I hardly know her. How very extraordinary. Why should she come to me?"

She hesitated. "I will see her," she said indifferently. She went into the cool dim drawing-room, so cold and unfriendly these sad days. The Frenchwoman rose nervously upon Therese's entry. Therese stood in silence, fingering the card, her manner forbidding.

"Frau Erlich!" said the woman. Her normally hoarse and affected voice broke.

"Please sit down," said Therese. Her sharpened senses detected the note of anguish in the other's voice. She sat near her, and waited, shrinking a little, her nostrils pinched against the exotic scent that floated from Madam Cot's person.

Madam Cot was a small, beautifully corsetted, buxom little woman, very smart, very chic, very dark, and extremely artificial. The typical beauty culturist. Her sallow face was exquisitely enamelled; her shining lacquered hair perfectly waved. She wore her usual black satin, and a pair of silver foxes. Her tilted hat was in the latest mode, her satin slippers revealing her small dainty feet. Her features were small and pert and vivid, her mouth heavily rouged, and her eyebrows beaded. She had sparkling black eyes, which resembled bits of black-currant jelly. Her only ornaments were a large diamond ring and the large platinum and diamond cross she always wore around her rather short plump neck. Her age might have been anywhere in the region from thirty-five to forty-eight. It was one of her many mysteries.

Today, she looked more than forty-eight. Under the enamelled mask agony peered out. The red lipstick could not conceal the withered pallor of the mouth beneath. Wrinkles sprayed about her gleaming eyes. She kept touching the cross at her throat.

She smiled. The smile was a ghastly parody of her professional smirk, hard, blank, effusive and servilely dignified.

Therese had always detested that smirk, seeing above the wide red lips with their shining teeth to the jetlike eyes with their knowing and merciless expression. The woman's eyes had reminded her of Maria's; they had the same cunning and malicious look. She had often idly wondered of what such a woman thought, if there were any human softnesses or vaguenesses behind the lacquered mask. She thought not. But how disconcerting to have to live with that inner personality! How distorted, how obscene, how dirty and vile the world must seem to such eyes and such a personality! Her dislike and impatience grew.

Madam Cot, who was the shrewdest and most calculating of women, saw Therese's aversion, concealed though it was by a film of polite formality. A dull color crept under the enamel and suffused her eyes. All at once those eyes filled with bitter and reluctant tears.

"Frau Doctor!" she stammered, and her daintily gloved hands extended themselves to Therese with unaffected and simple desperation. "You—I know you think it extraordinary that I have come to you, and wonder why I have come! But I have felt that I have known you for a long time—I do not know where to turn, or to whom to appeal. . . ."

Then Therese knew that here was a soul bewildered by anguish. The mask had cracked. The human face was contorted behind it. She dropped her gaze considerately to the diamond cross, now trembling visibly on the woman's breast.

"How can I help you?" she asked gently.

The woman fumbled in her glacé-kid bag, and withdrew her cobweb of a handkerchief. It was impregnated with her own scent-invention, "Cot 121." Therese recognized it, a heavy and sensual odor weighted with musk. She tried to conceal her growing aversion, though her delicate nostrils whitened and drew in again.

Madam Cot put her handkerchief to her eyes, to remove the scalding tears. Such women cried reluctantly. Their tears were blood and acrid salt.

You know of my husband, Frau Doctor? Henri Cot, the broker? You knew that he dealt in international banking stocks?"

Therese murmured noncommittally. She had not known.

The woman gave a hard and wrenching sob. "They—the Gestapo—had accused him of smuggling stock and currency into France. You know we—we were born in France, though are now German citizens? They—they said he did this to prepare for emigration, or to help some former clients of his— Jews. . . ."

Therese glanced up quickly. "You may be frank with me, Madam Cot. Did he help his Jewish clients?"

Madam Cot hesitated. A sudden malignancy glared in her eyes, then vanished. "Perhaps, Frau Doctor. I—I warned him. He told me nothing, however. There was a softness in him, at times, though only I suspected him. But—they could find nothing. They had only their suspicions. Because some of Henri's Jews were able to pick up deposits in London and Paris. How could he be so indiscreet, and he always so sensible, usually! So unpatriotic! I do not know. I, too, have my suspicions. At first I thought: 'He must bear his punishment. He is no true German, to help those abominable Jews.'" Her voice dropped to a whimper, and she regarded Therese with a sort of wild bewilderment and amaze: "So I told myself. And then I discovered—how childish it is!—that I still loved him!"

Therese was silent. She averted her eyes, before the sight of that open nakedness, that passionate emotion and despair. They were foreign to her; they embarrassed her. But she was truly deeply touched. She tried to remember if she had ever heard of Henri Cot. Yes, she remembered something, faintly. A hard, fat, black-eyed little man, suspected of duplicity, fraud, financial genius and crafty manipulation. Really a despicable person.

She said: "I am sure, Madam Cot, that the Gestapo's suspicions were without foundation."

The woman sobbed again, shortly, painfully. "That is of no consequence now, Frau Doctor. They imprisoned him. They took him to Dachau. That was six months ago. I have tried to see him. It is no use. I know only that he is alive because a released prisoner came to me and told me so. What misery and sorrow I have endured! What agony, what hopelessness! And then the man came to me and said: 'Madame Cot, your husband still lives, though they have injured him so severely that he is practically blind. For God's sake, secure his release before it is too late.'"

Therese uttered a compassionate and embittered cry. "I can believe anything of them," she said. "There is nothing that these monsters will not do."

The woman wrung her hands; there was a faint ripping sound as she twisted her kerchief in her simple frenzy.

"That is not all, Frau Doctor. The Gestapo questioned me. Then—they confiscated my own accounts. They—they turned over the management of my salons to—to Germans. I am now penniless, Frau Doctor. I have nothing. To live, I have been compelled to sell all my jewels, save these. Henri's famous library, and collection of Old Masters. My furniture, my house, even my clothing. I—I received a pittance for all these. . . ."

"Do you need money, shelter?" asked Therese, forgetting her aversion in her indignant sympathy.

Madam Cot wet her withered lips. She lifted her head. To Therese's surprised admiration, there was pride and even offense in the woman's jet eyes. She saw at once that to this woman acceptance of money was the supreme degradation. She would not hesitate to ask any help, no matter how arduous or dangerous, but money she would not ask. Therese could not understand such a perverted set of values.

"No, Frau, Doctor, I do not need money, yet. I wish only a little of what is mine. I wish only my Henri's release. So that we can live in peace again, as good and faithful National Socialists. You see, we voted for Herr Hitler. We were devoted to him." (It was evident that the unfortunate, and now servile creature, was hoping to gain favor in Therese's eyes, and re-establish herself as respectable.) "Henri gave such huge sums of money. He lived only for the Party. He said: 'Now is the time for the renaissance of the German spirit, the throwing-off of chains, the day of vengeance and national triumph.' You see, my Henri was a fanatical Nazi. I was concerned the most with my business. That was my sole interest. But Henri, though born in France, was a passionate German."

Therese's aversion and dislike had returned with redoubled force. She said coldly: "How extraordinary for you, who are French!"

To her surprise, the woman colored. Her eyes dropped. She fumbled in her lap. It was evident that she was overpoweringly embarrassed. She did not look at Therese as she stammered thickly:

"You can see how it is, Frau Doctor. We are good Germans, now. We are National Socialists. We have given large sums. When our friends criticized, we remonstrated with them. You Germans are often so tender-hearted. Many of our friends were disgusted and outraged at the treatment of those horrible Jews. Those ghetto Jews! How I loathe them! I said: 'They are not true Germans, these Jews. They deserve their punishment. They have ruined Germany.' "

"What gave you that amazing idea, Madam Cot?" asked Therese, with increasing coldness and dislike. "Besides, I take exception, personally, to your remarks. My husband's adopted brother was a Jew, and a truly noble man. I will not have him insulted in my house." She made a movement as though to rise and dismiss the woman.

The woman was silent. The color was hard and swollen in her face. She regarded Therese with a pathetic and animal despair; her lips shook. She bit the lower lip. And then tears rolled down her cheeks.

"Forgive me, Frau Doctor," she said, humbly. "I was not denouncing the real German Jews, the loyal German Jews. It is just the—the outlanders, the Jews who would not be Germans—that I have disliked so intensely. The Jews who remained individualistic, who held themselves aloof from Christianity, who would not be absorbed, who criticized and stood apart, and would not remain silent even if they could not agree. . . ."

There was a sudden sharp long silence in the room. Therese stared deeply into those swimming and fainting eyes, those agonized and hopeless eyes. Her own face showed her troubled understanding and quick compassion.

"I see," she said gently, at last. "You are Jewish, you and your husband, Madam Cot?"

The color deepened still more in the woman's quivering face, as though she were overcome with some intolerable shame. She clenched her hands together with a kind of savage fierceness. "We—we were born—half-Jews, Frau Doctor. But we were truly never one in heart with the obscenity of those inabsorbable Jews. We came at an early age to Germany. We became Germans. We have always been Germans! We love Germany, and all that is Germany. We love our Fuehrer. We are Christians, German Lutheran Christians. Pious devoted Christians. We are Jews no longer. We probably never were really Jews. That—that is what is so dreadful to us." She sobbed aloud. "And now, the house where I live is daubed with yellow! When I go upon the street, the people spit at me. They call me 'Jew!' My former friends, my patrons, will not see me. They avoid me. They pass me on the street without looking at me." She beat her palms together in an enraged frenzy and grief. "But I am no Jew! I repudiate the Jews! I am a German Christian! I hate Jews! I loathe them, and would not care if they all died!"

The despicable creature! thought Therese, her compassion leaving her. Her eyes sparkled with her disgust. She looked at the cross on the woman's breast. It was large, obvious. So this horrible woman had tried to conceal herself behind that gaudy bauble, shouting her repudiations! It was not to be borne with quietness. She could not keep the loathing from her voice when she said:

"Is that the reason you wear that cross constantly, Madam Cot? To alleviate suspicions that you are a Jew? To convince potential enemies that you are not a Jew?"

"No, no," stuttered the woman. But Therese knew it was true. Then all at once she was compassionate again, in spite of her disgust. What dreadful creatures we Gentiles are! she thought, to visit such degradation on another human being! This woman's shame is our shame. We are guilty. This woman has tried to destroy her soul, but she did it at our insistence. To placate us, to save herself from our monstrous cruelty and abominable savagery, she wore our symbol. She does not know that we have made that symbol a badge of infamy, destruction and hatred, ignorance and death.

"Forgive us!" she cried aloud, involuntarily, her voice a cry. "Forgive us for what we have done to you!"

The woman gaped at Therese's pale and working face.

"You have done nothing to me," she whispered. "You were always kind to me, Frau Doctor."

Therese could not restrain herself. She sprang to her feet. She began to walk up and down the room. But wherever she looked, she could not shut out the vision of that derisively winking cross. The cross of the heroic and gentle Jew, who had loved all men, had ached and suffered for all men, who had died on a cross of wood and torment, hoping only that he had lifted other sufferers from darkness and death! And now the reasoning and the compassionate, the gentle and the good, must repudiate that cross, denounce it, turn aside from it, because of the foul thing the wicked had made of it! It was too awful.

She stopped abruptly before Madame Cot. "Tell me, what can I do for you?" she asked, trying to control her shaking voice.

The woman, all her defenses gone, seized a fold of Therese's dress, and clutched it with both hands, as though she were drowning.

"Frau Doctor! You can help me. When your father died, another took his place in his church. Bishop Franz Althaus. You know him. I—I have learned that he was your godfather, and your father's closest friend. We—we are members of his congregation."

Therese was silent. She had not seen her godfather for over a year. She despised and detested him, though he had always been affectionate and solicitous of her. His wife was childless; he had regarded Therese as his own daughter. But she had avoided him more and more as the years passed, hating to accept his generous gifts on her birthdays and at Christmas. She had known all the time what he was, a bellicose and narrow man, greedy, pious, avaricious, unctuous, brutal and cowardly, without a truly magnificent emotion or a single human goodness. She had heard that he was highly regarded by the Nazis. He had been very fervent in his sermons about Adolf Hitler. He had exhorted his people to bow down before this foul anti-Christ, this madman, saying that God had sent him to save Germany. She had often read his sermons, widely and conspicuously published in the newspapers. But lately she could not read them. They were like a stench to her nostrils. This cross-decorated panderer to the destroyer of Christianity! This betrayer of human souls to their seducer and befouler! She had not thought even he could be so base, so contemptible.

She became aware, through the stress of her seething emotions, that Madam Cot had been speaking.

". . . and so, remembering how gracious he had always been to us, and how we were his most generous parishioners, giving large sums, and devoting ourselves diligently to the work of the Church, participating in all its activities, I went to him, asking for help for my Henri. It was very terrible. He listened coldly. Then he said he could do nothing, would do nothing, for a disloyal man like Henri. A man who had helped Jews. Then he said: 'But that is understandable. You are Jews. One can never trust Jews.' It was in vain that I expostulated that we were not Jews, but Christians. He only glared at me." The woman swallowed painfully. Torment and bewilderment dimmed her eyes. "That is not all. When I went to church for consolation, and hope in my sorrow, I found that my pew had been taken from me. I found that I must sit in a segregated corner, in the rear, far to one side, as though I carried pollution with me. And—and," her voice dropped to a whisper. "I—I found others there. A few—like me. I had not known these were Jews, too. They sat there, shivering and terrified. And our friends, with whom we had worked, whom we had visited, and whom we had entertained, either looked at us with contempt, as we huddled there, or ignored us as though we were beasts. As though we were not good Christians!"

She swallowed again, convulsively. "There were half-Jews there, quarter-Jews. One could not, with sense, consider them anything else but devoted Christians, much more zealous and pious than those who called themselves 'Aryans.' Why, some of them were even the most violent anti-Semites!"

Therese said: "A year ago, a month ago, I should have denounced such degradation. Now I know who are the real guilty."

But Madam Cot did no understand. She went on, whimpering: "Some of them were accompanied, in that segregated corner, by their 'Aryan' husbands and wives. It was not necessary that these Aryans sit there. But they did, boldly and palely, staring at our Bishop with such hatred and scorn! It was not Christian, Frau Doctor, to stare like that. I was the first to decry it. I said to one of these 'Aryan' wives: 'Why do you sit here, if you hate our good Bishop so?' And she looked at me with such eyes! 'To denounce him, to prevent him from forgetting! To avenge all of us!' And the other Aryans nodded. They were not afraid. It was only the Jews who were afraid. They kept their heads down, weeping."

Therese smiled strangely and whitely. "Then, there is still integrity and honor, even among us! There is still hope for us!"

The woman sobbed, not comprehending. "I do not think there is any real hope for us, Frau Doctor. But still, I have come to you. I thought perhaps you might intercede for Henri and myself, with your godfather. I thought you might persuade him to speak for Henri, to the Gestapo. He has such influence. They would release Henri at his word, in his custody. I thought perhaps you might speak to him, assuring him of our Christianity, our devotion to the National Socialist Party, our piety and zeal for the Church and for Germany. We are not Jews. We are German Christians."

Therese sat down. She regarded Madam Cot with a mingling of contempt, pity, and bitterness.

"You are really a despicable person," she said, in a low clear voice. "But I do not denounce you too much. We have made you so. I will go to my godfather, not just because of your private business, but because of ourselves." She added, gazing hard into the other's bewildered and shifting eyes: "I should not go, even now, however, if I were not assured in my heart that your husband has been helping Jews." She stood up. "Remain here. I shall go at once. Perhaps I shall have good news for you when I return."

"God bless you, Frau Doctor! I know you have a good Christian heart!"

Therese's pale mouth opened on a sigh of disgust. But she said nothing.

ON THE WAY to the Bishop's residence, Therese thought:

22

"There is no end to the baseness of human beings. There is no end to their horribleness, their fiendishness, their shamefulness and evil. What few feeble stirrings of conscience they possess are easily quieted by expediency, by slyness, by avarice and complete atavistic wickedness. Men delight in evil and darkness. They delight in cruelty and malice and brutality. They love to gloat over another's suffering. If there is a God, how can He endure us? From what pit of horror have we arisen? From what foul cesspool have we crawled?"

She felt as though she were suffocating. She drew in deep gasping breaths. She gazed through the windows of the car, blindly. It was early autumn. The sky was gray and overcast; the air was ashen. The houses marched gloomily side by side, like forbidding walls. A few dark leaves drifted from the trees, like cinders. The car paused for a clearing of traffic near a concert hall. Therese could faintly hear the doleful muttering of drums, the dolorous wail of flute and trumpet. Beethoven, mourning for a world that hated him, and for which he had only sorrow and compassion. It was the mourning of all the heroes, of all the martyrs, of the Christs and the angels, of God Himself. The vast mourning of an outraged Universe for the obscenity and the fury of men.

Food and a victim. That is all that men required. Food for their belly; a victim for their lust. Hitler knew this. That is why he was successful. This man was no man. He was an arch-fiend who understood mankind. He gave men food; he gave them a victim. That is why they were no slaves following him blindly, but satisfied and exultant monsters who loved him for what he had done for them. He had released their lusts. That was the secret of his growing power. The Christs told them they had souls. But they had no desire for souls. That is why they hated the Christs.

But there were a few. Surely, there were a few! The Traubs and the Muehlers. Only a handful of men. Would they save the city from the wrath of God? "Ten righteous men" would save the city. Were there ten to be found?

But the "ten righteous men" had deserted Germany. They had fled from her travail, from the march of the legions of hell. Were they not, as Doctor Traub said, more guilty than the monsters themselves?

Is there no hope for Germany? she asked herself with despair. Does the world not know what is happening here? Surely it must know. England, France, America—they must all know. Why did they turn their eyes aside? Did they not know, in their stubborn blindness, or their craft, or their greed, or their selfishness, or their lust, that in Germany was their own abattoir, their own Gethsemane? Did they not know that all mankind was climbing the Hill of Calvary, today in Germany? Surely they must know. But they were full of evil and malignancy, also. They refused to see that when one man was martyred all men were martyred. When a single grave was dug for an innocent, the grave was dug for all men. God would not be mocked. He was asking all men everywhere: "Where is thy brother?" And all men, in all the world, were replying with an ancient and terrible cynicism: "Am I my brother's keeper?"

For this, the mark of Cain was set on the brows of every man. The mark of Cain was set there for a thousand generations, not only for today. It would be washed away only by the blood and the agony of multitudes. No, God would not be mocked. The day of doom had arrived. A day of doom that would last a thousand years. There would be no peace for mankind. It had betrayed itself; it had betrayed God. The rumblings of vengeance could already be heard. God would not be mocked. The heavens were already red with His wrath.

The world said, looking on the madness and the violence and darkness of Germany: "It is not my business." But one of these days it would know it was its business, and its children would be heaped in the gutters, its blood would flow through countless streets, its dying hands would be lifted to fiery avenging heavens. And there would be no reply. England —France—America. They would pay for their smirking and cynical silence. They would pay, until every last innocent drop of blood was avenged, and every child comforted. They would pay until every last grave was at peace. This was justice. This was the law of Almighty God.

It did not matter what lofty sophistries men used to excuse

their delinquencies. They could speak of "natural if violent phenomena of social change," and "convulsions in governmental systems which must inevitably reach a certain subsiding mean," and all the other infamous smooth falsehoods. The frightful fact remained, inexorable and simple, that one man's agony was every man's guilt. A guilt _he_ must atone for by his own agony.

Therese had a sudden curious sensation as though she had burst some last brittle layer which had encased her. She was free! She saw all things. The awakening of which Doctor Traub had spoken had come. She was conscious of a strange resurgence of courage and fortitude, of sternness and resolution. For an instant she was aware of a blinding surge of ecstasy and complete understanding and ineffable peace.

The car came to a halt. She was before the Bishop's residence. Or rather, before his palace. She knew the house well. How well she knew it! She had spent her childhood and girlhood here. Karl had rescued her. There was the window of her bedroom, in the round white-stone tower at the left. How often she had sat there, by that rounded large window, looking down at the street, unawakened, restless, sensitive, selfish. When Karl had come, he had come like Prince Charming, awakening a sleeper, absorbed in her own tiny affairs. And then she knew, with mournful prescience, that she had never really awakened until now. She had failed Karl. All those years of their married life, she had failed him. She had helped bring him to his present pass. Sometimes she had surprised a puzzled look on his quiet face. She had not understood. Oh, let it not be too late! she prayed, still sitting in her car and staring at the palace.

The great polished bronze door was opened for her by a shining and meticulous butler. She had not been here for some months, really over a year. But the smell of the place was as she remembered, musty, waxy, dim and pious. She stood on the dim reflection of herself on the polished floor of the hall, while the butler respectfully, almost cravenly, took her furs. Yes, the Bishop was at home. He was in his study. "Do not bother to announce me," said Therese, curtly, walking across the acres of crimson carpet towards the study. She did not want to encounter the Bishop's wife, a sly, mealymouthed, hypocritically self-effacing woman who disliked her.

All the enormous thin windows were covered with stained glass, like a church. The wan light of the autumn day came through them, changed and lugubrious. The ceilings were vast and high, and frescoed, gloomily. The furniture lurked along the dimly painted walls, and there were shadows on the walls, ecclesiastical portraits of bishops in canonical robes. She could see the gleaming white of their garments, though their features were indiscernible. It was a gallery of impotent ghosts, sterile and without humanity. Nothing had been changed from her girlhood. She remembered her hatred for all these echoing rooms, all this dolorous splendor and somberness. She remembered the deathly smell of polished decay, furniture wax, airlessness, bitter sanctity. The shade of Jesus surely never came here. He would have smothered. As I smothered, she thought.

She stood by the tall carved door of the study. Her body tightened. So she had stood a thousand times, her father behind the door. She could even hear his voice, unctuous and rolling with platitudes that meant nothing, for the spirit behind them had never lived. From this vantage point, she could see the spectral curving of the shadowy staircase, winding through the gloom. There was not a sound, not the breath of moving air, not a single opening and shutting of a door. Every door was muffled. Even the street sounds were lost here. She might have been in a chapel full of corpses. On a far distant table, through a vista of great adjoining rooms, she saw a tall vase of white roses. She could smell them. They had the odor of mortality.

She knocked on the door. The sound echoed and re-echoed through the ponderous silence. A grave rich voice bade her enter. She pushed the door open on its velvety hinges. There was the tremendous room she remembered, darkly polished floor, scattered oriental rugs, heavy and enormous tables covered with cloths embroidered in crimson and gold and decorously heaped with religious volumes, more gold-framed portraits of dead bishops on the crimson walls, churchlike chairs covered with crimson plush and enhanced by curving golden arms, high, pointed stained-glass windows admitting purple, blue and scarlet light, and, at the end, a muttering fire beneath a black-marble mantel flanked by black marble columns. Near the fire was the Bishop's desk, huge, mahogany and polished, covered by a pile of neat paper, a huge Bible, a brass lamp, now burning with a far cold light. She could barely discern the Bishop in his black garments behind the desk. He might have been her father. Then all at once, she knew that he was indeed her father, just as the other had been.

She had thought his secretary might be there, and had hoped this, thinking it would give her a breathing space. But he was not there. The Bishop was alone.

She stood there, near the door, the wretched suffocating sensation gripping her throat. She was a young girl again, called to her father's study, and hating and fearing him desperately. The lamplight threw a far glimmer on her white face and faintly gleaming fair hair.

The Bishop stared at her, then rose. "Therese, my child, my dear! How delightful to see you!" His warm voice was warmer, enriched by years of good living and excellent wine. He stood beneath the large wooden cross on the wall behind him, over the fire. He was a huge stout man. But beneath that cross he was dwindled and mean.

Therese fixed her eyes on the Cross like a sleepwalker. She came towards it, rather than towards her godfather. Her eyes were distended. The pure and simple Cross, that men had so defamed, had made so the mark of anti-Christ, and everything that was shameful! She wanted to fall beneath it, mutely crying for pardon, mutely pleading for mercy. She felt her hand taken in a big hot grasp, felt something touch her cheek. But she could not take her eyes from the Cross. She sat down near the desk. Her eyes were filling with tears.

The Bishop, who had retired behind his fortress desk again, was concerned. "Therese! What is the matter, my dear? Is Karl ill again?" He leaned towards her, assuming an expression of anxiety.

"He has never been well," she murmured.

The Bishop made a clucking sound of commiseration, and shook his head. "You received my messages, my flowers, my books, Therese? I wished you to bring Karl to me. I might have given him a small measure of consolation, and hope. But he never liked me. So I could not intrude. You understand, Therese? It is man who must come to God. God cannot come to man."

Her eyes dropped from the Cross. She regarded the Bishop in a profound and breathless silence. Her eyes grew large and intent in her pale face. She saw him clearly, gross, enormous, fat, sleek and compact. He had a large and ruddy face, with three chins, which rested on a broad black bosom. He apparently had no neck. She saw his tiny brown eyes, alert, opportunistic, crafty and cold. He had a big bulbous nose, faintly shining with oil, a brutal, insensitive nose with the wide flaring nostrils of the coarse man. Beneath that nose was a wide thin mouth, viselike and colorless, a thread of divided flesh. Above all this was a low wide brow and graying cropped hair. He was a Prussian. His head was square and boxlike, like a bull's. His hands were curiously small, almost effeminate, pudgy and white. On one finger there gleamed a huge signet ring.

Her hatred swelled and rose in her like a consuming fire. Beads of moisture broke out on her upper lip. She clenched her hands fiercely, holding back the torrents of her disgust and hatred, and weary despair. She saw his sensuality, his greed, his avarice, his craftiness, and his all-encompassing coldness. He was Nero, in the livery of Christ.

"I thought," she said in a strained voice, "that it was your duty to bring God to men, to take Him into strange places, and speak His word in the slaughterhouse, and the houses of pestilence."

He stared at her blankly, and then with affront. He said, coldly: "Therese, your late revered father often complained of your impiety and lack of understanding, and irreverence. I did not believe it. Now you force me to believe it."

She did not answer. She lifted her eyes to the Cross again. She smiled a little wildly.

But he was truly fond of her. He could see her plainly now, in the light of the lamp and struggling daylight. He saw that she was extremely ill. Her delicate bones were visible under her thin facial flesh. Her hands were gaunt and trembling. Her sunken temples throbbed. She was still a young woman, but there was a shadow of gray at those temples, blending into the fair hair which he had always greatly admired. He saw the violet shadows under her too-bright eyes, and the pinched blue look of her nostrils.

"My dear child!" he exclaimed, in genuine concern. "You are ill! It has all been too much for you! But surely God has sent you to me today, for comfort. I have been praying for this, and hoping very patiently. 'Some day,' I said to myself, 'my goddaughter will come to me, and remember that I live only to help her.'"

He reached for a crystal decanter of wine, and poured a portion into a tiny golden goblet. He got up and brought it around the desk and held it to her lips. She made a gesture of refusal, then suddenly put her lips to the goblet and drank swiftly. The wine ran through her whole body in tendrils of flame. Courage came back to her, but a deadly hopeless courage.

"Thank you," she murmured. He stood beside her, the empty goblet in his hand, anxiety wrinkling his fat brows. He saw that she was intolerably thin in her plain black dress. She might have been a widow. He put his fleshy hand on her shoulder and pressed comfortingly.

"My poor liebchen," he murmured, and he was quite sincere in his anxiety and distress.

Hesitating, he went back to his desk and sat down. He put his fingers together, forming a little tent. Over it, he regarded her gravely.

"Therese, there is nothing I will not do for you," he said in a changed voice.

He was suddenly taken aback. For she had turned to him fiercely, gripping the desk with her straining hands. He saw the knuckles spring out. He was hypnotized by the passion in her eyes, by her whiteness, which gleamed in the dusk.

"Do you know why I came here!" she cried, and her voice rose almost to a scream. "Not to see you, not for myself! Not even to help any one! Just to look at you, and tell you what you are, to your face, as you will not be told again, until you die!"

"Therese!" he exclaimed, unnerved. He glanced fearfully at the door which led to his secretary's office. "Therese, be calm! You are hysterical. You do not know what you are saying."

She flung up her hands with a dying gesture. "I know what I am saying. And in your heart, you know, too!"

She was trembling so violently. Her white mouth opened on a gasp. She began to weep. She pressed her handkerchief to her lips, and clenched her teeth on it. Rings of fire floated before her eyes.

The Bishop half started to his feet. He was no longer a clergyman, but only an average man confronted by an aroused woman. He was filled with terror. "I shall call Louisa," he muttered. He rarely thought of his wife, the silly, impotent goose! But now he thought of her with relief. There was something ludicrous in his dismay, in his fallen mouth and frightened eyes.

Therese struggled to control herself.

"No, do not call Louisa," she said, forcing her voice to

quietness. "I do not want to see Louisa. I only want to see you."

Doubtful, he regarded her intently. Then, seeing that she was becoming calmer, he slowly lowered himself into his chair again. He had to grasp the arms, and lower himself gently. Too rich living had made him a victim of the inevitable complaint of such men.

"My dear," he said gently, "I do not understand you. I do not understand your attack. I can only believe that you are unnerved by Karl's illness. Perhaps I should have come to you, in spite of all refusals. You must forgive my negligence. Believe me, Therese, I can only repeat there is nothing I will not do for you."

She dropped her hands from her lips. Her flesh took on a marble-like hue. She leaned forward to regard him more clearly.

"I heard a story today," she said, in a strangely quiet voice. "I know the woman only slightly. I dislike her. I despise her. But in despising her, I despise myself. And you. I promised her that I would appeal to you for help. . . ."

He was much relieved. He made another tent of his hands. He smiled benignly.

"Of course, Therese. You have only to ask. I help all who appeal to me, as you must know. And the appeal is doubly important when you ask it."

He was affronted by her suddenly cynical and derisive smile.

"I hope you are not a liar," she said, the smile broadening on her face. "Forgive me, but I am quite sincere. You see, the woman is Madame Henriette Cot, one of your parishioners."

The ominous silence which followed her words seemed to fill the great room like dark wings. The Bishop drew a long sharp breath. His benign smile faded. His face became dull and brutish, and a little fearful.

Then he said: "But—but what have you, Therese Erlich, to do with—with such a woman? A Jew? A cheap shopkeeper?" But he spoke as though preoccupied, and more than a trifle shocked. Color seeped into the folds of his flesh. His eyes shifted. "How could you know such a woman? How could she appeal to *you?*" His voice sharpened into outrage.

Therese's lips twitched convulsively. "Once I should have asked myself that question, too. But now I know that one woman's suffering is mine also. That is why I am appealing to you. She has told me the whole story. She thinks you can help her husband."

The Bishop's eyes dropped to his tenting fingers. His social sense was insulted. He was filled with brutal anger.

"I am amazed," he muttered. Then on a rising note of wrath: "How dare she come to you—that person! It is not to be borne. A cheap . . ."

"You took her money, and her husband's money," said Therese, relentlessly. "Or perhaps, mein Herr Bishop, money is not cheap to you?"

His ruddy color became purple. He regarded her with little sparkling eyes like an inflamed boar's.

"Therese! You are outrageous! I can only tell myself that you do not understand. Her husband is a Jewish criminal. He smuggled currency out of our Fatherland, in express defiance of the law, in order to aid other Jewish criminals. . . ."

Therese glanced at the Cross. "There was once another 'Jewish criminal,' " she murmured.

"Do not talk like that, such blasphemy!" He shifted violently on his seat, then winced at the pain. The pain increased his rage. "I shall not argue with you! You are impossible! You have forgotten yourself, your position—everything . . ."

"It is not I who have forgotten," she said, steadfastly, looking at him with her quiet shining eyes. "It is you who have forgotten. You, a Bishop, a minister of God." Nothing could have equalled the scorn in her voice. "These people were Christians. They were among your largest contributors. You accepted their money. They were part of your flock." Her voice changed: "Shepherd, where are your sheep?"

He was silent. He regarded her over his hands with brutal fury. A look of murder, and something else, stood nakedly in his eyes. He tried to make his voice calm and judicious over his turbulent violence.

"Therese, I need not explain to you. But I shall. In your overwrought condition, I feel impelled to talk to you, though I am afraid it will do no good. You are hysterical.

"It is no part of a minister's place to intrude into politics. I—I am well thought of among the Nazi Party because I have prudently refrained from interference with the State. I am not like those of the Roman Catholic persuasion," he added, with a venomous sneer. "I am no busybody priest. I render unto Caesar the things which are Caesar's and unto God, the things which are God's. That is a Christly doctrine which the Roman Catholic Church refuses to acknowledge. They interfere. They whine. They accuse, They complain. They kick against the pricks. They insist upon contradicting, if the policies of the new State touch their precious doctrines. I know of priests who have, out of sentimentality, or worse, smuggled wanted criminals and Jews out of Germany. They deserve their punishment. I, myself, know what it is bidden me to do. It is not the business of Christ's Church to interfere in temporal affairs. Our concern is the concern of the spirit. And so, because I have observed this sacred doctrine of detachment, and concerned myself entirely with spiritual affairs, I am on good terms with every one."

Therese interrupted. "I agree that it is a safe, and pleasant thing, to be on good terms with murderers. It is very comfortable. And perhaps, profitable."

His nostrils flared redly. He clenched his teeth. His voice was stifled when he spoke. "I repeat, you are hysterical. I shall ignore your wild words.

"I owe a duty to the new State, to Germany. It is not in my province, nor could I hold it with my conscience, to help criminals. This man and this woman are criminals. . . ."

"Because they are Jews?" asked Therese, with her bitter smile.

He shifted again, violently, and winced.

"Do not be absurd! As if that mattered!"

"It apparently must matter. You have segregated the non-Aryans in your church."

The purple tint rose more deeply through his jowls. "It was by request of the others in my parish."

"And you, a minister of Christ, could accede to that! That un-Christian, that depraved, that degraded request! You could so pander to degeneracy and madness, you, shepherd of Christ! You, shepherd of the Jew Jesus!" She looked at him straightly. "I do not believe your parishioners asked that. I believe you did it on your own initiative. Or, perhaps, at the demand of the Nazis."

"You do not know what you are saying, Therese. You do not know how dangerous your words are!" His rage was lost in his fright. He glared at the door of his secretary's room. "Do you not know that you are talking treason? But I shall not let you involve me in this."

He stood up, quivering like a great black jelly, dismissing her.

But she did not move. She laughed at him, thinly, wildly. He stood beneath the Cross, and the more she looked at him, and the Cross, the wilder she laughed.

"You are afraid you will lose favor, mein Herr Bishop? You are afraid the Nazis will not like you, if they hear of this? They will not believe your protestations of hatred for the defenseless and the persecuted. They will not believe that you are sincere when you deliver up your people to betrayal. They will not believe you are a good Nazi."

"Go! Go, you shameless woman!"

She stood up. She faced him across his desk. "I shall not go until I say what I came to say.

"There are many ministers and clergymen like you in Germany, and the world. Expedient, greedy, lying, hating, anti-Christ. Betrayers and mockers of God. Delivering the sheep, with unctuous fat words, to the slaughterer. Leading the world deeper and deeper into a pit of hopelessness and death. Singing the song of Christ, as you drag the people into the morass, holding up the lighted Cross over the abyss. Compromising with evil, for your self-gain and your safety. Betrayers. Murderers! Beasts!"

Her voice sank, became almost whispering, despairing.

"If the world dies, it will be your fault. Its blood is on your hands. God will not be mocked."

She turned away from him, as though he were a loathsome sight. He remained where he was, shaking with rage and apoplexy. She went across the polished floor, dragging her feet, her head bent. She had reached the door. Her hand was on the handle. Then she heard him scream at her, mockingly, furiously:

"You can tell your Jewess friend that no one can help her husband, now! He hung himself a month ago, in Dachau Camp, a fitting end for his crimes!"

She turned to him, slowly. She looked at him in a terrible silence. He stood beneath the Cross. He was in shadow. But the light of the lamp, piercing its top, shone on the Cross, so that it seemed to illumine all the room.

She was driven away in a dream, in a nightmare, leaning back in her car, her eyes closed. She felt the motion of the car, but did not know where she was. Then she opened her eyes, tapped on the glass which separated her from Frederick.

"Take me to the house of the Chief Rabbi of Berlin," she said, her voice hoarse and faint.

Frederick was so astounded that he brought the car to an abrupt stop. He stared at her over his shoulder, his eyes goggling like a fish's.

"I said, take me to the house of the Chief Rabbi of Berlin," she repeated. She fixed him with her eyes, and her face was grim.

"But, Frau Doctor, that is incredible," said the young man.

She sat back on her seat, and waited. He spluttered. He muttered something to himself. He swung the car about with a vicious jerk. "I shall rid myself of him today," she thought.

Life came back to her beaten body. She saw nothing, though she gazed through the windows. Then she saw the bronzed green dome of the city's chief synagogue. Its steps were smeared with obscene yellow signs. She felt an impulse to vomit. The car stopped at the large comfortable house next door. Frederick did not get out of the car to open the door and help her alight. His neck was crimson. His shoulders were ominously set.

She got out of the car herself, and calmly walked to the house. She lifted the knocker. It sounded within, hollow and frightening. A little maid came to the door, opening it fearfully. She stared without speaking at Therese. Therese gave her her card. "I must see the Rabbi at once," she said imperatively.

The girl took her card, leaving Therese on the doorstep. Therese pushed open the door and entered the warm dark hallway. Terror dwelt here. She could smell it. But under it, she could smell fortitude and peace.

The Rabbi, holding her card, came towards her, smiling a little nervously, bewildered, but very polite. "Frau Doctor Erlich," he murmured. He was a little man, bent and aged with suffering. His eyes were beautiful and steadfast.

She held out her hand to him.

"Come with me," she said gently, weeping a little. "There is some one waiting in my house, who needs your help and comfort."

"REST. You have the right to rest. There is a time when the most valorous soldier must fall out," said Doctor Traub, standing beside Therese's bed, and regarding her with affectionate gravity. In the wan sunlight of the autumn day, his clothes were uncomprisingly shabby and untidy, his paunch most evident. Never had he looked so small and stubby, so gray and stout and tired. But his kind eyes were gentle and indomitable, and full of compassion.

23

"I have never been ill before," said Therese restlessly, turning her head on her hot pillow.

"You have done too much."

She had just finished telling him about Madame Cot. The telling had agitated her unbearably. He had been forced to give her a sedative, and decided to remain with her until she slept. Madame Cot, she told him, had been assisted by the Jewish Emigration Society to leave Germany and go to her sister in New York, who was a prominent cosmetician, owning a replica of Madame Cot's own chain of salons in that city. Therese had given her a draft on her Paris bank for a cheque, also. "When I last saw her, she was an old woman. She was no longer wearing her cross," she added, with bitter irony.

Doctor Traub moved away from the bed and gazed through the windows at the cold withering garden. He said aloud, sadly and musingly: "In mankind's supreme hour, in his supreme agony, the Christian Church has nothing to give it but a sop of weak vinegar, timidly tendered, furtively offered. Now is the final hour for Christianity, the grim and final test. Christianity must decide whether it will keep on its ancient way: assisting the strong against the weak, expediently compromising with evil, upholding oppressors against the oppressed, keeping silent before anguish, deafening its ears to the cry of torment and injustice, seizing avidly on the spoils offered to it by cynical thieves, or whether it will lift its voice against the madness which has the world, and brighten its rusty sword and take up its stained shield in the last struggle of men against fury and violence. It must decide whether its gilded churches are more valuable than God, and whether mercy and compassion and love are dead words or living glories worth dying for."

He added mournfully: "So far, it is keeping to its ancient and cowardly and avaricious policy of appeasing force, and helping to subjugate the miserable and despairing. It has said: 'Governments are not my concern. It is my business to conciliate.' They forget that Jesus was concerned with all that concerned men, and that He never conciliated the legions of hatred and rage. It has declared, recently, that it wishes only peace. It forgets or will not remember, that Jesus declared there can be no peace between that which is evil and that which is good."

He sighed deeply.

Therese murmured from her pillow: "My old Lotte said recently that she believed that Jesus has come again, and is walking the earth." The sedative had blunted reality for her; she floated in a strange and boundless universe.

Doctor Traub turned abruptly from the window. The setting sun was red and golden against the glass; it outlined him in light.

"So I believe. And how sickened He must be! How terrible it must be to have to climb Calvary again!"

Therese's eyes were closed. She was sinking into a dream-state. She saw a round and barren hill, sterile-brown and afloat with fog. She saw a lonely figure climbing that hill, painfully, gaspingly, carrying a cross. It climbed in an awful and deserted silence, step by step, sweating drops of blood and agony. It climbed alone. There was no one there to offer consolation or help. She was filled with an overpowering grief, so deep, so profound, that it seemed to her sinking senses that a thousand worlds joined in her sorrow. Then she slept.

Doctor Traub stood beside her, seeing, with sadness, how emaciated she was, how exhausted. He smoothed the fair thick hair on the pillow, touched the strands of gray at the temples. He sighed again.

As this poor woman has awakened, so the whole world must awaken, he thought. As she has suffered, so the world must suffer. Time no longer. The final hour had come. Death and hatred and evil had shown their faces first in Germany. Soon every man would be familiar with them, everywhere. The supreme day had dawned.

He slowly climbed the stairway to Karl's rooms. He felt old

and tired and hopeless. He knocked on the study door. There
was a prolonged silence. He knocked again. He heard a vague
shuffling of feet, as though a blind man were approaching the
door. It opened. The gaunt and ravaged face, the sightless
eyes, of Karl Erlich confronted him, without question, and
only with bemusement and lack of recognition. The doctor
smiled genially, pushed the door wider, and stepped into the
study.

"Good evening, Karl," he said. "I have just left Therese. I
thought I might visit you for a few moments."

He glanced about the still room swiftly. There, on the desk,
lay a wooden doll with a prong sunken deeply into the head.
He knew what it was. He pretended not to see it. He sat down
in a chair. Karl Erlich slowly closed the door and then stood
near it, staring and blinking. He put his hand to his head as
though it ached unbearably. His smile was spectral and sly.

"I have not been well," he murmured.

Doctor Traub continued to smile. His alert physician's eyes
saw the red glimmer of madness in Karl's eyes. He saw the
violently trembling hands, the pulsing temples, the gray
mouth and sunken nostrils. It was a dying man who stood
before him, his clothing disordered, his cheeks unshaven.

"There is much sickness about," said the doctor, in a matter-of-fact voice. "I have a few moments. I hope I am not
disturbing you. But I thought I might talk to you about
Therese. She is ill herself."

For an instant the madness disappeared from those tortured
eyes, and sanity sprang to the surface of the livid flesh. Karl
came towards him, quickly. "Therese? What is the matter
with Therese?" His voice, though exhausted, was almost
normal.

Doctor Traub thought swiftly and carefully. Then he said
casually: "I hope I have not alarmed you. She has a cold. She
needs careful nursing for a few days."

"Oh." The sound was only a breath. Karl fumbled his slow
way back to his desk. He sat down before it, literally falling
into his chair. His eye touched the doll. He gave the doctor a
crafty and evil glance, then seizing the image, he thrust it
quickly into a drawer and closed it. Doctor Traub pretended
to notice nothing.

"But you, yourself, are indeed ill, Karl. I should like to
help you."

The wretched man put his hands feverishly to his head.

"There is really nothing wrong with me," he cried with sudden violence. "I do not wish to be interrupted. Every one tries to interrupt me. Why will you not leave me alone?"

"I am sorry," said the doctor, gravely. "I do not wish to interrupt you." He paused. Karl said nothing. His shaking hands hid his face. His body was skeletonlike. An untouched tray of food lay on a near-by table. The shades were drawn against the day, and a feeble lamp shone on the desk. The air of the room was fetid, as though a corpse lay hidden somewhere. On the mantel, the head of Gilu grinned foully. The doctor had a sudden horrible presentiment that a loathsome presence lurked in the room, filling the unclean air with corruption and death.

He started quite violently. For Karl had begun to speak in a low muffled voice. "There is something you can do for me. You can tell Eric to go away and leave me in peace."

He had dropped his hands. He was gazing at the doctor with the distended eyes of hatred and terror. "Tell him to go away!" he cried.

"What does he want?" asked Doctor Traub quietly.

The sick man's face was convulsed. His body tensed as though it might spring. He panted audibly.

"He wants me to listen to him. I shall never listen! Not until I have done what I must do!" Beads of sweat rolled down his death-head of a face. His eyes glittered with madness.

The doctor was silent. He forced himself to maintain an attitude of judicious calm. Then all at once the imminent presence of loathsomeness vanished from the room, and it was no longer a carnal house. It was as though a friend entered, gentle and compassionate, urgently trying to make himself heard.

"Why do you not listen to him for a little while?" asked the doctor, very gently and slowly. "He only wants to talk to you. If you will just listen, once, he will go away, and leave you in peace."

Karl still panted. Then slowly, his breath became normal. The glare died from his eyes, which fixed themselves eagerly and imploringly upon the doctor. The strained tendons of his face relaxed. He asked simply, tremblingly: "You are speaking the truth? If I listen, only once, he will go away?"

The doctor's heart began to beat very fast. But he maintained his calm. He pursed his lips. "Yes. I am sure of it. Remember, he was your best friend, your brother. Can you blame him if he wishes to speak to you? Would you not do the same in his position? You are really very unkind to him. He wants to have peace, too. You are denying him peace. Listen the next time he comes. Then he will go away, and you will both rest."

The tortured eyes searched the other's face, fumbled at it. The doctor could hardly bear that pathetic sight. "Listen to Eric," he repeated, softly.

He stood up. Karl still stared at him with that dying and imploring look. He touched his temples with the tips of his withered fingers.

"You are right," he murmured. "I believe you. When he comes again, I shall listen. Then he will go away."

The doctor went down the stairs again, not heavily this time, but with the steps of hope. He stopped in to see Therese. She still slept deeply. He stood beside her. "Sleep, my dear," he said aloud. "Sleep. It will soon be morning."

24 THERESE forced herself to rest. She knew that she had much to do, more than she had ever done. But if she were to do it, she must be prepared. So she resolutely lay quiet, taking her tablets and liquids, eating the good food the anxious Lotte prepared for her, not allowing herself to think. She created a calm vacuum about her, allowed nothing to disturb her. She was shocked at her physical decay, and called in a hairdresser and cosmetician. Each day her hair was tended and brushed for an hour or more, and creams and lotions were massaged into her flesh. She received no visitors, answered no messages, though her room bloomed with flowers from sympathetic friends.

One day she received a note from her godfather, the Bishop. He announced that he had forgiven her hysteria, and asked her forgiveness for his "rather heated language." "I should have remembered the condition of your household, and the close events of the past few months," he said gravely in his small precise black hand. "I should have remembered that you were always a kind and sympathetic girl, easily imposed upon by malingerers and exploiters. Had your conduct towards me been even a little less violent, your accusations a little less incoherent and inexcusably vicious, I would have remembered. My impatience with you, however, was also inexcusable, and so, I humbly beg your pardon, liebchen. I hear that you are ill. Will you allow me to call upon you?"

Therese, her hands wet and trembling, tore the letter across and across. She flung it from her with a gesture of loathing. And then, strangely and suddenly, she was filled with an overpowering compassion and sorrow. The Bishop was not a stupid man. He must have his hours alone with himself, also. He must have his hours of thinking. She saw his face as in a vision, lonely, terrified, torn and dark. He was no villain. He was just cowardly. He was expedient with the expediency of the weak and the frightened. Once he had been a young man. He had chosen the Church from some deep inward conviction, not from avarice. She knew his family had been poor if

232

noble, and he could not, in the beginning, have dreamed that he would rise so high. But he had risen, and he had lost his conviction. That was very dreadful. And he must know what he had lost. He must know what he had sold for his palace, his luxury, and his position. No wonder then, that having bartered the spirit, he desperately clung to the price he had paid for it. If he lost the thirty pieces of silver, he would be bankrupt indeed, having neither glory nor money.

Therese sighed deeply, and tears filled her eyes. She wrote him in return: "When I called upon you, I did not understand. Now I understand. I ask your forgiveness. You must ask yourself why I ask this. Do not come to see me. I have more grief than I can endure just now."

A few days passed. Then on the fifth day he sent her a sheaf of white roses, without a word, and only his card. She held the pale glistening flowers in her arms, so mute, so expressive, so dead and odorless, and her tears fell on their pure carved petals. She felt they were flowers removed from the grave and tendered to the living, silently, by dead hands.

One day she rose, feeling strong again, and very quiet. As she sat by the window on this first day of rising, old Lotte came to her with a puzzled and frightened expression.

"You know, Frau Doctor, that the Herr Doctor has been very quiet lately. He has not wandered so much at night. But during the day he wanders. He keeps looking in each room. I have passed his door at night, and sometimes it has been open. He just stares before him, as though waiting for some one. He has an attitude of listening. One night he said to me: 'Lotte, have you seen Eric Reinhardt? He was to come and speak to me. I am waiting. But he does not come.' "

Therese turned her head swiftly, her new color paling. Her heart trembled. But she dared not hope yet.

"What did you say to him, Lotte?"

"I said: 'Herr Doctor, the Herr Professor is very busy these days. But he has sent a message that he will come soon.' And when I said that, he nodded, and seemed satisfied. He even asked me for a glass of milk."

Therese clasped her hands together. The tears came easily to her eyes these days. But she said nothing further.

She had dismissed Frederick, through Lotte. "Tell him that under present circumstances we need him no longer," she said. Lotte later told her, with grim satisfaction, that Frederick had been much enraged, and had muttered things under his breath. So he was a spy, after all. The whole city was full of furtive and malignant eyes. It was terrible. The air was permeated with watchfulness and evil. No wonder every man and woman on the streets appeared to be suffocating. Therese shrank from entering life again, and walking abroad.

But she knew she must do it. In the meantime, she read Schiller and Goethe, Lessing, Shakespeare and the Bible. She had thought to find a retreat here. But there was none. Each poet was preoccupied with the terribleness of mankind, and many, with a desperate sigh, yielded themselves up at the last with cynical hopelessness to the general corruption.

She had always loved Goethe. She had loved his compassion and beauty, his understanding and subtlety. But one day she read: "When the masses fight, they are respectable; but their opinions are not delectable." She read his cynical boast that he had never quarrelled with the opposition. In that boasting she heard his cry of self-hatred, his timid fury against himself, his understanding of his degradation. He loudly admired Napoleon; he surrounded himself with all the fierce, angry and gigantic figures of his day. In all this, he was rubbing salt on his wounds with a masochist's delight and will-to-die. In his expressions of disgust against the people was the groan of his own self-disgust. A deserter always denounces the deserted. It is his self-justification, his rationalization. Even Goethe had not been guiltless of this cowardice, this mournful depravity. How dreadful his last years must have been, in spite of world adulation.

But he had given a revealing truth in his words: "When the masses fight they are respectable." Deeply hidden within those words was the urging voice of a poet to his people, that they must fight constantly, never to give up, never to surrender to oppression, tyranny and madness. But not often would they fight, just as he would not fight. Thus his hatred and despair. The people revealed to him, as in a gigantic mirror, his own pusillanimity, his own weakness, his own surrender to expediency.

Therese read the daily newspapers closely, after her recovery. She read the mounting lists of those who had been taken into "protective custody," and those who had been beheaded or shot for "traitorous activities," and "Marxist agitations." The lists were like the lists of those who had perished in a dolorous pestilence. She saw many illustrious and well-known names there. The great and the noble in Germany were dying. Soon there would be left only the maggots. Sometimes she would be seized with a despairing frenzy. Did not the world see that its own epitaph was written here, that its own doom was sounding from Germany on shrilling trumpets? But if it saw or heard, it refused to acknowledge it. . . . But some day it must see and hear, and then it would be too late, too late for a thousand years. The damage done to the human soul might forever maim it.

There was only one hope: a spiritual revelation, an awakening of men's souls. This was not a battle of politics, not even a battle of nations. It was the struggle of the powers of darkness against the human spirit.

One day she received an urgent message from Maria. "Please come as soon as possible. Kurt has been taken seriously ill."

She dressed herself with fumbling and shaking hands, and asked Lotte to call her a cab. She tried to control herself, but a dark and superstitious dread pervaded her. When she walked out upon the street, she was appalled at the weakness in her legs, and her slow and feeble step. Once in the cab she had to wrestle with an overwhelming nausea, during which her mouth filled with sickening salt water and her senses swam. This terrified her. She thought she had recovered. She thought she could control herself. Now she was shivering in every nerve, and her vision was dimming. She dared not go to Kurt's house in this demoralized condition. She tapped on the glass and told the driver faintly to drive her down the Tiergartenstrasse.

The last few days had been rainy and cool, smelling of decay and darkness. But today the autumn sun was the color of gold, and warm as May. Mists glimmered brightly down far streets; the sky was an opal. Never had Berlin seemed so beautiful, so white, so broad and shining, the new buildings chastely noble in the sunlight. Groups of noon diners sat out under awnings along the Tiergartenstrasse, arguing and laughing with a vehemence unfamiliar among this phlegmatic people. The winy air had made them gay, had quickened their voices and their gestures. They were not speaking of politics. Therese, as she slowly made her way to a small empty table, heard them talking of the most trivial things. And then she saw that this trivial talk was deliberate. They dared not, either from caution or from design, speak of anything else.

Many stopped their drinking and talking to stare at her, a lone pale woman in the midst of the hubbub. Strands of her fair bright hair curled into little tendrils under her black hat. Her thinness, her smart clothing, her fine features, impressed them as belonging to a distinguished lady. Her diamond ring sparkled in the sunshine as she removed her gloves and laid them on the table. Some thought she was a widow: her face was so sad and preoccupied. A widow. At this, uneasy glances turned away from her, and those nearest her table became thoughtfully silent. There were so many widows these days.

A waiter came up obsequiously and asked the gnädige frau's order. Therese requested a cup of coffee, strong and black and hot. She sat alone, the reflections of sunlight on the awnings glimmering on her colorless cheeks and lips and haggard eyes. She drank her coffee, slowly, forcing herself to drink. The liquid warmed her, quieted her shiverings. Now she was not so nauseated. Her fortitude returned. She listened idly as she heard a near-by man ask his companion if he were going to the Parteitag at Nürnberg. Their voices rose in enthusiasm; they looked about them self-consciously, as though they hoped they were being overheard. Ah, at the Parteitag, the world would know once and for all that the Reich would endure no further nonsense from it! Their voices were loud and excited. But Therese saw that their faces were drawn and tired and very strained. They seemed to be directing their remarks for the benefit of two quiet insignificant men sipping beer at a near-by table. Then she understood.

Her throat closed with a sensation of imminent suffocation. She paid her bill and returned to her cab. Berlin was no longer bright for her, but a prison of dread and darkness. Hardly knowing what she did, she ordered the driver to take her to the Lehrter Bahnhof. Once in the great station, she wandered through the hurrying throngs. Thousands of voices echoed hollowly. The roar of incoming trains thundered under the gigantic roofs, filled the air with a gray fog. A primitive instinct for flight had brought her here. She crept about through the crowds like a disembodied ghost. She and Karl must go away. It was no use. She could not stay. She must fly as hundreds of others had flown. Nothing mattered but sheer physical safety. Hysteria gripped her and tossed her like mighty and resistless winds. She would buy tickets. She would take Karl away!

It was not until she was actually standing in line at a ticket booth that she came to her senses. Then, abruptly, she walked away, sought out another cab. Once in the seat, she collapsed. There was no escape. She was a fool. There was no island of safety anywhere in the world. A heavy, calm, fatalistic despair settled upon her, gave her the strength she needed to go on her way.

She walked up the steps of Kurt's house steadfastly. Maria met her. Therese was appalled at the change in the stout and malicious woman. She had shrunk; she was the color of soft lard. Her hair, never tidy at the best, was disordered, as though she had not combed it for days. She came to Therese with a rush, and seized her hands. She said simply, loudly: "Therese, he is dying!" Her voice broke; she stared at Therese with a blank bewilderment and complete agony.

Therese tried to soothe her. "Oh, surely not, Maria. People do not die so easily."

Maria shook her sister-in-law with abandoned frenzy. "But I know he is! The doctors—they shake their heads. They have taken X-rays. They have probed and examined. His head— they have to keep him under drugs! The pain! He screams. Now he is blind in one eye. They thought it was a tumor in the brain. But there is nothing there! They can find nothing. Nothing! Yet 'nothing' is killing him! I cannot endure it! I would rather he died." She burst into hoarse rough sobs.

The house was dim, close and warm, but Therese felt death-like coldness in all her limbs. She murmured: "He has worked very hard. He has been under a strain. It is probably just a nervous breakdown. I—I saw him not so long ago, and I was sure it was a breakdown. It will take time, that is all."

Maria exclaimed, in her rage of helplessness and fear: "Therese, you talk like the other fools! 'Time, time!' But there is no more time. If only that silly, whimpering husband of yours would come here, and console my Kurt! That is what ails him; he is dying for his brother!" She smote her hands together in her frantic and rising terror and rage. "I tell you, he will not recover, he will make no effort, until Karl comes to him! Why will you not bring Karl? Why do you not tell him his brother is dying? Surely, even his ridiculous pique will be forgotten when he knows."

Therese said quietly, fixing the woman with her eyes: "You do not understand. Karl is dying, too."

Maria was silent, but her breathing was hard and violent. She stared wildly at Therese. Her eyeballs glared in the gloom of the drawing room. She was full of hatred and despair and incredulity. "It is not true," she whispered at last, then louder, pleadingly: "It is not true, Therese?"

"Yes," said Therese, still very quietly, "it is true."

Maria burst into tears. "Then all is lost. My Kurt will die, if Karl dies. What is wrong with these men? Have they no strength, no iron in their souls? They die of a malady no one can cure—"

"Yes, Maria, a malady no one can cure. Except God."

The two women gazed at each other in a silence at once dark and ominous.

The room was dim and empty. There was no sound in the house. Then Therese caught a faint movement near a far doorway. She almost cried out. For it seemed to her that the nebulous figure pausing for a moment in that doorway was Karl's. She saw his slender bent figure, his white agonized face, his blind eye-sockets. And then she saw that it was Wilhelm in his uniform, gazing across the width of the empty room at her.

"Wilhelm!" she cried, taking a step towards him, remembering that day, so long ago, when she had driven him cruelly from her. "Wilhelm, I must talk with you—"

But he had gone. He had drifted away like smoke.

THEY CLIMBED up the immense balustraded
stairs together, the two silent and hopeless
women. Therese saw, as always, that the alert
old beldame, Frau Reiner, had her room door
open, in order that she might miss nothing from her cynical
eyrie. Therese thought this was too much; she had never
liked the old woman, and had shrunk even from thinking
of her since the last time she had seen her. Now she said
to herself: I really cannot compose myself to see her or
speak to her. There was no sound within the avid room;
perhaps she could slip by the door unseen. But she had
hardly approached it, to pass it, when the old woman, who
must really have been able to see around corners, called out,
shrilly:

"Is that you, Therese?"

Therese sighed. Even in that miserable moment, she
exchanged a wryly amused glance with Maria. She approached
the door with as much dignity as she could summon.

The old woman sat near the dimming window, caparisoned
and jewelled and perfumed as ever, a queen on her throne.
She looked at Therese cunningly.

"Ah," she said, in her high cracked voice. "The impeccable
gnädige frau!"

Therese had always had a gift for making even the most
blatant irony complimentary to herself. She had always
smiled serenely at the old woman's sallies, which were never
too subtly barbed. But she had no serenity, no composure,
today. She said with quiet stiffness: "Good afternoon, Frau
Reiner."

The old woman was silent. She stared at Therese with her
sly wanton eyes. She pursed up her lips like an old monkey.
She was indeed an old female monkey in her finery, and her
elaborate coiffure. "Hum," she muttered, surlily, after her
long scrutiny. "So life has become too much for you, eh?"

"Very much too much," answered Therese, in a low still
voice.

25

The old woman was silent again, but her eyes brightened maliciously. She seemed to be experiencing some inner and malignant mirth, without mercy but with complete understanding. Then she said: "It is about time, you impeccable lady. But I am afraid it is too late."

"Come, Therese," said Maria, impatiently.

But Therese said: "It is late. But not too late."

Again there was a pause. Then Frau Reiner motioned imperiously. "Come in, Therese. I want to talk to you. Maria, your precious Kurt will wait. He will not die today." She chuckled darkly. "He will not die until he has seen his brother. Now, I shall not be crossed. Come in, Therese. Sit down near me. I like to look at the faces of the guilty. They are very amusing." She added: "No, Maria, go away. I do not want you here just now. Your appearance and your conversation do not stimulate me these days. Go and smooth your husband's pillow."

The two women were alone. Therese sat near the beldame. The pale waning light lay on her colorless face. Frau Reiner studied her closely, saw the quiet folded hands, the suffering gray eyes. Even in her anguish there was a calm and dignity about Therese, or fortitude that could not be completely shaken. Frau Reiner shook her head, as though with angry denial.

"I have told you: I have always despised you aristocrats. But I admit you do not go to pieces; you refuse to be naked. That is the best, and the worst of you. You loathe emotion. When things are bad, that is a crime. But when they are hopeless, it is a virtue. But we plebeians, we vulgar, shriek and cry out all the time, and beat our breasts. You have always loathed us for this, have you not? It is very humiliating that at the last the world must depend upon you."

Frau Reiner regarded her with cunning reflection.

Therese said nothing.

"But there always comes a time when you realize that it must be all out, total, for either good or evil. At those times you do not hesitate, while we shrink back and hesitate, and whine. Perhaps there is something to your old belief that in the final moments it is the aristocrat who will save the day. What are you doing, Therese, to save the day?"

"I do what I can," said Therese, smiling faintly. "I realize, as you say, that in these days it must be all out, for good or evil. There can be no half measures."

"Hum," said the old woman, thoughtfully. Then: "How is my Karl?"

"I think he is dying," said Therese, quietly.

Frau Reiner stared at her incredulously. "And you can say that so calmly, with such composure?"

"It is because I see that now not even Karl must matter much. I am doing what I can for him. I am waiting for him to see me. But in the meantime, there is nothing I can do of any consequence for him. I do other things, while I am waiting."

"And the 'other things,' I presume, concern yourself?"

"Quite often, yes."

The beldame grunted. "That ought to keep you very busy." She looked through the window. "I have lived a long time. I have seen madness before. But it has been a localized madness. Now the whole world is insane. Once I thought: 'It is always the same story. There is never any difference.' But now I know that there is a difference in these days. Men are universally corrupt. In an era where there has been so much said about mercy, civilization, goodness, decency and honor, there are none of these things. Never, in the history of the world, has there been such a universal absence of them. At one time, a localized pogrom against the Jews aroused world-wide indignation, oppression of the innocent in one country made other countries outraged. But today, persecution and torment of the helpless only make other countries envious. They only awaken their lust to do the same. I tell you, we shall see outrages beyond imaginations, and the world will be indifferent, or emulate them."

Therese did not speak. The old woman played with her rings and chains with a sudden impotent frenzy.

"The souls of men are dead, or decaying. They are full of apathy. The world is a graveyard, a house of plague. Sometimes at night, I can see the streets of Berlin, the streets of all of Germany, even the large countryside. I see the specters of pestilence wandering through all of them. The pestilence will not remain here. It will spread throughout the world. For the world is ripe for it. It is full of corruption. What is to happen in the coming years will be too frightful to contemplate. But it will be because of the disease in the minds of men, the faithlessness, the cruelty, the greed and the hatred."

"I know," murmured Therese. The suffocating sensation

seized upon her throat once more, and with it came the old impotence, the old despair.

The old woman gazed at her crucifix, illuminated by the ever-burning candle. " 'A faithless and adulterous generation,' " she muttered. "Yes, yes, these must be the days spoken of by Saint Matthew. It is a terrible thing. I hope I shall not live to see the end. After all, there must be some mercy for the old. I did not make these days. I have done some wicked things, but I never thought it did not matter. Men, now, do evil and all manner of vilenesses, and are not only not ashamed, but are cynically satisfied and triumphant. They are not even hypocritical about it. There is no refuge. There is no corner of the world where just men can be found. You can find only disease of the mind, and leprosy of the soul."

The autumn sun had moved behind a cloud. The air was full of the smell of ashes. Desolation enveloped the streets outside, the atmosphere in the house. The desolation pervaded Therese. Her flesh felt as though it were covered with dust. In the gloom the little candle appeared to burn brighter, with a reddish glow, and the crucifix was the only vivid thing in the dark room.

The old woman's face was a mask of somberness, its thousand wrinkles a parchment of melancholy. She looked at the crucifix for a long silent moment.

"Burn on, burn on, little candle," she muttered, almost inaudibly. "But soon, you too, will go out, and the Thing you light will be lost in the darkness, too."

"No!" Therese's voice was loud and echoing, not frightened, but resolute. "It shall not go out! Nothing can make it go out! Only a few candles left, but they shall not go out!"

The old woman burst into a sharp and bitter chuckle. Her face shrank and withered until it suddenly resembled the head of Gilu.

"You are wrong, Therese. They will go out. Do you know what the world seems to me, in these days? A tiny prison, with shut doors, and barred windows, and inside, madmen. Soon, you will hear their howling on every wind. Listen: you can hear the howling in Germany. Soon every corner of the prison will be howling, too. Where will you hide, Therese?"

"In myself," said Therese. Her gray eyes shone with a strange light. "Just as others are hiding in themselves. Nothing can touch us then. We shall keep our own candles burning, even though they kill us."

She stood up. The old woman sat deep in her cynical and cryptic silence, the web of cunning thick over her shrivelled features.

"Even in Doomsday," said Therese, with soft steadfastness, "we still have that one refuge: ourselves. No treachery, no faithlessness, no outrage, can penetrate there. Not even death."

"Even death," repeated Frau Reiner, hoarsely. She leaned forward a little, and her eyes were like searching daggers reaching to Therese's face. "Even death?"

"Even death."

The silence rang with pregnant meaning. The old woman's clasped hands lay on her knee; her many jewels sparkled in the candlelight. She no longer grinned sardonically at Therese. When she spoke at last, it was with no jibe:

"Go, Therese. Karl will come back to you, now."

She found Maria waiting for her at the end of the long wide hallway. Maria was sitting in an attitude of complete desolation in a tall, high-backed chair. Her elbow rested on an arm; her hand covered her face. Her whole large flabby body seemed collapsed together, as though her bones had softened. Above her head burned a single yellowish light, and by it, Therese saw that the other woman's mass of hair was thickly streaked with gray.

She put her hand on Maria's bulky shoulder. "I am ready to see Kurt now," she said gently. Maria lifted her head. Her face was ravaged and exhausted. She rose without a word, and opened the door to her right.

The vast bedroom floated in gloom. Beside the bed one dim lamp burned. The windows were shrouded in silk and crimson velvet. The great bed, itself, was a shadowy white island in a dark sea. A nurse, stiff and starched, rose at the entrance of the ladies.

"Is he better?" whispered Maria, and her flabby face quivered.

"The Herr Professor is no worse," answered the nurse. She smiled respectfully at Therese, who had approached the bed silently.

The nurse and Maria went into a whispered consultation, withdrawing a little. But Therese stood by the bed and looked down at its sleeping occupant. She was profoundly startled and shocked. She had been so shocked at her glimpse of Kurt in the University library. But today her shock was deeper, and more despairing. The face on the white pillow was the face of a corpse, yellowed, emaciated, hollow and still. Like the face of the dead, it had a secret nobility and haughty peace, withdrawn and impassive. Approaching dissolution had ennobled and refined it, and for the first time Therese was aware of the great resemblance between Kurt and Karl. This might have been Karl's own head, lying there so motionlessly, with its closed eyes sunken in webbed, empurpled shadows. The wide mouth, once so brutal, was now cold and stern and ascetic. His nose, once so blunt and thickened, was large and thin and chiselled. The hollows of the cheeks gave the whole face a contemplative and classic expression, as though behind the attenuated mask of flesh there were thoughts far removed from humanity and the world.

He hardly breathed. On his left temple there was a huge bruised spot, swollen and veined. She saw how one vein throbbed and leaped, as though with unbearable suffering. She had thought she had lost the capacity to feel horror, but horror, sharp and scalding, swamped her, made her mind reel with its impact. "No, no," she whispered, aloud, as though to deny the ghastliness of some terrible evidence.

Her whisper seemed to arouse the dying man. Slowly, almost imperceptibly, his eyelids opened. His eyes, dim yet feverish, fixed themselves upon her. She bent over him, tears on her cheeks. "Kurt?" she murmured, and touched his forehead. He continued that mournful and fixed regard, as though not recognizing her. Maria crept to the other side of the bed. She looked at nothing but her husband, and her soul, imbedded though it had been in her gross flesh for so long, stood in her eyes.

Then the dry and shrunken lips moved. A pale light, like the reflection of a dying candle, passed over his face. "Karl?" he whispered, imploringly. He tried to move. His struggle was an awful thing to behold. He tried to move upward towards her. Veins, like purple ropes, sprang out on his thin neck. "Karl?" he said again, and this time the sound was a hoarse cry. A glisten of sweat broke out on his livid face. The nurse came to him, tried to force him back on his pillows. But he ignored her. The whole summoning of his dying body for strength resisted her efforts. He was drowning, and Therese was the only one who could rescue him.

She could not endure those hopeful, those crying eyes, those imploring and sunken eyes. She put her hand on his shoulder; it was like touching bare bone.

"He is coming, Kurt. He has been ill, but now he is better, and is coming to you soon."

She spoke aloud, quietly and strongly. He continued to gaze at her; he panted shrilly.

"Kurt!" cried Maria in an anguished voice, approaching him.

But he saw no one but Therese. The two looked at each other in a quite dreadful silence. Between his opened lips Therese could see the glisten of his teeth, as he struggled for breath. His eyes burned in their distended sockets. She could see the dilated pupil, fevered and glowing.

Then slowly, he fell back on his pillows again. He smiled. It was like the grimace of a death's-head. But there was peace in it.

"Yes, yes," he whispered. "You do not lie to me, Therese." He closed his eyes. He seemed to sleep.

Therese led the weeping Maria from the room, her arm about her. The nurse followed them into the hall, and softly closed the door.

"Does no one know what is wrong?" asked Therese. "His physicians?"

The nurse shook her head significantly. "They say it is nothing physical. They do not know. It is his mind. . . ."

The pathetic mind of the innocent. Karl and Kurt. A whole nation of Karls and Kurts. Perhaps a whole world. Everywhere the innocent, deceived, bereft, betrayed, were dying.

Maria and Therese went downstairs together, blindly.

26 "I HAVE given up hope," said Maria, wiping her eyes and cheeks. "All I ask now is that he die in peace."

"He will," answered Therese, firmly. She felt exalted by her promise.

She was about to leave when she saw that there was a visitor, and though she wished nothing more fervently just then than to avoid him, she saw that it was impossible. The visitor was Captain von Keitsch. He was standing in the hall, and coversing with Alfred. Wilhelm stood nearby in silence.

"Ah, gnädige frau!" he exclaimed gallantly, at the sight of Therese descending the stairway. He took her hand with a flourish and kissed it, openly admiring her. "And how is Doctor Erlich?"

"Much better," said Therese coldly, disengaging her hand as quickly as possible.

"And the good General? I have not seen him lately."

Therese regarded him piercingly. She knew at once that he had heard about the poor General. Her heart swelled on a bitter tide. "He is well," she said.

He saw her aversion. He paused. He smiled his warm smile.

"I am glad some one is well," he remarked mockingly. He composed his face. He turned to Maria. "And how is the Herr Professor? I have heard he is ill, and, of course, had to come to ask about him."

His large colorful face, his great bulky body, expressed his concern. His uniform fitted him perfectly, despite his mighty girth.

Maria, in spite of her grief, was flattered by the attention of the distinguished man. She even simpered a little, as she led the way into the drawing room, holding Therese's reluctant arm.

"It is so kind of you, Baron," she said. She sighed. "I wish I might say he is improving. But I cannot. No one seems to know what is the matter."

"Too much confinement," he suggested. "These scholarly men! They need air and exercise."

"We are going in strongly for air and exercise these days, are we not?" asked Therese. "I have heard you deal out large quantities of them in the concentration camps."

If she thought to goad this detestable man, she was disappointed. He merely looked at her with a candid smile. "That is quite true, Frau Doctor. We do not overlook health facilities even for the enemies of the State."

Her pale cheeks flushed with her angry agitation. She forced herself to turn her attention to her nephew, Alfred. "How are you, Alfred?" She shrank, for a few moments, from speaking to Wilhelm, so silent in his distant chair, so white-lipped and blindly preoccupied with his own thoughts.

"I am well, thank you, Aunt Therese." He gave her his broad boyish grin. Then he became sober. "I wish I could say the same of my father."

She studied his exuberant face, his firm round coloring. Then she had to turn to Wilhelm, and her voice was hesitant and gentle. "Wilhelm?"

He stirred. His lips moved, but no sound came from them. He turned his face towards her, but his eyes were empty and dull. Then, very slowly, his gaze left her and fixed itself upon von Keitsch. Instantly, and startlingly, his eyes were no longer blind, but vivid with an insane wild hatred. His lips drew back from his teeth in a soundless snarl. He leaned forward, as if to spring. Therese was aghast by the implication of what she saw. But no one else appeared to notice. Von Keitsch was murmuring to Maria, solicitously questioning her about Kurt. Alfred was bending forward, attentively and respectfully, towards his officer. Relieved that no one had caught Wilhelm's naked look, Therese turned back to him furtively, his breath quick.

It was indeed Karl's face, murderous and mad, convulsed with despair and hatred, and yet so mournfully pathetic. She must do something to distract his attention, before the others saw. She leaned towards him, willing him to look at her. "Wilhelm!" she called to him. "I have wanted to speak to you. Will you come to see me tomorrow?"

Her voice was like a hand, tugging at him. He turned his head stiffly towards her, and the blind and passive preoccupation was there again. He did not answer. She was sure he had not even heard her, but had responded mechanically.

"Will you come?" she repeated, and now her lips trembled with her grief and remorse.

He averted his head. He shivered violently. "No," he answered hoarsely, dully. "I cannot come." He looked at her, and deep within those suffering and tormented eyes a spark lighted. "I cannot come, again."

She was silent. Something seemed to open wide in her chest, and bleed. It was too late. Too late for Wilhelm, now. But she forced herself to be calm.

"But I have a dear friend I should like you to know, Wilhelm," she pleaded. "An old friend, Doctor Traub."

The name caught von Keitsch's attention. He turned to her alertly. "Doctor Traub? An old fat man? I have heard of him." His tone was pleasant and noncommittal, but all at once a thrill ran through Therese, ominous and warning. "A gentleman of the old school," added von Keitsch, lightly.

"A gentleman," said Therese, and looked at him fully with her cold gray eyes.

Von Keitsch laughed lightly. "We have no need for gentlemen in Germany today. They are too apt to be obstructionists. The status quo is always their fetish. They do not know that there is a status quo no longer, that events move, that time moves, that the world moves. They refuse to face facts."

"But facts can change, also," said Therese, through chilled lips. "The fact of today is the exploded theory of tomorrow."

Von Keitsch merely smiled, inclining his head. He was evidently enjoying himself. Loathing him, unable to endure his presence another moment, Therese rose and drew on her gloves. The Captain and Alfred rose, also, but Wilhelm was lost again in his awful dream and saw nothing, except his enemy.

"I should hate to see Germany become an exploded theory," said Therese, regarding the Captain with her calm and bitter look.

He bowed. "I am sure you will not see it, dear lady," he said.

"I am not so sure, Herr Captain. I am afraid you have given Germany a very bad repute in the world, and a very bad stench. The world does not like bad reputes and bad smells."

"But the world already smells so bad, Frau Doctor!" he protested, laughing. "Did you think it was a rose-garden?"

She did not answer. She looked again at Wilhelm. But he was an image of intense hatred, fixed towards the Captain. Her heart sank with dread, and a sick premonition.

The early twilight was already closing in on the city. She was driven away. Again, she felt mortally ill and shaken. She could not go home! Not just yet, to that tomb, to that darkness, to that all-pervading atmosphere of waiting doom!

She gave orders that she be taken to the home of Doctor Traub.

27 "BUT FIRST," said Doctor Traub, after one thoughtful look at Therese, "you must dine with us. And I warn you, my child, that we shall converse of nothing more important than the weather."

Therese had to laugh, in spite of the hot pain that heated her nerves. She thought: Why not? We can always resume the load of suffering. It is not bad to put it down for a little, and rest, and pretend it is not there. The eased shoulders and tortured muscles were made stronger by this, and the burden not so heavy.

She went to the old-fashioned wooden bathroom where she had washed her hands a thousand times when she had been a child. In this dusty dull mirror on the door she had seen her long pale-golden curls, her round cheeks, her thin young shoulders. She remembered how proud she had been when from time to time more and more of her figure could be seen in the glass, as she grew, until the day of her first long dress and her first up-coiled hair. Strange that it was always the inconsequential that one remembered through the years. She remembered how fascinated she was at seeing her full form in the glass; how she had pirouetted! She had said aloud, exultantly: "I am full-grown now!" Remembering this, Therese stood in deep silence, gazing at herself in the mirror, looking into her own eyes and seeing the shadowy hollows of her cheeks. She said aloud, as she had said that long-ago day: "I am full-grown, now."

She bathed her face and hands, combed her hair. She was full of a mysterious peace. When she came downstairs, with a tranquil air, Doctor Traub looked at her and thought: My little girl has come to full stature. He was happy. He thought of how few human beings ever come to full stature, but must return to the mystery from which they had come almost as unformed as they had emerged. He could see the incomplete souls, like the clay and stone abandoned half-done by a sculptor. Here and there the vague outline of a face, or perhaps one awakened eye, or a shapeless body in which the living arms

250

were still unformed. They were like embryos, still in the
mother's womb. The world was full of them, these embryos,
painfully striving for form, or still sunken in semi-uncon-
sciousness. Horrible thought, that the world was crowded
with fetuses; unshaped, unconscious, in various processes of
becoming, and animated only by the most primordial instincts
of the fish and the crawling seaweed from which their life had
sprung! It was a nightmare of horror, to think of it. He
thought of the world as the womb in which the fetuses were
forming—but how many of them never attained form! If
one could look beyond the mere-seeming about him, he would
go mad. Perhaps that was the secret of madness: the sudden
ability to see.

He said to Therese: "Helene has a wonderful duck for
dinner." He added: "You were always so fond of duck, my
dear."

"I still am." She bent and kissed his grizzled fat cheek.

The little house was lighted and warmed. The lamps hid the
shabbiness of the furniture, the worn rugs. There was nothing
but peace and love in the quiet, old-fashioned rooms. The
clock did not toll tonight. It rang comfortingly, warmly.
Autumn flowers were thrust thickly in a dozen mismatched
containers. The mirrors reflected them, and reflected the newly
lit fires. From the kitchen came the absurd and happy shrilling
of a cuckoo clock. The table was already laid. The damask
cloth, though patched and mended, was a sheet of stiff white
satin on which the heavy old silver sparkled and shone in the
lamplight. The whole house was full of the delicious and reassuring odors of duck and dressing, of hot cake and good
coffee. It must be a gala occasion. One did not, in Germany,
these days, assemble so many delightful foodstuffs at one and
the same time.

Then she remembered. It was the doctor's birthday. No
wonder he had not been surprised to see her. He had expected
her. And she had come empty-handed. He must know by now
that she had forgotten.

She held his arm as they went to the dining room. "It is
your birthday," she said.

His old plump face brightened with childish pleasure. "So
you remembered! I might have known that you would not forget, liebchen."

Helene came in from the kitchen, wiping her hands, her
apron flecked, as usual, with flour, her gray hair tumbled and

wispy, her homely face flushed and smiling and damp, her manner flurried but affectionate, and her beautiful eyes, as always, shining, simple and tender.

"I knew you would not be late, Therese," she said, kissing the other woman. "The duck is cooked to perfection." She wiped her forehead unaffectedly on the back of her worn hand, and beamed with delight.

Therese fervently thanked chance for bringing her here tonight. She would have given disappointment and sadness to these two dear ones who loved her. Never had she so appreciated this love as she did now. Her chilled body was revived and comforted by it, made to feel safe by it. For it was unassailable.

The dinner was excellent. The sly little maid smiled egotistically at the praise of the doctor, though Helene, of course, had done the major part of the cooking. Therese, like all her kind, rarely noticed servants. But when she saw that foxy small face framed in yellow braids, she had a faint feeling of revulsion. I see specters everywhere, she admonished herself severely, and forgot the little maid, who most evidently did not like nor respect Helene, though she was goodness and kindness itself.

The doctor prattled. He told amusing and malice-free stories of anonymous patients and their vagaries. Suddenly a little cloud of soberness came over his face. "Almost every one who comes to me is suffering poignantly. But it is not physical suffering. It is a torment of the mind. I have never seen so many neurotics. I do not like the word: 'neurotic.' An easy and lazy word to dismiss a condition which we do not understand. That is the trouble with people. They label something, and think they have disposed of it. What is a neurotic? Many psychiatrists, the fools! say that a neurotic is a man who is suffering from some maladjustment rooted in forgotten childhood, a present condition from which there is a cowardly flight, or a glandular disturbance. I say it is none of these. I say it is a desperate hunger of a starving soul for something which will make life significant, beautiful and satisfying." He added: "The world is full of neurotics. That is very terrible. And very dangerous."

"What do you do for your neurotics?" asked Therese.

The doctor was very grave. "At first I was naïve. I sent them to pastors. Now I know better. I give them the Bible. I must have bought hundreds of little cheap Bibles!" He smiled ruefully. "And then I tell them to walk alone in the woods, under the trees. Every day, for weeks, until they are cured, carrying their Bibles, and reading, and meditating. There are some that say it helps a neurotic to be plunged into social life and social contacts. This is wrong. At heart, the neurotic is sick of his fellow men. He is intelligent; he sees too much. So I send him away, to be alone. The neurotic is full of inner resources and strengths; the presence of his fellows disrupts his contemplation, disperses his fortitudes. Alone, he can reestablish his strength, coordinate his power. He can see beyond men. He can draw faith and courage from an uncorrupted atmosphere. All intelligent men, that is to say, all neurotics, are Narcissi. But strange to say, in worshipping their own image, they worship God, and are renewed."

They went into the shabby living room with its quiet lights and its snapping little fire. They sat about the hearth. Therese looked at her burden, and shrank from it. But she took it up at last with a sigh, and told the doctor of Kurt. Doctor Traub listened in silence, his face heavy with compassion. Then he said: "Kurt and Karl are both committing suicide, perhaps subconsciously. Yes, most probably subconsciously. They believe that in killing themselves they are killing what they hate. Just as the German people are killing themselves to avenge themselves. Hitler is their weapon."

"That loathsome man!" exclaimed Therese in a low voice. "Why have we not a David to kill him?"

The doctor shook his head. "It is not Hitler—it is the German people. It is not Hitler—it is every man everywhere. The world, in its hatred, is committing suicide."

Helene, who was sewing at his right hand, looked up in silence, and gazed at him. At one time Therese had thought her stupid, for her eyes were so open, so clear, so shining. She never had anything to say of any profundity. Now Therese knew that she was not stupid at all.

The doctor went on, as though musing aloud: "We are in a state of revolution. The revolution has started in Germany; it will spread everywhere. For there has come in these times a revolt against materialistic, industrial Protestant realism. Modern science, with its zealous hunting-out and destroying of all forms of Mythos, has urged man to lose faith in everything but himself. It has not learned that there is nothing in man, as a being, to create and sustain faith. There must be something beyond himself, some great spiritual and divine head, to lift him out of his primal swamp. Man, today, is in revolt against a realism which offers him no hope, no joy, no reward, except the bare bones of reason, and the dry desert of materialism. Man cannot live by reason alone."

He filled his pipe. Crumbs of tobacco spilled over his fat untidy paunch. But the firelight lay in his wise, sad eyes. "Reason!" he murmured, with sorrowful contempt.

Therese was silent. She listened to the rising autumn wind as it growled impotently and restlessly at the windows. The fire threw up showers of golden sparks. Helene no longer sewed. She looked only at her husband, and there was such a light of love in her tired eyes that Therese felt reverence.

The doctor resumed his musing voice: "There is a hunger in man which cannot be satisfied by industrial progress, by material prosperity. Civilization in itself, with its buildings, its comforts, is not enough. Nor can man be deluded by the high-minded but stupid altruism of those who urge that his faith should be centered in his species, and that it is his sole duty to advance the 'educational' and material welfare of other men. That is all right as far as it goes. But it does not go far enough. Man, the individual, cares, at the last, and rightly, for his own inner joy alone. He cannot secure that joy by building new buildings, or paving more roads, or putting more money in the bank. The joy is secured only by an inner sense of spiritual growth, of mysticism, of God-awareness. He will have his faith, if he dies for it. But sometimes faith can take the most frightful forms. As it is taking it in Germany today."

He got up, slowly, as though impelled by some deep dolorous restlessness. He walked heavily up and down the room. It was evident that he was very distressed. He stopped before Therese, and stood looking down at her. But she knew he did not really see her.

He resumed: "The leaders of German National Socialism say that we are now in a process of revolution. I have read the comments of other countries in answer to this. How smug they are, how stupid, how ridiculously amused! The dreadful fools! They do not know that our leaders in Germany are right! So right that it does not bear thinking of. But it is not a social revolution. It is a revolution of the human spirit, which has become distorted and crippled. Therese, do you remember the description in Victor Hugo's *Notre Dame*, of that section of Paris called Thieves' Alley? Do you remember his description of that dark and tortuous place, leaning and grotesque, fetid and unclean, swarming with cripples and the blind and the evil? Well, that is the world today."

He had conjured up such a fearful vision that Therese could only sit in paralyzed silence. Leaving her, the doctor resumed his pacing. He spoke aloud, but almost inaudibly:

"Robbed of the Mythos by twentieth-century realism, the German people have swung back to their ancient Wagnerian gods. Denied true faith and beauty, as all the world is deprived, they have recreated demons and angels, heroes and warriors, grandiloquent attitudes and Thors and Odins. A violent faith, but faith in truth, subconscious, deep and powerful, primitive and destructive. Bereft by fools of the Mythos of God, they have created a Mythos of Satan, in which there is still a wild and terrible beauty, a passionate escape from bitter and untenable reality, and a faith beyond humanity. Denied the powers of light, they have taken to themselves the powers of darkness. Faith can be evil and violent, as well as good and noble. The new faith will destroy the world, for it is beyond good and evil."

He added: "The whole new faith of Germany is turned inevitably towards war. But war is only one manifestation of it, the manifestation of hatred. Yes, we shall have war. Every nation will be involved in it. They will think that war the beginning of the end. But the beginning was in the despair of men, and the end will not be victory or conquest or defeat. The end will be in the complete destruction of men, or a spiritual rebirth. Germany will provoke the initial attack, and the world will then attack her completely. It will not know that in destroying Germany it is really avenging itself on its own faithlessness, and committing suicide. But nothing can halt the course of events now. Nothing but a universal awakening of the soul of all men."

He paused, then murmured: " 'The desolation of abomination. . . . For then shall be great tribulation, such as was not since the beginning of the world to this time, no, nor ever shall be. . . . And except those days should be shortened, there should no flesh be saved. . . .' "

For two thousand years those words had lain dormant, forgotten, covered with dust, sunken into the grave of time. But now they had emerged from the darkness like flaming torches into the present. With them came the imminent muttering of the drums of dooms, and every mountain, every plain, re-echoed them until all the world shivered and reverberated.

Men thought of the punishment of God. They did not know that they punished themselves.

"The National Socialists are right," said the doctor. "The order of the present day is corrupt and decaying. But the National Socialists merely feed and fatten on it, like vultures."

Therese's heavy vague glance encountered the mirror over the fireplace. She saw the foxy peeping face of the little maid. For an instant the two pairs of eyes met, and the face disappeared. Alarm ran through Therese. She tried to tell herself that all servants peeped inquisitively. But she could not quiet her alarm. The ominous words of Captain von Keitsch, uttered so negligently, came back to her urgently.

She waited until Doctor Traub had approached her again in his pacing. Then, with a quick glance in the mirror to be sure she was not overheard, she said:

"Today, in Kurt's house, I saw that odious man, Captain von Keitsch. Do you know him, Doctor?"

He came out of his sorrowful musing with obvious effort. Then he nodded slowly. "A little. I knew his father well. He was one of my patients."

Therese paused. She suddenly felt ridiculous. She was hysterical! She could not, even with so much evidence in her mind, quiet a feeling that she was more than a little absurd. She said reluctantly, in a low voice:

"He spoke of you today. Quite lightly. But—but I had a feeling there was something there beside lightness. He implied you were an obstructionist—among other things. It was all very casual, and there seemed nothing to it. But I had the most curious sensation. . . ."

She paused again. And then to her intense surprise she saw that Helene had started. She heard her utter a faint cry. But Helene was not looking at her; she was staring desperately, with terror, at her husband.

Turning from Helene, Therese regarded the doctor in astonishment. He had taken his pipe abruptly from his mouth. He held it quietly in his hand. His whole body and attitude were quiet. He stood looking down at Therese with sudden sharpness. His face was very pale.

There was a long, and to Therese, an inexplicable silence. Helene continued to stare at her husband with frozen terror. The clock in the hall ticked loudly. Therese heard a faint and furtive shuffling of feet beyond the hall. Perhaps the doctor heard it, and understood it. He lifted his head abruptly, and appeared to listen. Then, with that same hard abruptness, he left the room and went into the hall. Therese heard him pick up the telephone. There was another silence. And then at last the doctor's voice, calm, matter-of-fact, quite loud:

"Gottfried? This is Felix. How is your mother tonight? Did she respond to those tablets I left for her?"

A pause. "Good. I am glad she is improved. I do not think it necessary for me to see her tonight. I will see her soon, however, I have a visitor." He repeated, slowly: "I have a visitor, and do not wish to leave. In the meantime, continue with the treatment I prescribed for your mother. That is all I can do. I can do nothing more at present."

Therese heard the click of the receiver. She glanced at Helene. The poor woman was as white as old ash. Her hands lay over her sewing, and trembled violently. It was nightmarish; it was incredible. The doctor came back into the room. He had aged visibly. But he was quite composed. He looked at his wife: "I could hardly hear Gottfried," he said. "The connection was very poor. I must notify the company."

His commonplace words seemed to inspire fresh fear in Helene. She paled even more. Her hands shook, and her sewing fell from her lap. Therese stared, dumbfounded. She shook her head a little. She felt the cold wind of terror in the room. She heard the ticking of the clock, the sighing of the wind at the windows. She shook her head again, incredulously.

The doctor turned to her. His voice was still quiet. "Therese, my dear, I am afraid we shall have a storm. I will take you home at once."

"No, please, Doctor. I can call a cab."

But he shook his head. He looked deeply into her eyes. He was trying to tell her something. Helene rose. She tried to speak. She had to try several times before she said: "I will get you your coat and furs, Therese." The doctor left the room. Tears were thick in Helene's eyes as she brought Therese's things.

The little maid came in, carrying Therese's bag, which she had forgotten. She was demure and smiling. Therese, in her confusion, thought nothing of it until she saw Helene's distended eyes riveted in horror on the girl. The old sickening suffocation clutched Therese's throat. She was beginning to understand.

She heard the chugging and spitting of the doctor's ancient car outside. She kissed Helene warmly, and said in a natural voice: "Thank you so much, dear Helene, for a delightful dinner. May I come again, soon?"

Helene nodded, tried to smile. She embraced Therese. Therese felt the desperate clutch of her arms, the beating of her shaken heart.

Then she went outside and climbed into the car. The doctor did not speak.

THEY RODE in a profound silence. The old car, far past its usefulness, swayed, groaned, creaked, lurched, through the quiet dark streets. Here and there a street lamp made a glow of orange or russet fire deep in the heart of some autumn-colored tree. The huge yellow "hunter's moon" stood in the black sky, motionless. The air was crisp and smoky, yet fresh and cool. Doctor Traub avoided the more populous streets. He drove past still walls of houses with their narrow rectangles of golden light. He drove past quiet gardens and dark shops. Here there was peace, with only an occasional footfall, or the passing lamps of other cars.

Therese waited in silence. She knew he had something to tell her. She prayed internally that it would not be important. The restful evening calmed her fears, reclaimed her fortitude. Finally, the doctor drove more slowly. He entered a street empty of trees, with houses set far back from the pavement. He stopped under a bright street lamp. Therese could see the street stretching emptily to the front and back of the car. Then she knew he had chosen this spot deliberately. No one could approach the car for a long distance without instantly being seen. They were isolated by the brightly lit solitude.

She still waited. For a considerable time, the old doctor sat beside her, staring absently before him. Then he began to speak in a very low voice:

"Therese, watch ahead, and tell me if any one comes. I shall watch in the rear mirror. Lift your hand at an approach. Do you understand?"

"Yes," she murmured. She tingled with apprehension.

"It is evident I am being watched," he said, so softly that she could barely hear him. "Therese, God must have sent you tonight, with your warning. I do not care for myself. But— there is Helene, and those I have been helping."

Therese was terrified. But she did not remove her eyes from the open street. "Oh, do not do it! What shall I do if they arrest you, and kill you? You are all I have!"

He pressed her hand, warmly and comfortingly. But that was all the reply he gave to her pleading.

"Listen to me carefully, my child. I should have taken you

into my confidence before. But I thought you had enough burdens, without adding anxiety for me to them. But now I must confide in you." He paused.

"I am a member of the Underground. We help those who have a price on their heads to escape. I know it is only a temporary escape, that flight into Austria, into Czecho-Slovakia, into France, into England, into America! Murder and fury and madness will catch up with them eventually. But in the meantime, they have a little while left to work, undisturbed. That is all that matters—our desperate work. Those who flee are sworn to persuade those countries in which they have taken refuge to arm, morally and physically, against the madness and rage which is Germany. Perhaps their work is futile. We dare not think of that. We hope for the best, and pray. We know that in five or in ten years, Germany, armed with violence and insanity, will attempt, either by propaganda or by force, to subjugate the world, to infect the moral bodies of men with her own virus. We know that that virus is still dormant in other peoples, but we also know that at the coming of Germany, at her breath of plague, the virus will become active. It is our duty, and the duty of those who have fled, to urge immunization, both spiritually and with great armaments. There is time no longer for cries of 'Peace!' For the demons of hatred and treachery and violence have been invoked everywhere.

"The world must awaken. It must dedicate itself. It must conjure up a vision, and take up the sword. That is its only hope. If it will not do these things, then not only is Germany lost, but all men everywhere."

Therese said nothing. Fear had frozen her body again. She started intently at the empty street. Once, glancing away, she saw the doctor's eyes fixed vigilantly in his mirror.

He sighed. "But look at our enemies in other countries! Greedy merchants, blind or treacherous politicians, silly idealists with dirty noses, idiot intellectuals with their bleatings of 'social consciousness,' crafty or short-sighted pacifists with their wailings for disarmament and peace, traitors who hate their own people and viciously wish to see them enslaved or destroyed by the virus, haters of men everywhere, avaricious mountebanks whose bellies will never be satisfied—and all the impotent, fearful, timorous, ignorant masses in every land. And last, but not least, God pity us! a Christianity which has not only failed Germany, but all the world. For if Christianity had been a living vital force in Germany, we should never have countenanced Hitler and all his unspeakable atrocities. Germany would never have been enslaved. The rest of the world would have had its noble fortitude to resist its own traitors and fools, its betrayers and seducers."

Therese looked at the quiet and peaceful night, at the repose of the great city. "Oh, surely you are taking too dark a view! Germany is suffering and tormented, but it cannot last. Surely it cannot last! All extravagance is finally reduced to moderation. Germany, beaten and wretched, convulsed by crazy malefactors though she is, is too impotent, too weak, to threaten other nations."

The doctor did not turn to her, but she saw his dark and sorrowful smile in the mirror.

"What you say is true, at present, in 1933. But wait until 1938, 1939, 1940! I may not be alive, then, Therese, but probably you will still be living. Then, you will remember what I have told you.

"If Germany were ostracized now, quarantined now, avoided now, there would be hope. But think of the shopkeepers in England, the industrialists in America, the haters and crafty in France! I tell you, all of these will help the new Germany. They will help Hitler. They will lend him money, advance his interests, encourage his violence. Because of greed, wickedness and their private hatreds. You think me extravagant. My God, if I only were!"

His breathing became quick and panting. He shook his head.

"It is not Germany I fear. It is the evil men everywhere, the evil men who destroyed the German Republic, the greedy men who want markets, the pusillanimous and envious men who detest men of other nations. I fear, not Germany, but the wicked of the world, who have made German National Socialism possible, and who will do all they can to make it possible in their own countries. I fear the breakdown of the souls of men by moral disintegration, by cowardice, avarice, by irresponsibility, by hatred and exigency, cruelty and rapacity. These are the threats I fear. It is our duty to combat them, to awaken other peoples to the enemy without and within."

He was silent for a long moment, then resumed:

"You say it is only Germany. But it is not! Look at Italy, Russia. There is the same virus, under only a slightly different form.

"At the present time Hitler affects to despise Italy, privately calling the Italians impotent actors. He affects to hate Russia, declaring that National Socialism is the mortal enemy of bolshevism. But he is a fiendishly clever man. He is inspired by all the powers of darkness, which hate God. He knows that bolshevism, National Socialism and fascism are one and the same manifestation of the will-to-power, the will-to-destruction, the will-to-hate, the will-to-enslave. Some day, perhaps not too far away, he will combine with them, recognizing them openly as part of the world-revolution against modern civilization, decency, tolerance, peace and love, goodness and God."

He sighed, mournfully. His thoughts seemed to shift.

"All the conquerors of history have been animated by one desire: to expand their boundaries, to seize land. But in these days the conquerors and potential conquerors have but one awful objective: to destroy the souls of men. Therese, can you understand the horror of this?"

She was silent. She shivered.

He continued, sighing deeply: "The wars and the convulsions which will take place will be psychic upheavals, for all their outward manifestations of fury and violence. Below the clash of arms will seethe the earthquakes and tidal waves of souls in the process of dying and souls in the process of awakening. Which will win? I do not know. I know only that we who understand are doing what we can."

Overpowered as she was by the dreadfulness of what she had been hearing and thinking, the human heart of Therese cried out:

"But I cannot bear to think of losing you! What shall I do, then?"

He was silent a moment, then said gently:

"You can wait for Karl. When he comes back to you, awakened, you will both know what to do."

Therese began to weep, as one weeps for the beloved dead. Doctor Traub held her hand warmly, strongly, but never removed his eyes from the mirror. Two men approached the car slowly, seemingly engaged in deep conversation. They hesitated when they saw the car, then went on. The doctor did not speak until they had vanished at the end of the street. And then he saw that they lingered at the corner, apparently having forgotten the car under the light.

He spoke hurriedly:

"Listen to me, Therese. I have only a little time left. Two

men have just passed us. Probably they are only innocent neighbors. But there is a chance they are not.

"I will give you a name and address. Remember them. Do not write them down, but repeat them to yourself frequently so you will not forget."

She lifted her tear-wet face and listened. He put his lips to her ear and whispered the name and address several times. She nodded, wiping her eyes.

"And then, Therese, when Karl has come back, you will give him that name and address. He will know what to do, after he has seen this man and talked with him.

"Tonight, I was to take a refugee into my house, and hide him for a few days until he could get away, until a forged passport was prepared for him. He is a great scientist and philanthropist. He is to go to America, and there help with the work. He is hunted by the Gestapo. His capture means his instant death, and the death of those who have sheltered him.

"When you told me about von Keitsch, I knew the Gestapo was watching us and suspecting us. When I lifted the receiver to call 'Gottfried' I heard the unmistakable sound of wire-tapping. I might not have noticed it, but for your warning. 'Gottfried' knows, by my message, that he must immediately hide the refugee somewhere else, get him away at once. You have done a wonderful thing for us, Therese."

He started the car. He turned it about and hurriedly proceeded down the street, away from the direction of the lingering men.

They did not speak again. Therese looked at the doctor's face by the passing street lamps. He sat beside her, pudgy, short, the personification of the undistinguished German petty bourgeoisie, his snub nose glistening, his straggling little beard untidy and ragged, his clothing shabby and wrinkled. It was hard to believe that this small, comfortable old fat man was engaged in a heroic struggle, without malice and violence. Her heart shook with her love and fear for him. What could he do at best? And then she saw his expression, grim and resolute and very calm.

Her attention was suddenly distracted. She pointed to a red glow in the sky.

"What is that? A fire?"

He peeped. "Another Reichstag 'fire,' probably," he said bitterly. "Let us see."

29 THE RED GLOW became scarlet as they approached it. Now the quiet streets were alive with running, excited, conjecturing people, honking cars, bellowing and ringing fire-engines. "What have the accursed Jews done now?" shouted a wild-faced man at Doctor Traub and Therese, as he ran beside their automobile. "Another Reichstag fire!" shouted others. The light carved faces and running forms out of the darkness with a red ax. Therese, in the midst of the confusion, thought of harsh woodcuts. She could smell the acrid odor of smoke, and now could discern the faint far crackling of flames. She could see gray, fire-shot serpents of flame coiling up against the black sky and the huge yellow moon.

The congestion increased until it was impossible for a car to proceed. The upper windows of shops and houses reflected scarlet light, like a sunset. People were tumbling and running from every doorway. The streets roared with voices. Doctor Traub inched towards a curb, and then abandoned his car. He took Therese by the arm, and they left the car together.

They were immediately absorbed by a river of humanity, surging to one objective. Therese clung tightly to the doctor as she was buffeted and swirled along. She saw a group of young working-girls struggling through the crowds. Their mouths were wide open and their eyes glittered with an idiotic insane glee. They chanted shrilly: "Down with the Jews! Down with the Jews!"

Doctor Traub glanced at Therese with a bitter look. Suddenly she cried to him, striving to keep her hat on her head: "Let us turn back! I want to go home!"

If he heard her, he gave no sign. He was strong, in spite of his age, shortness and bulk; he pushed her through wedges he made with his arms with a sort of concentrated grimness of purpose. She could not resist him; he gripped her arms with stern strength and resolution, pushing her on. She smelled the sweat and the excitement of the throngs, and was nauseated. It was like being in the lion house at the Tiergarten. There

was the same acid stench of brutality and ferocity, the same
savage undercurrent.

They could go no farther. They had pushed up against a
wall of humanity, static, roaring, shrieking, whistling, laughing and jeering, even leaping in an excess of ecstatic joy. The
crackling was at hand; sheets and towers of flame leaped upward against the sky. The smoke and heat were stifling.
Therese could see clearly. The crowd was gathered about a
great burning synagogue. She could see the mighty round
copper dome, glowing with fire like an enormous sun in the
midst of a pointed crown of flame. Shadows of darker or
brighter incandescence wavered over it, like sunspots. From
where she stood, she could see only the dome and the narrow
upper windows, from which long tongues of fire flickered
out. The sky above the conflagration pulsed with rose and
crimson, pierced with bursting sparks like rockets, or exploding stars.

But the most terrible thing of all was the faces of the watching and shrieking and laughing and howling multitude. It was
a disembodied multitude consisting only of those closely
packed faces, on which the bloody light of hell was reflected.
She saw the countless evil glittering eyes, the opened screaming mouths, like dark caverns. No distinguishing features were
revealed. The crowd was one bestiality, one madness, one
mouth.

She felt Doctor Traub's grip again; he was pushing her on-
ward, inch by inch, through the crowd. She tried to protest,
feebly. But she could not resist him. She saw his white round
face, his narrowed cold eyes. The heat burned her face, made
sweat leap out upon it. Once or twice she would have fallen
but for his crushing hold upon her. Dimness came over her
vision; there was a confused murmuring in her ears. She began to whimper, deep in her throat.

When she could see clearly again, she saw that she was
quite close to the synagogue. Her arms were crushed to her
side. Near by, laughing, jeering, spitting obscene jokes, were
a large group of Storm Troopers. The crowds extended about
and behind her, endlessly, constantly replenished from the
side streets. Everything was as bright as day, with a vivid red
glare. Before her was the synagogue, its dark stone walls punc-
tuated and exploding with flames. Through the dull roaring
she could hear the chant of thousands of hoarse voices:

"Down with the Jews! Kill the Jews!" The majestic copper dome glowed blindingly.

It was evident that the multitude was waiting for something, gloating. Their thousands of eyes were fixed exultantly on the great open doors of the temple. Suddenly a harsh and deafening and fiendish roar went up from them. Two old men were staggering through the doorway, gasping, scorched, smoke-blackened and burned. They were carrying the great shining scrolls in their arms. They were all Israel, bearing the Covenant through the flames, the fury, and the madness of a hell-ruled world.

Therese heard a groan like death at her elbow. It was Doctor Traub. She hardly recognized him. His round fat face was ghastly; tears ran down his cheeks. The fire engines had drawn up, but the crew sat grinning on the heaps of hose and ladders, doing nothing. Some of them smoked casually, and exchanged witticisms with their neighbors.

The two old men with their scrolls stood on the steps of the synagogue. They looked down at the red-lit bellowing crowds. They did not move. Exhaustion, despair, hopelessness, suffering, stood on their faces, bowed their scorched bodies. Their legs trembled; they swayed. But they held the heavy scrolls in their arms with a desperate devotion, a desperate courage. Somewhere a woman's cry of anguish rose above the dull subterranean uproar.

The smell of hatred and fury and demonic joy was an overpowering stench. The hoarse chant of "Kill the Jews!" rose again. The multitude began to surge and sway; scores were thrown to their feet and trampled. No one cared. Violence and madness blew over them like fetid whirlwinds. The Storm Troopers forced a passage for themselves, leaped up upon the burning steps of the synagogue. They lifted their truncheons. They brought them down upon the skulls of the bowed old men. In spite of the deafening roaring the brittle crack could be heard clearly.

The old men wavered grotesquely. Blood ran in streams down their faces. Then they fell, suddenly. The scrolls crashed on the steps. The Troopers jumped up and down on the prostrate bodies of the old men. Then they turned upon the scrolls and kicked them savagely. The ancient scrolls with their silver tops fell out. The Troopers crushed them under their feet with insane savagery. The crowd, watching, shrieked, screamed, foamed with erotic rage and joy.

The Troopers, having accomplished their foul purpose, ran down the steps, for the flames were too close and searing. The old men lay where they had been murdered, the unrolled, befouled and torn scrolls blowing about them.

Therese was certain she was going to faint, and with dim eyes looked about for Doctor Traub. But he had disappeared. She called to him, weakly, wildly, in a frenzy of fear. She extended her hands, searching for him, like some one gone blind. But he did not answer her. She heard a sudden wild roaring, as of excitement or astonishment. But she continued to call for the doctor, with growing despair and terror. Her hat was lost; her hair fell over her face. Her clothing was torn, and her bag had somehow been wrenched from her arm.

She began to weep. No one heeded her. A sudden silence fell abruptly on the multitude, and in that silence the crackling and vomiting of flames could be heard sharply and distinctly. That silence was profound, almost deafening, in its intensity.

Finally, even she, in her distraction, was aware of it. Sobbing, she looked towards the synagogue again. Then a wild thin cry broke from her. Doctor Traub stood on the smoking steps, astride the dead bodies of the old men.

He had lifted his arm. It was that gesture which had silenced the crowd. Little, fat, round though he was, there was majesty and an awful dignity about him. Behind him the dark, flame-split walls were a background of dreadful splendor. The throngs surged closer, peering over each other's heads, trampling on each other, the better to see. The crimson light glimmered on their astounded faces, their open but soundless mouths.

"Oh, no!" moaned Therese. "Oh, no!"

But no one heard her. Thousands upon thousands of eyes were fixed on the little doctor, standing there in his majesty, with his upraised hand, his face glowing with the scarlet light. He was a statue, stern, quiet, heroic. Far above him palpitated the enormous incandescent dome.

Then he spoke. His voice rang over the sea of faces, clearly, sharply, yet with a strange carrying quietness.

"People of Germany!" he said. "Look closely. Look at your victims. Look at your fire. It is not this building which is burning. These poor old men have not been murdered. It is Germany which is burning! It is yourselves who have been beaten down and destroyed!"

The crowd was utterly silent. He might have been addressing a multitude of graven images in a forest of fire.

He bent down and lifted a tattered scroll. It was enormous, and blew about him in the wind from the flames like a great, torn white banner.

"Look closely, Germans! This is not paper you have trampled and desecrated. It is the Word of God!"

The silence became more intense. Somewhere, behind the thick façade of the walls of the temple there was a dull thunder and crashing, as the interior collapsed. The effect of this was terrifying. From behind the walls gushers of renewed fire and flame sprang upwards, like a volcano. The red glare became blinding, too intense for eyes. But the crowd could not look away. It stood, paralyzed, looking only at the little man with the sacred torn scroll in his arms.

"Look closely, Germans!" he cried, and his voice was like a trumpet of doom and prophecy. "Look closely, world of men! This is your funeral fire! This is your destruction! This is your hell and your end! This is the vengeance of Almighty God on a faithless and evil people. Do not think you can escape. Do not think you can hide yourselves behind a wall of your victims. Do not think you can run away. The anger of God will find you out, no matter where you hide. He will not listen to you when you cry to Him: 'We were deceived. We were misled and betrayed.' "

He paused. A furious shout rose somewhere in the packed throngs of sweating humanity, but was instantly silenced.

And now his voice reached them again, somber, stern, ominous. His face ran with tears.

"What you have done tonight, Germans, shall be done to you. Where you kill, a hundred shall die. Where you make homeless, you shall be homeless. Where you exile and drive away, you shall be exiled and driven away. A thousand times a thousand, justice shall be meted out to you. God will not be mocked. For you have opened all hell to demons and fiends. You have set madmen and criminals over you, to lead you. You have put the mark of anti-Christ on your arms and your foreheads. All your blood shall not wash them away.

"I tell you, you are dying tonight. The Fatherland is dying. Germans! Prepare to meet your God! Wicked, lying, callous World, prepare to meet your God!"

He stood with the scroll in his arms; the white torn paper

reflected the conflagration. The silence about him was more terrible, more doomful, than any roaring or shouting.

"O God!" moaned Therese, in her throat. "What good will this do?"

But the people stood in that silence. Their faces were whiter than parchment. Their expressions were transfixed with terror, shame, and wretchedness. Here and there a woman sobbed aloud, but the sound only intensified the silence. The fire crackled; the dome brightened; the flames shot upward as from the pit of hell. No one moved. No one saw anything but the little old man against his background of destruction and fire, fearless but weeping. They saw his tears. They saw his bent head.

Then there was a sudden uproar, a sudden confused surging. The multitude cried out. Several Storm Troopers were bludgeoning their way through the mobs. Their truncheons came down with vicious cracking force on near-by heads. The people fell back, screaming. The Troopers neared the steps. They sprang up upon them. Doctor Traub lifted his head, and calmly saw them coming. He did not move. He did not raise his arms to defend himself. He gazed at them, unafraid, calm.

They struck at him in unison. They surrounded him like lions about a small dog. He disappeared. They bent over something and struck and struck again, lashing out viciously with their boots. Then, with a shout of laughter, they covered their heated faces with their hands, and ran down the steps again. Doctor Traub, mangled and bleeding, lay beside the two old men. The scroll near him was bright red with his blood.

Therese could feel nothing. But she moaned over and over, automatically: "They have killed him. What good has this done? What good?"

The crowd was still petrified. Then, suddenly, the great black wall of the temple shivered, thundered. Slowly, horribly, it buckled, bent outward, and then, with a dull, earth-shaking crash, it fell. Its great loosened stones seemed to fly through the burning air. They fell, thundering and crashing, over the three bodies on the steps, burying them under tons of smoking debris. Behind them fell the mighty incandescent dome. Eruptions of renewed flame and smoke belched upwards. The heat was terrific.

Again, there was a sudden fateful silence, as though the multitudes had stopped breathing.

All at once that red silence was torn by a single savage, despairing, inhuman scream. In the midst of the throng there was a swaying, a bestial movement. Shrieking, the crowds tried to see, trampling each other. And when they saw, they screamed also, exultantly, despairingly, savagely. For the mob had turned upon the Storm Troopers. They had seized upon them. They were tearing them limb from limb. They were gouging and stamping and tearing. They foamed. They frothed. They stamped. From their throats came a horrible beastlike growling, as they worried the mangled fragments of the Troopers. The street had become an inferno, an arena, while wild animals twisted and devoured, in the midst of columns and clouds of crimson smoke and shooting sparks.

Hundreds, seized by primal fear, struggled and fought to run away. They poured into side streets, fleeing like frenzied animals. The thunder of pounding feet enhanced the frightful confusion. There was a shrill whistling, and scores of Troopers and police fell upon the mob, shooting, beating, stamping. The masses were now in full flight.

Behind them, the fire smoldered like a vast funeral pyre. The funeral pyre of mankind.

A BROWN LEAF, flecked with gold, flew up into
the dull air, caught a wan gleam of sunlight,
fluttered down. There was another leaf, and
another. The wind sighed restlessly, as though

30

bored with the sad sport. The pale far sky seemed formed
of the very essence of silence, filtering it down upon the earth.

Therese watched the fluttering of the leaves, gazed at the
sky emptily. She willed herself not to think. In these days, one
dared not to think. If one thought, madness came, and overwhelming despair, and the bitterest and most inconsolable
grief. She forced herself to be very quiet, to go about the days
serenely and calmly, like a robot without emotion or sorrows.
When the hot anguish rose up in her like a fire, she would say
to herself sternly: "Tomorrow. But not today. There is too
much to be done."

She forced herself to be absorbed in the most inconsequential things. And so she watched the leaves, compelling her
thoughts to rise and flutter aimlessly with them, until she had
hypnotized herself into unthinkingness.

When she was able to control herself, she dressed, drew on
her gloves, adjusted her hat. She passed her husband's room.
She knew he paced most of the night, every night, and only
slept at dawn. She did not glance at his door. She felt that he
was dead, that he would never rise again, and that he was no
longer part of her life. The closed door was shut on emptiness.

Lotte was dusting the hall below when she saw Therese descending the stairs. "Good morning, gnädige frau. But are you
having breakfast?"

"No, Lotte. I do not feel like it."

Lotte gazed with anxious shrewdness at Therese's pale
strained face. "Not even a cup of coffee?" She sighed. "The
Herr Doctor did not sleep until an hour ago. He wanders
from room to room, searching. He asks me: 'Have you seen
him yet, Lotte?' " She shook her head. "It is too terrible to
see."

Therese's face remained coldly indifferent. Lotte resented

such heartlessness. "He has been ill, Lotte. You must not attach too much importance to his ramblings."

She went out into the cool smoky autumn morning. She walked through the quiet morning streets. Servant girls were scrubbing doorsteps and washing windows. Their uncultured flat voices were the only sound in the stillness, and the scraping of their chairs and pails. Late autumn flowers bloomed on window-sills, and behind the sleeping houses lay old gardens, drowned in misty light. Sparrows fluttered across Therese's path, the pale sun on their gray wings. Chimney pots smoked. There had been a rain last night, and the old roofs shimmered with a dim wet silvery patina.

Therese proceeded calmly, as though with purpose. It was not far to Doctor Traub's house. She saw the little maid washing the steps. The girl stared as Therese came up; she held her mop in her hand, standing in the midst of a froth of wet soapsuds, blinking.

"Is the Frau Doctor up yet?" asked Therese.

The girl curtseyed. "Yes, gnädige frau. She is up early. She is drinking her coffee."

Therese went into the house. It was cool and fresh and dusky in the hall. The old clock chimed eight. Fingers of colorless sunlight streaked the frayed rugs and polished floor. Therese went into the morning-room. Frau Traub was sipping coffee near a bright window.

"Good morning, Helene," said Therese, casually, smiling. "Do you mind if I join you, and drink a cup of coffee?"

"No, Therese, my dear. The coffee is fresh and hot. But it is very bad, I am afraid."

Frau Traub smiled gently. She reached for another cup and poured it full of steaming brown liquid. She had become very old. Her hair was almost white. Her face had shrunken to half its usual size, and was wrinkled and gray. But her beautiful kind eyes were steadfast behind their spectacles. Her hands did not tremble. Glancing up, an expression of concern for Therese changed her smile. But she made no comment.

Therese sat down and removed her gloves. She sipped the coffee. Only then was she conscious of her faintness and exhaustion. But she kept her voice matter-of-fact. "Your train leaves at ten, Helene? I have come to go to the station with you, of course."

Helene's face took on a look of apprehension. She glanced

swiftly at the door. Then she leaned towards Therese. "My dear, do you think it is wise? For you?"

"Why not?"

Helene did not answer. Her smile did not appear again. She was old, and sick, and full of sorrow. The two women finished their coffee in silence.

The little maid furtively passed the door, seemingly intent on her work. Therese raised her voice: "And do not forget, Helene, to give my dearest love to the doctor. And please tell him not to keep you and himself too long in Berne. Of course, he must not return until he is completely rested. But you ought to be back before Christmas?"

Helene drew in a deep sighing breath. "Oh, long before Christmas, Therese." The two women exhausted a desolate look. "I shall write you, Therese, but you must forgive us if we are not good correspondents."

Therese forced herself to laugh.

Helene went on, pretending animation: "I heard from him, yesterday. He is very impatient, because I have delayed joining him for so long. But I thought it best for him to be alone a little while. He is so very tired."

"Yes," murmured Therese, "he was so very tired. We ought to be glad he is—resting, now." She added, quickly, as though to quell some inner torment: "You ought to be happy in Berne, Helene. Are you not often homesick for Switzerland?"

Helene smiled piteously. "At times. But I have many relatives there. We intend to stay with them, of course."

They went upstairs together. Helene walked haltingly, her step like that of a very old woman's. Therese closed the door quickly behind her. Helene turned to her. Her lips opened, and there were tears in her eyes. Then she pressed her mouth tightly together, and turned to her open trunk and cases. Therese helped her pack, in silence. Only at the last did Helene finally turn to her as though to speak, eagerly, despairingly. At this, Therese put her hand firmly over the other's mouth and shook her head warningly.

The little maid tapped at the door, and Helene, forcing her face to serenity, opened it.

"Ah, yes, child," she said. "I am going now. You have called my cab? Thank you. You will remember, after you have finished, to take the keys to Frau Doctor Erlich? And here is an envelope for you. It contains two months' wages.

I will let you know in plenty of time, so you can prepare the house for our return."

The girl curtseyed briefly. She regarded Helene inquisitively. But she only said in her high peasant's voice: "A day's notice is all that I require, Frau Doctor. I wish I were going with you to Switzerland."

Helene smiled gently. "Yes, it is a beautiful place, child. I was born there. The doctor, I hope, will entirely recover his health."

She closed the door softly. She went to her dresser and put on her old shapeless hat and black cotton gloves. Therese could see how her hands trembled, in the mirror. But her homely wrinkled face was without expression, except that of sternness and utter stillness.

Only at the last did this stillness break, and that was at the moment of leaving the large old-fashioned bedroom. She stood beside the great empty canopied bed. She was like one who gazes down, speechless, at a corpse. Here she had lain with her husband for nearly fifty years. Here, she would lie with him no longer. No, never again would she lie with him. Her white head was bent, her gloved hands folded as though she prayed. Tear after tear stole down through the furrows of her old face. But there was no breaking in her, no lessening of fortitude and courage.

She looked about the room again, steadfastly. "Good-bye, good-bye," she whispered. Her face wrinkled and worked. Then she smiled, and at that smile, Therese was forced to turn again. "Good-bye, my darling, my dear," whispered Helene.

She gazed through the window at her beloved tangled old garden, which she was leaving forever. She gazed earnestly, as though searching for some one. There were the bending ancient trees, crowned with misty light, and the high thick grass. She looked at the old red-brick wall, upon which sparrows were warming themselves in the last warmth of the year. The air was full of their cheeping. "Good-bye," said Helene. She put her hand to her lips and blew a kiss to the garden.

"Let us go. It is late," said Therese, who could not bear any more. Her will kept her body rigid and her voice composed.

She helped Helene down the stairway. The older woman walked blindly, stumbling. Two men went upstairs to take the luggage. The little maid stood by the door, blinking slyly, and curtseying. The two ladies entered the cab, and Therese briefly gave directions. Then they sat in silence. Therese did not touch

Helene. She dared not invite either her own or Helene's collapse. She stared sightlessly through the windows, watched the streets roll by. Crowds on the way to work now filled the streets, comfortable bourgeoisie hurrying to catch their busses. The tops of the buildings shimmered with brightened sunlight. The city hummed and murmured.

They passed a small wooded park. It was too early for children and their nursemaids. Therese tapped on the glass, and the man brought his cab to a stop. "We wish to walk a few moments," Therese said. "Wait for us."

She and Helene left the cab, walked into the park, and sat down. They were all alone. The golden and scarlet autumn trees were drenched in cataracts of awakened light. Birds and squirrels ran over the grass. For a long time the two women sat in silence, watching the little animals. The sunlight flickered on their pale drawn faces.

Then Therese spoke, very quietly: "Helene, I have a cheque for you. My Paris bank has transferred funds for you to its bank in Berne. If you need more at any time, you shall have it."

"Thank you, Therese," responded the other woman, as quietly. "But my relatives are quite wealthy. I shall remain with them."

"Nevertheless, even among wealthy relatives, one is more welcome if one is independent. Whatever I have is yours."

"But, Therese, you—you may need it yourself, if you and Karl decide to leave——"

Therese looked at the sky as the dead look, sightlessly. "We shall never leave, Helene."

Again they were silent. They clung desperately to their last moments together, so much unspoken between them, of which they dared not speak.

Then suddenly, terribly, Therese's composure broke. She burst into broken sobs. She bent her head. Her tears spilled down her cheeks. She could not control herself. Her sobs wrenched her throat. Her hat fell off, and her gray-streaked fair hair shone in the sunlight. She abandoned herself to her everwhelming grief and anguish.

"Oh why, oh why, did he do it? What good did it do? What good could it do?" She clenched her hands together in the access of her suffering. "He died for nothing, nothing at all! And now, I have no one in all the world!" Her voice, shattered and smothered, startled the birds and the squirrels, and they scurried away.

Helene did not weep. She put her arms about Therese, and drew her head to her broad flat breast. She held her as a mother holds a child. "Hush, hush, my darling, Therese, will you listen to me, just a moment? Hush, my child. You must listen. I have such a little time. I must talk to you, as we have never talked before since—since he had to go away."

Therese still wept, brokenly, but more quietly. Helene lifted her face to the sky, but her features shone with a brighter and more steadfast light, calm and unshaken. Her eyes were full of the splendor of faith. She smiled, and her smile was sweet and gentle.

"He did not die for nothing, Therese. Some few, perhaps only a handful, in that mob heard him. Only a few. But that is enough. Only a few awakened, only a few made to listen, and see, and understand. But it is still enough. Do you not see? They will make others, many many others, listen and see and understand. His voice, and the voices like his, will be heard. He must have known that. He must have been so happy, knowing it. Do you not understand, Therese?"

Therese lifted her tear-wet haggard face. She looked at Helene, saw her sweet serene smile, her faith-lit eyes.

"Yes," she whispered, after a long while. "Yes, I understand. He used to speak to me of this. But I did not understand, then. Now, I know."

Helene said: "When men like him die, they do not die in vain. It is only when they run away, that other men are lost."

She lifted her head again, and gazed at the sky, the light brighter on her old wrinkled face.

She held Therese more closely, and kissed her wet cheek. "Therese, you know I have to go. You know that Felix never carried any identification with him, knowing that this must happen to him sometime. You know they are still trying to find out who he was. If they do, then they will be able to trace back, and finally they will find the others who worked with him. Felix once told me that if—if he died like this, I must go away. Immediately. For the sake of the other workers. And that is why, as you know, I have had to pretend he is in Switzerland and that I am joining him. You do not know what I have endured these last days, Therese, while waiting for my passport! I thought that at any hour they would come, and say: 'It was your husband who created a riot that night, and we have come to question you, and trace those behind him. We have suspected for a long time that he was engaged in treason.' Therese, you cannot understand what I have endured, forcing myself to show no emotion, no grief, no loneliness! And with that girl watching me every moment. It has been so frightful." But there was no expression of what she had endured in her gentle, smiling face. "And I have had to pretend he is still alive, waiting for me to join him in Switzerland, for a holiday!"

She pressed Therese's hand. "You told me he gave you a certain name. Do not forget it, Therese. You keep it in trust for Karl."

Therese shook her head despairingly. "That is hopeless. Karl is dead."

"No, no, my dear. He is not dead. He will come back. Then you will stand with him, as I stood with Felix. You will understand everything then."

Therese gazed at her through her tears. She saw Helene's courage and gentleness, faith and sweetness. Then Helene said softly:

"I am not so unhappy. I have my memories. And I know that some day, perhaps very soon, I shall see him again. I only hope he will let me work with him once more. For he must still be working."

She wiped Therese's eyes tenderly with her own handkerchief.

"Have faith, have courage, my child. These things are the only hope for the world. You dare not forget them."

Therese put her hat on her head, rearranged her hair. Then she lifted Helene's hand to her lips and kissed it with her trembling lips.

"I shall not forget."

They returned to the cab, and drove away to the station.

31 THERESE struggled with her sorrow, which be-
became worse and more unendurable as the long
silent days passed. She remembered what Helene
had told her. She wept no longer for Felix
Traub. She wept for herself. She had no one. Her house was a
graveyard. The streets were the corridors of the dead, where
an unreal and spectral life went on, without substance. She
immured herself. She refused to answer any calls, or pay any
visits. A pall of heavy mist appeared to float through all the
rooms of her house, in which every sound was muffled. For
hours on end she would sit alone in her room, lips and eyes
as dry as paper, staring blankly before her. "The poor Frau
Doctor suffers so about the Herr Doctor," said Lotte compas-
sionately to her kitchen assistant. "It is worse, rather than
better."

But Therese was not suffering because of Karl. Her grief
was too great. She almost forgot him. Sometimes, subconsciously, she heard his pacing, heard his ghostly sighs behind
his doors. But these things did not enter into the still black
solitude where she crouched, mourning and stricken.

She was not a weak woman. Grief and adversity did not
dissolve her in a warm flood. She hardened in it, became
more resolute. And so it was that on a certain day, near
Christmas, she felt a hard blade of hatred push through the
heavy clay of her sorrow.

She began to hate Karl. Not suddenly, not with an explosive burst, but with a bitter and sullen thrusting upward
from the depths of her misery. She began to hate him, for
he had come to represent all Germany to her, the Germany
which had killed Doctor Traub, Gerda, Eric and Henri Cot,
which had fired synagogues and churches, which had beaten
down the helpless and defenseless, and which had begun to
poison all the earth with hatred, force and violence.

There were times when she tried to recall that Germany
had suffered, and this suffering had taken this frightful form.
But she also remembered that France, during the war, had
suffered more, far more, that Britain had suffered, and Bel-

gium. Their victory over Germany had brought them nothing but starvation, distress, torment, hunger, bankruptcy and hopelessness. They had forgotten the victory. They suffered as Germany had suffered. But they had not gone mad, and had sought no vengeance. Germany had gone mad. She screamed against the Versailles Treaty, which had never been enforced. She was outraged at her own torment. It was insupportable to her. It did not matter to her, and she would not see, that other nations suffered also. Her egotism revolted against her own anguish. She had told herself that she was surrounded by remorseless and gloating enemies, upon which she must be avenged. And so, from the abscess of her intolerable vanity, her sick egotism, her brutelike indifference to the grief of others, she had drawn a virus to make herself mad, knowing that only in a state of grotesque and vivid unreality could she take vengeance on a world she imagined chuckling over her misfortunes, and revelling in them. She lifted herself to a fourth dimension, invoked demons and fiends from the steaming pit of her dark insanity, and spewed out horrors on an appalled world. Worst of all, in becoming mad, she had breathed out her effluvia of madness through the aisles that led to other peoples, and had infected them also, or had at least awakened the latent infection in the souls of other men. Doctor Traub had been right: it was not Hitler. It was the German people. Had Germans been less egotistic, less rigid, less criminally innocent, less ferocious and intrinsically uncivilized, Hitler would have been a name lost only in a cloud of anonymous names forever.

And now Therese saw that hatred is the last weapon of weak peoples. Only the weak, the fundamentally unsound, the inadequate and the inferior, hated. In their hatred was a confession of inferiority. In their hatred was the seed of death, for only the strong can survive, and they were not strong.

She realized now, coldly and bitterly, that Karl was the personification of Germany. He was wounded and stricken. But his suffering had not made him strong, compassionate, resolute and faithful. It had not inspired in him a passionate and wholesome desire to reform outrages, without envy and without egotism. It had only inspired a self-induced madness in him, in which he could hate and take a loathsome vengeance.

Like a small but healthy minority of Germans, Therese detested weakness and extravagance and lack of fortitude. She detested them in her country, and now she detested them in

Karl. Out of the deaths of Eric and Gerda (if he had been strong), he would have taken a stern resolution to help destroy the corruption which had destroyed those he loved. Just as Doctor Traub had taken that resolution. He should have grown in stature, shocked, all-seeing, passionate, yet filled with pity. But instead, he had allowed himself to be absorbed into the anonymous and seething madness of his country. Therese saw now that it was only an accident which had made him hate that which had killed Eric and Gerda. Only a small accident. He might just as easily have hated what Eric represented, if he had not known an Eric. The German intellectual was not superior to the German peasant.

She had come to have a deep suspicion of intellectuals. In spite of their acknowledged mental superiority, they were fundamentally no more than the lowest among their people. Their greater brain-power made them only more ingenious in wickedness and foulness, made their recovery less possible.

And so it was that Therese began to hate Karl. Her compassion was consumed in her bitterness and understanding. She was coldly disgusted. She forgot him more and more, deliberately. Sometimes, when she heard his pacing, his fumbling, she had to clench her fists to control her anger and detestation. She also experienced fear. She felt that she harbored a danger in her house, a danger which was part of the fury outside. Karl was the enemy of Felix Traub. He was one with the violence which had killed her friend.

Sometimes she had an impulse to leave him and his house forever. She would pack her belongings and quietly flee from him, hoping to forget him. And then she thought that she dared not. Her going would open a door to release him into the sea outside. There were the defenseless, outside, struggling in that sea. She dared not release another fury upon them.

She saw now that those who hated, unreasonably and ferociously, were all one, no matter what it was that they hated. They were no better, no worse, than all the other haters. Hatred was a condition with no distinctions.

One day she really thought she would leave. Karl was dead, she told herself. There was no point to remaining. But, at the last, she could not leave. Some mysterious compulsion kept her there, like a guard, like a watcher.

But out of her revulsion and bitterness she drew a new, waiting strength. Perhaps Karl would die, as his poor brother was dying. That was her only hope. She had no real belief that he would awaken to a new self.

If he was a victim, he was a victim of himself. For that, there was no forgiveness.

Daily she called Maria to inquire about Kurt, Kurt who was not a victim of himself, but the bewildered and shattered victim of the madness which had Germany and his brother. At these times, Maria hysterically demanded that Karl be brought to his brother, and would unreasonably shout down Therese's explanations and excuses. Kurt was dying, but he could not die. He could only suffer and wait, coming alive only for brief moments when the door opened and he thought that Karl was coming. Maria wanted nothing more these days but that her husband should obtain relief from his torture, in death. She could not endure the daily anguish of watching his suffering, for which there was no hope. But Karl's absence kept him alive, though every physician said he should have died long ago of his mysterious malady. Maria could not forgive Therese for what she extravagantly termed her squeamish concern for her precious husband. "You are afraid he might be 'disturbed'!" she screamed violently. "You are afraid he might be 'upset'! What does that matter? He has always ill-treated my poor Kurt, in his sly derisive way. Yet he will not come to him, even though he is dying inch by inch!" And then when Therese patiently repeated that Karl was ill, was not himself, and was, at times, literally insane, Maria shrieked with wild and contemptuous laughter. "You lie!" she said. "It is you, only you. You want your petty revenge on Kurt, because you blame him for the deaths of that cursed Eric and Gerda!"

After this, Therese gave orders to Lotte that she must not be called to the telephone when Maria called her.

She went to see the old General one day. She was horrified at the change in him. He was old and broken, shrunken to apparently half his usual size, almost senile. He sat in a chair by a sunny window, wrapped in plaid blankets and robe, his massive head shaking unceasingly with an uncontrollable tremor. But he was very gentle and abstracted, even to the poor silly Martina, who found him less arduous these days. His memory was failing fast. Sometimes in the midst of a remark, he would fall abruptly into a doze, or a stupor, from which he would awake, dazed and blinking. He talked no longer of the National Socialists; he was completely unaware now of the changes in Germany. He spoke only of the campaigns of his youth and his middle age. He repeated, endlessly, and with chuckles, stories of Ludendorff and Hindenburg. He spoke reverently of the Kaiser, who he had come to believe still lived and ruled in Potsdam. Once he said: "I must get better soon. Ludendorff is a good marshal, but stupid. He is no match for the French, who are tough fighters. What is the news from the Western Front today, Therese? And is there really a revolution in Russia? Some one said that the Czar is a prisoner."

He had been very upset when he noticed that the portrait of Hindenburg no longer had its place over the drawing-room fire. Martina hastily explained that it had been taken down for repairs to the frame. He was not satisfied until it was rehung. Then he would hold long, amiable or querulous and bellicose conversations with it. He no longer knew the name of Hitler. When Therese tentatively introduced the name into a conversation, he merely stared, puzzled. "Who is this 'Hitler'? I have never heard of him," he said belligerently. "A plebeian name. Or is it von Hitler?" He shook his head. "A plebeian name. I do not know it."

He liked to recount the tales of his youth, and then he would blink at her archly, in the midst of them. "Ah, that is no story for a maiden, liebchen. You are so young. You would not understand. Ah, we were gay dogs!" And then she knew that he did not see her as she was, but as she had been as a young girl. It was too piteous for her to bear. She could not endure the sight of this broken, senile old man with his shrivelled throat and withered face, who believed himself a virile middle-aged man who was home, invalided by wounds.

While Therese was still with him, some of his old army friends came, old generals and colonels and field marshals. They sat near him, impotent and senile. They did not talk about the present; they talked only of the past. Therese listened to them, felt strangely soothed. She looked at their medals, saw the grim flashings of their ancient eyes. This was another Germany, rigid, honest, proud and fearless, unbending, perhaps, and inexorable. Once, one of them said in a hard low voice:

"The army! The hope of Germany is still in the army. No low fellows there, no upstarts, no aliens, no riffraff! The tra-

dition goes on. Some day it will sweep away this filthy chaff—
some day!"

Therese wanted to believe it. But when would that day
come?

She had friends in England, France and America, and received significant magazine and newspaper articles from
them, for censorship had not yet been fully established. She
took heart at some of the denunciations, vigorous and indignant, of German National Socialism. But many of the articles
enraged her. She read, for instance, the calm, cynical and
hating article of a certain prominent American woman writer:

"The thoughtless, the race-polluted, the trouble-makers and
the ignorant frequently denounce the new order in Germany,
for private or stupid reasons. They do not realize that new
orders are inherent in a vital world. It may be true that some
of the excesses of Germany do not appeal to us. But we must
remember that both Mussolini and Hitler are an expression
of revived vitalism, and this should be heartening to those
who have feared that human dynamics have become static.
Mussolini and Hitler are symptoms of a resurgence of activity;
they have mounted the galloping horses of a new era. They
have taken advantage of a renaissance of world-quickening.
. . . If we wish to preserve our own form of democracy, we
must understand this world-quickening, and apply its dynamics
in order to destroy our national inertia and sluggishness. No
good will come of interference, and only harm will be the result of any denunciations on our part. After all, we shall have
to deal with these new forces in the world of tomorrow,
and it is better to do so on our terms by conciliation and understanding, rather than in a mood of antagonism and deliberate
misapprehension."

She read many similar. At first she thought these articles
came from a lack of understanding. Finally, with disgust and
bitterness and anger, she knew they came from only too much
understanding. The writers of such were no fools. They were
traitors, in spite of their smooth words and their air of
reasonableness.

The men who urged "reasonableness," or set themselves
up as apologists for Hitler, were either the old and impotent,
or the woman-driven and effeminate. They too experienced
the resurgence of eroticism in the command for obedience and
subservience. But the men who were strong and fearless and

intelligent were the real enemies of Hitler. If the world were to survive, one of its first necessities was the masculine spirit, reborn and virile, uncompromising and inexorable.

She was so filled with disgust these days that she felt that she was wandering in some subterranean chambers of slimy corruption, where everything was darkness filled with quick hot breaths and foul smells. She knew now that there was no escaping this corruption. Its galleries were dug out under every nation. They were the Augean Stables which must be cleansed by light and sun, by vigorous hands and hearts. Perhaps even by war.

ONE BY ONE the first flakes fell, first dark specks against a pewter sky, and then white feathers drifting silently. But when they touched the ground they winked and disappeared, for it was **32** too early for a lasting snow. However, the eaves were fringed with faint and fragile whiteness, and the bare trees in the garden were flowering with the melting blossoms of an artificial spring. There was no wind, only a ghostly silence and muteness.

Therese watched the snow fall. Her mind grew numb and still under it, as though her pain and sadness had begun to sleep. A largeness and peace took their place. Quiet shadows drifted through her thoughts, formless, cool and spectral. She felt that she sat in an aura of unreality, that the world that had existed for her had forever disappeared. Suffering was gone. She believed she had lost the capacity for emotion, for fever and terror. Surely the dying felt so. This was greater than indifference. It was no turning away. It was not even negation. It was the formlessness of eternity.

She had not seen Karl for a long time. He rarely emerged from his room and study. He was a ghost, haunting two rooms, to which she had become accustomed. She thought of herself unconsciously as a widow. The idea no longer disturbed her. At first, her loneliness and desolation had been anguish. But she had gone beyond death now. She was accustomed to its silence, and to its inevitable peace. She rarely heard, consciously, the slow dragging footsteps of the distracted man upstairs. She slept at night, dreamlessly, as under a drug. When she thought of Doctor Traub it was like thinking of some one who had died many, many years ago.

She was resting in her small sitting-room, after breakfast. The unopened newspaper was on her knees. She doubted that she would read it. She rarely read any papers now. She never listened to her radio. Germany, like all the rest of the world had ceased to exist for her. Upon her features was a motionless tranquillity.

She heard a faint sound at the door. Karl stood there. She

285

looked at him without a stir of the heart, as one might look at a ghost or a shadow.

"Therese," he said.

She said nothing, merely gazing emptily at this unreal visitation.

He hesitated. But she could not move, nor gesture towards him. The snow-dimmed light was uncertain. She knew there was something there for her to see, but she could not arouse herself to see it. She struggled faintly against her inertia. And then, while she still struggled, still fought to see, he had gone away, without a sound.

I should have spoken to him, she thought. But her heavy thoughts would go no further. She closed her eyes, and for a time, she drowsed. The snow continued to fall. One thought floated dimly through the hollow of her mind: I must wake up.

It was the sudden wind which finally awoke her. The light was almost gone. She thought it was twilight. But it was just past noon. The snow was thicker, and swirled and danced in skeins and garlands in the wind. The wind was hollow and echoing, standing at the windows and the eaves, and calling in its dolorous voice. Now the trees outside were draped in white.

Lotte came in with coffee and small cakes. She set the tray on the table at Therese's elbow. She was much disturbed. "The Herr Doctor has left the house. We do not know where he is gone."

"Gone?" echoed Therese, dully, rousing herself heavily. "How long ago?"

"I do not know, Frau Doctor. It may be an hour. It may be two hours. No one heard him go."

Therese forced herself to her feet. She felt the renewed and painful throbbing of her pulses. She went upstairs. Karl's study door was open. His desk was shiningly empty. Eric's African box was nowhere in sight. The tiny mummified head still grinned from the cold mantelpiece. But that was all. Therese went into his bedroom. His dressing-gown and slippers lay neatly on his smooth white bed. She examined his closet. His coat and hat were gone.

Now she was trembling. Should she call the police, and tell them that her deranged husband was wandering the streets? He had not been outside his house for months. Where had he gone? What dark urging had made him go out? She wrung her hands in her distraction. She glanced through the windows, hoping to see his bent and emaciated figure. But the street was silent and white and deserted. Had the sight of the first snow aroused in him some dormant and healthy desire to be out in it? Had the first faint stirrings of sanity come back to him? He had stood near her that morning. He had wanted to say something. She had driven him away. As she had driven Wilhelm away.

She uttered a thin sharp cry. She ran to the telephone and called the police. The young man who took her message was sluggishly indifferent. She could not arouse him to any interest. He finally took Karl's description. She gathered that he was contemptuously amused. These hysterical women!

She went downstairs again, conscious of faintness and weakness. She forced herself to drink the coffee, but could eat nothing. I must be calm, she told herself. Perhaps Karl had merely gone for a walk. She must believe that. After all, he was not bedridden. Perhaps the fresh keen air would revive him a little. All at once a curious quiet came to her, as though a gentle voice had spoken to her, soothingly. Hardly knowing what she said or did, she turned her head and spoke aloud, wonderingly: "Felix?"

The sound of the name in her ears and heart increased the quiet, steadied her nerves. Tears filled her eyes, but they were not painful tears. She was sure that Doctor Traub was in the room. She could feel his warm and wholesome presence, his strength and comfort. It was very strange. She tried to see him. She was certain he was beside her, and the dim room seemed full of his smile. Her heart swelled, but it was not with pain. How ridiculous to believe there is any death, she thought. All at once, there was a still joy in her heart.

"Thank you, dear doctor," she murmured, and smiled through her tears. Then the presence was gone. But she was no longer terrified or distracted. She sat down again, and waited for Karl's return, positive he would come soon.

The unopened newspaper was still lying where she had dropped it. She picked it up, glanced idly through it, avoiding the larger and more vociferous columns. But there was no avoiding the largest. It leaped at her through the medium of a familiar name. The name of Captain Baldur von Keitsch.

She learned that he had been murdered two nights ago, in his apartment. Evidently he had been expecting feminine company, for he had dismissed his servants. When he had been alone, the murderer, or murderers had come. From the wording of the paragraph, Therese deduced that this was merely a repeating of news previously printed, which she had missed because of her disinterest in the newspapers. The Gestapo now had a clue. The clue shrieked from the paper. It seemed that a certain wealthy half-Jew in Berlin, a former publisher, had been seen entering the apartment building where von Keitsch had lived, at seven o'clock in the evening. This Jew had been importuning von Keitsch, whom he knew slightly, to intercede for him in order that he might continue his business. Von Keitsch's kindness, the paper averred, was famous. (Oh, that smiling ominous man, thought Therese, with sickness.) The Jew, in his defense, had alleged that he was a convert to Christianity, and several of his "white-Jew" or Gentile friends had been interceding for him, and badgering von Keitsch. Von Keitsch had apparently, in his goodheartedness, invited the Jew to call upon him that evening, for a few moments, to discuss the matter with him. The Jew's reply had been found among his papers, joyfully accepting the invitation. He had come; he had been seen. But no one in the building had seen him leave. Apparently von Keitsch, as gently as possible, had told the Jew that nothing could be done. Thereafter, there was no doubt that the foul Israelite had murdered him, out of wanton fury.

"But let not Jewry think it can escape the consequences of this dastardly crime!" shrieked the newspaper. "The hunt is on. When Baptist Werner is found, and his guilt confessed, the whole German nation shall take vengeance upon his race. Too long has Germany suffered in silence the crimes and outrages of this degenerate race! Let Jewry beware! The day of judgment has come for it!"

Therese experienced a wave of enormous illness. She sat down abruptly, the paper slipping from her hands. The poor, unfortunate, foolish broken wretch! Why had he done this thing? Did he not know that his whole race would suffer massacre, torture and flagellation for this? What had he done! No doubt he had been driven to despairing madness by the fiend to whom he had come, pleading. But he should have remembered the German people. He should have known what madmen there were abroad in Germany today. But he had lost his head. He had been seized by the pure and primitive reaction of all tormented creatures against their tormentors. One could not blame him. But he should have remembered.

The paper hypocritically implored the German people not

to be premature in their revenge-seeking. The world was too often alleging these days that Germany was full of violence and injustice. Let the German people show the world their true dispassionateness and love of fairness. The law must take its course. Baptist Werner must be found. Then, and only then, would the German people take their vengeance on him and his race. "However," pleaded the lying paper, "let there be order. The German people are no irrational Latins or brutal Englishmen. We are civilized."

Therese flung the paper from her, and ground her heel in it. She had reached that lofty plane, now, where her own private miseries could be forgotten in the contemplation of universal calamity. She forgot Karl. She forgot her sorrows. She was filled with an active despair and apprehension for half a million Jews. She was glad that von Keitsch was dead. A poisonous serpent would no longer spew his venom. Germany had one enemy the less. But there were still the helpless Jews. If she could have given von Keitsch back his life, no matter what her private detestation and comprehension of him, she would have done so, for the sake of the victims.

While she sat there shivering, staring blindly through the window at the drifting mistlike snow, old Lotte came in.

"Frau Reiner has telephoned, Frau Doctor. She wishes to speak to you."

"Frau Reiner!" Therese aroused herself. The old woman had never called her before. Therese had heard her frequently express her dislike for the telephone. "Telephones," she had said, have done more to spread German women's buttocks than anything else." She had declared herself unable to use "the things." But she had called, that was evident. It must be something about Kurt. Kurt was dead.

She went to the telephone, and answered it in a shaking voice. "Therese?" the old woman's voice, sharp and hard, came clearly to her ears. "You must come at once. We need you. Something has happened."

"Kurt?" asked Therese, faintly.

"Kurt? Nonsense. Not Kurt. He is dying, and taking a long time about it. But it is not Kurt."

Pure terror clutched Therese's heart. "Karl? You have found Karl? He left the house this morning . . ."

Now the old woman's voice was loud and furious. "Karl? You have not watched him? You have left him out of your sight? Where is he, you careless, silly woman? Where is my Karl?"

Relief flooded Therese. She sank down into a chair, her dry lips quivering. Then it was not Karl. She forced her voice to be calm. "Do not be so excited, dear Frau Reiner. Nothing is wrong. He went out for a walk; his strength seems to be returning. I—I thought for a moment he had had an accident, and they had somehow notified you. . . ."

There was a little humming silence. Then Frau Reiner said in a lower and fainter tone: "I am glad there is nothing wrong with Karl. Forgive me, Therese. Will you please come at once?" Now the tone was commanding again.

"Yes, certainly. I shall come immediately."

But when she mounted the stairs to her room, her limbs failed her. She was forced to sit down on the steps. Sweat poured down her face. The sickness was thick in her vitals. Prostration paralyzed her whole body. She leaned against the wall and closed her eyes. One cannot go on this way, she thought, in the throes of reaction. Behind her closed lids the face of Gilu appeared, huge, fire-rimmed, grinning, filling all the darkness of the universe with a wide evil smile. His empty sockets were gutted with flame.

Finally she was able to gather some strength. She went to her room and put on her hat and coat, picked up her muff. Under her hat, and between the soft pale waves of her hair, her face was dwindled and small, as though she had been through a prolonged illness.

THE SNOW pervaded the world with a spectral light. Therese dimly remembered her grandmother's house, where long dripping bead fringes had filled every doorway. She had delighted to run through them, feeling them whip against her face and run over her body. She thought of them now. The snow was like that: long skeins touching her face, blowing about her. The snowy wind blocked her breath; fingers of ice darted down her furry collar. The streets were almost deserted. Mechanically, she peered at every one she met, hoping it was Karl. But he was nowhere. The air grew colder and sharper; pellets of ice mingled with the snowflakes, stinging her forehead and cheeks. She put up her muff to shelter herself, bending against the wind. The physical exertion made her blood flow more strongly, blew away her almost constant headache. She was quite calm, really invigorated, by the time she reached Kurt's ornamental but gloomy house. She thought, with a sort of pale wonder, that during that walk she had thought of nothing, nothing at all. In not thinking was peace and strength.

The servant who opened the door had a white excited face. Servants always gloated over misfortune, the vulgar creatures! They derived a sadistic, if, at times, sympathetic pleasure, from the miseries of their employers. Was it a hidden desire for revenge for injustices and harshness? Or just the plebeian reaction to all sorrow and calamity? Therese asked for Frau Reiner, and was led upstairs.

The unusual shrouded quiet of the house frightened her. It was as though death were already here. She expected to see a bier through every open doorway. Where was Maria? Thick curtains were half-drawn against the half-light and the relentless snow. Occasionally there was a faint hollow echo, undetermined. She passed a mirror, and saw the silent shadow of herself in its somber depths. The air was chill. It was a deserted house.

There was another unusual fact: Frau Reiner's door was shut. Therese knocked. The old woman's voice peremptorily bade her enter. She opened the door. A dull red fire burned on the black-marble hearth. The old beldame was in her usual place by the window. But Therese saw, even in that uncertain light, that the old woman's face, though still indomitable, had subtly altered, had lost color even under its thick crimson rouge.

"Come in, Therese," she said, in a changed voice. "And close the door tightly after you. Thank you. Sit close to me."

Therese sat down. Her nostrils tightened instinctively against the mingled odors of ancient flesh and heavy exotic scent. The firelight danced on Frau Reiner's multitudinous rings and bracelets, showed the artificial tint of her elaborately curled hair.

"Ah," said the harridan, "it is good to see the impeccable gnädige frau. Such fortitude and quietness." Her tone was cynical and jeering as usual, but Therese saw immediately that it was forced.

"What can I do? What has happened?" she asked.

Frau Reiner bent towards her, and whispered, her eyes probing Therese's pale face. "My grandson, Wilhelm, is dying."

Therese choked back a sudden hard cry. She clenched her hands. Her face became rigid. But she said nothing, merely staring at the old woman.

Frau Reiner nodded somberly. "Yes. Last night he took a large dose of sleeping tablets. He must have stolen them from his father's room. The doctor and Maria are with him now, and his brother, that red-cheeked idiot!"

Therese cried: "But why? Oh, why?"

The old woman said nothing. Her shrivelled, Gilu-like face darkened, shrank. "You will hear, yourself. First, I want you to hear."

Tears rolled down Therese's face. "Poor Maria," she whispered. But she told herself that she was the guilty one. Poor Wilhelm, she thought. Poor, wretched, bewildered, agonized boy. She said: "Perhaps they can save him."

Frau Reiner clicked her false teeth grimly. "No! They can do nothing. He wants to die. So, they cannot save him. Besides, it is well if he dies."

The old woman tapped her black silk bosom, laden with its lockets and chains. "He left a note. I have it here. They think it disappeared. They have searched frantically for it.

They have turned the whole house out. I have helped them look. It is here. You shall read it, later."

There was a prolonged silence in the dusky, red-lit room. Therese wiped away the stream of tears she could not halt. The blackness of grief filled her heart. The grief seemed to float out of her body and encompass the whole suffering world. Through her tears she gazed at Frau Reiner, and all at once her dislike of the old woman was washed away. She saw that there was something heroic, something strong and powerful and steadfast about the harridan, something immutable. She felt that she had in her hands something terrible and momentous, and that nothing would shake her. Therese realized that the old were not really defeated by life, but that in some strange way they had mastered it, and could control it.

The house stood transfixed in horror, as though it had an enormous mouth open on a great gasp. Beyond this room lay the dying Kurt, and beyond him, the dying Wilhelm. The whole house was dying. And in the midst of this awful dissolution sat this indomitable grave old woman, aware of everything, in control of everything. She was not frightened. She was the human spirit, fully comprehending, stern and inexorable, which calamity could not overpower, could not turn aside.

Therese listened to the silence of the house. Apparently, nothing was stirring in it. The snow whispered at the windows, and the light steadily darkened. Suddenly, Therese thought to herself: I am sick of living. If only I could die!

Frau Reiner watched her. The gibing, cynical look was no longer on her mummified painted face. Rather, it was full of gravity. They were two women who understood each other. "I have called you for a specific reason, Therese," she said in a low voice. She fumbled for her gold-headed cane, and painfully rose to her feet, her black silk rustling about her, her chains and bracelets jingling. "Come with me."

Therese felt that she could not rise, so weak were her limbs. But Frau Reiner stood above her, seeming to tower, for all her shrunken smallness, seeming to command. So Therese got to her feet. Frau Reiner leaned on her arm and shoulder. "Come with me," she repeated.

They left the room together, slowly, feebly. The hall outside was deserted. Again, Therese heard the faint hollow echoing from the depths of the house. She heard the wind sobbing at the windows and the eaves.

They passed Kurt's door. There was only silence behind it. They approached Wilhelm's door. Frau Reiner opened it noiselessly, without knocking. Therese saw the room, where only a dim light burned near the white motionless bed. Wilhelm lay there, his young emaciated face already fixed in the mask of approaching death, his eyes sunken in purple pits. On one side of the bed sat Maria, a frozen statue of grief, with bent head, tearless. On the other side stood Alfred in his uniform, the black swastika on his arm. The doctor was listening to Wilhelm's pulse, and gazing fixedly at the dying boy's face.

Alfred was the only one who looked up as his grandmother and aunt entered. He inclined his head courteously to Therese, and then shook it, as though warning her not to make a sound. Therese came to the foot of the bed, still supporting Frau Reiner. She stared heavily at Wilhelm. Her only thought was: He is at peace. At last, he is at peace.

Guilty pain divided her heart, and she told herself that she had had a part in this. But after a moment she was not sorry. Such as Wilhelm could not live in this frightful world. They were better out of it. One might almost rejoice at their release.

She turned to Maria and whispered her name. After a long moment the distracted mother lifted her head and regarded Therese blindly. Her face was white putty. Anguish had sharpened her blunt features. In her eyes was a tortured question. And something else. Therese saw that this was a terrible and frenzied fear. The poor woman did not see Therese fully. She seemed engrossed in some awful preoccupation, in which her spirit wrestled frantically behind her dry broken face. But she did not appear to breathe.

The doctor lifted his hand warningly. "He is becoming conscious again," he whispered.

A change had come over the poor boy's sunken face. The purple lids were fluttering, the gray lips moving. His hands trembled, fumbled, on the white counterpane. A pulse leapt to life in his temple. His struggle to awaken was horrible to contemplate. Strange sounds came from his throat, as his will wrestled with death for the privilege of a last word, a last cry.

Therese could not bear it. Faintness seized her. She caught the post of the bed. She covered her eyes with her hand. The floor seemed to sink under her. She lost consciousness of where she was.

Finally, she dropped her hand. Wilhelm was gazing stead-fastly at her. He knew her. He was aware of her. From his pillow his gray sunken eyes regarded her sternly, inexorably, not with accusation, but as though he was willing for her to hear him, as though once again he was trusting her.

She understood. Her whole soul cried out soundlessly to him, knowing mysteriously that he heard: "Wilhelm! I shall not fail you again. Forgive me for failing you before, but I did not understand. I understand now. Only trust me!"

A strange, sweet, peaceful smile lifted the boy's gray swollen lips. He had heard. Therese, through her tears, returned his smile, leaned towards him.

He tried to speak. The doctor shook his head. "No, no," he said, gently. With a deep dry sob, Maria took her son's hand, cold and already dead, and kissed it frenziedly, rubbing her cheek against it, turning it over and pressing her mouth pas-sionately to the palm. But Wilhelm did not look at her, or at any one else but Therese.

There was a faint sound in the room, like the rustling of a withered leaf. It was Wilhelm, whispering.

"Aunt Therese." The sound could hardly be heard.

"Yes, Wilhelm," she said, forcing herself to stop her weep-ing. "Oh, yes, my darling."

He struggled to lift himself towards her, as though what he had to say must be heard and completely understood. The doctor pressed him back. The secret terror that had Maria sprang into the open, like a flame. She glared at Therese. "Go away!" she cried, loudly savagely. "Leave us alone! Leave me alone with my child. We do not want you here!" She half-flung herself across Wilhelm's thin body, as though to protect him from some most dreadful danger with which Therese threatened him.

Then Frau Reiner spoke, coldly, clearly: "I have brought Therese here. I have brought her here to listen to Wilhelm."

Then Maria, crimson of face, insane of eye, made mad by her fear and hatred and agony, turned to her mother, and called her a foul and unspeakable name. The name rang through the death chamber like the cry of some unclean beast. The two women, mother and daughter, regarded each other in the sickening silence after that one cry. Maria, fat and bloated and broken, panted from her position half across the bed. She had flung her arms about her son, and one of

her hands was on his lips. Her panting filled the silence
with a tearing, bubbling sound.

But Frau Reiner, leaning on her cane, was an inexorable
figure of doom at the foot of the bed. She was no longer
ridiculous and obscene in her outmoded finery and ornaments
and dye and rouge. She was judgment, which would not be
turned aside, which was immovable, dignified, filled with
splendor. Her old wrinkled face was grave, even noble, and
not without pity.

Alfred, no longer red cheeked, no longer composed, but also
seemingly filled with Maria's own mysterious terror, turned to
Therese and his grandmother.

"You can see that you must leave at once," he said, coldly,
fixing them with his pitiless eye. He made a motion towards
them, his hand outstretched. Frau Reiner turned to him,
sternly, with a calm fierceness. She lifted her cane like a
weapon.

"Back!" she said, quietly.

The young man was astounded. His hand fell to his side. He
stared at her, blinking. But before her will he was powerless.
He stood like a graven image, his eyes alight with impotent
hatred.

Wilhelm was struggling against his mother's hand. The
doctor had to intervene. He was Maria's cousin, a stout
plebeian man who had cultivated a beard in order to acquire
dignity. He understood nothing. He forcibly removed Maria's
hand. "You are smothering him," he said, severely.

Wilhelm, sinking again, fought sternly for the last wisps of
his life. And never once did he remove his drowning eyes
from Therese's face.

Frau Reiner glanced briefly at the doctor. "Will you please
leave the room a moment, Hans?" she asked. Her request was
a command, and the doctor was forced to obey, reluctantly,
shaking his head.

Maria burst into loud crying sobs, like a tormented animal.
She rocked back and forth on her chair, wringing her hands,
throwing back her head as though she were being strangled.
Alfred could not move. He clutched a bedpost with sweating
hands. He regarded his brother, not with grief, but with hatred
and terror. Beads of sweat ran down his face. He was willing
his brother to die before speaking. His fingers on the post
worked. They were strangler's fingers. Frau Reiner moved an

inch or two towards him, holding her cane like a lethal weapon. "Speak, Wilhelm," she said, gently and clearly.

The boy still looked at Therese. His faint whispering was stronger.

"Aunt Therese, I killed him. You must understand, I killed him."

Bubbles of foam appeared at the corners of his lips. His will made him stronger. He lifted himself on his pillows. It was as if he wished to impress his ghastly words clearly on Therese's consciousness.

"Yes, Wilhelm," she answered softly, mechanically. "I understand." But the black faintness had her again, smothering her, beating her down. She did not understand.

He shook his head impatiently. His eyes started from his head, as he implored her to listen and comprehend. "No, you do not understand. I—I killed Captain von Keitsch. I had to kill him."

Suddenly a white wild light passed over his face, like the reflection of joy. He could sit up. He was animated by a strange and supernatural strength. Alfred stared at him, terrified. Maria continued her prolonged groaning. But the dying boy saw only Therese, still.

Therese's mouth opened as though she were dying, herself. Her lids half-fell over her eyes. She fought to control her impulse to fall to the floor. But some inner will power made her say aloud: "Yes, Wilhelm, I can see you had to kill him."

He nodded. The light brightened on his face. "Yes, yes, Aunt Therese, you understand! I could not kill them all. But I could kill one. He was one of the worst. . . ."

"You are lying!" shouted Alfred, frantically. He turned savagely to Therese and Frau Reiner. "He is delirious! He is lying!"

"Quiet!" commanded Frau Reiner, lifting her cane at him, and compelling him with her ancient fiery eyes. "Quiet, animal!"

His terror urged him to oppose her at all costs. But her gaze quelled him. He subsided with something like a whimper in his bull's throat. His big fleshy face worked.

Wilhelm's whispering went on. "I planned it carefully. No one saw me come or go. There—there was a man there, pleading for something. I had gotten in before the Captain came; I was in a closet in the same room with him and the man. The man was a Jew. . . ." He had to halt. His breathing became thicker and hoarser. The stern look of preoccupation appeared on his face again, as he forced his dying flesh to obey him. "It was no use. He kicked the Jew and hit him with his fists. The Jew went away. Then I knew that I really had to kill him. He was so wicked, Aunt Therese. When I had gone there, I was not sure just what I was going to do. I—I was mad. I had been mad for such a long time."

"Yes, yes, darling," said Therese, softly, smiling, not wiping away her tears. "I know."

He regarded her pleadingly. "I knew it was not wrong to kill him. I knew it was just. He has killed so many men." The poor boy shuddered violently. "I have seen him kill them. He took our division to a concentration camp. . . . "

The remembrance transfixed him. His eye-sockets widened. His mouth fell open. There was something dreadful in his expression.

"Fool! Coward! Criminal!" said Alfred, between his teeth.

But Wilhelm had not heard him. He wrung his hands. The death-damp was thickening on his skin. He lay back on his pillows, and gasped. Again, he resumed the struggle to live until he had spoken.

After a long moment, he opened his eyes and once more fixed them on Therese. It was evident that he could not live much longer. Only his will was compelling his heart to beat.

"I knew I had to kill him. It was like killing a tiger. It was just." His words and breath came in short tearing gasps. "No one saw me. I was happy. I had done something good in my life. And then—and then—last night they began to say the Jews had killed him. I knew what that meant. Pogroms. Massacres of innocent people. I thought I would go mad again. I could not let that happen. Aunt Therese?" he pleaded, piteously. "I cannot see you."

"I am here, dear one," she said, gently and clearly. "And I hear all you say."

"I thought I would go to them and tell them that I had done it. But I have always been a coward." His dying voice was a thin breathless cry. "I could not go. I knew what they would do to me. So—so I wrote a note last night. And then— I stole some of my father's morphine. . . ."

He was at his last gasp. He could only say: "I could not let the Jews suffer. I had to die. It was the only way. Aunt Therese? You will not let them kill innocent people?"

Over her mounting faintness, and the deathliness of the

taste in her mouth and throat, Therese said: "No, dear one, I shall not let them kill the innocent." Her voice came clearly, fully, sternly, and he was satisfied.

He closed his eyes. He smiled. His hands and lips fluttered. Then he was still.

They all watched him for a long time. But he no longer breathed. That harried, innocent, tormented soul had gone. The tortured flesh was at peace. The dead face took on a look of calm and dignity and fulfillment.

Then Maria uttered a loud ferocious cry, as though her heart were being torn from her breast. She fell on her son's body. She kissed him wildly, holding him in her arms, uttering strange incoherent words. It was appalling to see. They turned from her. The two women stood side by side, pale and inexorable. Alfred faced them. His lips were white and stiff.

"Of course, you will not repeat this—this lie. You must know he was insane, and lying."

"It was not a lie," said Frau Reiner.

"It was not a lie," said Therese.

He smiled grimly. His breath was uneven.

"You have no proof. Mother and I will deny you were even in the room. You are not going to save the lives of filthy Jewish criminals by defaming our family name, the name of my father, and destroying my own career."

"Your family name," said Frau Reiner quietly, but with such terrible old eyes. "What is that, compared with the lives of the innocent? What do you matter, you inhuman animal? You uniformed beast? You swastika-decked foulness? The whole world shall know."

He gave a short snarling laugh. "You have no proof. The note he left is lost. We have searched everywhere. . . ."

"It is not lost," said Frau Reiner. "I found it. Do not look for it, Alfred. It is not in the house. It is already on its way to a man in high places, who has never countenanced violence and murder."

He dwindled, crumpled. He fell back, and stared at her, with hatred and fright. Then he began to whine, to plead.

"Grandmother! You cannot do this thing to us!"

She lifted her face, and again it was full of heroic dignity and gravity.

"I can and shall do this to you. It is justice. It is truth."

He burst into tears. It was a sickening thing to see this

young man, burly and fleshy, in his flamboyant uniform, weeping. He kept passing his hands over his face to wipe away his tears. Frau Reiner regarded him with disgust but also with compassion.

"Take counsel with yourself, Alfred. And may God have mercy on your soul."

She leaned on Therese's arm. The two women left the room. They went back to Frau Reiner's apartments. The old woman, with unusual vigor, locked the door, went to the window, and beckoned to Therese. She then removed an envelope from her withered breast. She leaned towards Therese and whispered in her ear:

"The confession is in this envelope. The address is upon it. Take it at once. Put it in your bosom. Hold it tightly. Do not delay an instant."

Therese took it and put it next to her warm breasts. "At once," she said. She was no longer weeping. "At once," she repeated.

Frau Reiner drew a deep quivering breath. She fell into her chair and covered her face with her hands. She was now only an old, old woman, with not many days left to her. Therese watched her, not moving. Finally the old beldame removed her hands. Her mummy's face and eyes were quite dry.

She said calmly: "I am glad that Wilhelm is dead. In my heart, I rejoice. It is good, in these days, that the young die. It is very good. We must really rejoice. We must always rejoice, when death comes."

THE NIGHT BEFORE, Karl had been pacing rest- **34**
lessly for hours. An unbearable tension was in
his body. He was forced to wipe his hands and
face repeatedly. His breath was short yet heavy.
His mind was like a pit, afloat with dark fogs and formless
movements. He kept glancing about him, despairingly, blindly,
his step growing more and more feeble, his expression more
and more fevered. At intervals he stopped and called aloud,
imploringly: "Eric! Eric!"

At moments he was devoured by an almost delirious expec-
tation. He walked through the silent sleeping house. He peered
into the deserted rooms. At each doorway he whispered:
"Eric."

He knew that Eric was in the house. Every night, for
months, he had called to him, despairing, knowing there
would be no answer, for Eric was not there. But tonight, he
knew Eric was here, that he would speak. But when?

His mind, clouded for almost a year, torn and wounded
and crippled and tormented, came suddenly alive with a
terrible clarity. He was conscious that much time had lapsed,
that grave events had taken place. He was like a victim of
amnesia, suddenly awakened, and horrified. Only Eric could
help him now, and save him from complete despair.

He returned to his study, and looked about him, pale,
emaciated, bewildered and dreadfully ill. His eye wandered
over each object, and sickened. The old fearful pounding in
his temples began again, as his spirit again engaged in its old
struggle with his will-to-madness and will-to-die. But now his
spirit was stronger. The conflict, in consequence, was more
powerful, grimmer. Karl felt in himself the war of mysterious
and implacable forces, to which his tortured body responded
with physical agony. He closed his eyes, groaned, covered his
face with his hands. He knew that the end had come. He
would become alive again, or die, tonight. He could think of
nothing. He was merely a mass of nerves and unspeakable
pain.

Some one called his name, quietly, urgently. He dropped his

hands. His lamp burned on his desk. Near-by, bathed in the soft lamplight, sat Eric, calm and smiling, his bright black eyes shining, his vital personality filling the room, which, all at once, was warm and safe.

Karl had not drawn the heavy curtains at the windows. The light of the lamp streamed beyond the sill, revealing the skeins and movement of the snow. Everything was silent, breathless. There was only Eric, smiling and waiting.

Karl stared at him. All at once, his face worked and tears blinded his eyes. Something like black ice cracked in him, divided, melted. He said simply:

"Then, Eric, you are not dead at all?"

Eric smiled, as though with deep amusement. "Dead? How foolish! Of course I am not dead!"

Karl sobbed aloud. Eric regarded him with compassion.

"Neither is Gerda dead," he said, very softly.

Karl's weeping filled the room with a broken and moving sound. The tears ran down his pale gaunt face.

"It is only you who are dying, almost dead," said Eric, and now his face was stern. "That is why I have been allowed to come to you, to save you."

He stood up. He came to Karl, and placed his hand on his shoulder.

"You are killing yourself, with hatred and madness."

Karl put his cold and trembling hand on the other's. It was warm and firm, and infinitely reassuring.

"But—they did that thing to you—I had to avenge you, Eric."

Eric sighed. "You avenged nothing but yourself, Karl."

He went back to his seat. His face was full of stern sorrow. He regarded Karl somberly.

"Hatred destroys the hater, my friend. They never hurt me, Karl. They did not kill me. How could they? I did not kill myself, and so, how could I die?"

He paused, then went on in a low voice: "Nothing can hurt a man but himself. . . . I was allowed to come, because there is so much work for you to do. You would not see it. But the world needs you. I have come to tell you this, to awaken you."

He regarded Karl with eyes suddenly brilliant with light.

"So much to do! Men are going mad. The whole earth is mad. Perhaps this is the end. If men are utterly lost, it is because you, and others like you, failed them. Doom and destruction are approaching closer every hour. Will you not see? Will you close your eyes forever? How will you reconcile this with your conscience, your soul?"

Karl was silent. He listened, holding his breath. His eyes were dazzled and dim. Through this dimness he was conscious of nothing but Eric's voice.

"Today is only the beginning of sorrows. The tragedy which men have been making will overwhelm this generation, and the generations to come. The disease which afflicts them is universal. There are no voices in the wilderness. There is only the chatter of cynical apes in a jungle. The storm is rising. Listen, and you can hear it, Karl!"

Karl listened. He heard nothing. He lifted his head and listened again. Then, as from an immense distance he heard an ominous muttering and roaring, the hollow groaning of thunder. These did not come from the sky or the earth. They seemed to come from out of the depths of cosmic space, like an avalanche from the stars, from the outer borders of the universe. Karl saw the quiet snow at the windows, was conscious of the quiet of the sleeping house and the city. But over and under them all was the deep and terrible thunder, shaking men's souls, shaking the pillars of the world. The thunder of the future.

"When that day comes," said Eric, in a strange voice, "men will say everywhere: 'Why are we so afflicted?' They will not know that the affliction has come from themselves, because they are faithless and treacherous, cruel and greedy, tormenters of their brothers, haters of each other. They will cry out for peace, and will not know that there is no peace, because it is not in their hearts. There will be frightful wars, and massacres, and famines, and pestilences, and they will try to hope, telling themselves that when all this passes there will be peace and quietness again. But this will be a lie, which they will tell themselves. For the things which are to come are only the red shadows from their own spirits. The pestilence is in themselves. Even when they lay down their arms, exhausted, the cause will still fester within them."

He paused again. It seemed to Karl that everything listened, and waited, not in quietness, but with horror.

"Where is there any hope?" asked Eric, mournfully. "There is no hope, until each man has a revelation in himself, until he sees God again in the darkness he has created. Each man must forget himself for his brother. Each man must have a rebirth of fortitude and faith, of simplicity and goodness, of gentleness and justice, of pity and passion. He must forget his own miserable life, his own self-love and greed. He must be prepared to die, heroically, and with joyful courage. He must never compromise with evil, nor try to appease madness and fury. He must say to himself: 'It is not I who matters. It is my brother.' "

Eric sighed. "Who can teach men these things?"

He said: "He who saves his life shall lose it, if he saves it at the expense of his suffering brother. That is the law of God. Men have heard it before, but now they laugh at it. It must be your work, and the work of others like you, to show it to be the truth it is, and that only by this truth can men live."

Karl asked simply: "But how, and where, can I begin, Eric?"

Eric smiled at him. "First of all, you must have the will and the desire to begin. Then, everything shall be shown to you, and you will see the way yourself."

Karl passed his hands over his face. "Forgive me," he whispered.

"No, Karl, I have no power to forgive you. You must forgive yourself."

He went on, very gently: "You will not see me again, until you come to me. But I will be with you. Only call on me, at any time, and I will help you."

A sensation of unbearable grief and loss seized Karl. He looked up. "Eric, do not leave me! Do not leave me again!"

Eric shook his head. "I never left you. It was you who left me."

He stood up again. The wooden doll with the prong in its head lay on the desk. Eric lifted it and regarded it sadly.

"You did not do this to Kurt, poor Kurt. You did this to yourself, Karl!"

He laid down the doll and regarded Karl intently.

"I must go. I have done all that I could do. You must do the rest."

He stretched out his hand to Karl, and Karl took it. A warm and comforting fire ran into his body at the touch. Even when Eric removed his hand, the fire remained, dissolving and thawing the ice in his heart. Then, all at once Eric had gone, and there was only the still lamplight and the snow at the window.

Karl sat motionless for a long time. His face was without expression. His eyes were closed. The wind rose and the snow came faster. Then Karl began to look about him. An enormous tiredness overwhelmed him, but it was the tiredness of peace. He stood up and walked slowly about the room, his head bent. He began to weep again, but with a feeling of release after great torment.

He went into his bedroom, and threw himself on his bed. For the first time in nearly a year he slept at once, without dreams, without pain. He slept profoundly, as though he had died. He slept until the daylight was gray at the windows.

He bathed, changed his clothes. He was still shaken, still weak. But his mind was clear and steadfast. He felt that he had been reborn. But he knew that there was much he must think about, and understand.

He went downstairs. He found Therese sitting sadly and without movement at the window of the morning room. He called to her. She turned her heavy face and dead eyes to him. But she made no motion to him, nor did she answer him. Then he understood what she had suffered because of him. He wanted to go to her. But something held him back. He turned away, and went out into the snowy street.

He had the strange sensation that he had come up out of the grave, on a reprieve. He walked through the city, and he saw all that was to be seen.

35 WHEN THERESE returned from the delivering of poor Wilhelm's confession, she was hardly able to get out from the cab. Her flesh was cold and numb. An overpowering sickness engrossed her whole stern attention. She walked into her house with a feeble step, as though she had become blind. Tears seemed to flood her heart, but none rose to her eyes. She fell into a chair, and her head dropped on her breast.

Old Lotte found her there, in the dark hallway, still in her hat and coat. Her muff had fallen to the floor. Her arms drooped as though she had fainted. Her attitude was one of profound prostration and collapse.

"Frau Doctor!" cried Lotte, frightened. Therese did not answer. Lotte removed the hat and saw Therese's face. She cried out again. The little servant came running from the kitchen, and Lotte shouted to her to bring some wine. When it was brought, Lotte forced the wine between Therese's white lips. Therese drank mechanically, like a sick child, her face ghastly in the gloom of the hallway.

"You are ill. Let me help you to your room," said Lotte, trembling.

Therese forced herself to smile. "Do not worry about me, Lotte. I am just a little tired." She made herself sit up, touched her disordered hair with shaking hands. "Just a little tired," she repeated. Her voice was hoarse.

Lotte wrung her hands in her apron. She tried to find something comforting to say. "Doctor Erlich has returned. He is in his room."

She started back a little, for suddenly Therese's face had become almost horrible. Rage and fury had started into her eyes, and even hatred. She visibly trembled. She clenched her hands on the arms of her chair and pushed herself to her feet. Standing there, she fought with her faintness. A fire raged in her, a furious and deadly fire. Then, without looking at Lotte again, she went up the stairway, walking swiftly as though with an ominous purpose. Lotte, terrified, watched her go.

Therese went down the hallway to Karl's study. Red lightning flashed before her eyes. She knew now the urge to kill, to destroy. She flung open the closed door with a loud crash. She stood on the threshold, panting.

Karl was sitting quietly before a new fire, watching the flames. He looked up at Therese. Had she been less agitated, less enraged, she might have seen what was there to be seen. But she did not see it. She saw only a man she hated and despised. Her breathing was loud and hoarse. Between the masses of her fair disordered hair her face was thin and white and almost mad. Karl's own face swam before her in a red mist.

"There you are!" she cried, loudly yet shrilly. "There you are, you fool, you madman, you murderer! There you have been, for months, dreaming your idiotic dreams, plotting your imbecile plots, when better men are dying all around you!"

Karl sat up. His pale face paled even more. "Therese," he said.

But she made a wild gesture. "What do you know of anything, you fool and coward, you traitor! Do you know that Herman Muehler is dead, and Felix Traub, and your own nephew, Wilhelm? Do you know that men like you have killed them? Do you know what is happening? Do you know that all Germany is a graveyard, full of vultures? Do you know that everything is dying? Germany, the whole world. . . ." She flung out her arms, and burst into the most dreadful tears.

She advanced towards him as though she would strike him. She raised her clenched fists.

"But what does that matter to you, you coward and fool? What does it matter, so long as you have your silly dreams, so long as you can hide yourself? You and your imbecile wooden dolls?" She laughed suddenly, shortly, madly. "Well, let me tell you something: I have known all along what you have been doing. You have been trying to kill your miserable brother! You have pushed a nail into a shameful doll's head! But I should not have expected anything else from you. Yes, Kurt is dying, and calling for you. But you have not killed him! Do you hear me? You have not killed him. I changed the dolls, a long time ago. The doll with his name is not the doll . . ."

She choked. Her breath twisted in her throat. She gasped. She pressed her hands against her breast to stop the agonizing and mortal pain in it. The room swirled about her. She felt some one take her arm and hold her firmly. When she could see again, she saw that it was Karl who was holding her. She saw his sunken face, his strange fixed eyes.

"Kurt—is dying?" he asked.

She tried to throw off his hand. He saw her loathing and detestation. He stepped back and regarded her without speaking again.

"Yes!" she screamed. "Are you not happy? Why do you not smile with your madman's glee?" All at once she could not control herself any longer. She lifted her hand and struck him savagely across his face. Not once, but several times. And he stood before her, not moving, only gazing at her intently.

"Therese," he said, gently. "My poor Therese."

But she hardly heard him. She fell back. She caught the back of a chair to steady herself. Her tears ran down her cheeks. She sobbed hoarsely.

She averted her head. "Go away," she groaned. "Go away. Never let me see you again."

She closed her eyes. Her head fell on her breast. Her sobbing filled the silent room. Her body bowed itself over the chair she clutched. She sobbed as though all her life and blood were draining out of her veins.

Finally, she could weep no more. She lifted her head and looked about her. She was all alone, Karl was gone. She had vented her fury. There was only a sick emptiness left. "Karl," she called, faintly.

There was no answer. The firelight leaped up, mockingly. She tried to take a step, but her limbs would not move. She looked at the fire. Then for the first time she saw a curious object in the fire. It was the half-consumed wooden doll, burning steadily. It must have been thrown there before she had entered the room.

She stared at it. Her eye-sockets widened. Revelation like a sword of lightning ran through her. She staggered forward, bent, gazed at the doll. The flames leaped up, shining redly on her wet face.

Then she stood up. "Karl!" she called loudly. "Karl!"

She ran to the window. Only the dusky snow-filled street met her eyes. She ran down the stairs, calling wildly. Lotte appeared, with renewed fear.

"The Herr Doctor left the house a few minutes ago," she stammered.

Therese stood on the stairs, clutching the bannister. She

stared at Lotte emptily. "I have driven him away again," she said, in a dull voice.

Lotte's old frightened face enlarged, blurred, before her. She uttered a faint sinking cry. She staggered. She heard Lotte scream.

Then, she knew nothing else.

36 THE STREETS were dark and empty, the lamps haloed in a mist of driving snow.

As Karl hurried along, he had the dazed feeling that time had collapsed together, that it was tonight that he was going to Kurt's house to see Eric Reinhardt. It was tonight that the long tragedy was to begin. Here was the snow, here was the serving-girl running along with her red shawl over her head. Here were the lighted windows and the crisp white curtains and the dark houses. In Kurt's house Eric Reinhardt waited for him, back from a long journey.

He stopped. His heart plunged. Yes, it was true. Eric was there, waiting, back from his long journey. He put his hand to his throbbing head. I have been given another chance, he thought. It is yesterday, and I have been dreaming, and now there is another chance for me. His eyes filled with moisture. He went on his way, his head bent, his thoughts mournful and filled with sorrow. So many thoughts, so heavy, so profound, so understanding, now.

He passed a small marching group of Storm Troopers, and he stopped and looked after them, as though he were a stranger and they were new to him. Yes, they were new. He had been away a long time in a strange country, and had returned to find his people convulsed and dying. What have I done? he thought. Where have I been? So much time wasted, when there was time no longer.

Forgive me, he said aloud, simply, looking at the sky, dark-purple and alive with silent snow.

Like the world, he had been living in dreams. The foolish, self-absorbed, dreaming world! And now, like himself, it must be awakened, called back to life by the urgent voices of the dead, and the despairing voices of the living. So much to do! So much to do.

He reached Kurt's house. It loomed, somber and dark and lightless, above him. He struck the knocker, and its long doleful crash resounded through the silent street. A servant opened the door, his old face white and streaked. He did not recognize Karl.

"I am sorry, Mein Herr," he began, "but no visitors . . ."

"Franz! It is I, Doctor Erlich."

The old man started at the familiar voice. He bent forward and stared incredulously at Karl. He studied the gaunt and spectral face, so changed, so feverish. He gave a little cry.

"Herr Doctor! Is it possible? I did not know you!"

He was still incredulous. The dim lamplight from the bleak hallway fell on Karl. The old man thought that this was a ghost, not a living creature. He fell back from the doorway and admitted Karl. He could not take his eyes away, but continued to stare vacantly, helplessly. When Karl began to remove his coat and white-rimmed hat, the old man came back to life. "I am sorry, Mein Herr Doctor! Allow me. I was so startled. . . ."

They regarded each other in silence. Karl then glanced about the old familiar hall. His features worked. Yes, it was yesterday again, and Eric was waiting.

The old man spoke again, stammering.

"I am sorry, but the Frau Professor is in no condition . . . You understand, Herr Doctor? The little Wilhelm died today."

"Today? Yes, I have heard."

Karl sighed heavily.

"There are to be no visitors admitted. There is great tragedy here, Herr Doctor. The Herr Professor is dying, and he does not know yet. But perhaps Frau Reiner will see you."

"I will go up to her, Franz. Do not announce me."

He went up the great stairway. No rooms were lighted. Tragedy and death were thick motionless smells in his nostrils. He passed rooms so familiar, yet so strange in the far struggling light. He heard, as Therese had heard, the dim echoing boom of distant echoes in this sorrow-filled house. The air was cold and stagnant. He held to the balustrade for a moment, trying to shake off his dizziness. When his father had died, in this house, it had been like this. Every room, every hallway, had had this dusty silence, this crushing emptiness. He heard the stifled sound of weeping now. It was his mother, weeping behind her door.

There was no past. There was only the present. There was always the present, and it was always the same.

He reached Frau Reiner's door and opened it without knocking. The sound of weeping he had heard had come from this room. There was no light in the room except that which came from the single dim candle burning before the crucifix he had given the old woman. Its faint deathly rays glimmered on the walls and the ponderous furniture. Frau Reiner was sitting near her window, her handkerchief to her eyes. She did not hear Karl enter. He spoke her name. She dropped her hand and glared at him, blinking.

"It is I, Karl," he said, gently.

She did not believe it. She stammered hoarsely: "Are you a ghost?"

"Yes," he replied, very quietly. "I am a ghost."

She gazed at him silently, leaning forward a little, the better to see him in the candlelight. Her shrivelled painted face quivered. The false curls on her ancient head trembled. The chains sparkled on her breast.

"But you have come back, Karl?" she whispered.

"Yes, I have come back. I have been away a long time."

Again she gazed at him silently. Then, all at once, she uttered a thick strangled sound and held out her hands to him. He came to her, and took her withered hot hands. Tears ran down her face, streaking the paint more and more. He bent over her and kissed her forehead. She clung to him.

"Karl! Karl! Thank God, you have come back!" Her hands fumbled at him, seizing his sleeves, his shoulders. "Karl, you do not know. . . . It does not matter. You have come back!"

"I have heard Kurt is dying. I must see him at once. I have so much to say to him."

She wiped her face. She continued to clutch him.

"He is dying. Perhaps tonight he will die. And his son, our little Wilhelm, is dead in his room. Maria—she is prostrated, unconscious. So many terrible things."

"I must see Kurt. That is the only important thing to me."

"Yes, yes! And then he will die. The terrible pain. . . . They said he could not die until you had come to him. . . ."

"Until I had come," repeated Karl. He breathed sharply, as though he felt a knife in his heart.

"No one knows why he is dying. They said it was a sickness of the mind. Some mysterious malady. I, myself, think that he wishes to die. There are things that men cannot endure, Karl. Do you know that?"

"Yes, I know. O God, I know!"

They held each other's hands, and wept together, openly, the old broken woman and the sick, trembling man.

"You must go to him at once, Karl. You must go now, so he will have peace."

She pushed him away resolutely, and pointed at the door. "Now."

"Yes, I will go."

He left her, walking with a feeble step. He passed the crucifix. The candlelight leaped up in the draft from the open door. It shivered over the ivory figure in its death agonies. Karl regarded it for a long moment. The deepest and most solemn silence stood between the man and the cross. Then he went out.

He reached Kurt's door. It opened before he could touch the handle. Alfred, in his uniform, came out, tears on his round hard cheeks, which were no longer red. He started when he saw Karl. "Who are—" he began. Then he cried out: "Uncle Karl! It is you!"

Karl looked at him heavily. Then, without speaking, he entered the room and closed the door after him, leaving Alfred outside.

The nurse sat beside the bed, peering intently at the unconscious face on its pillows. She looked up as Karl approached. She had never seen him before. But his aspect frightened her. She rose to her feet.

"I am sorry," she murmured, "but the doctor said no visitors. . . ."

"I am his brother," he answered quietly, but he did not look at her. He looked only at Kurt.

"Doctor Erlich."

He motioned to her. "Please leave me alone with him."

"But—but he is unconscious. The doctor says he will not recover consciousness again. I must ask you to go. . . ."

"Leave me alone with him," he repeated. He looked over his shoulder at her with terrible eyes. She was terrified. She backed away, wetting her dry lips. She thought to herself that this was a madman. But some mysterious force seemed to be pushing her from the room. She went out, closing the door after her.

Karl sat down in her chair. He bent over Kurt. It seemed to him that this was his own face on the pillow, discolored, emaciated, dying. Yes, it was his own face, the reflection of himself, the image of a dying self. All that he had been for long was dying here, never to live again. He moved the lampshade, so that he could see the better.

He took the cold claylike hand which lay impotently on the sheets. He held it tightly. "Kurt," he said softly, and then louder: "Kurt!"

A strange change came over the sunken, haggard face. The spirit behind it, preparing to leave, halted, looked back at the sound of that beloved voice, then trembled with recognition and dim joy. It came back, slowly, opening doors it had closed behind it, entering corridors it had abandoned, and then, coming back into the chamber where Karl waited, looked about it wildly.

Kurt's glazed eyes opened. A film lay over them, glaucous and thick. He stared through it, trying to see. The hand moved in Karl's. A little warmth returned to it. Then recognition was full, through the mists. The dry mouth parted, and a strangling sound bubbled through it.

Karl could not endure the sight of that joy, that passionate recognition. Shame, sorrow, remorse struck at him like heavy blows. He closed his own eyes for a moment. When he opened them, he saw Kurt staring at him in ecstatic realization.

"Yes," he said, very softly, "it is I, Karl."

"Karl," breathed the dying man. His bony fingers clung to Karl's hand. Mucus was thick between his parted lips. But his eyes shone with light.

Then another change came over him. His face took on a dark look of remembrance and agony.

"Forgive me," he said. Karl could barely hear him. He had to bend low over his brother. But he heard.

"No," he said, in a shaking voice. "You must forgive me." He took both the other's hands. "You must forgive me. If you do not, I shall never forgive myself."

The words were few, but they understood each other. They understood the long years of misunderstanding, grief, hatred, longing, love and despair. There were no reticences between them now, no reserves. They moved through forgotten years, remembering everything, understanding everything, forgiving everything. They looked into each other's eyes, and both knew peace.

Then, after a long time, Kurt struggled to speak again, in his low panting whisper.

"Karl, I am sorry. Eric—Gerda . . ."

"Hush. It does not matter now."

"But I killed them, Karl."

"No, no, you did not kill them. Hush, be still. Rest."

But Kurt fought with his death and his cold choking flesh. He tried to sit up. Karl put his arm about him, to support him. The bones of his brother's body were hard against his arm, and again he felt the shock of sorrow and remorse. Kurt's face was close to him, his cool breath on his cheek, his eyes fixed passionately on Karl's.

"When—when it was done, Karl, it was like a light to me. I saw things I never saw before." A convulsion made his body arch, become rigid. "I could not bear it. The things I saw. . . . They killed me."

"Yes, I know, Kurt. But even all that does not matter now."

He held Kurt to him, tightly. His brother's head rested on his shoulder. The tortured breathing became easier. He relaxed.

"It was a long time—the seeing. I fought against it. But I could not escape seeing. Then I knew I could not live any longer. Karl, you understand?"

"Yes, I understand. Everything."

Karl laid him gently back upon his pillows. A translucent light of peace and joy wavered over Kurt's sinking face. He still held his brother's hand. Karl heard the voices of the wind at the windows, the hissing of the snow. He held Kurt's hand tightly, warmly, and smiled.

"Rest," he said. "Sleep."

"Yes," whispered Kurt. "Yes. Sleep."

He closed his eyes. He slept. He smiled deeply to himself. His breathing became lower, more shallow.

Karl released his hand. Kurt's hand fell back inertly on the sheet. Karl stood up, and for a long time watched his brother as he slept. Then he forced his aching body to its feet, and left the room.

He went downstairs, holding to the balustrade to keep himself from falling. No one was about. He opened the hall door, and a gust of wind and snow-fresh air blew upon his face.

He was about to go out when he heard the nurse's shrill cry as she re-entered the room where Kurt lay, at peace at last.

He closed the door silently after him. Then, standing on the steps, he wept again.

37 OLD LOTTE was just passing through the hallway when Karl returned. She had always maintained an attitude of normality towards him, shrewdly believing that those who suffered from mental agony and distraction should have a normal atmosphere about them at all times, and a normal approach. So, though she was frightened by his appearance, as always, her fat wrinkled face smiled.

"Good evening, Herr Doctor. I have kept your dinner warm. It is waiting for you."

She helped him remove his snow-soaked coat, and competently shook it out. She expected that he would leave her silently, as usual, and in his dazed condition, mount the stairs to his rooms. But instead, he waited for her to hang up his garments. She started nervously when she saw him there. Then she was astonished, for he was smiling at her kindly, as he always used to smile before "the trouble." Moreover, his eyes were no longer dim and wild and distraught.

Her old heart beat with a strange mingling of hope and fear.

"Good evening, Lotte," he said. It was evident, from his pallor, that he was very weak and tired. "Where is the Frau Doctor?"

She stammered, her face working. "She is not well, Herr Doctor. I called a physician. She fainted. She has never done that before, to my knowledge. Now she is resting in her room, and the physician said she must not be disturbed."

He was silent a moment. He rubbed his cold thin hands together, and she watched him fearfully, wondering if what she saw in his face was true, and not a delusion. It was true that his expression was dark and thoughtful, but there was no madness nor confusion about him. He felt her watching him. He looked at her and smiled again.

"Good Lotte," he said. "What would we do without you?"

Her eyes filled with tears. All was well again, she thought. She could not speak for her overpowering emotion. So, trying to smile feebly, she turned and went away to her kitchen, where she could shed her joyful tears in privacy.

Karl went up the stairs. He reached Therese's door, and opened it.

The room was lit by a small lamp near the bed. On her chaise longue Therese was half-lying, feet covered by a shawl. She wore a white lacy negligee, and her long fair hair streamed over her shoulders. Her eyes were closed. An expression of extreme exhaustion and collapse gave her features the aspect of prostrating illness. Karl watched her for a long time. His face was quiet and grave, but as he watched her, he understood her sufferings and the long months of her loneliness and pain. It was not the old Therese who lay there, calm, selfish, composed, always the gnädige frau, whom nothing could disturb overmuch, and who lived in a cool serene world of her own, selfishly insulated against the miseries of others. This was a new Therese, worn fine and thin by pain and torment, and if she was calm, it was with the sad and terrible calm of understanding.

It is not only I who have come back, he thought, mournfully. It is not only I, who see at last.

He thought that both he and Therese had been away on a long and dreadful voyage, alone. And now they had both returned, and were together in this room, full of experiences and suffering.

He said, very softly: "Therese. Therese, my darling."

She opened her eyes, dull, heavy eyes, ringed with the shadows of despair. She looked at him. She did not speak. He went to her, knelt beside her, and took her in his arms. She did not move for a long time. Then, all at once, she burst into dry and violent sobs, and clung to him. They did not need to speak. They held each other, as though they were two who had thought never to see each other again, but had met once more in an alien and appalling land, where the most frightful voices resounded, and the heavens were lit by the red shadows of hell.

Finally, she was a little calmer. But she still clung to his hand, her piteous eyes fixed upon him.

"I have been to Kurt," he said. "He is dead. But I saw him before he died."

"Yes," she whispered. And again: "Yes."

Now her tears came, soothing, filled with compassion. She kissed his hand, his cheeks, his mouth. Her lips quivered.

She began to tell him everything. An hour went by. He listened silently and intently. Sometimes a spasm ran rigidly across his face. But he showed no other emotion. The wind trembled at the windows. The snow had turned to rain, and beat against the glass like volleys of bullets. But there were no other sounds but the slow shaking voice of Therese, and the wind and the rain.

She told him the name Felix Traub had given her. He nodded, silently. Then he said:

"There is so much to do. And so little time. But what I can do I shall do."

She kissed him again, clinging to him.

Then suddenly, she was filled with terror. She had regained Karl only to lose him again. She forgot everything in the extremity of her terror. Now she wanted nothing but to hold him, to keep him safe, to fly.

"Karl!" she cried, in anguish. "What, at the most, can you do? Karl, let us leave Germany. At once! Tomorrow! We can still get passports. England! France! America! Oh, I cannot have those things happen to you, Karl!"

He held her in his arms. She shuddered. Her hands clutched him, despairingly. He listened to her pleading. He looked at her wet distracted face. He tried to soothe her. She felt strength and fortitude in his arms.

"Therese," he said. "Would you really want us to run away?"

"Yes, yes! Immediately! I can stand no more, Karl. It has been too much. Now I have you again. We must go away. How can I stand by, and watch them kill you? For they surely will. They are devils. They find out everything. They know everything. It will only be a matter of time. . . ."

He forced her to meet his eyes, holding her face in his hands.

"Therese," he repeated. "Shall we run away?"

She tried to cry out. And then she could not. She saw the faces of Herman Muehler and Felix Traub. How could she betray them? She began to weep, hiding her face on Karl's shoulder. She collapsed against him. He held her closely.

But he looked beyond her, and his face was stern and dark.

"I had a dream," he said softly. "I dreamed that Eric came back. He talked to me. He told me what I must do. There is nothing else for me."

"Yes," she said. "Yes, there is nothing else."

And they clung to each other again, without words.

IT WAS Christmas Eve, and very quiet. It was also almost Christmas. Therese had hung up the holly. Children were singing in the streets. It was very still. There had been a new snow, and the roofs of the houses were white with it.

38

Therese was very tired. She had not seen Karl since the evening meal. He, too, must be tired, working so long in his study. She must call him to bed, remind him that he was still not completely well.

She went upstairs. His study door was ajar. She pushed it wider.

He was sitting at his desk, writing swiftly, his graying head bent, his face severe and absorbed, and attenuated. His fine thin hand moved rapidly. He was not aware of her.

She tried to call him, but something kept her silent.

So Voltaire and Rousseau had sat, at midnight, and later, writing. Their delicate pens had attacked a terrible era of oppresssion, misery and despair and death. These pens had overthrown a nation, a philosophy, a world. The sound of them had moved through generations. The sound had become flutes of liberty and justice, equality and fraternity. Now, savage and barbaric hands had seized on the flutes, had silenced their calling.

Now the fateful drums were booming through the world again. Now the shattering trumpets blazed at every wall, everywhere. Now the thunder was shaking the frail minds of men, and multitudes stood aghast in the darkness, listening to the drums and the trumpets, not knowing where to flee, or where to hide.

The mummy head of Gilu stood on the mantelpiece, near Karl, who was writing below. The evil face smiled ferociously. It was all madness and fury. And below it was Karl, with his smooth delicate pen, writing at midnight.

So it must always be. So the saviors of men must always work, forgetting everything else. Forgetting self and safety, greed and expediency, treachery and frightfulness, and fear.

Therese knew what the end must be. Soon she would be

alone once more, and this time for always, in this world. Soon they would find Karl and kill him.

She lifted her head, as though she heard the flutes of Voltaire and Rousseau, and all the voices of those who had died that other men might live in peace. Her pale face became heroic.

Nothing mattered now. Not even Karl's torture and death. Not even her coming loneliness and desolation.

She heard the carols in the street below. She heard the whispering of the snow against the windows. She heard the faint scratching of Karl's pen.

"For greater love hath no man . . ."

She closed the door softly behind her, and went away.